THE HOUSE GUEST

Barbara Anderson is the author of three novels, *Girls High*, *Portrait of the Artist's Wife* (winner of the 1992 Wattie Award) and *All the Nice Girls*, and a collection of stories, *I think we should go into the jungle*, described by the *Guardian* as 'the sharpest collection in English since Carver's *Cathedral*'.

GW00492985

Barbara Anderson

THE HOUSE GUEST

VINTAGE

Published by Vintage 1997

2 4 6 8 10 9 7 5 3 1

Copyright © Barbara Anderson 1996

The right of Barbara Anderson to be identified as the author of this work has been asserted by her in accordance with the Copyright, Designs and Patents Act, 1988

First published in Great Britain by
Jonathan Cape Ltd, 1996

Vintage
Random House, 20 Vauxhall Bridge Road,
London SW1V 2SA

Random House Australia (Pty) Limited
20 Alfred Street, Milsons Point, Sydney
New South Wales 2061, Australia

Random House New Zealand Limited
18 Poland Road, Glenfield,
Auckland 10, New Zealand

Random House South Africa (Pty) Limited
Endulini, 5A Jubilee Road, Parktown 2193,
South Africa

Random House UK Limited Reg. No. 954009

A CIP catalogue record for this book
is available from the British Library

ISBN 0 09 959951 1

Papers used by Random House UK Ltd are natural, recyclable products made from wood grown in sustainable forests. The manufacturing processes conform to the environmental regulations of the country of origin

Printed and bound in Great Britain by
Cox & Wyman, Reading, Berkshire

For Jetta

One

He still wore her ring. He didn't like them, never had, not for men. But she had wanted it. It gave her pleasure, the wide gold thing rolling around his third finger left hand. She had chosen it with care, loved the difference in sizes, compared his and hers endlessly, teased him and loved him and teased him again as she demonstrated cross-legged and solemn beside him—there is a vein that goes straight from this finger right to your heart, see.

She traced the route up his arm, stabbed his chest. 'Bong. Did you know that?' Robin held the finger in mid-air. 'I wonder who first found out. Did the dissection. Someone should have told us.'

Smiles rewarded him.

Everything about her enchanted him: her smallness, her tough fragility, her bounce. She had always been a bright kid, streetwise before the word hit Wellington, but now her quick alertness, her knowing innocence, her How, Wow, Do-it-again approach to bed and board and life itself astounded him, let alone in this day and age. Wouldn't you think, said Miss Bowman next door who was politically informed and kept up, wouldn't you think in this day and age politicians would have learned that *people* matter.

'It's funny you know,' said Lisa, watching the old woman as she crept up the path bearing an egg-beater because she had two and would they like one. 'It's funny. She polishes her outdoor taps and yet she smells. You wouldn't think they'd go together somehow, would you? I mean I don't mind or anything, but it's funny isn't it?'

Yes please, they would love an egg-beater, how kind. Robin's one was completely shot, she said, stowing the gift in the cupboard beside Robin's shining battery of beaters, straw and aluminium whisks and stainless steel bowls. Why he hadn't thrown it out she would never know but that was men all over wasn't it. She would keep a piece of wedding cake for Miss Bowman seeing she wasn't well enough to come. Lisa knew it would be lovely. Yes, the wedding of course, but actually she meant the cake. Mum was scared it would all flow out when they cut it but they all liked it moist and Lisa knew it wouldn't. Mum always washed the fruit first even though you don't have to now but Lisa felt it was a fault on the right side, not that she could cook. None of the girls at the lab could, and anyway she had Robin.

'I wonder,' she said as Miss Bowman retreated down the concrete past the Phoenix palm and the cinerarias and the shrieking red geraniums. 'I wonder sometimes about her and Emmie.'

Robin sat on the back porch dubbining her boots, three fingers cramped into the bull-nosed toe. He straightened, looked thoughtful. The most unexpected thing will do it and his mother was out. He dropped the cloth, circled her ankle with his hand. 'Lisa?' he said. She was more than happy. She always was.

'What did you mean,' he said later, 'about Emmeline?'

'Who?' murmured Lisa, her nose in the woven straw mat. She sat up, tugged, adjusted, reached for her pants. 'Oh her. I don't know. Nothing.' She touched the bridge of his nose. 'I must pluck out those hairs. It doesn't matter like now when you're not wearing your glasses but when you are they sort of bang about behind and it doesn't look nice.' She sat on his chest, hooked a child's foot each side of his hand, leaned to kiss his bruised mouth. 'And I like my Robbie to look nice.'

Where had she came from. How had she happened. She was a throwback to a romantic age which had never existed, an anachronism in shifts that clung or twelve-inch black leather minis topped by crocheted tops the size of dishcloths. She wore heels and her hair shone, her lipsticks were pale or else plum which stained like a dye. She loved the whole world and what she could not love she did not see. All small snub-nosed creatures delighted her as how could they not, those flop-eared puppies in baskets, beribboned kittens and solemn wide-eyed infants dressed as bumble-bees. Meerkats on TV pleased her as did baby chimpanzees, wondering, nervous prehensile fingers to their chins, when they had last phoned their Mum. Her heart melted. Look! Look! She wanted things to be nice and did what she could to make them so. She was kind and loving. She could not understand how people could be so awful to each other. Those black babies. No. It was too much. It didn't bear thinking about.

Sad movies made her cry. Old dogs and deathbeds and children at risk finished her, let alone violence or brutality. They were not for her. Strong meat was not her cup of tea. Robin could go alone if he must, but no, not Lisa. (He stopped going.) The world was cruel enough already in Lisa's opinion, without paying to watch. She hid her eyes when it was famine.

Her mother Maureen was a cheerful hard-working woman but by no means romantic. She had little reason to be. She was a splendid woman. Splendid. Look how she had coped when George disappeared and never a penny paid in maintenance for either Lisa or Murray then or ever; two babies rolling around on the kitchen floor and never a word of complaint. Amazing. Maureen Shield had rolled up her sleeves, oiled her Bernina and got on with life which was certainly no picnic but there you were. She put a notice on the board in the New World. (Dressmaker. Ladies and girls. Large sizes a speciality. Phone Maureen.) They phoned and kept phoning. They phoned in droves, they came clutching their lengths. Lengths for two-pieces and spring outfits, for change-of-season and jump suits and mother of the bride. Occasionally for a big wedding when things were rushed Maureen sewed all night. The well-oiled hum of the Bernina backed Lisa and Murray's childhood dreams. Scraps of bridal satins, tulles, taffetas, velvets and double-weave brocades were hoarded by Lisa in a shoebox labelled *Brides* in red. Occasionally she wrapped her fabric treasures around Betty or the faceless Rhonda, but mostly she sat and stroked them, crooning to herself.

Robin stared at the baby in the wicker pram with distaste; the mouth moved, made sucking motions, burped. There was a bubble of milk.

'Lisa,' said his mother Eileen. 'That's pretty. Where did you find that?'

'Oops,' said Maureen, one hand scrabbling down her leaking front. 'Won't stay in place these pads, will they? Judy Garland's daughter. We thought it was nice, didn't we George? Mind you hers has got a Z but I don't like names with a Z, well not at the beginning except Zoë. I like Zoë, especially with the little dots. It's not the same without the little dots. It means Life and that's nice but we liked Lisa better, didn't we George?'

'Aye.'

'It means Chosen of God and that's nice too. But not with the Z. She's Lisa with an S and we like it pronounced Leesa too, don't we? She'll have to explain, poor poppet.' Infinitely gentle, Maureen touched the button nose with one finger. 'Leesa with an S,' she told it. She sat back on the sofa, fussed with her pads once more and lay back. 'There's lots of names like that,' she said. 'Cathleen say. It's quite a different name with a C. Or Randall with two Ls. Isn't it George?'

'Aye.' George sat on the sofa, , the fingers of his right hand moving in rhythmic circles on his chest as he stared out the window. Aye was his answer to any question or statement. At any situation, at any time and in any place, the word eased his path through life. 'Aye,' he said as he slipped the Morris into gear and backed down the drive. 'Aye,' he said as the long day's picnic ended, the shades lengthened and the wind dropped and the return drive to Seatoun was accomplished.

'How did she get out?' asked Robin as he and his mother walked up their drive next door, past the concrete bird bath and the blood-red petals of the Crown of Thorns splashed on the rockery below.

'Who?'

'Lisa.'

Eileen Dromgoole, widowed by a freak accident on the building site ten years ago, looked at her son and sighed. His steel spectacles enhanced his air of concentration. He wished to know. Presumably he had already picked up the basics from the boys' toilets or the playground beneath the straggling pohutukawa of primary—though certainly the process of getting out was difficult to believe, let alone visualise. Oh dear. Eileen put on the kettle, tweaked the venetians. 'Get the little red teapot, Robin,' she said, 'and I'll try.'

Robin obeyed. He had always been a helpful child and facts were important.

So he had known Lisa since she was born, before she 'filled out' and became human, had minded her since the days her arms had waved without volition as he pushed her pram along the waterfront past the changing sheds to the play area, though of course she was too little for any of that.

Glimpses stay with him. George's laconic Aye when they returned. The only thing which excited him was pigeons. 'Have you ever kept pigeons, lad?'

Robin continued to rock the pram. He didn't want her to cry. He liked it best when he pushed and her eyes were wide and her hands moved. He liked her hands, the way the fingers grasped his outstretched one like a telly advertisement for a bank. A lifeline.

Robin is a lifeline.

'No,' he said finally.

'Why does no one have pigeons here? We all had pigeons in Skegness. Lofts we had.' George glared at him, sandy eyebrows locked together. 'Every man jack of us. All fanciers we were, took the magazine, races and all. Why not here, lad? Lovely pigeon country.' His arms weaved about the quiet street, sketched updrafts, defined the beating of grey-black wings. 'I had pouters and rollers as well but they were just for fun. Not racers.'

'They might get blown away in the northerlies,' said Robin, offering a finger as the eyes opened. 'Cook Strait is windy.'

'Aye, but you never know till you try, do you?'

Lisa was two and Murray four when George left his family. He took the Morris and went and was never heard of again. No message delivered or sent. Robin took over Lisa's pushchair on a permanent basis. He biked home each day from Rongotai, his legs pumping as the wind boomed in his anxious face. He knew she would be waiting. Arms out, bare feet bouncing on the wicker stool, Lisa and her curls waited in the glassed-in porch.

'Robbie, Robbie!'

'I can't understand it,' said his mother to Maureen, 'why he doesn't mind? I mean he's fourth form now after all. You'd think . . . I mean don't they laugh at him? The other boys.' Quick anxious fingers plucked at her white cardigan which was inclined to pill. 'I don't know,' she said. 'I just don't know.'

Maureen's thumbnail was busy extracting a scrap of apple peel from between two molars. Royal Gala. 'Well, he's different, Robin,' she said. 'Always has been. I've said since he was tiny. Robin is his own person and he likes Lisa.'

He had changed her nappy once.

She climbed out of her pushchair, lay on her back on the stubby grass of the playground and flung round pink legs over her head in anticipation. 'Damp,' she said.

Robin had never told her of this incident. He could see the bright

12

eyes, hear the emphasis. 'I *like* it.' Why had he not? She would have loved it, this extra flick of happiness compounded by endless recall.

'Robin changed me when I was two. No, I mean really *changed* me. My nappies and that when I was two, wasn't it? On the playground. And I flung my legs back, didn't I, Robbie?'

Aye.

'Only son of widowed mother.' The phrase had pleased him when he met it as a child. It had leaped at him from *The Home Fires Kept Burning. A Nation at War, 1914–18*, one of the books trapped between brass horse heads on the mantelpiece in the front room. These were all that remained of Nana Dromgoole, who, his mother told him, had been a reader. Perhaps that was where Robin got it from. Terence hadn't been but things do out. Eileen had kept only the ones with squashy red or blue leather covers and embossed gold titles. *The Wide, Wide World* was her favourite. Scrolled in gold leaves, it remained unread by either of them, but Robin enjoyed *Home Fires* and the photographs were interesting. Slim veiled nurses stood by lines of cheerful men in narrow beds, pushed smiling amputees in bath chairs, smiled themselves. Red Cross volunteers met trains, lit cigarettes, assisted the blind. There were photographs of casualty lists and reproductions of death notices from provincial papers which were more interesting because they told you more.

Robin murmured the phrase to himself—only son of widowed mother. He was glad to have acquired definition. A phrase for himself alone. He did not know any other only sons of widowed mothers. Mr Ramsay down the road (car smash) had left three boys, but second or third son of widowed mother had not the same edge, the same plummeting sense of family demise. (Daughters were not mentioned.) Robin gave up hitching bike rides on the backs of speeding trucks for a few weeks, though he missed the blast, the hysterical pedals, the shouts tossed to the wind. He stopped playing chicken at the Coutt Street crossroads. Later he drove his mother's aged car sedately. He had imagination, both as a driver and a son. He was aware of mortality. He had lived with it all his life.

His mother's grief, gentle but all pervading, a miasma of incompleteness, of lonely days and endless nights, changed in time to dreaminess. Eileen spoke little of Terence (Terry before the scaffolding collapsed). At first she had not wanted to upset Robin. He was only a baby after all, and a solemn one at that. Sometimes he smiled, but not often. 'Funny kid,' said Bernie at the dairy watching the multicoloured plastic strips sigh and resettle behind the skinny back. 'Never know what he's thinking. Deep I shouldn't wonder. Not bubbly like some.'

Later there seemed little point in going into it. It was a long time ago.

He grew into his face, they said, and his hair darkened. 'Hasn't Robin *grown*,' they said.

'Yes,' said Eileen brushing the curved shelf of her bosom. 'And he's got a prize at college too. Overall Attainment.'

The careers master advised the humanities. Not as an academic, he didn't mean that, not for a moment. Teaching perhaps. Robin looked at the cadaver in front of him in horror.

'No? You're probably right,' said Lawson. 'How about social work? They give you time off from the Department to study.'

'What do they do?'

'Do? There's an enormous range.' Lawson burrowed in drawers. 'I had something somewhere. I'll look it out,' he continued, coming up breathless from the drawer and grabbing his inhaler. 'Later. Later.' He honked a couple of deep puffs. 'Welfare, counselling, probation, there's always a need for carers.' Another honk. 'It's a growth industry.'

A carer. Robin saw himself caring. He had always minded strays, had never hurried past featherless fledgelings or dumped kittens. The SPCA knew him by name. 'You've got a lovely nature Robin,' the one with the diamond in her nose had told him last week as he handed over the latest crippled seagull. 'Any problems getting him into the sack?'

'Emmie helped me.'

'Good on her.'

Lisa thought he had too. 'Ooh Rob, you shouldn't.' 'Ooh Rob, you are naughty.' 'Ooh *Robbie*,' she said birthday after birthday as she unwrapped dolls, hugged bears, books or bright shining things to her chest. She always kept Rob's present till last. When she was little he had given her an unyielding doll capped with nightmare yellow hair. Battery-operated, Betty crawled relentlessly onwards. When Lisa picked her up to love, Betty's moulded pink arms and chubby legs swam against her as though struggling against an outgoing tide. Once he met Betty face to face at the front door, banging her smiling head against the other side of the glass in endless sorrow. Lisa had left her to her own devices for a moment and Betty, programmed as a battery-powered lemming, had motored on.

When Lisa was twelve he gave her the best present of all. A music box with a tiny ballerina in a plastic tutu perched on one toe. 'Though I say not / What I may not / Let you hear,' tinkled and creaked through the sparsely furnished rooms and narrow hall as the ballerina revolved. 'Turn the bloody thing off,' yelled Murray who now had a desk of his own. He was going to be a doctor. He said so, but how. You need money for medicine. Six years. More. Maureen sewed harder. Lengths and more lengths and remnants burst their wrappings throughout the house or lay heaped in corners awaiting transformation.

'I'll get a loan.'

'It won't be enough,' worried Maureen.

'I'll get another one.'

Lisa cut tiny squares from her favourite bridal fabrics and glued them to the base of the dancing lady's plinth. She nicked a bottle of natural-coloured Cutex from Woolworths and applied it to the edges to prevent fraying. It worked quite well.

There were few expeditions from Seatoun and little money. 'Three in a row and not a man in sight,' said Bernie at the store. 'Funny isn't it? You don't often see it in a row like that. Four kids and not a father between them, if you count Emmie.'

*

The first time Robin went into the bush was a school trip to the Orongorongos before the Five Mile Track was tarted up. They had been to Butterfly Creek at Eastbourne on a day trip from primary but there were too many screaming kids. The best bit had been the kidney ferns, but all the birds, if there were any, had been scared songless. There were few in Seatoun except the gulls which he watched for hours. He went to the Central Library; they'd have more books there, wouldn't they? More real books, not kids' books; he wanted proper books, he wanted to find out. He saved up for a starling box. But never pigeons.

The first time in the Orongorongos and the last remain with him. The first memory is shredded, munched bite by bite as the martyred Saint Veronica ate her spiders. Fragments only remain: the first sight of the tin hut buried in the bush, the macho feel of boots, their sweaty superman power. The waking to the strong socks of others in your face. To still mornings and the bird calls and the silence.

The humanities went for a burton. 'I want to study birds,' Robin told Lawson.

The man looked at him. Sick, riddled with stomach ulcers plus asthma, Lawson did his best.

'Birds?'

'Yes. I like birds.'

'That will be more difficult. You can do a BA while you're earning. It's the lab work in science that employers jib at.'

'I've got a job with a caterer, nights and weekends and I can live at home.'

Lawson crawled away to die but his replacement was helpful. Robin enrolled at Victoria.

A woman on the bus moved from her seat beside him on his way home from rat dissection. She had crashed down next to him, her behind working pink stretch knit into vinyl, then sniffed. Robin stared straight ahead. The rats were the worst, they made him gag,

16

a smell like nothing else on earth; strong, sour and choking, it stayed with him for hours. The woman sniffed again. She levered herself upwards and swayed to the back muttering. Perhaps he had a bit of rat still on him. He gave a surreptitious sniff but was unconvinced.

He kept his eyes on the neck of the bus driver. Enthroned and dignified, she sat high-rumped on her own bus, endlessly helpful, endlessly calm. 'What you need lady is a forty-nine.' 'Over the road man, over the road.' Black leather gloves sliced off at the tips frayed and flapped around brown fingers and ruby nails. She was in charge and had not smelled a thing.

Lisa also had an acute sense of smell. 'Betty hates it too, don't you Betty?' The curls bent to catch the answer as Rob lifted her ancient bike from the concrete with one foot. Miss Bowman had swapped Emmie's Junior Girl's with Maureen in exchange for running up three lengths of cotton, though what anyone would want with sleeveless in Seatoun Maureen would never know.

'I'll give you a practice on the road if you like,' he said. 'Come on.'

Lisa looked doubtful. The road was forbidden and she wasn't all that struck on the bike.

'The thing is,' she said, 'Betty's hair's falling out.'

'Give us it.' He put out his hand for a hank of yellow acrylic. 'I'll stick it back. And when you're older,' he said, 'I'll take you tramping in the Orongorongos.'

'Orongorongos. Yeah!' Lisa dumped Betty. Excitement always resulted in action. Hands clasped, legs working, she could jump for ever. Betty, still smiling serenely, was banging her head against the table leg.

Young women liked him and had always done so. Years ago he had wondered why, had felt tempted to ask one or two of the more forthcoming for reasons, but there were no words, just a mystery he learned to accept. Angie told him in the sixth form he had neat ears and she liked the way his hair grew and how he looked sort of vulnerable and sexy at the same time if he knew what she meant.

Guys with glasses did sometimes, she said, though not always. Later Nicole in physiology liked the way he sat. She couldn't put her finger on it but she liked the angles, the way the top leg hung straight. His weird resigned smile was a relief, she said, after the leering hunks in biochem. It made him look contained, she said, as though there was something there and by the way Mum and Dad were going to Levin at the weekend.

He was grateful but had always known he would marry Lisa. He was twelve years older but that worked out well if you thought about it. It would take him years to finish his degree, to get established.

It did not work out like that. To his surprise he disliked zoology. To his bewildered astonishment he hated the whole thing. He had not thought it would be like this. It was not the smells. Everyone told him he'd get used to them and they were right, as the inhabitants of Rotorua become used to the cauldron blasts, the all-invasive subtleties of their thermal wonderlands. Become, if anything, attached to the hard-boiled eggs of home.

The first-year labs were full, the students busy. Smelling of talcum powder or rank as goats, they hacked at the meticulously prepared specimens, the demonstrations, the recumbent rats. Scraps of mangled flesh littered the benches after they had finished with the nerves.

But the smell was nothing. His dislike lay deeper and was more disturbing. Of course zoology must involve the study of dead animals, even in this day of conservation, distribution studies and the holistic approach to life upon planet Earth. What else could it possibly do? How could you understand flight unless you knew the mechanism, how appreciate economy of effort until you had traced ligaments, muscles, nerves?

But everything in the place was so irredeemably dead. This limp bedraggled lice-ridden pigeon, how could it once have soared and swooped and returned to base, either in Seatoun or Skegness. It was impossible to visualise, as was the former attack, the rat-pack vigour of the rodents which now lay flat on their backs in hands-up capitulation, their claws locked in rigid appeal. It was not so bad once you started; finding out is always interesting, but the non-viable content was high.

The freshly killed rats for muscle study and the raddled yellow of the preserved ones depressed him equally, as did the specimens in vast glass-stoppered jars; a scramble of pickled salamanders, a deep pile of toads, a preserved elephant fish fringed with purple gills which drifted sideways when disturbed. 'Adrienne's green gecko guts,' said the reminder on the noticeboard. 'Freezer under Bob's stuff.' Where else would they be. His mincing distaste depressed him further.

And, Christ Almighty, the dropped gut stench of hens.

He worked hard, though not at his own desk like Murray next door. He sat with a plank across his knees in his narrow room beneath school photographs Blu-tacked to the wall by his mother. He achieved good grades and made his decision. It was a momentous one. Other guys he knew dropped out, dropped in, changed courses at will or inclination. On impulse they abandoned psych, took up drama, ditched law, couldn't stand the shit another minute. Not Robin. He had wanted to study birds and still did. But it was all too dead.

He switched to arts.

Lisa applied for a job in the medical laboratory at the hospital the minute she left school and was accepted though dozens were turned away. 'Turned away,' she said sadly, her hands clasped in sympathy for the failed. She loved the work, and everyone loved Lisa. She was on A Bench under Padma. A Bench was the best, everybody said so, well not to their faces but the doctors and everyone knew and Padma was marvellous. There was no one like Padma. Honestly, she meant it. Padma knew everything and never flapped even when they were flat out and things got really hairy. Padma didn't know how to flap, you should see some of them on the other benches when it was nearly time to knock off and six specimens appeared out of nowhere. *Six* including a spinal fluid. Ask yourself. But Padma just kept calm, you should see her. She wouldn't let any of the juniors flap either. She couldn't handle people who flapped, she said. If the juniors were going to flap they could leave right now OK? She was that quick and she never made a mistake, and she knew where to look everything up if she didn't know straight off, and she was never scared to go to Dr Biddle if she couldn't find what she wanted because she knew, and he knew, that she would never ask him unless it was something impossible to find by herself, not like some of them. And you know everything grew for her? It was amazing. Even the anaerobes, if there was anything there in the first place of course. Some people couldn't get anything anaerobic to grow it was that difficult, but with Padma if nothing grew you knew somehow there was nothing there anyway and the same with the blood cultures which were tricky as well. Blood cultures are boring everyone said so, but Padma didn't mind. She just got on and did them straight off and her technique was perfect. One or two of the others seemed a tiny bit, well sort of sloppy, but Padma! And Padma had told her in the tearoom the other day when there was no one else there and they had rinsed their cups and left them upside down to drain on the bench by the window that she thought Lisa should think about trying for her exam, because you could always tell the juniors with potential. Imagine.

She also loved the other two lab assistants, Janice and Sandy. Lost in his maze of love and longing, Robin learned a great deal about both of them, how they laughed, the particular ways they perched on their high stools, their differing techniques as they planted pus swabs on blood agar. Their social lives, narrated in detail, rolled before him.

We went to the Embassy last night, Jake and me.

We didn't. Si and I went to *Parasite*. Si likes horror.

Jake doesn't. We went for a coffee after at the Deluxe.

We didn't. We went straight home.

I don't like going home straight off, it's boring.

We do. We always go straight home. Always.

We don't.

Robin met them frequently and had seen them in action. Neither appeared to listen to the other's stream of consciousness except to snatch key words; names of new cafés, soaps, movies were pounced upon so that Sandy or Janice could give her own response and judgement as soon as possible.

Sandy, he learned, couldn't *stand* films about the Inquisition. She wouldn't cross the road. She and Si had seen *The Piano* but Si thought it was crap. Janice sighed, waited for her turn to communicate. She and Jake had checked out that new café in Willis Street but her cappuccino went flat.

He could never remember which was which but had been told too often to ask again. Janice was either the dark one or the one with yellow hair tufted either side and the engagement ring. They had both passed their exams recently and it was getting harder every year. Everyone said so and Lisa could see why.

'It has to, doesn't it, I mean,' she said standing before him in parrot-pink shorts, 'there are more and more bugs and more and more drugs; it stands to reason it'll get harder. I was at primary with a girl from Greece. Marina her name was. She started school in Athens. She said it was awful, you had to go way back beyond BC, Greece has been going that long.' Lisa scratched her leg, a long thoughtful slide up her brown thigh.

'I'm going to see Dr Biddle on Monday. I'm going to train. Sit the exam.' She held her bottom lip between her teeth in gentle recognition of her daring and stared at him. 'What d'y'reckon?'

It was the combination that did it. Sensual yet innocent, naive yet self-aware, Lisa stood waiting for answers from the guy next door. 'What d'y'reckon?' she said again.

He shook his head, held out his empty hands. There was no answer. Just something that had to be said. 'Lisa,' he said.

Lisa took a step back. 'What?'

An aircraft roared in to land at Rongotai drowning words, sense, giving him another chance. A chance to laugh, to fling it away, to get them both out of this frozen stare, this poised-for-flight stance.

This error.

'I love you,' he said beneath the telephone wires and the Phoenix palm tossing in the wind.

She stared for a moment then ran, bare feet slapping the concrete as she jumped the glue-eyed spaniel huffing its way down the street.

How could she not have known? How could she be so *interested*, so passionate in her love of brides, babies and the whole of creation and not know how he felt about her? Everyone was lovely, except those who were weird or odd or toffee-nosed and even they couldn't help it probably. She had no right to such ignorance. She was a seventies baby, in love with life and especially love. How could she not know about desire, sex, sheer bloody longing. She had known the mechanics at an earlier age than he had. 'Robin,' she'd said years ago, snuggling up beside him on the divan in the sunporch. 'What's the definition of a virgin?' She watched him slyly, wriggling with the suspense of her rude joke.

'OK. What's a virgin?' he asked the clear eyes.

'The ugliest girl in Form Two.'

His heart moved for a second. 'Oh.'

'That's a lady who hasn't been, you know.'

He said it. He said it when he made love to Karen, an angular botany student who fancied him. Fuck, fuck, fuck, he gasped as he lunged against her. At first she thought it was kinky. It's only words, he said. He didn't know why he said it. He'd remember next time if she didn't like it. He forgot, but Karen became used to it, quite liked it in fact, flung it back at him as they rolled together. She was a good girl Karen. He liked her.

He never thought at such times of Lisa. Not then. It was about the only time he didn't. So how could she not *know*?

He began the long haul back to reason, working out what to do, arms hanging limp as he stood on the grass verge of the quiet street. An empty plastic bag tangled in a power line soared and leaped beside him, hung limp then filled again, snapping and crackling like a windsock above his head. A speckled thrush hunted a late worm at his feet. Ten, twenty times the spike hammered. Robin exhaled and ran up the next-door path calling her name.

Maureen opened the door. Her double-ended pin cushion was around her mottled neck, her hands deep in gathers. 'Rob?'

'There's something I've got to explain to Lisa.'

He shoved past her, the pin cushion nudging his chest.

She was sitting on her bed winding the music box. The ballerina began to turn, the halting tinny flicks of sound began. 'Hullo,' she said.

'Lisa.' He sat beside her, put his arm around her. She moved slightly. There was shyness, unprecedented shyness and silence. Robin cleared his throat. 'Lisa,' he said.

He 'had a word' with Maureen.

'But she's just a baby, Rob.'

Sixteen isn't a baby. Not in this day and flaming age.

'And she thinks of you as a brother.'

Worse. Much worse. Oh shit.

An uneasy truce was established after a few days. He was very gentle, he could wait. He took her to the movies. 'You choose, Lisa.' He had taken her hundreds of times; *Indiana Jones* to *E.T.*, *The Princess Bride* to *Who Framed Roger Rabbit?* had all been enjoyed. This time was different; their hands brushed over Jaffas, jumped away. (She had fed them to him once, sitting on his chest on Maureen's lawn dropping them into his mouth till he nearly choked.) They sat silent while *Fried Green Tomatoes* lapped her in schmaltz and Robin thought about tide tables at Waikanae and the estuary and his chances of seeing the spoonbills before they left. He saw the thrust of the wing beats, the sudden downwards lurch, the surge of power regained. Poetry, you could say, in motion.

'Would you like to come to Waikanae?' he whispered. 'On Saturday.'

Her eyes didn't move from the screen. 'Why?'

'I want to check on the spoonbills. At the lagoon.'

'Oh, I don't know.'

'We'll have a swim after. Get an ice cream at Lindale.' He swallowed. Ice creams. Older men. Humbert Humbert. No one could think that. Certainly not Maureen, never read the book for starters. Not even Murray who had never liked him. Murray was a prick and would make a packet. Robin could see that a mile off.

Her eyes turned to his, pale, moist and gleaming.

'Oh, all right.'

'Would you like coffee?' he said later.

She hesitated, glanced inside the Deluxe. Rock blazed at them; the place was full, steaming, jumping with sound. The espresso hissed, importunate as a steam train in an old movie. There was little food left in the glass cabinet; a collapsed slice of quiche, a bagel, a hefty muffin with knobs. A man with a brimless hat danced alone, an anorexic-looking woman in a wide-brimmed one with a sunflower screamed at him. People argued across tables, held each other tight, kissed gentle as fishes. Lisa shook her head.

Robin got it. In one swift jolt he got it. His jacket was wrong, his glasses, his hair. He was too old. Or not old enough.

He must keep as calm as Padma; must woo the woman he loved, the child he planned to marry. The very word made him wince. Not marry; woo. Nobody wooed for God's sake. They had it off or they didn't. They fucked. They screwed. But he would have to woo Lisa like some moustachioed ex-creep of the silver screen. A where-are-they-now? A dead. In the midst of career decisions, statistics, spread sheets, graphs on tidal populations and private ornithological research viz-à-viz English Literature he must play the male. 'Be of good comfort Master Ridley and play the man,' said Bishop Latimer as the flames licked. There had been graffiti on the memorial plaque recently. He had seen a photo. Someone had tagged it.

Maureen was on his side but it would take time. 'Years maybe, as she seems determined about this exam thing, doesn't she?' Wide by now, generous to a fault, Maureen still spent the same impossible hours at her Bernina. Grey hair cropped, calves rounded above ankle sox and Murray's outworn Reeboks, Maureen motored on, conditioned as the now motionless Betty had once been. Lisa did the cooking, Murray did nothing. He was studying.

Rob's mother knew nothing about his passion, but then she knew very little about him at all, or about anything else much except 'my work'. Her wistfulness had found refuge in the local church, a no-nonsense building where Eileen spent as much time as possible.

Robin's faith in Eileen's God had departed early. Eileen had been disappointed at the time but passive as ever. 'He went to Sunday School,' she told the new curate, 'and was in plays, but there you are.'

She overcame her shyness to become a hospital visitor, although each new patient was an alarming experience. How did you know they *wanted* to be visited. Some made their distaste obvious, which destroyed her for days until the next challenge. But like many soft women Eileen was persistent to the point of brutality. Her gentle manner made her welcome with the shut-ins and the olds. She liked to get round her widows once a week.

Robin did the cooking. From earliest childhood Robin had cooked. Not with his mother who would not let him because it was dangerous and wasn't it a bit sissy for boys and what would Terence have said. Robin retreated to Miss Bowman next door. That dour figure and her red-haired niece Emmeline made him welcome in the dark kitchen out the back. The children stood side by side on stools, beating and rolling and stamping with cookie cutters sent from Miss Bowman's sister Martha in Cold Lake, Alberta. There was a set for Christmas; a reindeer, a bell, a tree and a star. Emmie, two years older, sang one of Aunt's songs.

> I went to the animal fair,
> The birds and beasts were there,
> The big baboon by the light of the moon
> Was combing his auburn hair.
> The monkey he got drunk.
> He slid down the elephant's trunk
> The elephant sneezed and fell on his knees

And what became of the monkey unky unky unky unky
unky . . . ?

Robin punted one up from the bike sheds.

Ask your mother for cash,
To see the big giraffe
He's whiskers on his pimples
And pimples on his . . .
Ask your mother for . . .

'Robin,' said Miss Bowman. Shamed by her strong eye, he stirred
harder.

They progressed as cooks, they became dedicated. Later they
shared their interest in food, swapped recipes, tended their herbs
and discussed problems. Fines herbes for example. The chervil is
always over by the time the rest are ready. Did Emmie find that? By
the time he was fifteen Robin had taken over the cooking completely.
Birthdays were recipe books. Christmas was money 'for all those
weird things you like, dear'. The narrow slice of Eileen's kitchen
shone with Robin's *batterie de cuisine*. He had the sense to hide his
interest from the other kids. It was a secret shared only with Emmie
who was scatty and becoming more so each day.

'Very nice dear, very tasty,' said Eileen dabbing a napkin to her
lips after a triumphant *tarte citron*, a succulent lamb shank. Sometimes he wondered if there was anything she would not like. He
had never found it, though she had had to be brave about garlic
and he knew without asking that raw meat was not on.

The evenings when there was no meeting Eileen sat and watched
television. All programmes pleased her until ten p.m. when they
ceased to exist. They were too late. The blue square changed to a
blink as she switched off and turned to plump her cushion. 'Bed,'
she said, kissed his forehead and went. Sometimes Robin watched
with her as she sat making little mews of approbation or dismay at
successive images, trying to find if there was any programme which

she did not like. He wondered if she would be just as happy in the launderette watching the periodic surge and slap of the washing cycle, the exuberant tsunami crash of the first spin's wave, but decided this was a smart-arse thought and buried it. They lived in faintly uneasy harmony. Robin mowed the lawns. The garden had long since ceased to exist though rhubarb and parsley flourished. 'That's the thing about parsley,' said Eileen. 'Either it likes you or it doesn't.'

Gradually, over the year, Lisa became accustomed to his new persona, his suitor's face. She had always been pleased to see him; now she leaped up laughing to greet her boyfriend who was mad about her. She took him to staff parties, worried over his clothes, put him right on socks.

'Hi, I'm Robin!' he yelled to a guy with a can of beer above the thump and grind of 'Modern Love'.

All right, keep your shitty name to yourself. I am here because Lisa works here and thank God I don't.

Something moved deep in the beard alongside. It was alive, there were pink lips. 'Hi, I'm Sandy's partner. Si. Futures. We were talking about the crash.'

'Oh.' He tried harder. 'Eighty-seven?'

Si looked at him for a moment in silence then dragged his palm over his nose and mouth. 'Yeah,' he said. 'Eighty-seven.'

These people had shares. Money. Spare money they had put into shares so they could lose them when the market crashed.

He was getting sour. Sour kinky old dropout son of widowed mother. Oh God.

'Sandy says,' said Lisa as they drove home, 'she thinks you look just like Yves Saint Laurent. When he was young, of course.'

Wasn't he gay? 'Oh.'

'She thinks that older men are really sexy.'

'Which one is Sandy?'

'You know. The one with the neat little ring.'

'Oh.' He paused. 'That one.'

*

One of the few things Eileen had told him about his father was his hobby.

'He loved his stamps, you know.'

'Yes.' The stamp album was now Robin's. He tried to like it, to imagine his unknown grandfather and father's hands on the Side Faces, the 1898 five-shilling Mount Cook. The book had a dry wrinkled closeness, the pages crackled. He could not imagine a more boring occupation in the world than collecting stamps. King George V had been a philatelist. He had also shot birds; hundreds of them lay at his feet in faded photographs of triumphant massacres. A few of the legs stuck upwards. The beaters were at the back.

'He loved his stamps so much that he wanted me to love them too and you know what he did?' Eileen stopped, her hand at her mouth.

Robin smiled. 'You've told me before, Mum.'

'Yes, but wasn't it lovely of him? He wanted to get me interested so he started me off with my own collections of flowers and birds and fish stamps even. They were so pretty.'

Did they sit side by side across the table, the lamp shining on the excruciating boredom beneath. Did she like it. Did she 'take off on her own'. Had his father thought and hoped and longed for her each night as he came home from his day's work to his collection. Robin had never asked. There was no obvious evidence, just the faded memory of togetherness, of sharing a hobby. A grisly word.

No one could call tramping and the bush a hobby but he could see he would have to be careful in introducing Lisa to his passion. He did not want to put her off. She had never even been to Butterfly Creek.

To his delight, his grateful down-on-your-knees wonder, she loved it all. It was all so pretty, especially the filmy ferns. Only one cell thick? No wonder they dried out, but weren't they pretty when they hadn't. In his excitement he bought her boots, a light pack, a floppy hat. She had always loved dressing up and was quick and agile. She crashed through creeks, was wary with rivers, used her head and loved everyone in the huts. They were so nice, each and every one of them. Sometimes they were even nicer than the last lot, didn't he think?

Robin, who sometimes had to force himself to talk to the clowns who were lousing up his space, sat beside her and her steaming enamel mug of tea and smiled. Billy tea really did taste different too, didn't it? She'd never believed it before but what did the other guys think and had they really done the Saddle in three hours? Wow, had Rob heard that, it would take us miles longer wouldn't it, Rob?

It wouldn't, or not him alone. He nodded.

The hut creaked around them as he lay on the bunk below her and ached with longing. They would hear him he supposed. Wanking is not for huts.

She tracked down a waterfall next morning. He had never seen it before and he had walked the track dozens of times. There was a sound of splashing, thin squeaks of laughter. Lisa turned and dived off the track to the left.

'Don't ever do that!' he yelled, ducking beneath the spines of the bush lawyer to blunder after her.

She turned, her hand pushing back ropes of supplejack. 'What?'

'Leave the main track like that.'

'For heaven's sake, Rob. Don't be so bossy. I want to find the pool.'

She turned, crashed on through the rough side track and rounded the corner. Sitting in the middle of the stony pool beneath the waterfall cascading from the bush was Emmeline; small breasted, skinny, henna hair piled high, her nipples dark. Beside her a naked child lay on his stomach kicking the shallow water into myriads of shining drops. Rays of sunlight shone through green.

'Emmie,' yelled Lisa. 'What on earth are you guys doing here? Hi, Calvin.'

Calvin kicked more strongly, water leaped higher, was caught in a mini-rainbow. A top-heavy wood pigeon achieved lift off, clattered above them in a glint of grey and blue.

'Hi.'

Emmie.

Not here. Or not now. Not just now when it was important for everything to go right.

Two

So how would you begin. How would you start on the adult Emmeline O'Malley. She wouldn't see thirty again according to Bernie, which was true but not by much. She had been brought up by her aunt in steely poverty and pride. Robin's earliest memories included Miss Bowman and Emmeline riding stiff-backed on ancient bicycles through wind and rain, through sun and drifting sand to track down the Specials in Kilbirnie, the Best Buys in Miramar, the Library. Miss Bowman, large, layered and strapped about the middle like an ill-assembled and badly tied parcel; Emmeline a pale-skinned follower, her flaming hair plaited and dragged around her narrow head. They wore black woollen stockings summer and winter. They spoke to few. Their woolly hats were of no known pattern; their histories were unknown. They were different.

Maureen and Eileen agreed it was odd that Miss Bowman (no

one knew her first name) should keep herself to herself. That there should be little popping in. She was friendly but distant, a mysterious bundle of a woman. She gardened, she cleaned the taps in the garden, she raked the gravel in her purple hat, in the fullness of time she sometimes wet herself. She loved Emmeline.

She admitted Robin, but only by appointment. When he was about four he had climbed over her fence to watch her raking. 'I've come to play,' he told her.

Miss Bowman scarcely glanced at him. 'No, you haven't. If I want you I'll ask you. Off you go. Tout de suite and the tooter the sweeter.'

Emmeline, swinging from the tyre swing with her mouth open, had smiled. He remembered that.

Miss Bowman spoke differently. Not only the accent but the care with which she chose her words, the attention she gave to each. Bicycles, photographs, televisions, advertisements, apartments, Emmeline; none of them was short changed, all were delivered in full. Which was unexpected when you thought about it, her being American and the way they shorten worse than the Aussies. And where had all her stuff come from? Family. It must be family. She couldn't have bought it here. It was not only old but weird. On entering Miss Bowman's front room you checked the airlock, dived deep and sank onto an Edwardian seabed. When they did *The Forsaken Merman* at school, Robin felt at home. Pale light filtered, slid down the edges of drawn blinds onto green plush covering the round table. There were books bound in leather hungry and cracked as seaboots: *The Ingoldsby Legends, The Scarlet Letter, Leaves of Grass.* A stuffed ermine's winter coat, snarling mouth and pointed yellow teeth were trapped beneath a bell of glass. There was a barometer, a button hook, three pieces of scrimshaw and unlit candles. An ancient naval sword hung on the wall, its handle covered in sharkskin so the wielding hand would not slip. In what Miss Bowman? Blood, boy, blood. The sofa and chairs were rounded reefs of ruby red or scratchy green with smooth mown areas around anemone flowers and swaying seaweed leaves.

There were more flowers on the hooked rug on the linoleum. Egg-yolk daisies flowered before a log cabin. An eagle with widespread wings perched on one end of the roof, a windvane at the other. A briskly trotting black horse sped by.

The pictures were not marine. Each one told him something. Everyone had a question. Why did the man ('Napoleon, Robin, Napoleon') have his right hand inside his coat? Why was the lady with the drooping head sitting all alone on top of the world? What was a Tiff and why had the lady and man had one? And tell me again, Miss Bowman, oh tell me again about *The Old Shepherd's Chief Mourner*. The bare room, the faithful border collie, the only one who really cared keeping Vigil throughout the Night, head outstretched on the humble coffin. What's humble, Miss Bowman? Poor, boy, poor.

There was only one photograph on the plush-covered table. A woman stared straight at the camera, her hair hanging beneath the wide framing hood of a cloak clamped tight at the neck, the other hand resting on a long stick. Her face was unsmiling which surprised Robin. Seaward suburbs ladies usually grin like mad in photographs. He had seen them in chemists' windows.

'A friend of mine,' said Miss Bowman and put it behind the ermine.

Miss Bowman told them stories, her voice lilting as though echoing through water like dolphins on TV. She sat in front of the one-bar heater before the fireplace in the front room and told them stories of mystery and terror. About the little boy who put his hand through the wringer when he had been told not to and it was squashed flat as your hat, about the even smaller boy who went to the dump when he'd been told not to and got shut in a fridge and whose bleached bones were found years later. 'Bleached bones,' murmured Miss Bowman, her eyes on the glowing coil of the heater. About the seagull with only one leg at Lyall Bay which was always hungry because seagulls give no quarter and nature is red in tooth and claw and not only nature.

Little Degchie-Head was one of her favourites. It had been her mother's and its subtitle was apt. 'An awful warning to bad babas.'

'Robin's crying, Aunt,' said Emmeline from the comfort of Miss Bowman's wide lap.

'I am not.' And he wasn't either.

They popped corn in a corn popper also sent from Cold Lake, Alberta. Emmeline and Robin took turns, tense with delight and careful of the hot stove because of *Little Degchie-Head* and Willy in his bright blue sashes who fell in the fire and was burnt to ashes.

They did not go to the same primary school. Miss Bowman, for reasons known only to herself, took against the local one. She and Emmeline rode off each morning through the tunnel to Strathmore Park. Miss Bowman and her BSA were there to meet Emmeline each day as the bright gaggle streamed out the school gates by the safety crossing to be bossed across by the big kids with whistles and lifted barriers. Emmeline mounted her bike and rode home with Aunt to silence and dreams and ballet.

And that was another thing. You couldn't take ballet or indeed anything unless somebody paid. How did Miss Bowman afford it? Obviously she didn't have a bean. They lived on the smell of an oily rag—ask Bernie. Their clothes were another layered secret. And Valentine's Dance Studio was a tough outfit. Charity, according to Miss Valentine as well as Miss Bowman, was for the birds. There would be no reduction of fees for the impecunious, however talented.

And Emmie was talented. Extremely talented and hard working, with none of the distractions of overheated girlish friendships or winsome boy-niggling charm, Emmeline seemed destined for a dedicated and brilliant career. Her skinny body was supple as a reed, her plaits had disappeared at secondary, her Medusa tangle of leaping red hair was once more wrapped around her head, her arms and legs were born to move.

She began to be noticed. Murmurs were heard. Scholarship, overseas, the Royal Ballet even. Emmie O'Malley with the cast-iron belly, Emmie the loner, the 'Don't-Care was made to care'

34

nutcase, grew from ugly duckling to cygnet, from cygnet to young swan with a future.

Wrapped in dance, in movement, in the slow tuning of an efficient instrument into a near-perfect one and the sweaty painful slog of achieving same, Emmie had remained on another planet even during her late teens. She practised three to four hours daily. Dancing was her life until she discovered Gary.

Gary. Ah Gary. Little is known of Gary. His only point of interest is that he was the first. The first of tall guys and small guys and loutish apes and smooth bastards and mellow veterans who beat a path to Miss Bowman's back door to see Emmeline because she was friendly and good fun.

'Emmie there?' they shouted at the bundle by the back door.

'Do you mean my niece, Emmeline?'

'Yeah.'

Ballet was not tossed aside lightly nor immediately. It just faded from the scene. Eileen and Maureen learned not to ask Miss Bowman when they met at the store about the latest medal, the next recital, the possibility of a TV appearance.

Emmeline, clear eyed and graceful and draped in garments even more unusual than those of her childhood, gave no explanation. Her sartorial range was wide. She had the eye of an op shop falcon for camouflage combat fatigues, for shimmering diaphanous fabrics which might have been discarded by Scheherazade, for lace. She shrank the relic of a fifties twin-set to body-stocking dimensions. You couldn't put your finger on her. She had class but no centre. She was splintered, flaky, generous and loved men.

Was Emmie the town bike? Hating himself and the phrase, Robin had denied the thought. And it was nothing to do with him, for God's sake. There was Lisa growing daily in beauty and in grace next door on the other side. Lisa.

Miss Bowman kept her own counsel. If she was disappointed at the abandoning of ballet no one would ever know. If she was heartbroken they would know even less. She remained silent.

*

Ballet became too time-consuming and labour-intensive but there were other avenues for grace, for movement, for head-held-high attack, for the combination of dignity and up-yours approach to life Emmeline had learned at her aunt's knee. She auditioned for acting parts. Nobody had ever heard of her. She had no agent. She joined Equity. She read the scripts offered, she stared the directors in the eyes, blinked and stared again. Both men and women gave her parts. A walk-on in Lorca, a dancer in *Bohème* (no singing required) a miscast Masha in mourning for her life. She worked her way up. There was something about her. She could act for one thing and her voice carried.

She continued to live with Aunt. They liked each other and male visitors seemed of little interest or concern to Miss Bowman. She made them welcome as did Emmeline and returned to her front room.

'Good night,' she called from the passage. 'You'll let your friend out will you Emmeline? Good night, Sebastian.'

'Night, Miss Bowman.'

No climbing of silken ropes was required, no love-sick cries for Rapunzel, Rapunzel to let down her long hair were needed in the quiet back street of Seatoun.

Emmeline's acting career (*Talented newcomer scoops pool*) flourished. Several years later it was interrupted, but not for long.

Even Robin realised she was pregnant. They seldom spoke nowadays; a wave sufficed, a smile. Their relationship was compounded of childhood goodwill, mutual lack of interest and stuck-with-it propinquity. Over the next few months she seemed to inflate slowly but inevitably like a balloon which has been filled with technical assistance, helium perhaps, or a foot-pump at a party. Her clothes did not change. Emmeline drifted about, floating in virtually transparent shifts or waddling in dungarees, clutching her stomach with affectionate wide-stretched hands.

She came up the concrete path one Saturday morning when he had his head under the bonnet peering morosely at the engine. The brake fluid was down again. Engines, plumbing and people have something in common. Once they have been opened up you need experts, specialists who charge like bulls and what can you do. And the spare tyre was shot and tutors get peanuts and he was trying to save and stuff it.

'Hey Rob,' she called.

He lifted his head.

'Oh. Hi, Emmie.'

'Hi.' She leaned one arm against the thing and smiled at him. Vast, friendly, hair floating, tendrils wafting, Emmeline was pleased to see him.

'Would you like to sit down?' he said quickly.

She looked around, still smiling. 'Where?'

He opened the door of the driver's seat. 'Here.'

She laughed. Full-throated and infinitely happy, Emmeline laughed. 'I might get stuck, matey.' She patted his arm. Some Orthodox Jewish women don't touch men other than their husbands. Not even to shake hands. And Chinese women dislike being kissed in public. It just goes to show, as Maureen would say.

'The other side maybe.' Emmeline waded round the back, opened the front passenger's door, lowered herself gently into the seat, held her stomach for a moment then patted the driver's seat. 'Don't you like being called matey?'

He took off his glasses, wiped them and put them back. 'I don't mind.'

'Robin then.' She patted the seat again. 'I want to ask you something.'

He climbed in, watched his feet and waited.

She was looking at him with attention, excessive attention, her eyes bright. 'Would you do me a favour?'

He hesitated for a moment, spoke quickly. 'Yes, of course. What?'

She laughed again, patted his knee.

'Oh, Rob,' she said. 'Now promise me you won't say yes unless you're quite happy with the idea.'

Oh shit.

'What?' he said again.

37

'Would you drive me to the Maternity Annexe when . . .' Again those cradling hands, that stomach. 'When the baby's coming.'

He could feel his dropped mouth.

'Well . . . But what about? I mean . . .'

'What about what?' Her eyes were candid, she was not kidding, she simply hadn't caught on.

This was ridiculous. Why should he be the one to be choosing his words with care. 'The father,' said Robin loudly.

Her voice did not change. She was calm, serious. It was no joke. 'He's gone. He shot through.' She glanced at him. 'Wouldn't you?'

He was disgusted with the windscreen. 'No, I would not.'

Her hand brushed his for a second. 'No.' She paused. 'Well, will you?'

Why the hell should he? Even as the thought surfaced he felt the sands shifting beneath him, the quicksands of decency dragging him into embarrassment at the best, into God knows what at the worst. His shoulders moved.

'Why not a taxi?'

'I've hardly ever been in a taxi,' she said dreamily. 'It's amazing when she moves.' She took his hand. 'Do you want to feel?'

He snatched it back. Unwilling, ungracious, Robin tried again. 'Is it a girl?'

'Oh, I haven't had a test or anything. I just assume it is.' Vacant in the mind if not in body, flaky as peeling skin, Emmeline smiled yet again. 'Aunt and I wouldn't know what to do with a boy.' She began climbing out of the car. Mountainous, heaving about like a cast cattlebeast, she hauled herself up and bent her head again. Amiable as ever, Emmeline had something else to say.

'Don't give it a thought, Rob. It was dumb of me to ask. I'll phone a cab.'

He was out of the car, clutching her pale arms, insisting, 'No. No. Of course I will. I was nuts.'

He had to work hard to convince her that nothing would make him happier, that it would be both a pleasure and a privilege for him to drive her to the Maternity Annexe when the time was, he almost said ripe, rephrased: 'When the time comes. I mean it.'

She was pleased. Delighted in fact. 'You're an old smoocherama.' Her mouth brushed his cheek, light as Lisa's first baby kisses. She smelled fierce, musky, drenched in something distilled from ambergris and sex glands. No floral overtones for Emmeline.

'I could ask dozens but you're so reliable,' she said. 'Of course I shouldn't ask anyone. Girls can do anything. I just thought it'd be more fun.'

'Just give me plenty of warning. Time, I mean,' he said. 'I wouldn't want to . . .'

She didn't, of course. For years afterwards the night of September 14th 1989 stayed with him.

She came beating on his door at one a.m., Miss Bowman's plastic raincoat over something long and trailing, her feet in jandals, an unravelling kete in her hand. 'Rob, you've got to believe me, Rob! She's coming.' She jumped into the front with unexpected agility. Both hands clutched the kete to her stomach in a disturbingly matron-like gesture. 'Why didn't you answer the phone?' she said crossly as they hurtled across the sleeping streets of the eastern suburbs.

'Didn't hear it.'

'Huh.' Her body, he noticed in glancing terror, had stiffened, arched. 'Christ,' she panted. 'I didn't think it'd be like this.'

'How long's it been happening?'

'Not long.' She relaxed, breathed deeply. 'Have you got a watch?'

They took a corner at speed. Robin's arms were rigid, his glasses misting. 'Why?'

'I'm meant to time the contractions. The time between. They said.'

He tugged it off, flung it at her. It fell to the floor.

'Don't worry,' she gasped. 'Just get there.'

Her hair was damp. He could see the glint of anger on her sweating face. 'I won't tread on the damn thing,' she muttered.

'You promised we'd start early.' He couldn't see, he couldn't think, his back was stuck to the seat, she was moaning beside him.

'I didn't know,' she gasped. 'It's meant to take hours. That's better, that's better. It's just in the—*Christ!* Just get there man! Get there.' She was writhing, slipping to the floor, out of control. 'Get there!'

They made it. Robin fell in the sliding doors. 'Quick! Quick!'

They were calm. This sort of thing had occurred before. They were pros. They assumed, not unnaturally, that he was her partner. 'This way please, Rob, is it? Aren't you lucky. It's going to be a quickie, this one. Must be a girl.' Large, cheerful, steeped in the miracle of birth and death, Carole and Kura took over. 'Come on,' they said. 'This way.'

'The poor guy's not the father,' muttered Emmeline, now supine, breathing deeply, doing what she was told to do. 'Just gave me a lift in. Shove off, Rob.' She stopped, overtaken by concentration and a breathy moan to Jesus.

'That doesn't matter,' said Kura. 'It's nicer with a friend but it's over to you. You didn't say, did you Emmie? Not on the admission sheet.'

Gasping, sweating, Emmeline dragged the word from somewhere. 'No.'

'Would you like to come, Rob?' Rooted to the spot, his feet clamped to the ground in horror, his head began the brisk shake of dismissal. His eyes met hers above the huge draped stomach.

'Shove off Rob,' she muttered again. She heaved in sudden convulsion, a gasp, a scream, something.

He grabbed her hand. 'I'll stay.'

She moved her blind head. 'No.'

'You'll tell Aunt,' she said, long bony fingers draped around a cup of tea.

'Yes.' He wouldn't take his eyes off her or the bundle in her arms, the slick of orange down on the scalp. 'What're you going to call him?'

She lifted her face; dried sweat and hollows grinned at him.

'How about Robin? Just kidding,' she said quickly. 'You'll break

40

it to Aunt. About him being a boy.'

'Sure.'

'She won't mind, of course, but she's not very well. You've noticed?'

How could he not have noticed. Weight was falling from Miss Bowman. She was now gaunt, her face yellow, her hair tugged back in sparse grey wisps. She was undoubtedly far from well.

'Otherwise of course she would have come with me, but I didn't tell her all hell had let loose. I think she'll be still be asleep. It's the pills. Don't wake her, will you? Leave it till the morning.'

'Yes.'

She put her cup down on the saucer on the locker, centred it carefully and told him, 'She's my mother, you know.'

Twice in one night someone had trusted him. With transport. With a secret which had once seemed necessary. 'Oh,' he said.

One finger circled the rim of her cup. 'Yes. Well, she's never said a word but she must be, mustn't she? Wouldn't you say? I wish she'd tell me, tell me the lot.' She hugged her child. 'We need to know, don't we, matey?'

'She must've said something.'

'Oh yes, there's the whole scenario, farming in Vermont, maple syrup, antique butter churns I shouldn't wonder. Photographs. All that. But not much about the Mommas and the Poppas.'

'But why did she come here?' He must stop nagging. She was exhausted.

'That's the big one,' she murmured. 'Or one of them. There's Aunty Martha who married a Canadian in Cold Lake and an uncle who died. And my mother Marie who died. The only thing that's missing is the family bible. And me.'

She shook her head in dismissal, glanced around the gleaming white room, sniffed briefly. 'If this is hospitals I don't think much of them. But Carole and Kura were great, weren't they, and I couldn't handle a home birth. All that aromatic oils and herbal massage and homeopathic potions and the music and loved ones in rows sounds great but . . . And can you imagine Aunt?' She shrugged, a large

41

generous heave of skinny shoulders. Her lips touched the sleeping head.

'He's going to be a redhead,' he said.

She grinned. 'Mustn't grumble. I hope Aunt's all right.'

He put his hand on hers. 'She'll be fine.'

She nodded, dragged her hair back. Victorian maidens with consumption, he had read somewhere, had had their hair cropped short. It was thought to sap their strength when they had so little left. Looking at Emmeline he could understand it. Even as drenched rat-tails her hair was a threat.

She put out her hand; formal, gracious, Emmeline O'Malley was offering her thanks. 'You were fantastic.'

'That's OK.' He kissed her cheek and left.

He sent her flowers. He sent her chrysanthemums and lilies and alstroemerias and pittosporum for backing as the florist suggested. 'To you both,' he wrote, 'with love, Rob and Lisa.'

She came home by taxi the next day, without them. They were lovely she told him over the fence. She couldn't think how she'd forgotten them. She was so sorry.

Lisa thought the whole thing was a bit funny, well not funny but you know what I mean. 'And you were there all the *time.*'

'Yes.'

She stood in silence, processing the thought, letting it seep in. 'Why?'

'She had no one else. Miss Bowman's not at all well . . .'

'Anyone can see that.' Lisa paused. 'What did you do?'

'Nothing. Held her hand, rubbed her back. You know.'

In fact Lisa didn't. She was not over-pleased but her good nature plus a sense of drama came to her aid. The other girls were impressed by Robin's role. Padma less so. And the baby, oh the baby. Lisa crooned, she cooed, she knitted a kiwi. 'When he's older, I'll knit him a rugby shirt. No, no, for the kiwi I mean. Then he can be a mascot, eh Calvin? A mascot for the Seatoun Midgets.'

'Thank you,' said Emmeline. She and Lisa did not dislike each other but the age difference had always precluded much interest.

Emmeline's former passion for ballet had held no interest for Lisa despite the endlessly *en pointe* ballerina tinkling through her life. And Emmeline looked a mess and Bernie said it was just what she'd been expecting for years and who was the father.

Emmeline thought of Lisa, when she thought at all, with a kind of awe. She was astounded that a bright little snuggle bunny like Lisa should wear the clothes of a funky up-front player, should love her job and do it well and at the same time assume the persona of some goddamn lady-in-waiting. Someone holding herself in readiness, waiting for her white wedding to the groom of her choice whereupon she would live happily ever after. In this day and age! With a sensible down-to-earth old bat like Maureen for a mother and a father who had walked out on her. It was beyond comprehension. And look at Murray. Why didn't she take a good look at her brother occasionally. A warning surely. Murray glued to his student's desk, his dreams of white coats and stethoscopes and Yes Doctor and No Doctor and Please Doctor and Oh Doctor coming nearer every moment and the Bernina overheating in hopeless pursuit. On the rare occasions when Emmeline met Murray she watched him with interest. He puzzled her.

She watched him at Maureen's Christmas drinks party while Calvin did half press-ups on a blue fleecy cotton rug with clowns in hats. He heaved himself on his forearms, lifted his head and collapsed to resume the struggle. You would think he would have got tired of it, thought Robin, whose proprietary pleasure in Calvin's existence had lessened since Emmie had resumed her scrambling muddle of a life. Not from lack of enthusiasm but he seldom saw the child. Calvin was with Emmeline at rehearsals, auditions, productions. He slept backstage. He was fed in the interval. In buses and backpacks, by day and by night, he accompanied his mother while Aunt rested or crept about her garden.

Murray sat with legs spread wide, russet-cheeked and ready to tell them anything they cared to know about parasitology or endocrinology, neither of which he had studied as yet but which were of special interest to him. He sat in his own chair, a deep one with wide curved arms reminiscent of the thirties, built for comfort and almost impossible for Maureen to lift. Fortunately there was little need for her to do so. Murray's chair sat year by year in the same place, full frontal to both the television screen and the heater.

The rest of the party—Miss Bowman, Emmeline and Calvin, Robin and Eileen, Maureen and Lisa—sat in a semi-circle around him as though seeking guidance from a counsellor, a change-agent who could set them right for life, who could guide them on the road to recovery.

George had always asked the neighbours in for a 'spot' at Christmas. Maureen, angry and hurt, had not done so the first time after he left. The following year she collected her festive capon from her neighbourhood butcher whom she supported both from loyalty and not having a car.

'Hubby'll like that,' said Lance, slapping the immensely naked bird with a modesty square of greaseproof paper before shoving it in its plastic bag. He twisted the ends and presented it with pride.

Confused, heart thumping, money worrying her like a mauling dog, Maureen drew herself upright. 'I haven't got a husband.'

Lance dropped one eyelid. 'Good on you,' he said.

Maureen marched home, punctured the plastic bag for air circulation, put it in the fridge and rang Miss Bowman and Eileen. 'Come over,' she said, 'and have a Christmas drink with me and the children.'

They had done so ever since. Miss Bowman disliked crowds but Maureen was a good sort and once a year wouldn't kill her and she supposed someone should do something vaguely festive at this time of year. She was grateful it wasn't her and brought cookies.

Eileen's works did not extend to hospitality. If she was asked she came. Reciprocity was unknown to her. She couldn't see why Robin had to take a bottle but that was his business.

Having 'got her ask in', Maureen went back to the Bernina. Lisa made the guacamole and the sour cream dip as usual, bought the corn chips and the peanuts and more or less left it at that. At the

44

last moment she stuffed some dates with cream cheese for a change. Murray bought a bottle of Henderson Dry and a six-pack with the money Maureen gave him.

The living room had not changed throughout the years. Christmas cards marched or sulked or fell flat on their faces on the ziggurat of honey-coloured tiles surrounding the built-in heater. It was one of the few changes Maureen had been able to afford since he left. She had had the fireplace ripped out. 'Ripped straight out,' she told them each year, demonstrating with heaving gestures both the artisans and their effort. 'I said, do what you like with it. I don't want a bar of it. Nasty smoky thing and all that lugging wood and cleaning up.'

The Bernina sat on a wooden table shrouded in sky-blue organdie for camouflage; generations of pins had been dropped and picked up and dropped again on the maroon carpet squares. A magnetised pin holder, two patchwork pin cushions and Maureen's double-ended one for every day lay on a trolley beside the sewing table with pinking shears and cutting-out scissors and sharp pointed ones for fine work such as slitting button holes, which frankly Maureen found a bore, especially as they always come at the end. Reels of polyester and silk threads from blush pink to carmine, from palest cream to persimmon, lay jumbled in ancient chocolate boxes nearby. For years Maureen had promised herself one of those reel-holder things you can spin around for instant access to any colour instead of scrabbling. Maureen spent a good deal of time scrabbling; hunting for tape measures, crawling on hands and knees in search of a lost sleeve, a belt, a scrap of Velcro she'd had there a moment ago. Her flattened palm demonstrated, her eyes searched—right *there*. You wouldn't read about it.

None of which disturbed her cheerful goodwill, her pleasure in every aspect of her rewarding life.

'Why the hell, Mum?' said Murray each time she wheeled out her bike to ride to the appropriate church on Saturdays to check on the back view of Tina's or Diane's or whichever bridal gown would soon be viewed as it headed up the aisle.

'I like to make sure it's perfect, the pleats and gathers hanging straight and that. All it needs usually is a quick twitch but you have to know what you're doing. It's what people mostly see, the back. And it's their big day. I like to have it all lovely with flowers and white and horseshoes and proper music and everything.' Maureen's grin was lopsided. 'Then they fall into the sink and if they're lucky he stays, but honestly . . .'

She glanced around her kingdom, smiled at the hulking three-piece, the ziggurat bricks, the muffled Bernina and laughed aloud, 'Where would I put him now?'

Love of life and people flowed from her, as from Lisa. A trip to the dairy took her twice as long as most. There were babies to be clucked at, toddlers to be chatted up, old ladies ripe for escort at crossroads, high-tailed dogs with pricked ears to be applauded, old men who couldn't understand the form which had arrived that morning and could Mrs, er, just . . . Of course she could and let's do it right now.

And what about Bernie whose husband had been made redundant for the second time, a fully trained machinist and now look at him. What did they think they were playing at in the Beehive, giving themselves a pay rise while people like Tony, decent hard-working voters like Tony . . . Oh, she could weep.

Other people's problems appalled her. She strode through life marvelling at her own good fortune. Her cropped hair hung straight, her eyes, triangular as Mrs Thatcher's but more benign, snapped with happiness, her smile illuminated.

Robin could see where Lisa came from; the clear skin, the smile, the goodwill. But when had Maureen taken root? Could she ever have run, jumped, danced all night, this solid *planted* woman? Moved with speed, skipped, appeared and disappeared in moments like her adorable wisp of a daughter? Maureen's arms and legs now moved as though wading through swamp water. She soldiered on.

'Cheers,' she said, lifting her sherry glass. She only had four left now but fortunately the boys always had beer. Someone, the Barkers from Kelburn, wasn't it?—had given them six for their wedding which had been a generous present in those days and it was sad two had broken but that's life.

'Cheers.' United in fellowship the neighbours drank.

Maureen turned to smile at Miss Bowman who had knocked back her sherry in two swift gulps and placed the dregs on the glass table beside her with a faint ping.

Robin inspected his mother's new perm. As she had told him, the last row hadn't taken; the rollers had been too big. You can always tell when they skimp the bottom and Eileen had never liked that new girl.

Did he love her, he wondered. Of course he loved her. It wasn't her fault, her lost pitiful life. It was the scaffolding's. But if she had been a man would he have greeted her with enthusiasm, shouted her a drink at the nearest pub as he would Maureen. Eileen's maternal love had unexpectedly tightened, had pulled from both sides like the strings of an ancient sponge bag since he had told her about Lisa. 'Engaged!' Her laugh was merry. Merryish. 'To Lisa!' she gasped, her hands clutched in front of her chest like a supplicant squirrel. 'Isn't she very young?'

'We're not getting married for a while yet.'

'Oh.' Eileen picked up the faded velvet cushion from her chair, gave it a quick bang and replaced it. 'Well dear, I hope you'll be very happy.'

Robin put his arms around her. 'Mum?'

She pulled away, looked at him politely, touched her grey spectacle frames with a quick hand. 'Yes, dear?'

'And here's to the happy couple,' laughed Maureen. Miss Bowman lifted her empty glass, peered in it without hope and replaced it.

'Engaged couple,' murmured Eileen.

'Engaged happy couple,' crowed Maureen, happier than ever.

Rob put his arm round Lisa. She smoothed her mini, her head was down. 'That's lovely, thank you.' The nape of her neck where her hair parted, the deep pale hollow at the base destroyed him. He kissed it fiercely, would like to have bitten it.

Her hands flew upwards. 'Robin!'

Murray leaned back. His walk shorts had water melons on them, the bottom button of his shirt had come undone, his navel was hairy. 'Going to *Bohème* next week?' he asked.

Confused, aching with lust, Robin shook his head, the single swipe of a tormented beast. 'No.'

'Me neither. I can't understand for the life of me why all those arty-farty types go on about opera. Nobody likes good music more than me but I just like to get right into it, know what I mean?' Murray's hands waved, indicated total immersion. 'The composer, the soloist, the orchestra and me. That's it. That's all I want. Nothing else. With opera you've got all these clowns mucking about, right?'

Miss Bowman picked up her empty glass and stared through it. 'Some people do find the sheer richness of opera overwhelming,' she said. 'The passion. The drama. You don't have to like it, Murray.'

Murray glared. 'I know that. I'm just trying to tell you why I don't.'

'And achieving it.'

'They bang on. They won't shut up.' Murray's eyebrows were about to leave home, storm out the door. 'I don't know where they're coming from, those creeps. All that stuff.'

'Verbal appraisal in the interval can be distracting.'

'I didn't mean the audience!'

'Ah.' Miss Bowman held out her glass. 'Would you freshen my glass, please Murray? Thank you.' There is always a solution. Even an archaic home-grown euphemism can be called into service.

Robin watched her with attention. She was dying, this woman. What else could possibly be happening to her. What else could cause layers of fat, cushions of flesh to disappear, to melt away like snow from a rock face to reveal the indomitable old crag beneath. And still she bothered to take on the prick and demolish him. If they had all been in the same boat as children, as Bernie maintained, Miss Bowman's craft would have made it. Clinker built or carvel, Miss Bowman would have taken charge; rationed the water, stripped off her shirt for a makeshift sail and set course for the headlands.

She gave a large, expansive, reassembling heave and smiled at him. 'I have never thanked you properly, or not properly enough, Robin,' she said, 'for supporting Emmeline so gallantly when Calvin was born.'

'No, no I was glad. Very glad. Yes, I mean . . .' Calvin stared at him. He was now flat on his stomach chewing a clown. His eyes were dark, his cheeks scarlet, a dribble of sick appeared. Emmeline mopped.

'Why Calvin?' asked Eileen.

Emmeline's smile was friendly. 'Why not?'

'Calvin Coolidge. Vermont. Good man, weaned on a dill pickle or no,' said Miss Bowman, wondering if she should risk trying for a third. The sherry glasses were elfin in size.

'I'd really like to hear those people who're coming soon,' said Maureen who had not been listening. 'What's their name? You know.' Her fingers clicked, her face was tense with the effort of recall. 'They're coming soon. Two of them. They were here years ago. You know! Just the main centres, I think, though I'm not sure about Dunedin. They never seem to get anyone do they. Everyone said they were wonderful. No, no, not Kiri. I'd never be able to afford Kiri and anyway she's not coming is she. I just can't . . . They were married. Two of them. Man and wife.' Her fingers clamped the air in desperation. 'I almost had it. *You* know, Murray.'

'No.'

'Cleo Laine,' suggested Emmie, re-siting Calvin on his rug.

'Cleo *Laine*. That's it! That's the name! Cleo Laine and her husband.'

Oh the happiness, the relief of discovery and remembering. The room was filled with Maureen's pleasure. It is better to have lost and found than never to have forgotten at all. Her face fell. But what was the husband's?

Murray told them about his scholarship, how it didn't mean a thing. It was useless, absolutely useless. He'd have to live at home, he couldn't see any way round it. As for when he got to medical school, God knows. You just had to mortgage your life away unless you were rich or a Maori or preferably both.

Emmeline lifted her head. 'Murray,' said Lisa.

A jerk, a goddamn jerk. Robin, his nose deep in DB lager, considered the word goddamn. He had liked it ever since he heard Miss Bowman chasing a rottweiler down the drive years ago. Arm upraised, skirts tucked in, Miss Bowman had given it beans. The rottweiler, after one tentative stumpy wag, had disappeared at speed. It was a pity the word wasn't in common use. It was forceful, explosive and to the point.

Of course he loved his mother. He was goddamn programmed to love his mother. Only sons of widowed mothers are set in concrete. He drank deeply, caught Miss Bowman's eye and drank again. He watched the bubbles in his beer as they slid up the sides of blue plastic. In glass they come up the middle as well. He glanced at his watch, smiled weakly, stared at Lisa. 'No, no, I'll just perch here, Eileen,' she said settling herself on the wide arm of the sofa. The inside of her thigh was pale, secret, there was a blue vein. Oh sweet fuck. 'I'm quite happy here,' she said offering him a plate of stuffed dates. He shook his head.

'Oh come on, Robbie.'

'No, no thanks. I don't like dates.'

'How can you not like dates? It's like not liking coconut or something. Everyone likes dates.'

'No thanks,' he said to the succulent shine of her lips. 'Not for me. I just don't like them.'

Maureen and Eileen discussed the fence between their houses which was a worry. They agreed it was on its last legs. That's the thing about wooden fences. They don't last for ever. The two women, their faces earnest, discussed the problem. Did the boys think there was any point in them patching it up a little? It would be lovely if it would just see them out.

Murray looked thoughtful, pulled his lower lip. 'No,' he said, 'not a chance. Not an earthly.'

The women looked more worried.

Robin said he would have a look at it.

Miss Bowman said it was a pity it wasn't on her side. A slap of paint would see her out. She held out her glass. '"No moaning at the bar,"' she said.

Eileen, hands clasped once more, looked puzzled. Maureen who had caught the drift if nothing else threw back her head to laugh. 'Look, it's Christmas,' she said, 'and who needs a fence anyhow? Have another sherry.'

They talked about Robin's new second-hand car. Did he like the colour? Was it warm and comfortable? They hoped it hadn't got power windows. Eileen had been in a taxi with them recently and she wanted to put down the window to get rid of the air freshener which she always thought was worse than the nicotine and indeed most things. And when you got nicotine plus Summer Meadow it was beyond anything and she was fiddling about for hours trying to get the window down and the man got quite shirty. It was hopeless since taxis had been deregulated. Hopeless. Half of them can't speak English and they won't let on either. Just shoot off trying to pretend they know where you mean and half the time they haven't a clue.

Lisa was still handing and smiling and handing again. Murray, without a glance or a word, dug a fist full of peanuts with a quick downward scoop and flung them into his mouth.

''Nother beer?'

'Thanks.' Robin watched the large munching mouth, the angry eyebrows, the huge convoluted ears. Not a lovable face. Not a face to inspire confidence and trust when the doctor could finally see his way clear to see you now. A white coat might be a help but not much, and anyway did they wear them now? He sighed.

They discussed the problem of the milkman's unreliability. None of them trusted those cardboard packs and what other alternative was there.

Miss Bowman yawned.

Calvin gave a piercing wail.

Emmeline lifted him from the floor, heaved up her sagging T-shirt and buttoned the screaming child to her breast. The evening sun fell on the threads of orange draped like saffron stigmas across the naked skull.

The women gazed with pleasure at this maternal phenomenon which they would not have been able to practise in their day. Not feeding, not in public. Not with men.

Robin, who had last seen Emmeline's breasts overlaid with Calvin's cord-attached, flayed-rabbit body, watched with interest. Murray, torn between the professional detachment of a medical student and disgust at the crassness of the woman, swigged his beer and kept his head down.

He helped himself to another fistful of nuts. 'When're you and Lisa getting married?'

'When she's eighteen.'

'That's not for years.'

'Just over one.'

Torn once more between the rival put-downs of baby snatching and the bloody stupidity of waiting, Murray was silent.

The clock whirred, clicked, heaved itself together and chimed seven.

'Look at the *time*,' said Eileen leaping to her feet.

Three

The wedding. Yes, the wedding. They had been sleeping together for eight months but the wedding had to wait until April. Lisa insisted on Easter.

She sat on his knee on the back porch, her head against his chest, his hands cupping her breasts as she explained her reasons.

'It's traditional. I've always wanted to be an Easter bride.'

'But that's England.'

'Well?'

'It's spring there. Resurrection. New life.'

'But we're not having a baby straight *off*.'

'No, no. "The Lord is risen." Chickens. Lambs. All that.'

'Oh I'm not fussed about that. It's just that it's traditional. And it'll have to be tiny. We'll have to pay. Mum can't, not with Murray.'

'Yes, of course.' The heart does sink. You can feel it sliding down, slipping into the left shoe. Still it was worth a go. 'Why have the whole works? All that money. Why don't we save it for somewhere to live?'

'But I can't not have a wedding!'

It crippled them, leached them dry as export sphagnum moss, but she had it, that was the main thing, and was happy. She had the church and the vicar and 'Here Comes the Bride' and *The Prophet* ('For life goes not backwards, nor tarries with yesterday') and the friends and the caterers and the biggest triumph of all which was the wedding frock. For weeks Maureen had lived and breathed white satin. Had draped and pinned and ruched and fitted and redraped again. 'It's lovely to have a size eight to play with,' she said. 'So many of my ladies are sixteen or more. With one or two I don't use the tape even. The gap would be too awful. I just take a quick guess. You get quite good at it after a while.'

The girls from A Bench all came though Dr Biddle couldn't make it at the last minute; a few of Robin's ex-colleagues from zoology who shared his enthusiasm for the bush; one or two from the English department but not many. Karen from botany greeted the bridal party with wide-armed enthusiasm. 'Baby fucker,' she whispered in Robin's ear and moved on to kiss the bride.

The bridesmaid, Sandy, yes Sandy, wore pink and seemed happy. The bride was adorable. She had her wedding, her day, her apotheosis. She was a bride. Robin watched her across the hall; pink-nosed with delight, lips damp, eyes aglow. Literally aglow, he couldn't take his own from her as she danced from guest to guest. Yes, the ruching was lovely wasn't it, Mum had spent hours. Would Aunty Mavis like a chair? Was she sure? Oh well then, as long as she was sure. Hello! Hi! Great to see you guys. Thanks. Yeah, Mum made it. Well yeah, but she trained as a cutter. Hi. You made it then! Cheers. Good to *see* ya.

He found himself beside Emmeline. Rake-thin, relaxed, she leaned against the wall and watched. Her scarlet jacket fitted and flared above black leather jodhpurs and dusty boots, her bush of hair was tied back. Rakehelly, that was the word, Hellfire Club,

moonlit hell-for-leathers beneath gibbous moons. He was pleased
to see her.

'How's the actress?'

'Actor, dumb-bum. Actor.'

She really did look most unusual. 'I just wanted the kneejerk
reaction.' He rubbed the shoulders of his rented suit against the
wall beside her; it was a bit tight across the shoulders. 'I like the
way the non-sexist bias flips about. There's a sneaky policy change.
Cabinet Ministers have affairs with actresses, not actors. Unless of
course they do. Ever noticed that?'

'Sure. That's part of the fun.'

'"In this day and age"?'

They grinned at each other, surrounded by noise and food and
ritual practices and happiness.

'How is she?'

'Still battling on. You know what she said yesterday?'

He shook his head.

'I wonder which bit's going to drop off next.' Emmeline sniffed,
flicked her hand to her nose.

He glanced around looking for his glass. She handed him hers.
'Thanks.'

'It affects me like that too. That's why I'm drinking like a fish.'

'You are not drinking like a fish!' he snapped.

'Small fish.' She demonstrated, guppy fingers gulping. Calvin,
hair flaming at knee level, eclair drooping in one hand, hurtled
towards his trousers.

Emmie swooped, swung him high in the air. 'Not on the wedding
pants, honbun.'

'Hi, Calvin.'

The brief glance was framed by cream and chocolate. 'Hi.'

Surely he saw beneath the disguise. 'You remember me, Calvin.'

The child was busy, twisting and turning towards the mangled
chocolate eclair held beyond reach. 'Nah.'

Deflated, Rob ran his hand over the orange bullet head. It was
like caressing Miss Bowman's boot-wiper.

'How's your thesis?' asked Emmie, unleashing Calvin once more.

'OK.'

'I keep asking what it's called. Bit of a giveaway not to remember. Something about Henry James, isn't it? Too long. Heavy in the bottom. I like thin books.'

Robin tipped back on the heels of his new shoes, his eyes on his bride still meeting and greeting and having fun. 'So does Lisa.'

Emmeline ran her tongue in front of her top teeth. 'Is that *right?*'

'And it's not Henry James any more.'

'Good.' She grinned, shrugged off the weight of fat books. 'Who then?' Her face changed, became sly with self send-up. 'Anyone I know?'

'Alice O'Leary.'

'Oh, Aunt knew her.'

'Whaaat!'

Her eyes were following Calvin's flight course about the room. He was busy having a ball; being spoilt, hugged, cosseted or avoided. He ran round and round, up and down, in and out, weaving through the configurations of the party like a manic and diminutive figure at a hoedown. 'Yeah,' said Emmie. 'She stayed with us when she first came out. Weeks and weeks. I was about eight or nine. She came from Vermont as well.'

Rob shook his reeling head. She had no idea. No idea in the world. He wanted to seize her bony hands, to shock sense into her, to make her understand the astonishment of her gift.

'But that's amazing.'

'Why?'

'Well, because . . .' Because she's my thesis. I can talk to someone who knew her, a friend of hers, as well as the half-dead husband down south. All this and Lisa too. Robin stood still, awestruck, surrounded by revelry and the shrieks of friends. There were balloons, icing, icing on the cake. 'Hey.' He breathed the word out. 'Hey, I've met her.' Well, glimpsed her, heard her voice. He had met Alice O'Leary.

*

The hut was a hide for bird-watching; flattened grocery cartons begged from Bernie had been reconstituted into a lopsided structure stuck together with wide brown sticky tape (commercial grade). Rain had not yet reduced it to sludge but its days were numbered. The smell was distinctive, the sour furry smell of damp cardboard.

Robin had not told Eileen its real purpose. She had disliked the eyesore but been brave. All small boys had huts. She knew that, though she also knew she would have to wait for an inorganic collection to remove the mess eventually. In the meantime Robin hid. There were few birds, but those that came he watched and waited for and hugged himself with joy. He drank cocoa and sugar and cold water from a plastic medicine glass from the bathroom as starlings goose-stepped feet from the slits in the hide. A blackbird came frequently, his mate less often. Why? Why was that? The sparrows were regulars, known by name: Fat, Jim, Boss. He liked them but they came too often. They had not the rarity value of chaffinches or robber gulls or the occasional silvereyes.

The hide was at the back of the section by the nearly defunct woodshed. Rampant bignonia had almost engulfed it and moved on to overflow Miss Bowman's shed alongside a leather-leafed loquat and a straggling lilac. (Miss Bowman disliked pruning.)

A woman ran out Miss Bowman's back door and stood still, both hands covering her mouth as she stood rocking back and forward, back and forward.

He knew who she was. 'I have a house guest coming to stay Robin,' Miss Bowman had told him last week, polishing the glass of her pictures in her front room.

'A house guest,' he said carefully.

'Yes. A guest in the house. You know about guests.'

Did he? 'Yes.'

'A house guest is a guest who stays in the house.'

'Oh.'

'So, don't come over till I ask you again.'

He looked at her. She shook her head. 'No,' said Miss Bowman.

'Mum, why can't we have a house guest?'

The things they come out with. 'What on earth for?'

'I don't know.'

And here was the house guest, tall, dark and weeping on the back steps. She ran to the shed door and tugged hard. He could see her hair, more hair than he had ever seen, rolled and twisted about her head.

'It's locked,' Robin told her from his hide. It was always locked; always had been. The woman turned and headed for the lilac and sank down. 'No!' she cried at the late-afternoon stillness, the bright light. 'No. No. *No*,' wept the house guest.

Robin watched in alarm. He crouched lower, hid deeper in his shyness and waited for her to go away. But she was sad, so still . . . He crept out of his shelter and moved to the sagging fence. 'What's the matter, lady?'

Her head snapped up from her hands. She gasped and scrambled to her feet. There was mud on her frock, mud on her clutching hands, a streak across one cheek.

'How long've you been here?'

'Hours.'

She shook her head, mopped her eyes.

'You're the house guest,' he told her.

Her eyes closed briefly. Her voice was funny. 'Something like that,' she said.

'Can I come and see Miss Bowman?' he asked Emmie. 'Soon.'

There was a smear of cream on her jodhpurs. She wiped it angrily, then licked the finger. 'Bugger. What? Oh sure. She'll tell you all about her.'

'The bridegroom,' said a man by Robin's side, 'the bridegroom who should be dancing, stands without a glass at his own wedding. How can this be?'

Spiro Daskalakis seized his arm, planted a full glass of sparkling white in his hand and hugged him. 'For you Robin I break my rule. Never to drink on the job. My first rule. How many years is it since you came? Since you are with me and they say to drink. How many times? Tell me.' The fingers of the hand without the glass snapped open and shut begging for numbers. 'Many, many, many.' Spiro drank, wiped his moustache with the back of his hand and beamed at them. 'And the lady . . . ?

'Hi. Emmeline O'Malley.'

He bowed. 'Daskalakis. Spiro Daskalakis.'

'She's an actress,' said Robin.

The bubbles got up his nose.

Spiro Daskalakis came from Kalives in Crete; a small hill village near Chania where he had sat with booted friends in tavernas drinking raki as the piles of broad-bean pods and peanut shells mounted on plastic table-covers. Had burst occasionally into fierce stamping song, had danced with men weaving in arm-locked camaraderie. A war buff from childhood, Robin knew about Crete and Cretans. About Maleme and Galatas and 'Stand for New Zealand.'

People were called Agamemnon. Euripides, Spiro told him, had given him a kitten when he was small.

Spiro retold old stories. Stories of heroism, of dead fathers and uncles and child cousins and women during the war who smuggled food to Allied soldiers hiding in the hills. Of love and poverty and wild dances and caves where Gods were born, of a village by the sea where the hippies had lived in the nearby caves with their looseness and their drugs and their women who were whores. The caves, he told Robin, had been left filthy.

He had a good face Spiro, tough, honest and calm. Magnanimity flowed from the man. His trust had almost embarrassed Robin years ago as they sealed the deal with a fierce clench of hands. Three nights a week and weekend engagements starting as dishwasher but would move up. In time, if it happened. In time. No promise.

Robin, to no one's surprise, moved up quickly. He was neat, quick, kept his knives sharp and cleaned up as he went. His sandwiches were a dream. He was promoted to mains, had the right touch with souvláki and dolmades and not only the Greek. He was

Spiro's right-hand man, his offsider. He was still invaluable, even though he had now reduced his time to one night per week and weekend extras if required.

Dionysus Caterers worked in what looked like chaos but was not. My girls knew what they were doing, as did my casuals. Caterers' manners is what we have, boy. No please, no thank you, no excusings while we work. Just getting on, getting there is all. All done. Nice and easy, Spiro explained, leaping to an overflowing pot, his tongue clicking to calm it.

He was a childless widower and had lived for many years in a tall house on the hill in Island Bay, alone except for his tropical fish. 'They are the best thing, fish, for being alone. Every morning I come down and they are there. Swim this way, swim that way. Why do they do that?' he had asked Robin years ago. 'You know fish. You learn fish. How do they know which way to go? Which one decides? You study. You know.'

'No, I don't know.'

Spiro had put down his small coffee cup, patted Robin's cheek, his lips smacking the air with approval. 'Don't know,' he says. 'Don't know and says so.' He traced a dreamy circling spiral of approbation in the air with one forefinger. 'An honest man. A good man.'

Robin's move to the humanities had been a wise one. It was not just that too much of zoology was dead. Statistics and computers bored him and you couldn't get into the back row of the research chorus without them. Dionysus Caterers kept him solvent and he had broken free from the contents of the steel tubs and pale shapes drifting.

He crossed the road to the English department, two floors of which crawled between German and classics in a tower block designed around a lift well. The tutorial rooms were boxlike after the labs. There was no shiny technological equipment, and few teaching aids. The pursuit of English literature was assumed to take place inside the head; eyes, ears, books, an occasional film or tape were all that was required. The minimalism suited Robin. The spectrophotometers and the other machines across the road had held little charm. The Vibros respirometer shaking its guts out, lights flashing as for blast-off which never happened, had been impressive at first but soon palled.

He had a second chance and was lucky. He had found his natural habitat and dug himself in, put down roots and settled in like a gentian on a well-drained scree.

He planned his course with his usual caution. He must have a firm base on which to build. He must leave his options open at this stage. The thought of school teaching appalled him as much as ever. He would become an academic despite Lawson's adverse comments, ulcers and miserable death.

He thought fondly of the poor old guy when he discovered how much he enjoyed the release from 'relevance'. He had enjoyed English at school and the academic approach to books and their authors slipped on like a well-powdered surgical glove. It dawned on him after a while that it was possible to get good marks without too much effort. You did not have to worship the stuff, though some did. Not the law students of course, most of whom suffered their year's grind through English literature with distaste ranging from catatonic silence to yawning obscenities. But there were some.

The range of enthusiasm for their subject among the teaching staff also interested him. Some of them were so emphatic, so fiery and insistent that you should love the dead writer to whom they had devoted their lives, that it was advisable not to sit in the front row during lectures. Some were so laid-back they could scarcely get in the door before, sighing deeply, they grasped the lectern for support and held on. One or two were brilliant; made him see, briefly, that passion and commitment might be the only way.

But only briefly. Robin became adept at tracking down references, looking up sources, studying the text and not the author. Sylvia Plath's life and death held little interest for him, that of Lawrence surprised him. Literary influences researched for years by dead critics seemed obvious to him, strange bedfellows of admired and admiring did not surprise him, comparisons could be approached analytically, a pecking list of writing and writers as rigid as the Periodic Table could be established with ease. The precision appealed to him.

He was workmanlike also in his approach to exams. He studied old papers with care and picked likely questions with accuracy. His prepared answers seldom failed him and he enjoyed the spin-of-the-wheel challenge. He was pleased with life. He had made the right decision. He and Lisa would marry and move to Lyall Bay. The study grant and Dionysus Catering should be enough to survive.

He accumulated As as an undergraduate and moved on to his Master's. He nodded at members of the staff in the lifts, washed his tea cup, worked harder and nodded again. He refilled the Zip. When he was appointed a tutor in 1988 he had hoped for something slightly more in the way of . . . well, not friendship, of course, not even conversation, but some faint acknowledgement from his colleagues of this able student now working on his doctoral thesis on Henry James.

His first choice, as Emmeline remembered, had been *The unreliable narrator. A contrary view.* It was obvious to Robin from the moment he read *The Turn of the Screw* that the female narrator was stable and unbiased, both as a witness and woman. It was some of the critics, in his view, whose games were suspect; who flew their own kites, pushed their own barrows, then dumped their own eggs in the well-feathered nests of their lit crit opponents and waited for carnage.

'I think you're making a mistake, Robin,' said his supervisor Owen Braithwaite, his brown curls tight as carpet wool as he turned from his computer to peer at him. 'It's been done to death, *The Turn of the Screw* and the reliable/unreliable narrator business. Far too often, surely.' His face brightened momentarily. 'Perhaps I exaggerate, but then again . . . I agree there's always room for one more in anyone as convoluted and subtle as James. But that particular controversy . . . Is it still,' his hand touched his mouth to give warning of the joke, 'still relevant? There's been so much. Stern of the Crew, all that nonsense, quite apart from the rest. Of course, Robin, it's your choice. It must always be but . . . Well, let me know when you've thought about it. Read it again. It won't take long. Great deal to be said for novellas.' Owen pressed a button. The winged toasters of the screen-saver disappeared. 'Let me know,' he said again. 'Think about it.'

Robin thought about it and was convinced. He could get bogged down in an over-ploughed field. He would find someone un-expected, different, new: somebody like Alice O'Leary (1928–1979).

The man jumped the other way when he proposed *Alice O'Leary. A case in point.*

'A bit slight, isn't she? For a doctorate?'

'I don't think so.'

Owen puffed air through his nose, adjusted his spectacles. 'I agree of course that as a symbol of sudden cessation of creative endeavour, blasted hopes, etc, she has few equals but . . . She's such a *rara avis*, that one. A one-off. And so little to go on.'

'We know all her early life,' said Rob. 'While she was writing in Vermont, marriage, no children, widowed, came to New Zealand, remarried and stopped. Why she stopped will explain a lot. There must be something more than just that "married and gone to New Zealand" crap.'

'Yes,' murmured Braithwaite drowsily stroking his chin. He sighed, tugged a long pink ear. 'Possibly, possibly, but all that loss, that bitter acidity.'

Robin smiled. 'That's why I like her. I think she's clear-sighted.'

'Yes, yes, I do see that. And you're going to rescue her.' The lips smiled. 'Suffrage year's over, you know. You do realise that.'

You dim prick with your stroking fingers and your *rara avis* and your flying toasters. Robin breathed deeply, was filled with forgive-ness. He had found his subject. The more he read of her stuff the more he liked it. A few grim stories, fragments, poems, four novels. Why had she stopped writing? Why had she come to New Zealand, married and stopped? A case history. A case in point. He disliked the implication and wished to prove it wrong even though it meant he would have to change his thinking. The texts alone would not be sufficient here. He would have to dig further. A misfiled quotation from Henry James surfaced unexpectedly on his screen. *Here truly is the tip of a tail to catch, a trail to scout, a latent light to follow up.*

He agreed with Owen Braithwaite about one thing. It was odd that Alice, a woman of talent prematurely silenced, had not been done before. Very odd. Not a good role model, perhaps.

'You still have this one,' said Martha, touching the head of the surviving twin. *'That's something.'*

It is best to learn betrayal at an early age. It strengthens the heart muscles and the sky does not fall.

No woman has wet her pillow for her sister's grief.

When babies open their mouths their gums are new and their teeth, they tell me, are pearls. They have not been here long.

All grief is self-pity.

His colleagues did not consciously avoid him. It was probably the design of the place: no common room, no tea room, pigeon-holes for mail. Plaintive notices begging for individual responsibility and cleanliness in the cubbyhole with the Zip. Men and women padded to and fro to their rooms clutching steaming mugs of their own Instant. Dead-mouse teabags lay stained and leaking in the sink. A certain amount of hissing together beyond closed doors went on but very little. Occasionally someone laughed. They worked hard. There was much to be done and not enough money.

Robin joined the Staff Club when he was offered the tutorship; he ate explosive egg sandwiches, read the *Guardian Weekly* and the *New Scientist* and watched the tie-dyed cloud shadows drift across the harbour. Somes Island floated on air, the marina was half empty. Where had they gone, those sleek shining toys which normally berthed there. It was too calm for sailing, too calm by half. They must be lying on their sides with their keels showing, being scraped for barnacles which feed by standing on their heads and waving their legs in water. Emmie, he remembered, had had a tie-dye phase. The results had been variable.

*

His English One tutorials were held in room 4B. He knew it well, had sat for years among men and women almost identical to those who now lounged or stretched or fidgeted in front of him, indolent, bored, inattentive or hopelessly pathetically keen. An older man sat fussing in the front row with a tape recorder beside a blond hunk in ripped jeans and a shrieking T-shirt. Two mature women students, colour co-ordinated and smiling nervously, sat in the next row; attentive, pens poised—wood from the neck up. A dark well-barbered man opened a briefcase (law). There were a few other men and several women; dark and silent, wide and chatty or sleek as mice, they looked at him. One cushioned her breasts on crossed arms and stared. An Asian woman with club-cut black hair waited in what looked like a trance. She was sweating lightly. He glanced at his list. Japanese? Yes.

'Today,' said Robin firmly, 'we start with D.H. Lawrence as a poet. What did you think of his poems?'

Silence. The sun shone. A bus snorted and farted its way up the hill.

Total crippling silence.

'Anyone?'

The hunk, whose name was Clyde, stroked the black hairs on his arms into whorls and kept his head down. He put one finger up his nose, rotated it, inspected the result and wiped it on his jeans.

'My own feeling,' said Robin, 'is that Lawrence's poetry has been underrated. His novels of course are better known. How many of you have read anything by Lawrence?'

A small fly hovered over the hand of one of the mature students. Cara flipped it away. It came again, persistent, onto a good thing. She slapped, shooed, flapped as though it were a tsetse fly about to inject her with a particularly virulent trypanosome. 'Go away,' she muttered. 'Go *away*.' It stayed for some time, cruising and drifting in the silence.

'Lawrence,' said Rebekkah with the breasts, 'is a turn-off.'

'Yeah.'

'Total,' said Clyde.

They were in accord, all except Helen, the middle-aged woman with horseshoes on her scarf. She stirred on buttocks tight with tension, got her commitment out in a rush, stuck up for the man. She had adored every one of Lawrence's books and didn't mind saying so.

The Japanese woman looked as if she were about to be sick. Her eyes were glazed; beads of sweat lay on her upper lip.

Robin leaned forward. 'Do you feel all right?' He glanced at his name sheet. 'Taeko.'

She nodded; her polished blue-black hair did not move. 'I am confused,' gasped Taeko and vomited. The copper-coloured projectile of disaster hit the floor followed by the stampeding feet of 4B's first tutorial.

Robin cleared it up. He never saw Taeko again.

He moved back to his bride and her delustred satin, sidestepping Calvin and his snatch of imploding wedding cake, took her hand, kissed her ringed finger. 'I love you,' he said.

'I know.' She laughed, tossed back the veil. Her hair was tied up in knots. He could see she wouldn't have wanted it plaited which was how he liked it best. The bleached gold entwined with endless variations of darker strands from below fascinated him, turned him on man, turned him on. Plaits were not on offer. But why do they do it? Ritualised as shaven Hasidic brides, their hair is tied in knots for their wedding day. Lisa's multicoloured richness was now manipulated into pouches, poufs, loops and holes for bats to die in.

'I wish we'd had dancing,' she said.

'We couldn't afford it.'

'You always say that. It's not *quite* a real wedding without dancing.'

He kissed her, took her in his loving arms and kissed her hard. The crowd parted, clapped, loved it.

His mother was at their side, abandoned, tremulous, forgiving. 'Robin, can I have the flowers later for poor old Mrs Parkhurst?

She's got weeks of physio coming up.' Eileen's head moved, she gave a damp cluck of sympathy. 'Stretched nerve,' she murmured.

'Yes, yes, of course.'

'Who's Mrs Parkhurst?' asked Lisa.

He shook his head in defeat. 'When can we go?'

'Oh, we can't *go*. Not for hours.'

She moved away, laughing and bubbly as ever.

'You can't mean it!'

She grabbed her going-away clutch purse to her breast. 'Of course I mean it.'

'*Carry* you. No. I won't. No. This is the nineties.'

'That's not my fault,' said Lisa. 'Come on.'

His heart was thudding. Not from effort, she was light as a drifting leaf, but from something like shame, dislike at the phoniness of the yo-heave-ho gesture of satin-filled arms in once-aboard-the-lugger pretence. He had seen a Fire Service calendar recently of a muscle-bound hero oiled and stripped to the waist, carrying a limp blonde to safety; eyes closed, hair hanging down, the redeemed one's nightgown was neck-to-knee cotton. The mannered pose, the cheerful face of the pretend rescuer had made him shout with laughter. A good night's work.

He set her down gently.

'Well,' he said.

She smiled at him. 'Robbie.'

'Do you want anything to eat?'

'Heavens, no.' She patted her concave stomach. 'Do you?'

'I'd like a sandwich.'

'A *sandwich*.'

'Yes. I'll get it. You get to bed.' He felt tempted to tell her she had had a big day but thought better of it.

She was sitting up in bed propped by white pillows, expectant and pink-cheeked in her trousseau nightie. Her hair, he was pleased to see, fell around her shoulders once more. The nightgown was chaste; white, virginal, the blue ribbons tied.

She had never worn one before. Not as an adult. Not in her whole goddamn life. He laughed, fell on the bed and reached for his bride with shaking head.

'What is it?'

'God, I love you,' he said.

He tried to tell her about his tutorials but what could you say.

Hamlet's a terminal wimp.

No worse than Ophelia.

'Why,' said the old man in the front scrabbling at the tape recorder with arthritic hands, 'is the gravedigger meant to be funny? He's not funny. Not funny at all in my book.'

'I agree that some of Shakespeare's comic characters can be, shall we say, uncomfortable to us,' said Robin carefully. 'I don't mean the comedies themselves of course, but some of the characters, well, I think we have to regard them as comic in intent.' A tutor had told him this a few years ago and he was happy to hand it on. 'Humour,' he added all by himself, 'changes over the years. Most verbal humour doesn't last. Probably the audiences at the Globe fell about at funny peasant stuff like this. Whereas Chaucer's *Miller's Tale* or *Lysistrata* say, well, nothing dates bawdy. Sex,' explained Robin, 'is part of the human condition.' There was a flicker of interest; heads lifted. He paused. 'Satire lasts if it's good enough. Wait till we get to Swift.'

Clyde, he glimpsed upside down from the desk in front of him, was reading a recipe for apricot jam.

The briefcase yawned.

They sat in silence. The brutal sullen silence of bored adolescence. He discovered later that some of them, Barclay with the briefcase, Jeanette with the pony tail and the psychedelic pencil-case, the one with the teeth, were all very bright. On paper they shone. Their Browning essays had shown that.

'*That's my last Duchess on the wall, painted as though she were alive.*'

Using this quotation as an example, discuss the tensions achieved by

68

Browning in his dramatic monologue 'My Last Duchess'.

In room 4B, week after week, month after month, the intelligent ones, the ones who could have contributed, who could have lifted the gloom, who could have bloody well *helped,* sat mute.

As time passed the matrons and one or two of the others thawed, which brought its own dangers. They wanted him to know what they thought and why they thought it in their *own words.* They brayed, they hesitated, they insisted. They would not shut up. They asked questions which ranged from the eager to the banal to the abysmal.

'I think,' said Helen, 'that this one's the most wonderful poem I've ever read about a baby.' She placed her palm on her Sylvia Plath, flattened 'The Night Dances' with gentle reverence.

Her friend, Cara, who favoured the drifting pale creams and off-whites of Edwardian memsahibs, peered at the page with increased interest. 'You mean there's a *baby* in it? What do you mean it's obvious, Hen? I can't see it.' Cara peered again, her face troubled as she searched for babies, waited for them to boo at her from behind dense thickets of words. 'Oh,' she said. '"Small breath." Is that it? Is that the baby?'

She had trouble also with Larkin. Look at 'Church Going'. 'Proper to grow wise in.' What did Robin mean he was not religious? He wouldn't have said that otherwise, would he? Not if he didn't have faith.

All this and more he tried to explain to Lisa as he stir-fried vegetables with the brisk competence of the professional cook. Lisa sat on the kitchen bench with the sun on her back, her eyes on her pink strappy sandals, a can of Sprite in one hand. She lifted her head; her eyes were kind.

'But why does it worry you, Robbie? I'm sure they like you really.'

He turned quickly, the opened can of shrimps still in his left hand. 'What on earth's that got to do with it?'

There was a problem with one of her buckles. 'Oh, I don't know.'

'I don't give a stuff whether they like me or not. We're not there to make friends.'

'No.' A long swig of the Sprite. 'And anyway they couldn't. Not, I mean.' She put the can in the sink, lifted her legs, held them close. She told him about her day at the lab. She told him how many specimens they had had on A Bench and how they were just having to work harder and harder and harder and how the sinking lid was making things virtually impossible and how every single piece of equipment, even swabs if you could imagine, had to be accounted for because of the cutbacks, and how Padma and all the seniors were ropeable, in fact everybody was, you should hear them. It was all Admin, Admin, Admin, everywhere you looked. Completely top heavy. They just walked around all day doing nothing or else sat there with their fat salaries and their car parks and goodness knows what else and expected the people at the cutting edge where it was all happening to make bricks out of straw. It couldn't go on like this. You should hear the nurses. And it's the patients who'll suffer. Everyone says so. People will be hurting. You can only do so much.

He turned the gas down and looked at her. It was true, all true. The country, as Miss Bowman said, was being thrown to the dogs in the name of progress. That was all that mattered. That was all you had to fight. And yet her attempt to console nettled.

But wasn't that love. Caring. Concern for the other.

He thought of Sandy and Janice and the last conversation he had overheard. Their self-absorption never failed him. I did this. I did that. We went here. We didn't. We did. He said and I said and he said and I said No. My bassinet was frilled with pink. Mine wasn't. Mine was blue. Mum said. Mine wasn't.

He realised he was being ridiculous. It would not always be like this. He and Lisa would have other things to talk about, more interesting things to discuss together than their daily whinges from the cliff face of work. I did, I didn't, I did. What Lisa and Robin did at school and how difficult it had been for both of them.

He knew also that sharing is one of the joys of a stable relationship. Her A Bench problems, her regrettable tendency to split ends, the plastic shower curtain which would cling to her legs with amorous enthusiasm instead of hanging straight, were his problems as well. He *wanted* her to share, to confide. They would crack the problem of the mould in the bathroom between them. It concerned them both. It was theirs and he loved her. His heart lurched each time he turned into their cul de sac after a catering session and saw the bedroom light shining. Come home, my lurve, come home.

So what on earth was he on about. All was well and would become better. Things would grow and flourish between them, interests would blossom, nourished by the hand-held watering of togetherness, of love.

Cooking was not even a starter as a shared interest. Never had been, but that was good. Lisa was meticulous about the washing-up ('No, no Robbie, it's my turn') and they were both neat. Robin's love of cooking did not include a prima donna disregard for muddle. It is a myth engendered by the mucky that Mess = Talent squared. He looked forward to the savouring, the presentation, the lift of her lips as she reached for the Bordelaise minus bone marrow. Yummy.

Even the shopping did not bore him as he sought the perfect melon, tracked down Florentine fennel, the best pawpaws, polenta. And always, of course, the freshest coffee.

He had assumed that her lack of interest in birds stemmed from the comparative dearth of interesting ones in Seatoun. It was not that she did not enjoy them in the bush; the limpid call of the bellbird delighted her as did the tramper-friendly fantails and the clockwork charm of the bush robins. But she was completely non-specific, she liked them all, they were all nice. 'Listen!' she whispered, one hand palm-out in blessing. But she had no concern as to which was which. Was that plangent call across the valley a tui or a bellbird? Lisa did not care. Whatever it was made a nice noise and she loved it. It was the same with all bird calls. She was happy to ask him which it was, nod happily and forget immediately. Glimpses and flashes which left him haunted at not knowing worried her not at all. Bush wren, grey warbler, what did it matter? He had thought she would want to learn, would catch on to the fact that knowing is part of it. But of course it didn't matter. As she said, she adored the bush. They must get away more often. Yes, she agreed, they certainly must. It was just that things seem to happen in the weekends, don't they. Parties and that.

The Ornithological Society held no charms. She was happy to go with Rob on his gull counts or dotterel checks, was glad to picnic on river banks surrounded by lupins and cicadas. She loved it. But not the actual counting, not standing for hours with binoculars and *counting*. She sat on the bank or in the car with her knitting until it was time for afternoon tea and she called him, waving the signal tea towel with oystercatchers from Forest and Bird. The exception was chicks. Chicks she had to see. Bundles of black or grey fluff, the maternal behaviour of a banded dotterel mother feigning injury as she flapped away from the nest in her attempt to entice the predator, left Lisa speechless with joy. Wasn't it clever of her? Brave too. I mean she didn't know Rob wouldn't hurt the chicks did she. Lisa was a great enjoyer. They must indeed get away more. She needed a break as much as he did. As Padma said she was a lovely little worker.

She had no objection, for example, to the Saturday-morning roster at the hospital laboratory. You had more responsibility somehow. Not really of course, there were plenty of seniors about, but it was all urgent stuff and very varied and it kept you on your toes and was good experience. 'I'm on next Saturday, remember.'

Robin rang Emmeline. Could he come and see Miss Bowman? Ask her about Alice O'Leary? He had tried straight after the wedding but she had had a relapse and returned to hospital. He must be quick; quick, careful and considerate, but most of all quick.

'Yes,' said Emmie. 'She says she'd like to see you.'

'Did you mention Alice O'Leary?'

'No. Why?'

He'd always known she was nuts.

He would go to the supermarket first. Do his stuff with Eileen and Maureen. Save the treat for the end as he had always done. He strode about the echoing aisles of the barn-like place flinging things into his trolley with precision. He wasn't after anything interesting, just stocking up on basics and a box of Roses for Eileen and something for Maureen. He checked the tabloid covers at the checkout—'Half-man half-plant battles evil in Louisiana bayou.' 'Di's secret sweat obsession.' 'Bishop denies rort'—and drove on to Seatoun wondering why it seemed so much flatter than Lyall Bay when it was not. His memories were of flat gardens, flat houses, flat roads stretching to the sea; of biking to school and back in head winds. The bobbles framing the hood of Lisa's pram had tossed in the northerlies as he pushed.

He sat motionless in the car, hands flat on the wheel, his eyes on his mother's house. Two bedrooms, tidy condition, handy to bus, one careful lady owner—and lucky to have it as well she knew. He was, he supposed, a reasonably good son; he 'kept in touch', mowed her lawns, intended to fix the dead fence eventually. Robin dragged his hand through his hair and stayed sitting. When he woke in the night, which was seldom, he instinctively put out his hand to the warmth of Lisa beside him, heard her breathing. Always in these moments; intrusive, unwelcome as Witnesses with *Watchtowers* came the thought of his mother lying alone.

He snatched the box of chocolates and leaped out. Of course she would be sleeping alone, what else would she be, and had been for years and would continue to be till death did them part. He ran up the drive and hammered on the back door. No response. He banged again, then moved to the rust-ridden mint in the kerosene tin, lifted one corner and removed the key.

He called her name, walked through the narrow slab of the kitchen into what had once been a dining-room before cosying itself into a den. Two well-rounded autumn-toned chairs had moved in; the television waited vacant as an unlit oven beside the large heater in front of the boarded-up fireplace. The mahogany formica table and chairs had been shoved to one side—tea was nicer on the knee she found nowadays and why not? The formica coffee table remained, its legs splayed for the unwary, its surface unscarred by use. Limbs had been sliced by flying shards in the Falklands campaign. And drip-dry shirts cling to the skin when alight. Nothing is perfect.

He moved to straighten the beaked half-man half-bird chocolate-paper collage inscribed in early joined-up writing—*Mum, Happy Christmas from Robin.* The crocheted afghan folded neatly across the back of Eileen's chair waited as did a pile of 'my little papers' on a stool beside it. The top cover smouldered at him, New Zealand's own supermodel's pout was his alone.

He stared around, his face blank as the TV. Clutching his chocolates (was the birdman Roses?) he moved on. He had no reason to fear a collapsed corpse and did not. Empty rooms and still air surrounded him. She would be out doing her rounds. Popping in to cheer Miss Bowman perhaps. So near, within such easy popping distance, and so ill.

His shoulders twitched as he rejected the thought. Miss Bowman was not pop-in material. Miss Bowman was a rock who chose solitude or by appointment, who was not to be peppered by the casual or bored by the uninvited.

He scribbled a message, placed it under the chocolates and shut the door. His faint annoyance at his mother's absence was illogical, ridiculous and present. Here he was bearing gifts and where the hell was she. He gave a quick snort of self-disgust and tried next door. Maureen was not at home either. She too would be on duty, biking around the flats in search of the day's bride, the train to be tweaked, the veil to be spread wide with quick concertina-playing movements of both hands.

He left the chocolate almonds in the letterbox with another note and headed for Miss Bowman. He must make an appointment for next time, bring the tape recorder. He was on the trail, a scout padding.

He walked up the cracked concrete path thinking of the house guest, saw her eyes, her heavy hair. He had never seen hair like it since, so heavy, dark, coiled so low on the back of her neck.

The garden was overgrown, the taps dull. Years ago Miss Bowman had transformed the gravel drive which led to the shed at the back into a flowering field. In the summer miniature blue and white harebells flourished beside creeping thyme and tangled with mats of green. Diminutive white trumpets flowered around miniature irises and resisted overlay by a thug with frilled leaves and powdery green flowers.

The exuberant fight for survival of such small things had pleased him, lack of restraint had added to its charm. Now it was a wreck.

He rang the bell. A quick thudding of bare feet was followed by Calvin's shadow against the stained-glass panel of the door surround. Robin could see the triumphant stretch as the key turned. Calvin was a trier. He flung the door open and held out his arms. 'Hi!'

It must have been the poncy suit at the wedding which had put him off. Robin swung him up, buried his nose in the warm neck. 'Hi, mate.'

Calvin wriggled free, skidded up the bare hall which ran to the back of the old house and returned to give him the news. 'I'm in the big kids' room at day-care now.'

'Good on you.'

Emmeline came down the hall, friendly, cheerful, her arms imitating her son's. Calvin, she explained, was finally dry. She gave a quick chop with one hand, bony fingers carved the air. 'Phht. Straight into the big kids' room. Neat eh. One of the reliefs is we're no longer lousing up the environment with disposables.' She scratched her behind thoughtfully through a trim little op-shop number covered in yellow and green sunflowers. She looked like Doris Day gone wrong. 'Come in.'

Calvin was now chewing his way around the equator of a Granny Smith. His head, caught in the crimson shafts from the door surround, had caught fire, exploded to burn-off. He handed the ring-barked thing to his mother who held it in both hands and munched, elegant and meticulous as a chipmunk on *Wild Life*.

Calvin, his hair now faded to its usual orange, disappeared down the hall.

'How's Miss Bowman?'

Emmeline shrugged, her uplifted palms told him. 'No longer with the big kids sadly. Aunt,' she yelled, 'do you want to see Robin now?'

The voice was surprisingly strong. 'Yes, please. Very much.'

He walked in. He had never seen Miss Bowman's bedroom before. It was both satisfactory and unexpected. He had not known Miss Bowman was a believer, let alone a devout one as her choice of pictures seemed to indicate. He had never seen Miss Bowman striding off to either church or good works. Yet here she lay, surrounded by a collection of holy pictures. *Praying Hands* hung in the front room but you didn't have to be devout to appreciate that. These were different. A Holy Family featured an ill-favoured Christ Child. A Sacred Heart on the opposite wall appeared to pulsate at the viewer's gaze directed to it by one long pink index finger. Strangest of all was a lithograph of a dreaming sensuous Christ; an intense visionary who gazed through the long floating hair of an early rock star; a Messiah who loved his flock but especially, oh especially, the believer who gazed back.

There were swaying shadows and muted submarine colours in this room as well, purple-blue chairs, a dull ruby bedcover, faded silks draped and hanging in swatches over a screen, and a sharp smell of ammonia.

Robin held the back of a wicker chair. 'How are you, Miss Bowman?'

'Rotting away boy, just rotting away. Sit down, sit down.'

She heaved herself up. He and Emmie both sprang to help, narrowly avoiding collision in the process. She flapped them away. 'Tell me what's going on in the world. They've got to do something about Bosnia.' Fingers insubstantial as x-rays insisted. 'But then again what? And how? Tell me. Fitzroy Maclean said it would be hopeless and he knows the place. Built for guerrillas apparently. All very well thundering on like that wretched Thatcher woman. Tragic. Tragic. We must go in, but then we'll go out, and then what? People go on as though there's one answer. A or B. Not like that, is it?

Never has been. Never simple. Some things, some things, what *is* the answer? But, yes,' she panted. 'Can't not. Can't not.'

They talked politics, economics, market forces, funding sources and user pays; agreed then disagreed, got cross, slogged it out like the thugs and ground-covers outside. Anger could not be good, not for that face, that dragging breath. He tried to calm her, to humour her which enraged her further.

You cannot storm in on the dying and start grilling them immediately, but he could feel his breathing, his anxious heart. She had been in hospital for months. Major surgery. No visitors. Home for two weeks and he was the first visitor, Emmie had told him. Now. Spit it out. Now. Tell me Miss Bowman.

'Miss Bowman, I'm doing my PhD thesis on Alice O'Leary.'

Eyes, black hooded eyes too bright for the yellow pleated face beneath, snapped shut and reopened. 'Why?'

'She was a good writer.'

Miss Bowman scratched a fingernail at a yellow mark on her winceyette nightgown. 'Egg,' she said.

'You were a friend of hers,' he insisted.

She had shrunk, grown smaller, turned inwards. Her hands were claws. She was not old enough to look like this. Neither as fiercely ancient nor as collapsed.

'At one time,' she murmured.

'Why did she stop writing?'

She was silent. His heart squeezed to a stop. She was not going to tell him. He was pleading now. 'She was a good writer and I must find out all I can and the fact that you know her . . . It would be the most enormous help if you could talk to me about her.'

She thought of something. 'Emmeline could show you her books. We have her books.'

'But you must remember her. Tell me. Tell me anything you can remember. Did you know her as a child? Her parents, anything. What was she like? Why did she stop?'

She closed her eyes. He could feel the lump in his throat. 'Miss Bowman, *please.*'

Shock tactics. There was nothing else. Robin got it out. 'I heard her weeping. Alice. I heard her when I was a child.'

Her eyes flicked open, closed quickly. 'Miss O'Leary to you.'

'Why was she crying!'

'You'll have to go now. No puff.'

He could hear Emmie dispensing juice in the kitchen, her voice calling. He stood up in silence. 'Miss Bowman?'

Her eyes opened. 'Nnnh.'

Filled with the impotent despair of frustration he bent over the gutted body. 'I just want to thank you.' Why was he attempting anything as impossible? She didn't deserve it anyway. He saw the woman weeping by the lilac. Why? And this old boot could tell him the answer and would not and he needed to know. He swallowed, tried again. 'Just to thank you for all the fun I had as a kid. The popcorn and . . .'

Her eyes glinted, an old witch savouring her brew. She took his hand. 'You've got to make the most of dying while you can, Robin. Remember that.'

'But I can come again? Please.'

She shook her head. 'Goodbye, boy.'

'I'm sorry about the whiff,' said Emmie as they stood gazing at the harebell seedheads. 'But like your mother I think no-pongos are worse. And even if they weren't, how could you go round spraying above someone flat on her back below you? You might as well carry a sign. "This room is being sanitised for your convenience."'

She hid her head for a second in her hands, sniffed loudly. 'The trouble with heroes is they make the rest of us look so feeble.'

He looked up from his blasted hopes, dead as the fucking harebells.

'Don't be dumb,' he snapped. 'You're not feeble.'

'Good,' she said fiercely. 'That's nice.' She sniffed again. 'I get mad you know. Fed up. So does she. It's not a barrel of laughs this dying stuff. Ministering. Being ministered at. She *hates* it. I lost my cool the other day. I roared and screamed and . . .'

'You're meant to.'

She was furious with him, fists clenched, face too thin. 'What the hell do you mean?'

'I read it somewhere. You have to let go occasionally otherwise you explode.'

'Huh. You mean the "Don't shoot the pianist, he's doing his best" stuff?'

'That's the one.'

She bent down, tugged a frilly leafed clump from a nest of thyme. She was too quick, too angry. The plant came away in her upraised hand, showering his shirt with the deep rich friable loam of garden writers.

She brushed his chest, her quick fingers streaking black across white.

'Hey, that reminds me. Wait here.' She ran up the steps and reappeared waving a batik cotton shirt. 'I put my hand straight on it. I never put my hand straight on anything. Amazing.' She held it out. 'This any use to you?'

No birds, just a kid whistling. He fingered the soft cotton, the melded pinks, blues, mauves; glanced at the collar. Malaysian. 'It's great. Why don't you want it?'

'I bought it in a day-care bring-and-buy. It's ten times, fifty times too big. I like things big but jeeze. Come here. Turn round.' She held the back of the shirt against his shoulders, her fingers busy on his back, a child borrowed for a quick check at a street market. He stood still as you are meant to. 'Any good?' she asked his shoulders.

He must remember. It was not her fault. Miss Bowman's silence. Her dying. Any of it.

'Yeah, I mean it. Thanks a lot. Great.' He kissed her cheek. 'And let me know if I can do anything to help.'

She shut her eyes briefly. 'I hate that phrase, that "let me know". Think about it. "Robin would you care to slip round with a litre of chicken soup easy on the onion and no rice, and make that two while you're at it and I'll freeze some." Why don't people just *do* it?'

'But I will now you've asked. I meant it.'

'I have not *asked*.'

Hopeless, hopeless as ever. 'What do you want?'

'I want you to bugger off.'

They stood side by side in silence. He put out his hand, touched her shoulder. 'Thanks for the shirt,' he said.

She kicked the dislodged clump of roots. Shrugged. Her hair really was the most extraordinary colour. Henna and dried blood tinged with Chinese Wild Man red.

'Why do you dye your hair when it's red already?'

'I just give it a little tickle-along. Doesn't everyone?'

'Not Lisa.'

'Huh. How is she by the way?'

'Good.'

'I don't doubt that for a moment.' She paused, stood on one leg, replaced it.

'See you,' she said and ran.

Four

He tried the shirt on as soon as he arrived home, inspected himself in the long mirror Maureen had handed on to them because it was broken and some of her ladies were superstitious, although if anyone copped it it would be her not them as it was her fault; the scissors had hidden themselves beneath a pile of scraps by the overlocker and slipped when she tidied up, to splinter the bottom-right-hand corner into shards, darn it.

The shirt was light, cool, you wouldn't know you had it on. Imagine ditching a shirt like that. Deceased estate perhaps. Dead man's batik. Bung Daddy off to day-care.

Lisa ran to meet him at the Mein Street exit of the hospital, a snatched frond of wild fennel in one hand for tonight's fish as requested, her Saturday over, her Urgent done. It was always Saturday or Urgent. Sandy had had a really shitty Saturday last week. They were one short and it was hell in haemotology as well. Complete chaos, know what I mean? Blood on the floor haha.

She stopped, one hand on the car door. 'Robbie! Where'd you get it?' Her face was ecstatic; for him, for his shirt, for how beautiful he looked, for how it brought out the blue of his eyes. He should always wear blue—and pink of course but it was the blue in this one that did it. She was stroking, patting him, frisky as a kitten released from Urgent.

'Where'd you get it?'

'Emmie.'

A mere flick of silence. The smile remained. 'Why?'

'She bought it in a bring-and-buy at day-care. It was too big for her.'

She shook her head at his amazing luck, clucked her tongue in approval. 'Choice eh.'

He was never quite sure about her slang. It sounded dated to him, something left over from primary but how would he know.

'Let's have coffee at Deluxe. I'm starving.'

He changed when they got home. He wanted to wear it on Monday. It might cheer him up after the debacle of Miss Bowman's silence, which he would tell Lisa about but not now.

Lisa's Mondays also pleased her. They had none of the sealed-off completion of Saturday, fewer prospects of drama, less chance of independent discovery of some esoteric bug no one else had noticed in the direct slide but which she had picked up on the blood plate and Padma had been pleased. But Mondays, like all her days, were welcome. She enjoyed the loving seemliness of their work-day routines as much as he did. The fact that they never wanted the toilet at the same time was lucky wasn't it, when you came to think about it. Rob was tidy as well, a happy coincidence which added to her ever-rolling stream of pleasure in her marital state. Breakfast for example; she quite enjoyed making the toast, the satisfactory clop as the thing disgorged mixed grain or sometimes kibbled wheat. Whereas Rob preferred the grind and hissing slurp of coffee-making so it all worked out quite well. And they both liked marmalade which was good too. Some people didn't like marmalade at all but they both did. Some people didn't even like breakfast. Imagine.

And it didn't take them a minute to clear up before they were on their way and she was wondering aloud what the weekend cultures had grown. Sometimes she couldn't wait to get to the incubator but fortunately they always read the blood plates first thing. Always.

Her zest for life was infectious. Rob drove across the city after her brief garlic-scented kiss, trying to work out his fascination at the way her mind worked.

It was like any other energy equation. Input equals output. Well, not equals. Friction, entropy, wear and tear will catch more than the internal combustion engine: things will fall apart, drop off. But by and large. In this day and age. He grinned, surprising a lean blonde sniffing her armpit in a Mini beside him.

And Lisa knew this. Lisa whose legs often dangled from normal chairs, who wore little boys' shorts, whom he could have held over his head with one hand like some goddamn ice skater flinging his partner about.

The blonde swept past him.

And it was not only Lisa. Teaching had helped and his excitement about Alice O'Leary. The more he tried to overcome the inert indifference of most of his tutorial the more determined he became that they should not miss out, should get excited about something or someone who could get inside your head to delight, terrify, tighten privates or appal, and why not start with Eng Lit? His previous mark-grubbing exam-passing techniques had been senseless. Passion is the thing. What did fooling the sods matter. You land up gutless, unkindled as a damp sack, a time-server. He must get on with his abstract, dive into his research, slap in for copies of the letters from the Newbery, attempt Miss Bowman once more. Though he had blown that and the thought was sour in his mouth. But he could talk, glean, catch nuances. See her.

See the books. They would be signed. He could touch them. Touch the book that came from the hand that broke the heart of

Miss Bowman. If it had. God what a fool. Why had he rushed the old woman—bounced her, clammed her tight as a tube worm around her treasure.

He parked the car and headed up the hill. Everything about the new building pleased him, the cavernous clanging coffee space, the glass and the light, the soaring height. Some of the students were less cheerful. Ripped jeans and layered grunge sat in corners, weeds of despairing hair draped a couple of tables. Cuts were tough and getting tougher. The Minister had been mobbed last week.

Rob strode across the wide overbridge to the arts building, wondering as always who had chosen the carpet. Its diagonal stripes were reflected as looped green garlands in the slick chrome bellies of the garbage bins. Below them drifted discarded paper, greasy bags, a misfired can or two. He glanced at the languid intertwinings on one or two of the padded benches. One couple were male. He hadn't noticed that before. Not on the overbridge. The usual group of Asian students sat beside a drooping rubber plant; two Muslim women glided by with draped heads and deep-laden arms.

There had been another PhD student sharing his room originally —*Aspects of Religious Imagery in James K. Baxter: an Interpretation*— but she had disappeared for reasons unknown which was a help. Space was at a premium.

He sat at his desk reading, making notes, dissecting Alice's mind, puzzling at the occasional naiveties of her sexual images; the naked arrows poised to strike, the fastened doors, the stolen keys seemed too well-worn to express such bitter grief, such loss.

The titles also puzzled him. *The Mystic Scroll, The Hand of Time, We All Fall Down, The Load.* Surely she could have chosen better than these dim uninformative *Wide, Wide World*ers. She had been born in the nineteen-twenties, not eighteen.

Another misfiled quotation surfaced on the computer screen. 'The three hundred and fifty or so images drawn from the realm of music are never technical and usually not elaborate or even very interesting,' wrote the critic. So why mention them huh, why spend your life digging for irrelevancies; for 'something of Schubert's', for

'Wagner, four times', 'Mozart, three times', 'Beethoven, twice' and 'Paganini, once'?

Robin could understand the critic now. He also was hooked. He also had something to demonstrate, to disclose, to tell the waiting world, and not trivia either. Better by far to be first on Alice than seventy-fifth on Henry. He would find the answer, tell them why she had stopped writing. The thicko husband presumably. He must get down south. With Lisa.

The sun was warm through batik. A satisfactory shirt. He picked up the telephone to ring Emmeline then remembered she would be rehearsing.

Squatting on his heels, stirring the contents of his pack in search of *Kangaroo,* Robin glanced upwards as the door shot open followed by Clyde. One hand clutched a knife, the eyes blazed. The man was drunk.

'A C. A fuckin' C!'

Mouths dropped, backs straightened, someone gasped. The tape recorder pressed in error whirred in the silence.

Clyde roared like a rutting stag. 'Where's the boy wonder!'

Robin stood. 'Here.'

'You heard then?'

'Yeah. Linguistics are probably recording you for their corpus.'

Clyde was both ridiculous and alarming, the wild eyes, the spitting rage, the boozer's breath. The man was blind drunk and had a knife. Rob's neck pricked. He could be sliced. He could be dead. He stiffened, the whirr of the recorder continued. Another bus stormed up the hill.

'I need a better mark. A B at least.'

'Sit down Clyde. We'll discuss it later.'

'I need a pass. If I don't get a pass I'm out. El foldo.' He grabbed Rob's collar. 'Kaput. Get it? Stuffed. Out!'

4B were staring, wide-eyed in silence and in fright. The mature students were less concerned than the rest. It was awful for Robin who was a nice boy and couldn't help being shy, but they had not seen the knife. Astonishment was uppermost on their faces. Imagine demanding better marks. They would never do such a thing. Never. They were ruffled; their rears stirred, their heads lifted like hens' at a whiff of ferret but they were not seriously alarmed. Helen touched Cara's arm briefly. It was all right. She was here.

The rest were different. They knew about the drunk and the stoned. Irrational behaviour had been seen before, passers-by had been stabbed; on the Quay, Manners Mall, anywhere. Their faces were blank with the effort of invisibility. A born-again's lips were moving, her hands clasped tight.

Rob put his arm on Clyde's. 'Come on.'

Clyde swung at him. 'Get your shitty hands off me, dick-head.'

Adrenalin was pumping, producing unexpected calm. He clenched his fists.

Clyde paused, his tirade faltered, died on wet lips. He smiled a friendly drunk's smile, gave a loud building-site wolf whistle and held his arms wide. 'Who's a pretty prick then? Who's got a sexy shirt? Come on, tell Clydo.' He hugged Rob, pressed his tutor's face against the sweat and obscenities of his T-shirt for a moment then dumped him.

4B exploded. They exploded with relief, delight; the urchin glee of sucks-to-teacher engulfed them in waves. Clyde bowed and slumped beside Mr Tarrant and his recorder. The old man welcomed him, his tight mouth smiling, his finger on the button. 'Would you like to hear yourself, Clyde?' he said. 'I recorded it by mistake.'

Clyde rose in silence, swung his hand in a stiff-armed arc, threw Mr Tarrant's teaching aid out the window then subsided. He laid his golden head on his arms and slept.

No one was hurt but Mr Tarrant was shaken. Clyde was his friend. He had sat beside him for weeks, had helped with his tape recorder in a most gentlemanly way, had had his head screwed on and liked his cricket.

*

Robin made hamburgers for tea. His heart was not in it but Lisa liked them. They could have them in front of TV and there wouldn't be much washing up and it was more cosy somehow, especially now with the nights drawing in.

She came back from the hutch-like kitchen smiling, rubbing and rolling her hands over each other, her day's work done.

He took the sticky things she offered him and rubbed them in his. She sometimes squirted too much hand lotion by mistake and he knew what to do.

He kissed one, buried his nose in aloe-scented slime. 'Let's get out to the Orongorongos this weekend. A guy at work's offered me the key to his hut.' He paused. 'This afternoon.' He held up the key. 'Here.'

'By ourselves?'

'Yeah. That's the whole point.'

'Oh.' She pulled away from his chest, her face thoughtful. 'Your shirt smells all sweaty,' she said. 'And some of those private huts are miles away. People say.'

No, no. He explained carefully. People thought that but it wasn't true. There were some perhaps, but Owen Braithwaite's was virtually on the foothills, no distance. Easy.

'All right.'

They would go, they would get away. He was grateful to Owen Braithwaite and not only for the key. The man had been relaxed about the incident; the university's insurance, he assured Robin, would cover a replacement tape recorder, though the claim form might read rather oddly. One beautiful hand dragged over curls. 'The window's gone, you say? No one hurt?'

'No.'

'I'll get onto Maintenance. And I'll notify the appropriate people about . . . What's his name?'

'Clyde Benton.'

A brief edgy smile. 'Consult a higher authority. "Who supervises the supervisors." By the way, would you like our hut this weekend?

87

Not at all. Good idea to get away. Have a complete break. No, no. Penny's mother with us again. Teeth this time.'

There was no sun in the clearing where they parked the car. They shouldered their packs and set off with Robin in front. There was little sound but the rhythmic thud of their boots and an occasional bird call. Otherwise silence and damp and a few rays of splintered sun. They had been late getting away and there were too many people. The main track was becoming a trail for booted ants. They had already been passed by two.

'Have you been to this hut before?' she asked.

'Yes.'

She untangled a supplejack which slapped back at her. 'Oh. It's getting a bit dark, isn't it?'

'It's just because there's no sun.'

'Yes, but it's different without it. All the greens are the same colour and my hair's sweaty.'

He turned to wait for her. Legs her length must be a disadvantage in the bush. 'Is your pack too heavy?'

'No.'

'Give us it.' He restowed and handed the lightened pack to her smiling. She shrugged it on, her face distant.

'Better?'

She nodded.

It would be better when they got into their rhythm. When they arrived at the hut and he got the fire going. When the sun came out tomorrow and the bush shimmered with light. The weather forecast was good. Bright golden suns had trekked down the North Island on last night's TV. All would be well. He strode on.

'You're going too fast.'

Premenstrual tension perhaps. Physiological imbalance. Something. He slowed down, offered his hand, was refused.

They dumped their packs outside the hut two hours later. She certainly looked tired, her face was white, her skin pinched about the nose as though more was needed. He straightened his back, raised his arms to the sky. 'Stretch your back,' he said. 'Like this. You'll feel better.'

A half shrug is worse than a whole, the lift of one shoulder more of a rejection than two.

He turned the key in the lock. The door was stuck. He shoved with his shoulder, tried again and fell in an upended scramble as it gave way. He sat looking up at her, smiling at her blank face to show that it was fun, that life was good. 'I should carry you over the threshold.'

'Why?'

'Well because . . .' Because why? Because you liked it last time. Because I love you. Because I can't stand you sulking. 'I thought it might cheer you up,' he said still smiling.

Her face was a mask of deep sorrow. 'Why on earth would I need cheering up?'

'I don't know.'

She sat on the wooden bench staring out the window, her elbows on her knees, her face cupped in grubby little girl's hands. He looked at her in silence for a moment, noted the neat back, the tidy arrangement of crossed brown legs, then turned to light the fire. The bastards had not left much wood but he could start it and get more before dark. Disturbed spiders scattered; a pale brown one swivelled its abdomen and swung Tarzan-like across his field of vision. He stopped to watch, hoping for a repeat performance but it had done its dash.

'I can see why the Maoris didn't like the bush,' she said still staring into the half light.

'Like the Swiss didn't like the mountains?'

She swung to him, her mouth tight. 'You always do that. You always take what I say and turn it into what you want to say. You do it all the time.'

He stood on one leg cracking twigs against his knee. 'What do you mean?'

'Just what I said. I'm telling you about Maoris and the bush and you drag in the Swiss and mountains. I'm not *talking* about the

Swiss and mountains. I'm talking about the bush. You do it all the time.'

'But I think like that. Lots of people do. The mountains were a drag to the Swiss originally. They didn't climb them for pleasure any more than the Maori walked in the bush for fun. Analogously, that's the word.'

Her head was low, one hand hung from her wrist in a heart-breaking droop. 'Oh shut up.'

His arms were around her, hugging the sad crumpled figure on the bench. 'Lisa,' he said stroking her hair.

He wooed her with words, cajoled her with kisses. She sniffed. 'And it smells too.'

He brought her round, turned her about like a P class into calmer waters, loved her better, seated her by the fire. She sat curled in his parka, cherished and deeply loved, watching her backwoodsman mate who would deflect slings and arrows and sadness. The depths and mysteries of her overwhelmed him as he watched her unfold into contentment. The wooden hut sighed and creaked around them, a dusty primeval shelter, every slab of which had been manhandled through the bush by heroes. He stood up. Firewood. She would help him.

'Lisa?'

She was on her feet, screaming, an arm outstretched, a finger pointing to emptiness and bare wood. 'A rat, a rat!'

He dumped his log. 'Was it a rat or a mouse?'

'I said rat.'

'Yeah, but there's a difference. I'd say rat too if I were you.' Unwise. Unexpected. He didn't know why he had said it. He put out a hand. 'Come and get some more wood, honey.'

'No.' But then there was the rat. 'Oh bloody hell,' said Lisa, slamming out the door beside him.

They made love in the musty dark of the upper bunk. She felt safe in his arms, knew little of the climbing skills of rats and there were no rat droppings in sight. He had swept up the dried tea leaves of mouse spoor and set the trap.

He held her tight, explored her gently beneath his unzipped Mountain Mate. She was shivering. 'I do love you really,' she said.

'I know. I know.'

'It's just . . .'

He was as eager as ever as she lay waiting for delights. The soles of her feet itched when she had an orgasm she had told him months ago. That was one way you knew, Sandy said, though of course it was unmistakable when it happened. There was nothing like it. It was amazing but she didn't always have it. It wasn't a good idea for her to stroke him and kiss him down there. She had told him before. He got too excited and didn't wait for her and that wasn't fair. She turned to him and loved him dearly.

He lay beside her in the blackness thanking gods; leaned on one elbow, kissed her mouth. 'Good night, my sweetest love.'

She rolled over. 'Night.'

He put his hand around her, slid it between her legs, touched her. '"There tha shits and there tha pisses,"' he murmured.

The huddled curve of her back did not move, nor a hand; not a glimmer, not a grunt.

'I love you,' he said.

'Nnn.'

The weather forecast had been wrong. There was no sun in the morning. The air was cold, the creek icy around their distorted pallid toes. She couldn't find her toothbrush. She couldn't understand it. She knew she'd put it in her bag. Had he taken it? She couldn't stand dirty teeth. It made her feel awful.

'Have mine.'

She didn't want to. She had never used anyone else's toothbrush. She just didn't like the idea. She waited till he had gone to squat in deep bush before she overcame her scruples, bent over the stream and scrubbed and brushed and spat with vigour. Saliva and white bubbles eddied in tranquil calm behind a small rock. She kicked them on their way, watched them hurtle and disintegrate down small rapids. You have to spit somewhere. She gave her mouth a quick rub with the back of her hand and waited for him to come back and hand over the shovel so she could go.

The bush across the creek was dark, creepy almost. 'Rob?' she called. She wanted to tell him. Tell him straight off how it was all right in the sun with people around and fun and chiacking and that; but this dense green, the silence, the towering giants and the lianes that slapped and grabbed. She had never liked dark green. Like rhododendron leaves. Tough, lifeless, all the same. 'Rob,' she called again.

'Coming.'

She stowed the shovel by the ashes in the fireplace and stared at his stubbled face which had showed little interest in her reaction to dark green.

'Let's go home,' she said.

'But we've got the whole day. I want to head up Mount Matthews while we've got time.'

'I want to go home.' She shivered, wrapped her arms around herself for comfort. 'I'm tired.'

'Well, you stay at the hut and I'll go.'

'I'd be eaten by rats.'

'There are no fucking rats.'

She looked at him for a second, fists clenched, legs apart. Her playground bully stance softened as she moved towards him. 'Robbie, you know I love you,' she said.

She swung down the track, jumping logs, skipping from stone to stone at the creek crossings. Rob watched her back, his eyes red and itchy. He wanted to tear them out of his head, to fling the hayfever-ridden things at her. Get shot of the sight of her gleeful descent to 4B and the tape recorder and Tuesdays for garbage and Eileen's arthritis and his unwashed shirts mouldering in the laundry.

He was puzzled by his gloom. What the hell was wrong with him? What had he expected? Just because she had been so excited on their few previous trips didn't mean she would love every aspect of the bush. This trip had been too tough. The hut had been further up the valley than he remembered. Obviously she was not fit enough and lots of people were scared of rats even if there weren't any. Rats have a bad image. They leave sinking ships. No boy-stood-on-the-burning-deck stuff for them. They are too intelligent. They abandon. They spread plague. They eat corpses. Alice O'Leary had written a poem about it. Why would not Lisa, his rose geranium-scented Lisa, hate anything as outwardly repellent. It would be against nature for her to see that rats are interesting and spiders fascinating and that it's a good idea to save the ugly animals as well. A lot of people are racist about animals. Going bananas over penguins and dolphins, loving Russian wolfhounds and hating tarantula spiders which are also hairy and have long legs and whose bite is no more painful. Lisa's disappointment was completely understandable. He should have taken things more slowly, broken her in more gently, not bullied her into the grind of real tramping where the sunlight is fitful at best and hateful on a gut-busting hill. Where any shelter, however primitive, is enough. He had rushed things. He should have remembered his mother's stamp collection. He saw Lisa's face beside him, intent and happy at Butterfly Creek as he had explained the life cycle of a moss.

'Say it again, Robbie, which is the sexual and which is the asexual?'

He patted the mat with his palm. 'This is the sexual stage, and these are the capsules which release the asexual spores.'

Her face was thoughtful. 'That's funny isn't it? The asexual stage looks much more interesting. Like teeny wee pepper-pots.'

She was right too about the sun. It did bring the bush to life, transformed, glinted, lit the theatre. Without it subtropical rain forest could be brooding and dark. Some people did find it alien. He would have to work on it. Take it gently. At least she had agreed to go back by the other track—the crowded main track would have depressed him further.

*

'Slow down,' he called.

She lifted one hand and disappeared still jumping, skittering along the track like some bloody mountain thar.

The scream was sharp; one yell, then silence.

He raced down the track, fell on his knees beside her. 'All right?'

'It's my ankle.'

'I *told* you so. Why the hell did you go so fast?'

Her face fell apart. 'Ooh. Don't.'

He was gasping, insisting. No. No, he hadn't meant it. 'Tell me, tell me. Where is it? Where?' He loosened her left boot; she screamed with pain. The ankle was swelling before his eyes, enlarging, blooming like a time-lapse rose. 'I'll have to take the boot off.'

'No!' Her nails dug through his shirt. 'No!'

He took it off. With infinite agony-inducing care he removed the size-three boot of which she had been so marching-girl proud. She was writhing, breathless with pain, fighting him. As the boot came off she gave a shriek and fainted.

He strapped her ankle, tearing strips from his wet shirt, wrapping it firm but not tight, making use of every second of insensibility.

She opened her eyes, moaned briefly and rolled over to vomit. 'Oh. Oh. Oh.'

'That's good, that's good, I promise that's good.' He had no idea why it was or would be or ever had been. 'Good,' he said again.

He mopped her with his hay-fevered handkerchief, held her in his arms. 'It's all right. It's all right. I promise. It's all right.'

'What are we going to do?' she gasped.

What were they going to do. 'Don't worry, don't worry. It's all *right*.'

'Yes.'

His mind was racing. It wouldn't be dark for hours. He could get out, get the Ranger, get back.

'Don't leave me,' she said.

He kissed the top of her head, held her tight, talked her down like a would-be suicide, gentled her like a stable groom. Words streamed from him; gentle, loving, largely unrecognisable words told her it would be all right. Everything would be all right. He was here. It was all right.

She lay still, calm at last, her eyes on his. 'Yes.'

He still held her, stroked her for some time, shut his eyes briefly. Opened them. 'Lisa?'

'Yes.'

'Lisa, I'll have to leave you just for a couple of hours or so. I'll skid down and get the Ranger. We'll be back before dark.'

Terror. Pure terror in the scream, the naked yell. 'No, no, no!'

'It'll still be daylight. I promise.'

'No. No.' He held her hands, forced himself to look at her panic.

He tried. He explained. It was the only way that made sense. He would be back, the Ranger would have a stretcher. Get her out, safe, home in no time. He promised. He swore it.

'You could carry me.'

'Lisa, I can't carry you and the packs and . . .'

'Leave the packs. Just me.' She was shaking with shock. 'If you leave me here I'll die of fright. I mean it. It'll get dark. There are things.' Her voice sharpened. 'No!'

She did mean it. Her eyes told him, her hands, her whole body insisted. He looked at her, his face tight with despair. How could he explain, how could he possibly begin to explain. OK she was light but he must take at least one pack. Something else could go wrong, what if he had to leave her anyhow, as he very likely would. What if he tripped? He couldn't leave her without food, a sleeping bag, water. Things could go wrong in the bush and often did.

'Lisa, listen.'

'Don't say listen. How can I help listening? It's mad when you say listen.'

He grinned, was rewarded by calm. 'But listen, OK.'

She nodded.

'I'll carry you, you carry the pack.'

'Why do we need the pack?'

'Because we do. Otherwise I won't move.'

'But that's what I *want*. We stay here together till someone comes

95

and gets help.'

'It's quite possible no one will come. This track is much more isolated.'

'You were the one who said to.'

'I know, I know, but *listen*. Owen Braithwaite'll hoist something in if I'm not at work but he won't even know till Tuesday, if then.' He was firm, decisive. 'Now how are we going to play this?'

He had hoped to piggyback both her and the survival pack but she became hysterical with pain when he tried to hoist her up. He shouldered the pack and lifted her in his arms. The distribution of weight was impossible. Crippled, bowed as a felon incarcerated, he set off. 'OK?'

'Yes.'

They made reasonable progress; pathetic, but reasonable. Each foothold had to be checked, each step tested. It would have been better climbing up. Descent is always worse, real climbers say. Concentrate. Get there. Just get there.

She moaned at each jar, apologised, moaned again.

'Don't talk.'

'No.'

He shambled on, step by step, his arms dragged from their sockets by her weight which was nothing. He couldn't see properly. He couldn't see at all; his glasses steamed up constantly. He leaned his pack against a giant rimu. 'Wipe them,' he gasped. No breath, no breath at all. No breath ever again.

She unhooked them from his bowed head and polished them on the bottom of her stained shirt. He stared straight ahead with unfocused eyes, his mind dead with unfinished effort till she re-hooked them. A grey warbler trilled. There was a vague pattern of leaves before his blurred eyes. He closed them. He would have to have a rest.

'We'll sit down for a while. Hang on.' Infinitely careful, he edged the pack down the rimu, sagged his knees to lower her to the ground. When she was safe he lay back. He'd work out how to get up later.

They lay very still beside the track. Midges hovered, maintained their endless dance, a branch snapped. A bee, a fat idiotic urban bumble-bee circled above them. Another grey warbler.

'Robbie.'

'Nnn?'

'Look Robbie, I think we've got to . . . What I mean is . . .'

He opened his eyes, sat up quickly at the tone of her voice.

Her eyes were wet. 'This isn't going to work.'

He sat up, brushed himself angrily, reached for the pack. 'Of course it's going to work.'

'No. It's too hard.'

'I'm just having a rest. Can't I have a bloody rest?'

She took his hand, kissed it, gave it back. 'Yes. But the thing is.' He had to strain to hear her, lean nearer. 'I've decided. You must go and get help and get back.' She paused. 'Before dark,' she said.

He could drown in those eyes.

'Lisa.'

'It's the only way that makes sense.' She was still staring. She knew she could trust him. 'You said.'

He was firm, efficient. The thing was to be efficient. To leave her warm, as comfortable as possible, food to hand. He tore the drooping dead ponga fronds from a nearby tree and laid her on their brown crackling surface, wrapped a sleeping bag around her, added more fronds for warmth and kissed her.

'There'll be noises, but don't worry about them. It's like being in a house on your own. You don't hear small noises when there are other people. It's no worse. I promise.'

Christ those eyes. 'Yes.'

He held her close, kissed her gently and ran. Why gently, why did he kiss her so gently. Why did he do that.

He had been scrambling down the track, leaping and sliding for ten minutes, when he remembered he hadn't marked a nearby tree. She can't move, dumb-bum. He ran on.

*

'She couldn't move,' he yelled. 'Her ankle, she couldn't move!' The Ranger and his mate Shaun who had called in for a beer on his way home looked at him in silence. One large man and one small nuggety one stood panting, sweat coursing down their legs. They said nothing. Their eyes avoided his.

'You're sure this is the spot?' said the Ranger finally.

'Of course.' Rob slammed his hand hard against the rimu. 'Rimu, rata, karaka, like I said. And the rewarewa over there.' He was pointing, insisting, longing to shake.

Shaun's voice was gentle. He just wanted to get things straight. 'You didn't make a blaze then?'

'She couldn't walk! She couldn't fucking walk!'

Shaun touched his shoulder, the shoulder is safe. 'We'll just have a wee bit of a look round then. She can't be far away.'

The Ranger turned to him. It was beginning to get dark, colder. 'Where's the ponga fronds you mentioned, Rob?'

Robin spun around. There were none. There were no ponga fronds. He tore from side to side, bellowed her name to the hills. '*Leeesah!*' Silence until the echo. '*Eesah. Eesah.*' Shaun and the Ranger stared at their boots.

The Ranger took charge. They could give it an hour, no more. Nothing could be achieved after dark, not a blind thing and the ambulance would be waiting. He sent Shaun and Robin up the track, nodded at Shaun, was answered. Keep an eye on him. We don't want two of them. They checked their watches. Their voices roared her name, their feet crashed. The Ranger began his detailed search nearby. He would get on to Search and Rescue as soon as he got home. He pulled on his Swanni against the chill.

Rob had absorbed bush lore at primary where there were few trees in sight. You dried matches in your hair, you made sure your boots were worn in before you set off, you had dry socks, warm clothing, wool was best. You never tramped alone. Not unless you were extremely experienced and well-equipped and seldom then. You made sure. You told someone where you were going. You signed the book. You had bushcraft and were well prepared.

This teaching programme had been assisted by television. The searches were all televised, or rather the bush clearing where the Search and Rescue team was based was shown. Helicopter sweeps were filmed, the back views of the volunteer searchers, their bright parkas and muted Swanndries followed as they fanned out across the field of view. The exhaustion on their faces was caught on their return as they accepted mugs of tea from strong-armed women and shook their heads. Nothing yet. Not a sign. No. Not yet. There was the obligatory interview with the team leader; tough, serious, a man who had done time in the field. An experienced man. And always, always, always, the relatives. How did you feel, Jack, when you found your daughter had disappeared without trace? What chance do you think your son has now the weather is closing in, Beryl? Were you surprised when your wife wasn't where you thought, Rob? Yes I was. I hadn't expected it. I was surprised, yes.

He refused, flatly refused to be interviewed. He swung a punch at the ape with the camera and the kidney belt of films. They wouldn't let him join in the search. He would be more use at Base, they said. Men were coming in all the time. They left him alone eventually. He sat on a log and waited till the bush was lost in the dark and the day ended and no one spoke.

They found her on the third day, quite near the track as it turned out. She must have dragged herself from the track to hide better, gone deeper and rolled. He had not told her not to. He had not said Don't move. She couldn't, that was why. She couldn't move.

The rain blew horizontally across the clearing, mist swirled around the base caravan, the helicopter was grounded as they carried her down. Hypothermia.

The volunteer who had found her shook Robin's hand. He had a gut. They don't usually have a gut. Not Search and Rescue. He had done what he could. He was very sorry.

'I wanted you to know, Rob,' he said, 'I just wanted you to know how peaceful she looked.'

'Thank you.'

'Lying there like a little girl.'

Don't tell me, he screamed at the dark sodden bush, the empty sky.

'Peaceful as a baby,' the face continued. 'I just wanted you to know.'

Five

He stood in the church porch shaking hands, kissing weeping women, embracing their overwhelming grief. Yes, yes; it was sad. Very sad. Yes. Thank you for coming. Yes, she was. Expressionless as a toy dog nodding in a rear window, Robin agreed. Yes. Yes. Very. Thank you. Yes, wasn't she.

Emmeline was different. She ran in almost late; boots clanging on stone, head swathed in orange, one hand dragging Calvin in what looked like a miniature tuxedo. She flung her arms round him.

'Oh Rob!' she gasped. 'Oh Rob, good to see *you*.'

'What!'

'I mean, I mean. Oh God, I'm sorry.' She blundered on, all grace gone, her turban slipping. Followed by Rob's bewildered gaze, she caught Calvin's hand once more and fell into the church.

Eileen insisted on cooking the tea that night. Lisa's service, she explained, would have taken it out of him. The chop stared back at him from the foetal position, its flap curling, its fat charred by the pan. She never grilled; it messed up the oven.

'You'll just have to pick up the pieces like I did, dear,' she said, touching the corner of her mouth with a crumpled paper napkin.

Pieces. What fucking pieces. Show me a *piece* you sanctimonious old . . . No. Not cow. This is not a cow. This is a mother. My sad soft brutal mother who transmutes funerals to services, deaths to resurrections and chops to . . . He wanted to scream, to flaunt his disbelief in her face. There is no God. No God but no God. Nothing. None. Get it?

He shook his head.

'Aren't you going to eat your chop, dear?'

'No thanks. I . . .'

'Would you like something else?' Nervous fingers twitched as she watched. What else was there except two tins of baked beans cloned side by side on the bottom shelf for emergencies.

'No thanks.'

'Oh well.' Eileen heaved herself up from the mahogany formica, waited for her hip to click into place and headed off.

'Sit down, Mum, I'll get it.'

'No, no.'

'Mum!'

'No, no. I'm up now.'

He was on his feet, shouting, his fingers clenched. 'Sit down.'

She stared at him; her face melted, disintegrated, turned to pulp. 'I was only trying to help.' One hand dragged her hanky from her bust, another clutched the chair back for support as she sobbed her heart out in the stillness.

Robin stood across the table, his arms hanging, his heart thudding. 'I'm sorry. I'm sorry.'

'What's the use of being *sorry*?'

'I don't know. But if I see another weeping woman I'll scream.'

Her hurt was soundless now. Tears flowed unchecked. 'It's not as though I haven't been through it.' She paused. 'And you have screamed. You've screamed already.' Her sniff was half sob. 'At me.'

He stood there breathless, helpless, hopeless, teeth chewing the inside of one cheek.

Still grasping the chair back, she navigated herself around it and sank onto vinyl.

Rob kissed her forehead, put an arm round her shoulders and moved to the kitchen. 'Where's the coffee, Mum?'

'There's instant in the green tin. I can't afford real coffee like you and Lisa.'

He gripped the kitchen bench, stared at the red camellia blurring before his eyes by the whirligig clothesline. There were still a few crimson blooms left; the rest had turned to brown sog. It was late, of course, late in the season. Winter, he had been told several times during the day, was drawing on. Even clichés were not safe. Lisa skipping down the drive to tell him the latest from Standard Four. 'Winter drawers on!' Her anxious eyes watching his face. 'Get it?'

He got it, picked her up, hugged her. Put her down. He had to remember, he had to remember she was a kid. A little kid.

He poured the boiling water onto the granules and watched with bleak intensity as they turned to brown swirl. Tell me. Tell me. You must know. Tell me.

'Where's the milk, Mum?' he sobbed.

Puckered, moist about the eyes but pleased to help, Eileen came to his aid smiling. 'It's like I always say. If you want something done, do it yourself. It's done in half the time.'

They sat side by side in silence before the boarded-up fireplace. She rootled in a drawer, found some forgotten red-boxed chocolates bloomed with grey. He ate three.

She laughed, pleased by excess. 'And you're the one that doesn't like chocolates!'

He flung in another. 'Oh well.'

Eileen stroked her skirt. 'I thought they'd be nice,' she said.

He blew his nose, mopped up.

She put out her hand. 'It comes over you, doesn't it? All of a sudden. Just like that.'

Robin, his face hidden, snorted.

She nodded, gathered herself together with quick little straightening shrugs.

He watched her warily. He recognised the signs, the setting-up routine before action.

People often do it. He had watched a man in a café last week, doing . . . doing what? The memory had disappeared. What was it? *What*. Rob dragged a hand through his hair, made fists, willed the thing back. The man resurfaced, stretched his neck, flexed his fingers before using his cell phone. Strengthened for the task, one stiff finger prodded, an ear listened. Silence. The aerial was pressed down once more. Wrong number. Robin had been pleased. Why had he been pleased. The Germans have a word for it. I am going mad.

'Robin?'

'Yes?'

'I've been thinking.'

He ate another chocolate. Peppermint. The sweet slime of incipient nausea clung to his palate, slid behind his teeth. His tongue was busy, seeking, tracking, licking wide and deep. The thing is to keep busy. 'Yes?' he sobbed.

'Now that you're alone . . .'

He was on his feet again, his face a foot from hers. 'No!'

Her hands, her tiny begging paws waved, her red eyes were round with shock.

'But why not, Robin, now we're both on our own? Why not?'

He spat it out across the bleakness, the stale chocolates, the gap between them. 'I have to live my own life.'

Eileen reached for her crocheted afghan, pulled it around her straightened shoulders and faced him.

'Whose else could you possibly live?' She wriggled deep in her own chair, picked up her little paper and turned her shoulder. 'Thank goodness I have my work,' she said.

*

Maureen was different. Her world was laid waste; she had no pieces to pick up. Her lengths failed her. For a week she couldn't face the sight of them. The second week she sat at her Bernina, tears dripping onto jersey or poly or crepe. Murray came in and stood silent, his hand on the door knob till he walked away.

Maureen had no memory of that first week except wet pillows and people. She sat bemused, remembered no one, did not even thank them, clutched the plastic ballerina and waited for Rob to come and see her. Murray, stunned with surprise, took over; he heated things, stored things, cooked. 'What on earth's got into her?' he asked Rob every time he arrived.

'Her daughter is dead.'

'Yeah, but life must go on.'

She greeted Rob with love, clutched him to her, could scarcely let him go. They wept together. They loved each other. They understood how they felt.

It never seemed to occur to Maureen that Lisa's death might have been avoided, that Rob could have tried harder, looked longer, *told* her not to move. Never by word or deed did Maureen indicate she had thought of such a thing, let alone held him responsible. They sat for hours going over old photographs; sharing, laughing, howling their eyes out.

Maureen had not owned a camera and she was grateful for Rob's reprints. 'Why have you got so many of her when she was little?' she asked.

'I don't know.'

She straightened her shoulders. 'Well it's just as well, isn't it? As things have turned out.'

Yes.

'Rob?'

'Yes?'

'If ever you see an old high chair. It doesn't matter what it looks like, just as long as it's cheap, would you get it for me? I don't get out much you see.' She paused. 'I mean I'll look when I do but . . . I would be so grateful.' She slammed one hand on each knee and stood up. 'This won't overlock that two-piece,' she said.

Why the hell did she want a high chair? Rob's throat was dry. 'A high chair?'

'Yes.' Maureen waded across to the sofa, groped behind it and came up with Betty in one hand. The golden acrylic hair had virtually disappeared, the pink skull was hidden beneath a bonnet made by Maureen. 'I tried to tell her,' she said. 'I tried to say it doesn't matter, look at men, but she wouldn't have it, you know what little girls are like.' She lowered herself beside Rob, straightened Betty's legs, sat her on her knee. 'Who's a pretty girl then?' she asked.

Scrotum tightening. James Joyce was right. Rob breathed out.

Maureen glanced at him, her laugh friendly. 'Lisa loved her you see. And she's company. And if I can get an old high chair she'll sit up there at the right height and I can look up and she'll be there smiling and . . .' Her voice changed, became sharp. 'And why shouldn't I? We've all got to work things out for ourselves. God in heaven, why shouldn't I? I've seen in books, castles and that at the library. They had painted cut-outs in long corridors; flat, just boards, a woman peeling apples say. I can't remember what they're called.' She was weeping now. 'For company they are. To sit the other side of the fire. To be there! Why shouldn't I? When I come in especially. When I come in and it hits me, Betty'd be there in her high chair waiting.' Her voice rose. The anguished mouth widened. 'Why shouldn't I!'

He was on his feet, hugging her, loving her, agreeing, oh dear God, agreeing with every word. 'You'll get your high chair, mate.'

Too round, too red, staunch to the bone, Maureen sniffed. 'Good. And another thing.'

She glared at him, her face tight with decision. She had something to say and Robin could shut up and hear it. 'Don't you listen to anyone else. You find your own way. You want to . . .' She shook her head, baffled by pain. 'You do it. You're a young man.'

He looked at her in horror. Christ Almighty, what did she think he was. Appalled, disgusted and speechless, Robin sat with his legs apart staring at the crumpled wobble of her mouth. 'I know it's too soon to talk, but we don't get much time just the two of us, but like I say you're a young man Rob and all I say is . . .' Tears were streaming down the powdered runnels either side of her nose, splashing onto Murray's old sweatshirt. 'You do that. Don't you fuss what people say. It's easier for men, that sort of thing. You're young, Rob.'

This was too much. What was she offering him. What the flaming hell was she *doing*. Lisa, his wife, his love, his reason for being, was dead because of him. And this was her bereaved mother, offering him *The Pink Pussy Cat*, *Shady Ladies* or *Sex to Go*. There is no end, there never was and there never will be to the surreal ball-clutching insanity of grief.

'Please,' he said. 'Please don't, Maureen.'

She shook her head quickly. A tear splashed sideways, found a new track. 'Yes. Yes. Too soon. Sorry. But you know now.' She shuddered; a long convulsion mounted her heaving front. 'And don't forget the high chair.'

'No. No, I won't.'

Murray was different again. Yes Murray was different again and again and again. Murray wouldn't let it go. Murray, who through the entire period of their acquaintance had never shown any interest or affection for his younger sibling, who had treated her as an intrusion on his pilgrim path upwards, wanted the facts. Why hadn't Robin made a blaze on the tree? Murray was not a tramper, no way, but even he knew that the bush is confusing, right? You mark the tree. That's what bushcraft is all about. And what did Robin mean she couldn't move. She obviously had moved. She had crawled off the track and they had missed her and she had died. There was too much grey area around to Murray's mind. Why didn't she answer their calls the first time? Presumably they had called.

Wooden as a totara angled to fall, Robin answered. 'Yes.'

'Well then?'

'You've read the coroner's report.'

'Yeah, but like I said. There's too much unexplained.'

Robin leaned nearer. His eyes watched the scene from above,

the right-hand corner of the ceiling gave his perspective. Soon his body would fall. Crush. Destroy. Obliterate.

Tell him. Just tell him. That's all.

'She had abrasions on her head. The pathologist thinks she rolled down a bank, was knocked out, and came to much later.'

'And died.'

'Yes.'

'Well I don't know.' Murray's large jaw hung loose, shut again, his head shook. 'She was very precious to me, Lisa.' He sat in his own chair, drank from his own coffee mug. 'Cold,' he said. 'And Mum hasn't done a stroke of work since. Takes rests, for God's sake.' Another shake of the bison head. 'I don't know. I just don't know.'

Robin stood up and walked to the door in silence.

'Where're you going?'

'To see Miss Bowman.'

'She's dead.'

He was shaking the man. 'What d'you mean?'

Murray was fighting for breath. 'Jesus,' he gasped, one hand guarding his throat on release. 'You gone nuts or something?'

'When?'

'Last night.'

'Why didn't you tell me!'

'I just did.' Fingers massaged the neck. 'I could sue you, you know that?'

'How did you find out?'

'Emmie ran over. I took charge. Well, someone had to, you know what she's like. Total flake. Bawling all over the place. As for the kid!' Murray pressed the lever of his new La-Z-Boy chair. His legs tilted. He was an astronaut cushioned for take-off, a dental patient laid out for repair. 'She was very grateful. I'll say that.'

It didn't matter of course. Nothing mattered, but he would have liked to have said goodbye.

*

Calvin met him at the gate. He took Rob's hand and told him his news. 'I'm not happy,' he said. Robin lifted the child in his arms and held him tight. Orange spiked hair, every vertebra palpable, nose leaking snot. 'Why not?' he said gently.

The eyes were fish pale, the tongue licked the slimy trail. 'Mum's bust my trike. She fell on my trike in the night and squashed it. She's busted my trike and Aunt's died.'

'Calvin? Oh hello.' Sodden, depleted, damaged, Emmeline came towards him. 'Good to see you. Oh my God, I've done it again. I'm sorry,' she wept. He held her in his free arm till Calvin kicked his way to freedom.

'It's my fault you know,' she sobbed. 'I didn't sit with her last night. I wasn't *there*.'

His gut tightened. 'You don't have to be there.'

'But I loved her.' Her forehead puckered, the damp silky skin beneath her eyes was blue. 'Surely you can understand that.'

'Yes.'

'Well then? I let her down. She shouldn't have died alone.'

'Oh shut up,' he roared. 'For Christ's sake, just shut up.'

She leaped backwards, one skinny hand outstretched. 'Thanks a lot.' She ran to the front steps and turned. 'I thought you'd understand,' she yelled as the door slammed.

Robin had no idea how he had got into it in the first place. Margery was a friend of Eileen's which should have warned him. Why had he been persuaded to see this pleasant smiling woman who counselled? Because he had hurt Eileen too much. Because he had betrayed Emmeline. Because all he had achieved was a high chair.

He sat in Margery's warm crowded flat filled with mud-coloured pottery and snaps of her grandies and chairs with fat cushions and talked things through. He hated it. Hated every moment of it. He felt like Oscar Wilde sitting in his prison cell telling lies to his solicitor and he, Robin, was not even telling lies. It was just that he could not bear to talk about it. His grief was his, all he had. Margery could not share it. It was not hers. It was his alone like the proliferating mould in the bathroom and the shower curtain which licked his thighs each morning.

Grief, he thought later, is like sex, indescribable and different from anything previously experienced. There are physical manifestations you cannot explain, detailed descriptions of which would induce either prurient interest or embarrassment from the uninitiated. Elation and depression may be mentioned but not the intimate mechanisms of euphoria or misery. Not to the lay person. There are specialists in these things. There are counsellors for sex and those who counsel the bereaved. Those who have been trained to understand and may be paid to do so. Those who explain that grief is normal, as is sex. That obscene night terrors and wakenings to despair are part of the healing process, especially in such a case as yours Robin. Those who meticulously, sedulously and from near at hand avoid any mention of Time the Great Healer, who understand, none better, that the living must of necessity feel guilt for the dead. Especially in such a case, yes well . . . Next Thursday then, Robin.

Margery wanted him to remember, to think through, to verbalise. Was there nothing, nothing at all, she asked him after some time, no matter how slight, nothing which had irritated him about Lisa?

'No.' And if there was I would not tell you.

He stood up. 'Thank you very much Margery. You've been very kind, but I won't come again. It's not your fault, I just . . .' He leaned forward. He didn't want her to miss a word of Alice O'Leary's counsel. 'All grief is self-pity,' he said and left.

It was better at work. Much better. His colleagues shook his hand, murmured condolences, were reticent and superbly non-inquisitorial. They did not want the facts. How Robin felt when he found his wife had disappeared from the track was not queried. One or two may have watched the drama of the search on TV but very few. By and large in this day and age the men and women in the English Department had minds above such intrusion. They were sorry for

Robin who worked hard, appeared to have a few discipline problems and was probably not a first-class first. Nevertheless he was effective and willing and would doubtless move on in time and she had been a nice little thing. The whole thing was tragic. Tragic, they murmured and shook his hand again.

Tutorials also helped. He had to concentrate for an hour. The importance of Yeats's later poetry and Lawrence's early work had scattered like spilled mercury and must be recollected. Lisa's death was not the fault of his students, few of whom appeared to be disturbed in any way and why should they be. Sad of course for the poor prick/boy/sod but there you were. There was a slight awkwardness the first time they met after the funeral but little more. Helen and Cara pressed his hand on leaving, their eyes tender; the rest shuffled out with heads down. Clyde was no more. Life went on. Toni, the blonde with the furry pencil case, wrote him a little note. There was a kitten curled on the top of the page and another on the back of the envelope. She was a kind person.

The chairs scraped at the end of the tutorial. One of them fell over, was manhandled back on its feet with plenty of wrist spin, teetered a second and stayed stable. 4B English slouched, ambled or departed with speed. It had not been a successful tutorial. Rebekkah had backtracked to Lady Chatterley. They had finished Lady Chatterley weeks ago, had laid her to rest beside Mellors and her floral arrangements, but Rebekkah needed more. Breasts heaved as she clicked her fingers. 'Look, I just don't get it. If a man said "there tha shits and there tha pisses" to me, I'd hit him. Why's it meant to be such a turn-on? Why?'

Robin's heart stopped. He stared in terror, hung on tight. 'I don't know,' he gasped.

'I mean I understand the vision of tenderness and frank sexuality overcoming the coldness of civilisation and all that but . . .'

Helen's face was anxious. 'Yes, I agree in a way, but what I find even more odd is that he thought Lady Ottoline Morrell would like it. I mean.'

Rebekkah's glance was dismissive. Sexual analysis, like symbolism in Lit Crit, is for the lusty or busty or those who *know*. Pollen she found significant. Arum lilies reduced her to pulp.

'Who's Lady Ottoline Morrell?' asked Toni.

'She sucked up to talent and was rich.' Exit Lady Ottoline, kicked to leg by a scuffed boot in 4B. 'Everyone knows about her.'

'I don't.'

This was not Rebekkah's problem as her shoulders indicated.

Helen leaned forward eager to help. She was a good reader, always had been since *Gulliver's Travels* at nine sprawled on the living-room carpet thirty miles from Geraldine. Being a mature student was the most exciting thing that had ever happened after Ron and the girls.

'He quoted it to her in a letter,' she said. 'He thought she would like it if a man said it to her. In bed I mean.'

Robin's fingernails were digging his palm, dragging him back from the hut, the bunk, the warmth beneath his wandering hand.

'They corresponded,' continued Helen. It was not a word she used often. 'Corresponded,' she murmured again. 'The English used to be very frank sometimes in their correspondence. Those sort of people. It seems odd to us but . . .'

Ben at the back's army-surplus beret had a feather; mallard duck, blue. 'Jesus wept,' he muttered and laid his head on his arms like Clyde.

Robin was in shock, his head reeling. The room was hot, stuffy, and smelled of lilac. Or rather fake lilac. You never see lilac now, or smell it. The stuff squirted on erogenous zones by Rebekkah bore no resemblance to the fragrance which flowed in summer from the bush beside the weeping Alice. Lisa had smelled of rose geranium. Lisa in the bed with rose geranium. 'We were talking about Yeats's relationship with Maud Gonne, Rebekkah,' he said bleakly. 'Lady Chatterley was weeks ago.'

'But it's interesting,' insisted Rebekkah. 'It's at the base of the whole fundamental fallacy of Lawrence's so-called eroticism. If you ask me it smacks of coprophilia.' She was prepared to take them all on, the mute, the bored, the puzzled and the startled. She was a strong woman, Rebekkah.

She tangled with Robin a week later. She sat before him, proffered the deep scoop of her neckline and demanded an extension for her Yeats assignment—

'*We make out of our quarrel with others, rhetoric; but of our quarrel with ourselves, poetry.*' *W.B. Yeats. Discuss.*

'I've told you all before, Rebekkah. There can be no extensions for late work.'

'I have to have it. Both the kids have been sick and I've been up all night and there's no way I can handle it during the day with Haden around and Shelley's worse. All I need is one lousy week.'

The interesting thing, he thought, watching the surge of emphasis before him, was her tone. There was nothing placatory, apologetic or even hesitant about it. She was insisting on her rights, the due meed and rights owed her as a female crew member of spaceship Earth.

'No,' he said.

She leaned forward, explained carefully. 'I must have an extension.'

He wanted to shout into her pancake make-up and the deep crimson blush of her anger and tell her what she already knew. My wife is dead. The words were ringing in his head.

The loaded eyelashes lifted. You do the top ones last, Lisa had told him, and don't bother spending too much on mascara. They are all much of a muchness. Rebekkah's eyes searched his as she changed tack. 'Robin, I think I should tell you that one or two people in your tutorial are a little . . .' She hesitated, gave a sad little smile. 'There've already been two drop-outs.'

He heard his unspoken shouted words, watched them float paper thin and spineless to the floor, moved his feet.

'Robin,' her hand touched his as she changed again. 'I know about your wife. That's tough, that's very tough. Believe me, I know. Well, Wes didn't die. God no, but it's the same in the end only worse. It's not a clean break like yours. It festers.' One of her black eyelashes had come adrift. It lay beached on the lower lid, a minuscule scrap from the flotsam of emotion. Rebekkah was getting steamed up. 'Like I said I'm sorry but this is my whole future and Haden and Shelley's as well.' Her eyes were snapping at him. You don't often see eyes snapping, let alone lined and tarred with additives. She was a fighter, Rebekkah, a brave fighter like black-eyed Miss Bowman. Her kids would starve. Wes would win.

'A week. No more.'

She practically skipped out the door. Remembered. Pressed his arm in comfort and ran.

It was the best thing that could have happened. He would never do that again. And to Rebekkah. Rebekkah of all people to have been tempted to flash his grief at. Never again.

Her Yeats was a fortnight late. It was not bad, not bad at all.

Spiro Daskalakis offered more work. The ropes are in good hands tonight. My offsider Robin is with us. Quick sharp.

They went home together to Spiro's house afterwards, climbed the zigzag up the hill and shut out the night. They sat in the kitchen and watched the fish drifting and weaving in their heated tank.

'Do they sleep?' he asked.

Hands lifted, palm upwards, Spiro offered him doubt. 'Sometimes I was coming down when they were new. When it was dark in winter with my torch. Always they move.'

'Horses can sleep standing up.'

Useless. No help at all. 'But not swimming, not waving their tails.' The happiness of the image, the deep rumble of mirth starting deep and exploding with force, the sheer bloody joy of the man.

'People ask me if they have names. They think they are pets or have names. That I call this one Tom and that one Harry and over here is Dick like *The Great Escape* tunnels. Pets! Why would they be pets? I know their names, I know their real names.'

They watched the fish in their metre-long world; the singing pinks and oranges, the velvet blacks and virtually transparent silvers, the streaks of fluorescent colour which darted and the fish which drifted and trailed, dazed by their own glories. There were striped fish and plain fish and timid fish and fish with spots which cruised or hid in plastic castles or wove through hectic green aquatic plants as graceful as themselves.

Spiro was now pointing, making formal introductions. 'Rosy Barbs. Neons, a good name, no? See how quick. Black Neons, two there are, but one hides in his castle. Cardinal Tetra two, Angel Fish two, Golden Gourami and two Pink Kissing Gourami is all.'

Rob dipped his head at each name though they had met before.

'I had a Red Oscar once I did call a name. Icarus, I called him, he flew so high. Leaping for food. I fed him by hand and one day, Ppht! Up, up, he is leaping for more, and suddenly there he is.' Spiro's foot tapped in demonstration. 'My Icarus is on the floor. My Red Oscar lies stunned and gasping.'

Rob's mouth twitched. 'Was he all right?'

'A box of birds he was soon, but I had to take him to my cousin in Tawa who has a big, big tank.' Arms moved. 'He was too big for his boots, my Icarus. Yes,' he continued, 'fish are the things to watch because they are beautiful, things of mystery which I do not understand. Learning you can learn from books, from words, eyes, people, like watching with the filo pastry, the sharpening of the knife. That way you can learn. There is a right way and a wrong. Always. But not with understanding, not with knowing. That you cannot learn. I do not understand these fish. What makes them,' asked a hand, 'tick? Each move is different. How can that not delight me? Why? Why do they go this way that way? Who says, who is it that is boss? Look at him, this speedy Neon. This time he leads, this time he goes half way, next time who knows? Pfff!' Again the upflung doubting palms, the cheerful acceptance of the total unknowableness of any creature beneath the moon.

And this was fish. How did Spiro go on humans? He was now making Greek coffee—hot as hell, sweet as love and black as something, served in tiny cups with glasses of water.

'What about people?' asked Robin. 'How do you go on people?'

'Simple, boy.' Spiro's face was eager, his moustache on the move. 'It is words that are the trouble.' He demonstrated, waving legions of the things in the air. 'Words are all that is the matter. If I could say to him,' he pointed to a larger more complicated fish, 'why this way, why that way, and he could tell me then he would, no? But perhaps I am his boss say, or he is mine. Perhaps I think, ah now I understand, but he might have his own,' he produced the word with triumph, '*agenda* might he not? How can I trust him? It is not thoughts I hear. Not his. Not mine. Not yours. It is words.' Spiro shook his head. 'It is not that he lies. He is a good fish, no? See how honest, his eye firm, the streams of his tail float buoyed up by angels. He does not lie, but perhaps he feels he should say something when asked. It is more he does not *know*, this fish who is asked. None of us, none of us know why we do come, why we do go, why we do love and yet we ask and we ask and we ask again. Do you love me? Yes. Do you really love me? Yes. Oh yes. Do you love *me*? I am not sure but I think and hope so. Who can say that? Who is the monster who can say that? Even he who is not sure cannot say so. He can only hope and pray and try to love.' Spiro stared at the sludge in the bottom of his cup. 'And yet still we act as though all the passion of our words will not be turned to dust.' He crossed himself briskly, gloated over the word. 'Dust.'

He stood up. 'You do not have to hate yourself because your Lisa died.' He crossed himself again. 'There are depths and mysteries.' Spiro stood up and took Robin's little cup. 'Tell me about her,' he said. 'Talk to me about your Lisa.'

Time passed, as they had said it would. It passed as days and nights and weeks and months. Sometimes it went in circles or scrambled to hell. It was not as linear as they had told him it would be, but it passed. Robin had not yet gone south to see the husband. His research, you could say, had suffered since his wife had died. Eighteen months isn't long.

*

He stood at the back of the crowded lift as it sighed its way to the ground floor. 'Of course,' said the man from linguistics as the door opened, 'they let themselves become completely dependent on the potato.'

His companion nodded.

'It depends whose side you're on,' said a woman striding past, 'Bloomfield's or Chomsky's. You have to believe in something.'

The woman's hair as she marched up the Pirelli tiles of the entrance tunnel reminded him of Emmeline's. Robin's pleasure in the potato pundit sank. He had been rude to Emmeline, worse than that. Much worse. He would go and see Emmie. And Calvin. He had not seen them for months.

And Eileen, and Maureen and even, God help us, Murray. All of them he would see. All of them he would love (fat chance!), none of them he would understand, and none would understand him. He felt faintly elated, as though he had worked something out, or rather Spiro had; had tracked down the original resource material and handed it on so it would come in handy. Is your Dad handy?—the Jehovah's Witness at the door had asked him years ago. No. He's dead and you can skip the house either side as well.

Robin glanced at the posters for a Chainsaw concert plastered on the brick wall beside him. Why fifty small identical posters. Why not one big one. Why not fifty separate posters. A leaflet drop. He did not understand. But then he did not understand anything. But then he did not have to understand anything. Spiro had told him. His step quickened as he passed two strong-calved women. 'Of course there will be ongoing assessment, continuous assessment for relevance as well as content,' said the one with the backpack.

Of course. Of course and of course and of course.

The steps near the library were lined with students eating, peeling fruit, drinking juice and confiding. A neat line of orange peel decorated the tread of one step. They sprawled, supported each other's backs, drank coffee, belched and ate apples. Some were hauntingly beautiful. A young Maori woman sat reading *The Duchess of Malfi* with a man's pink cannon-fodder face cradled in her lap. He lifted a finger, curled tendrils of hair, dropped it when satisfied and started again. She had good hair. Strong, springy, plenty of it.

Robin's gut was sticking to his backbone. Two-thirty. Lunch. Yes. Lunch. He collected a precariously loaded roll, jammed a slice of cucumber back into position with a thumb, picked up a polystyrene cup from the stall in the corner of the quad and sat down to anonymity and echoing noise and peace of a sort. Smoke trailed from some jerk's face into his. The mandibular movement of a python was needed to get to grips with the roll, to catch the free-floating beansprouts, the tomato slices, the egg mashed with mayo. He opened his mouth wide.

The pigeons cocked satin heads and waited. One sat unblinking as a leading light on the step below him. A small grey feather flecked with white was stuck to one claw. The bird seemed unconcerned at the misplacement. Did it mind, wish to dislodge it as a human would. He would never know. He put out his hand to grey and black and crossed primary feathers. The pigeon scuttled. He thought of George's daughter.

His mother was home. She came out to greet him smiling in checked easy-care, an enormous star-shaped brooch stuck on her left front. She disliked her front. It was too big. She had always wished for a smaller one but you don't have much say do you.

The brooch was dazzling, a gold and red centre surrounded by the mangled rays of a scrambled sunburst. 'I haven't seen that before,' he said.

Her hand flew to it. Rays were still visible writhing beneath her hand. 'Oh, it's just costume.' She gave a little yelp of laughter. 'It's not real or anything.'

Well no.

He had seen that look before today, round-eyed, amber, unblinking, watchful. Of course. The pigeon. His mother's fingers moved against the brooch caressing shit metal. 'Where did you get it?' he asked.

'Someone gave it to me.'

'Good on them.'

'I think of it as a symbol,' she murmured. 'The Son of God's rays reaching deep into our hearts spreading joy.'

Ah.

She looked up at him, her eyes anxious. 'I wish you would get back into the comfort of the church, Robin.'

'You make it sound like some sort of padded playpen.'

If she was offended at his cheap crack she did not show it. Her pale cushioned face did not change.

He offered her a childhood memory in apology. '"I want to get back into the woods where bears are *bears*."'

She looked startled, but then she often did. One finger touched her lips.

'Kids' radio programme. Sunday mornings. *Maxi the Taxi*, you remember.'

'I would have been at church.'

'Of course.' He felt the cool stillness, the drawn blinds. American voices telling him of little tug boats and bright fire engines and bears who did not discover they were happy in their own backyards till they got into trouble in someone else's and went back to the zoo and made the kids happy. A cop-out. He had thought so at the time.

He picked up the battered hymn book from the table. 'Why the markers, Mum?'

'I mark them when I first go in. It saves time. And I keep the markers there till next week so I can check if I want to. Which hymns we had, I mean.'

He put his arms around her, kissed her soft cheek. 'I see,' he said.

'Mind my hair,' she said gently.

There was no answer to his knock next door. He peered through the venetian blinds. Maureen lay asleep on the cretonne-covered sofa. Beside her in the high chair he had found sat Betty, her battered face calm, her eyes blue. Rob laid his face against the cold glass for a moment then ran leaping up Emmeline's path.

He stopped short. Murray was mowing her lawn. Pushing and yanking at a smoking old Morrison, yelling the Hallelujah Chorus at the top of his voice, Murray was in action. He thrust the lever into idle. 'Hallelujah, Hallelujah,' he roared, seizing the laden catcher and heading round the back trailing clots of green. The sweat stain down the back of his shirt was T-shaped.

Rob clutched Emmeline's arm at the door.

'What's Murray doing?'

She removed her arm, held it against her with the other hand. 'Cutting the grass,' she said. 'What did you think?'

Six

'Yeah, but why?' said Rob.

Her purple pants were wide, her shirt knotted above her navel, her feet bare. 'He offered to.'

'Why?'

'King of *Kings* and *Lord* of Lords,' roared Murray, followed by the thundering roar of the mower as he set off again.

'What *is* this? The guy offers to cut the stuff. I say thanks.' Arms akimbo, body tense, Emmeline had had enough. 'What's it got to do with you? I've scarcely seen you since Aunt died. The first time I did you spat in my eye. What are you, some sort of . . .'

Her toes and heels beneath the purple were bright pink, the arches white. Why just the toes and the heels, he wondered. He lifted his eyes to a wedge of hair and sharp-nosed anger.

'Yeah, I know. I'm sorry about that. It's just . . .' He watched the clown roaring and belching along. 'When did you start liking the shit?'

'When he started offering to cut the grass.'

You had to hand it to her. He stretched his mouth into a grin.

She was looking at him with her usual attentiveness. 'Are you not feeling yourself?' she asked gently.

The banal phrase, the possibility of double entendre, was dirty fighting, as she would know. He looked at her, his eyebrows banging behind the bridge of his glasses as he disliked her.

There was a flicker, the merest glimmer of a smile as she led him inside. Her hand touched Aunt's bedroom door as they passed. Her voice changed, became conversational, chatty. 'You know it's weird. I always think of Aunt as smiling. Why do I do that? She didn't smile much. She wasn't a chucklehead. She was tough, grim even. Remember those grisly stories? Why did she tell us those blood-curdlers? She'd be lynched now. Even Sylvester the cat doesn't have his head burned off like Little Degchie-Head or thumbs lopped off like Little Suck-a-Thumb.' She scratched her head—couldn't work it out, didn't know. She offered him muffins and lemon drink from a jug with a sieved spout held at navel level. She was on an Earth Mother kick. A guy at the theatre had brought fruit and vegetables from up the coast and no one wanted lemons.

She would never change, he knew that. Till the day she died she would be frugal and prodigal, strong and self-doubting, a fiercely independent panhandler who could get under his skin when he was not feeling himself. Murray would never have offered to mow anything unless there was a reason. Robin would bet on that.

Her ability as an actor seemed to him another thing she picked up and discarded at will. Useful to have, and a pleasure to slip into, to fling to the audiences below when required; to bless the hands, the cheers, the sheer bloody enchantment. Yet he knew about her hours of research, her excitement at 'finding the walk', at 'getting inside', her willingness to work till she dropped. She was correctly cast as an actor. They are meant to be various. To stand like saints and fry like sinners before gliding into the final tango. The one constant in Emmeline was her love for Calvin.

She was now curled up on the old couch in the kitchen taking an interest in her pink and white feet as she told him how she had fixed the blockage in the back lavatory.

The Edwardian completeness of the old house fell apart at the back. There were passages to burrow down, half-empty rooms with speckled mirrors, a cracked hand basin in a corner. Rob's heart ticked. In a back room in Seatoun Alice had sat down and wept.

Emmeline was now on another tack. Did he know that the Aborigines along the Murray and the Coorong Rivers had used human skulls as water carriers? The skulls of choice were those of deceased parents and close relatives. Emmie snatched her feet to her, clutched the toes. 'Isn't that wonderful?'

Her navel had disappeared, folded away neatly in a pleat of her stomach. He missed it. 'Miss Bowman would have liked that.'

She nodded as though he had got something right, some minor cause for approval like the correct answer to a tricky clue. 'Yes.' She blinked. 'This lemon drink isn't bad.'

Talking to her had always been interesting. She leaped from topic to topic, whirred from grief to pragmatism like an out-of-control Catherine wheel. He was glad of the muffins and cordial and the now-absent tanned navel and the sleazy crackle of rayon against her legs. Her particularities, her contradictions could be ticked off on several hands, like six.

The scent of bruised grass filled the air. Murray was still at it.

Emmie was now backtracking. 'The "great long red-legged scissor man" haunted me. Just when I was getting over those bleeding stumps I read Kipling. Aunt had lots. I'll never read him again. Ever. An Indian girl falls for an Englishman. At the end of the story she stands outside his window and holds up her arms. No hands. Her father has chopped them off.'

'Kipling,' he said hopelessly.

'And Saudi Arabia. You've seen those photos? It's worse, it's worse if they do it surgically.'

'What!'

'The stumps are so thin. The ends of the arms.'

What on earth was she on about? She couldn't mean it would have been better, that they would have been thicker if hacked off on a block in the marketplace. How could he have thought she was 'all right', 'coping'? How could he have assumed for one moment that anyone as fragmented as Emmeline O'Malley could cope without her rock of ages.

'I had a dream last night.'

Oh God.

'Yes.' Her chin was now propped on the heel of her hand. 'I lost a thumb. I wasn't worried or anything, you know how you're not in dreams.'

Other people's dreams bored him. He was tempted to skip them in novels but obviously something was expected. 'I am,' he said. 'Often.'

'Oh yes, if it's that sort of dream. Anyhow, I looked down and there it was all neat and tidy, no blood, and I thought ah yes I must put it in the fridge.'

'Freezer.'

'No, no you're meant to pack it in ice. Not put it in the freezer. But I didn't have any ice, you know how you never do in dreams. Have what you want, I mean. But it didn't matter at all.' She wiggled her thumbs, stared at the tendons, stroked the generous back swing.

'Are you working at the moment?' he said quickly.

'I am and it's great. *Hedda Gabler*. You must come. But that's not what we're talking about.' She was hugging her knees again. He supposed it was because she was so thin she could slip from one position to another with such ease, her movements smooth as spilled water. Sinuous. That was the word. Sinuous. Lisa had not been sinuous. Lisa had been edible. He stared out the open window.

'We were talking about Aunt.'

Were they? He hadn't noticed. He had gone somewhere else. It still happened.

'I wish we had some dope.' She was on her feet again. 'I just might have.' Toes and heels moved with the precision of a ballerina ascending a gutter. She was reaching at full stretch for a jar inscribed *Unguentum Ultralanum* on the top shelf of an old dresser. 'What a bit of luck.' She sniffed the contents. 'Does it go off?'

She rolled the joint with quick hands. Even as a child, he remembered, they had combined the manual dexterity and brute force of a specialist in crown and bridge work. She lit the feeble-looking thing, inhaled and handed it on.

He had worked hard on dope in the eighties, had hoped to be enhanced, elevated, to shuck off a few layers, but nothing much had happened. He dragged deeply.

'Where's Calvin?' he asked after some time.

'Birthday party. Staying overnight. His father's in Australia,' she said dreamily.

Now that was interesting. Very interesting. 'Australia?'

'Yeah. He sent a platypus last year.' She giggled. 'Platypus catchymus.'

And that was funny. That was really good. '*Catchymus.*' He stretched his arms to the ceiling and let them flop. 'Murray must've stopped farting around with the mower. No hallelujahs.'

She was playing hair games, one hand twisting and rolling between drags on the joint. 'He goes home for a shower,' she said. 'He'll be back later.'

'Why?'

She leaned forward, picked up a pot-holder shaped like a pig, kissed its pink padded haunch. 'Rob?'

Perhaps it was working this time, he seemed to be mellowing out. That was the phrase. Mellowing out. Perhaps his previous tries had been duff stuff. 'Yeah?'

The marijuana was smoothing out the wrinkles of his brain— the sulci? the gyri? were flat as your hat, flatter. He must look them up. And Bloomfield. And Chomsky. But why.

She was beautiful. 'Yeah?' he said again.

'I want to tell you something.'

Dope-laden confidences take time. He listened, absorbed it into his cleansed mind and stared at the pig's haunch while she told him about Aunt's papers, how there were masses of them, photographs which meant nothing, letters, piles of the stuff. And lists. Endless lists. One headed 'Apples'. She pulled a yellowed piece of paper from the drawer in the dresser and read. '"Rhode Island Greening, Easopus, Spitzberg, Snow Apple, Sheepnose, Yellow Bellflower." Why did she keep that? It's so sad.'

'They're good names,' he said. 'I'd keep a list like that.'

Emmeline shook her head. 'But there are hundreds of different lists, well dozens. She must have gone through the house from memory. Where she'd lived before here; cupboard by cupboard, drawer by drawer.' Emmie peered at another one. 'Pots, pans, skillets, jelly bags, waffle irons, trivets. What's a trivet?'

He couldn't be bothered, waved a hand, handed back the roach.

She inhaled deeply, sighed it out. 'There's nothing wrong with standing on your head,' she said, 'as long as you don't talk about it at parties.'

He agreed, but there were more interesting things. 'You're wreathed,' said Rob happily, 'wreathed in *smoke*.'

Dead leaves hung orange and green from the cherry tree outside the window. One fell, another orange one with a bite out of it drifted down. Actually drifted, lay on the ground.

'Look at that,' he said.

'What?'

'A leaf.'

She was unimpressed. 'But why did she do that? Why did she make the lists?' Emmie leaned across the table. 'You know what I reckon. She was stitching on her past, that's what. Her hero was Calvin Coolidge.' Emmie held up the limp roach. 'I'm sick of this. Want it?'

He shook his head. 'Why Calvin Coolidge?'

'He came from Vermont.' She giggled. 'And he didn't talk much.'

It was very funny. He could see that. They laughed and laughed. Were happy. Couldn't remember why they were laughing or what was funny or tragic or make any sense of either which did not matter at all.

He was staring at her, examining the way her limbs moved as though he had never seen her in his life before. As though she were some sort of miracle. He put out his hand.

'Emmie . . . ?'

She sat upright, shook her head to clear it. 'No.'

She shuffled about in her pocket, produced an envelope. 'Look. This is the important one. Read it.'

> *My dear Emmeline,*
>
> *I will be dead when you read this but that is all right by me and must be by you honey, and Calvin will keep you jumping.*
>
> *Don't go back to Vermont. It is a cold place. Your father was an attorney called Jackson Purdie. He is dead now. My family was in lumber. My grandmother stood by me and the things we have were hers. They were shipped out after she died. Also the money, the capital of which is intact but I have had to use the interest.*
>
> *Mr Greenstone in Kilbirnie has the details.*
>
> *You have been all my joy, and Calvin also.*
>
> *Your loving Aunt.*
>
> *PS. Be careful with the money. Mr Greenstone is a man of integrity.*

'What the hell does she mean, Rob?'

'Just what she says. It's perfectly clear.'

'God in heaven, how can you be so hopeless?' She shoved her face at him, her eyebrows inches from his. He put out a hand to touch one. She snatched her head away. 'I don't know who I am,' she said. 'Can't you see? Aunt told me I was her sister's child . . .' She shoved the piece of paper at him again. 'Read it! Doesn't it sound here as though she was my mother?'

This was not the moment for important discussions. Robin was aware of that. He was stoned. His head was floating above his neck. 'But you told me she was,' he muttered. 'When Calvin was born, you said.'

'Oh yes I said. I've always thought so since I was about fifteen.

Earlier, when kids whispered, I guessed. But why didn't she *say*? Talk to me about it.'

'It's easy enough to find out. There must be a birth certificate.'

'That's not the point. I wanted my mother to tell me.' She snatched back the letter. 'Think man, think.'

Murray stood at the door. His white T-shirt was ironed. He was showered, shaved and smelled of Brut. 'Bit of a problem there,' he said. 'He hasn't got the equipment.'

'Lawns look nice, Murray,' murmured Emmeline, restowing her letter and scrubbing her face on a tea towel.

'You guys smoking dope?'

'We were.'

Murray sat beside Emmeline and held out a hand.

Robin stood up. 'Stay for a lasagne,' she said staring up at his face, her head bent back as though to a great height, a worm's eye view of the departing.

'No.'

Her head snapped upright. She held out one drooping gracious hand. 'How's Henry James?' she said.

'Dead.'

Nothing is more excluding than unshared laughter. 'Henry James came from *Baa*ston,' she said. 'I happen to know. He was a Boston Brahmin.' She sucked the roach and handed it back to the lawn man.

Rob turned on his heel.

'*Braah*min,' she yelled at his back. '*Braahmin*, y'dork.'

She rang a week later. Her voice was crisp and friendly. Emmeline never remained pissed off for long. Her occasional willy-willies of rage soon spiralled back to earth, all cheerfulness restored. She was buoyant as a float.

'How's Henry James?' she said.

'Still dead.'

The repetition of the laboured joke was typical, typical of her goading wanton bloody-minded silliness. Catchphrases, jokes, rags and tags of words and memories of no interest to anyone but herself churned beneath that hair and fell at random. Sometimes they hit the mark but by no means always. Emmeline was not concerned. Like Aunt, and indeed Murray, she pleased herself.

'I never know why he fussed about all that social high-life stuff in England,' she said.

'How do you know if you don't read him?'

'I have read him and I thought he was great but some of them went on too long.'

And suck on that. 'He was afraid he might be bored at night,' he said.

The silence was brief. 'Oh.'

'Yes.' He had meant to talk to her for hours the other night. To share with her his memories of Aunt, to support and comfort her without as much as a blink of the eye to indicate that he knew how she felt and that Time was the Great Healer. He did not know how she felt. Nobody knows how anybody feels. Ask a fish.

Also he wanted something. He wanted Alice O'Leary. Every memory, every nine-year-old's glimpse of the 1969 house guest must be described for him. Murray's scented presence had finished that. Rob's toes curled in remembered frustration.

'Emmie, there's something I'd like to talk to you about.'

'Sure. Which reminds me. I'm going to hear Chainsaw. They're on next week. Want to come?'

'Emmie for heaven's sake, I'm old.'

'And I'm two years older. And a solo mother. And so was Aunt and I'm going to hear Chainsaw.'

Over-egging it as usual. Throttling the wisp of self-irony with excess. At least he laughed. 'Come and have a meal first,' he said quickly. No woman other than Eileen had been to the flat since Lisa had died.

'No. It won't start till late. I'll ask Bernie's niece to have Fatso. We swap kids quite often. Come here about eight. I'll be rehearsing till then.'

'You're sure you wouldn't rather go to a movie?'

'Get real, Raab,' she said, the come-off-it smile still in her voice. He saw her on the tyre swing; a mocking bird, the shining cuckoo of the eastern suburbs. Grunge metal for God's sake. He must be mad.

Eileen was pleased with herself, she told him when he rang. She had remembered both hares and rabbits this month. It was easy enough to remember the rabbits last thing at night at the end of the month but the hares next morning were more difficult, especially on your own. Her endless superstitions; salt thrown, ladders avoided, fingers crossed, puzzled him. Why bother when she was already watched over, guarded from on high with every hair of her head numbered.

Emmie had boned, rolled, chopped and tasted before blasting off to work.

'She can get herself organised if she wants to,' Eileen had admitted long ago.

And change the look of a place. In this case by climbing on the table to remove a bulb, to soften the light which fell on the beat-up chairs, the scrubbed table, the last cherry leaves in the jug in the middle. Miss Bowman had had branches of crab apple in the same grey jug, another time a scatter of lime-green elm flowers. Where had she found them? He had never seen an elm in Seatoun. Like Emmie she could produce things from nowhere. It was enough to make you believe in genetic heresies—inheritance of acquired characteristics, a gene for legerdemain, for the quick nick, the sleight of left hand over right for the creation of small visual treats, of transient scarcely noticed pleasures. Get it or don't get it. I like it.

They talked about Calvin. What Calvin said, what Calvin did at the new day-care.

'You didn't tell me he'd changed.'

'I *didn't*?' Her eyes were shadowed but he could see her mouth. He grinned back.

'OK, OK. How long's he been there?'

'Not long. All I've heard so far is there's no doors on the dunnies.

This day and age, I suppose. Aunt would have hated that.' The edges of her fingers were blurred by the candlelight. 'And the next thing'll be school. You know how I'd sum up Aunt and me? Cosy. Life was very cosy once I'd calmed down about men. I loved Aunt. Aunt loved me. We both loved Calvin.' She straightened her shoulders. 'Cosiness. Who needs it?'

I didn't mind it. And nor did Lisa who died alone with her thumb in her mouth the man said and that I will not believe.

She touched his hand. 'Sorry. You'd think I'd learn, wouldn't you. Shut up. Stop trying to play both Hamlet and the Clown. Think occasionally. "But when he thinks he fastens / his hand upon his heart." Who's that?'

'Housman. He was an atheist. Buried apart from the rest.'

'Not out of wedlock and over the wall like poor Sorrow Durby-field? We'll be lined up in rows. But it was no joke then. Not in Vermont.' Her face changed. 'Or here. No joke at all. Don't tell a soul, but I think it's better with two. I don't mean when the parents hate each other. Hell no. But other things being equal, as Murray would say.'

He picked up their plates and rinsed them in a stone sink the size of a horse trough, his back towards her, his hands busy.

'Are you still seeing him?'

'Of course.' She seemed happy with the crass question. 'Murray and I,' said Emmeline, 'are very close.'

He propped the plates on the wooden draining board, examined it. The gouged track beneath his finger was grey and furry with age. It reminded him of a long white-haired cactus called Something senilis. 'No one could be close to Murray,' he said.

She was all attention. 'No?'

'He has jumper leads in his car. He carries jumper leads. You remember that caravan George had before he shot through? It was out in the backyard by the whirligig.' Rob's arms demonstrated towels spinning, pyjamas whirling. 'And you know what the guy did? He spent hours getting the levels right so he would know how to get the levels right when they went on holiday—and they never went! Or else he was banging on about pigeons. Or shooting through without a word. I bet he left after a meal.'

'What's this got to do with Murray?'

'He was his father.'

She looked at him with contempt, a slow lip-curl of distaste.

'Ah. Fathers. Sins of.'

'I didn't mean that.'

'Then what the hell did you mean?' she said and put her head in her hands. Her hair was too near the flame. He gathered it for safety and held it behind her neck.

'He's a shit, Emmie,' he said. 'I promise you.'

She snatched her hair back. 'I don't find him so. He's very kind to me.'

'He's ten years younger than you. At least.'

'Jesus. What *is* this? And what about you! You were twelve years older than Lisa.'

'That was . . .' No. It was not different. He held out his hands, palms upwards in defeat.

'Robin, Robin, Robin.' A dying cadence, the mocking self-awareness of an out gay admonishing a closet queer filled her voice. 'Watch it sailor,' snapped Emmeline. She stood up. 'Come on, time we went.'

Once again, Murray had sidetracked the conversation, deflected the course and got him offside. He didn't care for Murray.

He had been to the place once before. Some kids from the lab had had a twenty-first there a few years ago; had decorated the hall with streamers, turned up the disco, blown up the balloons and got down, man. There had been a few parents present, men with polished faces and women with cropped hair who danced and danced and yelled and screamed and had fun. It must have cost a fortune. 'I thought kids didn't have this sort of thing now,' said Robin.

Lisa had looked puzzled. 'Why not?'

'Well I don't know,' he muttered. 'It's . . .'

'You're no good at *fun*,' she said.

The place had changed hands. Definitely and decisively the ambience had changed. Gone were the bright lights, the starkness for renting. The smell of dope greeted them as they stood in the queue. Men and women slipped in and out of the semi-darkness to racketing blasts of sound from the hall. A long-haired woman in front of them was explaining to her friend that she had not minded licking the whipped cream off the male stripper's chest. Not in the slightest. What she had objected to, and still did, was being bottom. She was always top. Had always been a top person and always would be.

Emmeline touched her shoulder. 'Hey,' she said. 'Where were you?'

Robin put out his hand, gave a quick tug of her wide trousers.

The woman showed no surprise. She flicked back her hair to explain. 'Ladies' night. New club just opened. I've got a card somewhere.' She burrowed in a drawstring Indian bag. 'Here. Have fun.'

'Great. Thanks.' Emmie touched the bag. 'Do you find the mirror bits drop off?'

'No.'

'Mine did.'

'What'd you do?'

'Nothing.' They laughed. Emmie admired the electric-blue lace stockings. They were stockings? Yeah. Her friend's galumphing steel bracelet and Emmeline's trousers were also admired, made part of their instant rapport.

Robin watched in silence. The woman could just as easily have taken a poke at Emmie. But no, they had a base. Like gay men, they shared a freemasonry, an outlook. A gender bias. But presumably so did heterosexual guys. The thought did not comfort him.

Emmie was back on the stripper track. 'Was it, well you know? I mean it wasn't for real, obviously.'

'God, no. But it was pretty . . .' The rings tossed. 'Well, like you said. I mean otherwise I wouldn't have minded being bottom. If it hadn't sort of seemed real.'

Emmeline nodded. 'I guess not.' She took his arm. 'This is Rob.'
'Hi.'

Emmeline turned to him, her eyes glinting like a child's with a
treat. 'Wasn't that great? You couldn't come. Ladies only.' She cheered
up. 'Perhaps that's only Fridays. I'll ask.' But the stockings had
disappeared.

They queued again to get their wrists stamped Paid.

His childhood doctor had had a *Good Patient* stamp for kids. At
the end of a visit Dr Brabson, his teeth wrecked by pipes and
insufficient dental care, had leaned forward. 'Hold out your hand,
Robin.' He wondered when it had stopped, when the award had
become sissy, a shameful secret to be hidden from the other kids
instead of skited about. Five, he supposed. Or six. Not much older
than Calvin. It seemed pretty young.

A Maori guy beside them had a ring on each of the fingers on
his right hand and none on the left. A woman clung to his arm, her
crutch barely covered by a pelmet of leather. In the smoky half
darkness you could not tell where her tights ended and the teetering
heels began. A babe in invisible boots.

'You do know,' teased Emmeline, her body locked against his in
imitation of another woman eating her man alongside, 'that "Elvis"
is an anagram of "Lives"?'

He grinned, tightened his arm around her. A man and woman
shoved past them. Both heads of tough grey hair were tugged into
pony tails, both wore black T-shirts stamped with large golden lions'
heads. Her chest thrust out more than his but not by much. They
were together. Swingers. They had probably arrived on a Harley
Davidson, he stiff-armed, her body hugging tight into the corners.
They would not grow old. No siree. A black man in turquoise socks
and blue jandals danced alone, one protruding ebony toe beating
the rhythm.

Men with shaven heads embraced nearby, paralysed by the
wonder of each other.

'Come upstairs,' said Emmie. 'You see better.' She glanced at him, on her own ground, sending him up. 'Unless you want to dance?' He caught her arms, held them to her as the support band thundered around them.

'Drop it, Emmie. Just for once. Just for tonight, OK?'

'OK.'

They sat drinking sour wine at a table on the mezzanine, hands touching as the support band thundered and the crowds danced and waited. It was too long since he had been surrounded by such a blast of sound, such beat. The hedonistic anarchy of the sound was therapeutic. He was grateful to Emmeline. It was her idea.

The local group blared and screamed to an end. Chainsaw appeared to swirls of dry ice, strobe lights and roars of applause. You couldn't even see the drummer. He was lost in special effects. Occasionally he loomed frenetic from the mist, flicked sweat from his hair and sank once more.

The large man opposite (drunk? stoned?), a man in need of help, spilled his beer. The tide flowed slowly towards them across the table. Emmie mopped with tissues, the drunk held out his hand, Emmie, her smile gentle, gave him the dripping thing. He blew his nose on it and handed it back. 'Ditch it,' snapped Robin.

Chainsaw were warming up. The grunge chords, the full tilt power, the guitar/vocal's strutting hips and rumbling rasp were having the right effect; guitar riffs twanged and scorched and were rehashed with gusto. The band were transfigured, the crowd reaching critical mass. The dust-ridden streams of light swept and soared and soared again above the yelling, the screams, the endless driving thump and roar of sound. He could feel it in his crotch and knew it was a cliché and didn't care.

Rows of black shapes jumped up and down, pogoing in unison below the stage. The audience were away, gone, lost in ecstasy and dust and the passionate conviction of the true believer.

Emmie clutched his arm. 'He's going to dive. Watch the bouncer.'

'What?'

She slammed her palm on the damp table. 'Sssh.'

Her face was shadowed, lit from below. Downstairs was a cave, a darkened cave of worshippers pushing and shoving before the lit shrine.

He gripped her arm. 'Let's get nearer. Go down there.'

She shook her head. 'Later. Watch.'

A thin guy scrambled on the stage in front of the bass guitar, dashed across the stage, was chased by a man so tough, so beautiful, so trained to kill that Robin's heart moved. Emmeline's mouth was open, her lips wet. The crowd roared their support for the diver. The bouncer was stripped to the waist, a double-headed eagle tattoo moved between his shoulderblades as he ran, his trousers were rolled to the knee, his hands encased in leather mittens, his head cropped. He was a powder-monkey between the smoking decks of *HMS Victory*. Stooped, effective and hard as nails, he tossed the flyer through swirling gas onto the pogoers and slammers below. The crowd shifted, supported the arms and legs and head for a moment before the diver sank, disappeared, went with the flow and surfaced.

'It's regulation,' yelled Emmie. 'No stage diving. That's why he's here.'

The half-naked figure squatting at the side of the stage was hypnotic. Another flyer appeared, and another, a woman. Each time the bouncer uncoiled, raced, seized and flung with economy. He was pretty to watch. Each time the diver rolled and sank and the bouncer waited for more. His smile was amiable, deadly but amiable. Nothing personal. Chainsaw lifted their game. The crowd were alight.

'Let's go down,' yelled Robin again.

They shoved through the death-trap crowd on the stairs down to the front, to the action and the heartbeat, the anarchic arousal, the sock of excitement of the drums and the noise and the heat as the dry ice rolled and swooped. Robin screamed something at her against the noise, the throbbing in his ears. 'What!' She was dancing. Emmie was enjoying herself.

He tried again. Hopeless, but it didn't matter. He could tell her later of his astonishing discovery. Of ease. Of more than that. Of bliss. What a word. Katherine Mansfield, betrayal, bodice-rippers swam before his eyes. But still it was the word. The bliss of abandoning, of not trying, of not giving a stuff lifted the hair from his head, weaved his legs faster. Sharper than happiness and more ruthless, unsolicited and more dangerous, bliss is transitory and to be seized. Bliss from the cacophony of Chainsaw lifted his heart and head.

'Let's go home.'

Robin opened his eyes, saw the light jigging on the mirror at the foot of the bed and shut them again. Emmie was still asleep.

This should not have happened. He did not love Emmeline. Emmeline did not love him. Sex without love is death. An expense of spirit in a waste of shame. All that. But last night had not seemed like that. Anything but. It had seemed . . . Well. Yes. He lay remembering. What Spiro would call an opener for the eye. And Lisa was dead and all grief is self-pity and self-pity is sin and there is no God but God. Oh Jesus fucking Christ. Robin stormed out of bed, tripped on his abandoned clothes and headed for the door.

'Where're you going?' she murmured.

'For a pee.'

'Put the kettle on, would you?' Emmeline yanked the duvet over her side and snuggled down. Snuggled.

She was sitting up when he came back, the duvet wrapped chastely above her breasts.

'Didn't you make the tea?' she said.

Rob laughed. He sat on the wreck of her double bed and laughed and laughed and laughed. He laughed till the tears splashed on his naked legs, till he mopped his face on his underpants and pulled them on.

'You take milk, don't you?'

'Mmn.'

The room was resolutely shambolic. An old mangle by the window was draped with an unstable pile of clothes, a chaise longue covered in mock leopard-skin sleaze was piled with scripts and books and three pairless shoes and a green hat whose brim was pinned back with a purple daisy. Stills of past productions were Blu-tacked to the wall or hung askew. There was a squash racquet. Leaf-pattern reflections danced in the mirror, reformed and danced again as he climbed back into her bed. The languorous Christ figure with the floating hair stared him in the eye from alongside the mirror. Rob gulped his tea.

'You brought him in then?'

'The funny Jesus? Yes, I like him.'

'It certainly gives the phrase Bride of Christ a new slant.'

'Your arse is too smart, Mister.' She was lightening things, defusing so she could slip away from the subject they were talking about. He would not play.

'Last night . . .' he said.

She put up a hand. 'Don't say it.'

'Because we don't love each other.'

She put down her cup in silence and stretched. Her feet touched the end board, dorsi-flexed, lifted the duvet. She turned; that look of polite enquiry, the head cocked to one side. 'You think I'm a slut?'

'God, no. I meant me.'

'So that's all right, then?'

Hopeless. He changed the subject. Searched for something irrelevant. Something easy and long ago. 'What were you and Calvin doing up in the Orongorongos that time? In the pool?'

She blew her nose hard and stared at him. Her night-tangled hair looked even more dangerous. It looked like a pelt, a matted trophy of blood and fur, an end product of slaughter. 'Walking in the bush,' she said. 'Tramping. Why do you ask?'

'I didn't know you did.'

'I don't very often.'

He saw the skinny legs splashing the rainbow against the tree, the shot-silk chest of the matronly pigeon clattering above Lisa's head. 'Who carried Calvin?'

'Me, in the backpack, but he walked a lot of the way. He was nearly three by then.' She looked at him. 'And another guy at the end.'

Sun spots and long shadows were now jiggling above the mirror. 'Where was he?'

'Gone for a pee I suppose. It's years ago, remember.' She sat upright; the duvet which had reminded him of the whole incident in the first place, or rather not the duvet but its chaste placement when he had seen all and known all, had slipped. She readjusted it and turned to him.

'Drop it will you? I've told you before to lay off. The guy was a friend of mine, the same as Murray is a friend of mine. What do you think I am, what do you think I do? Grow up! I don't sleep around any more, who would in this day and age, and if I did, what's it got to do with you? Besides there's Calvin.'

Her muddled thinking left him breathless. Here was a woman lying beside her last night's lover telling him she didn't sleep with men and if she did it was nothing to do with the man she had just slept with. It should have been laughable but it was not. Robin chose his words with care.

'You've always fascinated me,' he said. She looked at him in silence. 'You and Miss Bowman. Both of you. Your amorality.'

'Gee thanks,' she snarled.

But amoral was good didn't she see, or rather not necessarily bad. Nothing to do with immoral, quite the reverse, well not exactly the reverse but . . . It just meant she was non-moral, was unconcerned with convention, didn't make moral judgements, didn't speak evil of her neighbours behind the iceblocks like Bernie.

'What've you got against poor old Bernie?'

He was banging the duvet now. 'You are unconcerned about restrictive traditional morality,' he said. 'And I admire that! And I respect the fact that you have a talent for friendship and are generous to a fault. But you've got to use your head. Otherwise you'll get hurt again and again and then you'll get mad and what's more you'll get more mad than you would have in the first place if you'd used your nous. You're thirty-five years old and it's time you grew up.'

She sprang out of bed, snatched an old kimono from the mangle and tied it with a vicious tug. 'You are the most . . .'

A slow smile spread across her face, lifted the corners of her mouth and widened. 'Where'd you leave your car last night? On the road? With any luck both Bernie and Eileen will have seen it, and all three of you can,' her voice was harsh, stiff fingers indicated direction, 'go jump in the lake.'

The idiotic school phrase finished him. He was back running to help her, jumping across concrete to defend her against thugs. Last time she had lammed it at him. This time he laughed.

She tugged her belt tighter. 'Oh, fuck you,' said Emmeline and marched out.

They drank coffee across the yellow daisies, the naked branches of the cherry tree grating against the silence.

'What time are you picking up Calvin?' he said eventually.

She was busy with her dregs. 'Thea's dropping him off.'

He watched the slowly revolving spoon, the wrist, the angle of attachment, touched one of the cherry leaves. 'These are the last,' he told her.

'Nnn.'

Everything was dead. Finished, blown, shot to hell. He might as well risk it. 'Tell me about Alice O'Leary.'

'What about her?'

'Everything.' He leaned forward, put his cards on the table. 'Please, I mean it. She was here for months and I need to know.'

Emmeline rubbed the nape of her neck. Both hands lifted the mane high on her head, twisted, held and draped the coil over one shoulder. She had other routines involving rubber bands but at least she didn't fling it about like a demented filly besieged by horsefly.

'Six weeks.' Emmeline inspected her fingernails, clenched her hand and inspected them again. He waited. 'I didn't like her,' she said.

He was very quiet, very professional, a mild seeker after truth.

He realised how lucky he was, that anyone less good natured, less easy going, as Eileen called her with emphasis on the easy, would have kicked him out long before: a man who had fucked her head off and been fucked back with enthusiasm, who had told her next morning it was all a mistake and he did not love her and followed it up by giving her a rundown on her inadequacies at best, her sheer bloody stupidity at worst. Shame swept his neck, scratched behind his eyes.

'Why not?' he said slowly and gently as a second applying ice to the battered face of his charge.

She chewed a red tendril, tucked it away, finished with it. 'Look, I was only eight or nine. It's . . .'

A black and white cat stalked along a nearby fence-top, black paw, white paw, black, then dropped from view. 'If you really want to know I thought she was a wimp,' she said at last. 'She drifted about looking sad and she sort of sucked up to me and wanted what she called talks, I remember, which made my toes curl and she—oh I don't know—kids sense these things. What was she on about? I kept wondering. She made me shy. You know how tough, how austere Aunt was. She hardly ever hugged me but I knew she loved me, which is all wrong according to those books I showed you in the middle of the night. The recovery ones. I mean it's meant to be the kiss of death not to demonstrate affection. That's what makes me wonder about the whole thing. Why I want you to read them to see what you think. But at the time, even when I was little, somehow I knew Aunt loved me even if it meant Emmie O'Malley with the cast-iron belly biking upwind for half her life to another school instead of the one here. I knew she was on my side. And all those years of ballet. Think about it. All that money, support, endless bus rides and her sitting around waiting for me and never a word when I ditched it. She seemed to accept I was me. Different. Not her. Right from the start. Whereas Alice . . .'

'You called her that?'

'I had to call her something, and there she was drifting and dreaming while shadows fell all over the place. There was a sort of, no, not phoniness, but something about her, an unease, a sort of hopeless . . . sorrow or something.' Emmie's hands moved. 'Oh, I don't know.'

'But I don't get it. You've read her books?'

'Yes.'

'They're tough, cynical. Brutal almost. "All grief is self-pity." La Rochefoucauld couldn't beat that.'

'It's not true.'

'It is for some.'

She placed both elbows on the table, cradled her face to mock him. 'You mean the abyss?' she drawled. 'Those who can face the pit? "Who thank whatever gods may be / for their unconquerable souls" and stuff like that.'

She leaped to her feet, her legs moving in dreamy concentration beneath her knee-length T-shirt. '*Strictly Ballroom*.' She circled around the table, her face blank with concentration as she danced her loopy dance, her dip and glide and dip again. 'The best bit is the old guy dancing all by himself. You see it?'

'No.'

'He's always wanted to break out like his son does—be innovative, imaginative, not strictly ballroom, but he's scared, or his wife won't let him or something and he dances how he wants to—alone at night. Sad. Sad. We'll go.'

Would they? Yes, they would. Apart from anything else, any apologies or concern for her, he must keep talking to Emmeline. Things must surface. If people can forget their childhood memories of sexual abuse, which admittedly seemed to him unlikely, then a house guest who drifted and dreamed and embarrassed a nine-year-old for six weeks must have had more daily impact than had been revealed so far. Robin wanted everything; Alice's thoughts, clothes, gestures, her walk, everything about her must be laid out for inspection if not dissection, so that he could understand, could dive into the depths armed with underwater camera and spear gun. His casual approach as a student to the lives of authors he had studied astonished him. How could he have been so cavalier about

Sylvia Plath, felt that Beckett was entitled to his privacy? The text? Oh yes, of course the text came first but it needed to be clarified and all Emmie had done so far was to muddy the waters. Where was the bitter observer of grief, the steely survivor of the work in Emmie's memories? Even Alice's doggerel did not sound to Robin like that of a moist and drifting dreamer.

> A cat swung by the tongue
> Cannot squeal
> The nail has got it.

His image of the dormant lilac and the locked shed and the all-engulfing tears of the woman filled his mind. It was all very odd. 'Verr inter–esting,' as Miss Bowman used to say. He must go and inspect, check on the lilac, and the back bedroom. Something must tell him something.

He was grateful to Emmeline who was loving and generous and loopy and beautiful. Who had revived his interest once more in his research subject. Had breathed life into the house guest and mucked things up, but then nothing is simple, is it. He held out his arms, grinned at his benefactor. 'Emmie?'

But Emmeline had stopped dancing. She was now washing up, her back towards him, her hands submerged in a plastic bowl in the horse trough. 'You don't have to,' she said as he picked up a tea towel with the Eiffel Tower stamped in black.

'Don't be nuts.'

'No, no. I meant *Strictly Ballroom*. You don't have to come.' She wiped her nose, left detergent bubbles, wiped again. 'I know your views. You told me last night.'

He was still miles away. He took off his glasses as though that might help. 'What?'

'Sex without love. You said. I'm going again anyway.'

What man could be such a monster? 'I didn't mean . . . I'm sorry.'

Her shoulders twitched.

'You're always *sorry*. You're the sorriest person I know. Maybe she was just no good with kids or something. Some people aren't.'

Calvin came chugging down the bare hall on his decrepit plastic trike, its rear-end design based loosely on that of a purple-shelled snail, its handles curved like drooping tender horns. He was followed by his friend Ruby pushing a cart, again plastic, but equipped with bells and a klaxon-like wail. She was a tiny brown child, one of those minute little kids you're surprised to see walking, let alone pounding along behind sirens in pursuit of drama. Her hair was wisps of black, her face cheerful. Bernie's niece Thea brought up the rear.

'Hi,' yelled Emmeline with outstretched arms to swoop. 'Good to see you.'

'There's one thing I haven't told you,' she said standing at the gate which leaned beside them.

He shifted the inscribed copies of Alice's books in the kete and kept his voice calm. Friendly but calm. 'Yes?'

'Aunt left a bit of money.'

What revelation had he been hoping for. 'That's great,' he said hugging her. 'Great. I mean it.' He could not find the words he wanted. Words to rejoice in her good fortune, to tell her she deserved it, to say he was sorry yet again for his crassness.

She did not look particularly happy. 'It's all very odd. I thought she didn't have a bean, the way we lived.'

He put his arms around her and kissed her.

'Thank you so much,' said Emmeline.

Seven

Robin sat in the car on Lyall Bay foreshore, his eyes on the grey surf as he tried Aunt's system for the denial of guilt. He found it interesting but not very effective.

Emmeline had turned to him after they made love, had stroked his chest, licked it. 'Doesn't need cream,' she murmured. 'Now stop feeling guilty.' He rolled into her arms. She held him for a moment then wriggled free to grab tissues, mopped her chest and handed some on in silence. 'Stop now,' she said, 'and I'll tell you Aunt's system.'

Naked beside him, backed by crumpled sheets, slipped duvet and tissues, Emmie told him how Aunt had taught her to deal with 'this guilt rubbish'. 'When I feel guilty I work it out. I say to myself there is no point in this unless I can do something about what's causing it, or don't *want* to—and that's the catch. It's all in the head. If I can't, or don't want to change things, then there's no point in it so shut up O'Malley and stop being wet.' She glanced at him, a careful sideways peek. 'Get it?'

He screwed the tissues tight, slid his closed fist along her thigh. 'And then what happens?'

One arm was reaching for the light switch. 'You've got a good smile,' she said. The underarm was carved not moulded, interesting in its hollows, its red tuft of hair.

'It works.' She paused, examined a hangnail. 'Usually. Like Aunt said. Face it, do something, or ditch it.'

'Leave it on,' he said. 'I want to talk.'

'I talk better in the dark.'

'I want to see.'

She lowered her arm, stroked her armpit drowsily. 'Lisa,' she said, 'is dead. That's tragic. But you can't do anything about that, right, because. . .' She turned to him, her nipples framed by a few pale hairs at eye level. 'What was that thing you had at your wedding?'

He remembered instantly, wished she hadn't.

'"For life goes not backwards, nor tarries with yesterday."'

'That's it,' said Emmie. 'That's what I mean.' She turned off the light and rolled over. 'Night.'

'Emmie?'

'Yeah.'

'I just wanted to say I didn't . . .'

'Oh shut up, for heaven's sake.'

He glanced at his watch. Four-fifteen. There was a heave of the duvet.

'Are you awake?'

'Yes.'

'Good.' Her arm reached for the light. 'Funny. I usually sleep like a log after.'

He lay blinking against the glare. Distance was a haze without his glasses.

'There are a lot of grey areas in my life,' said Emmeline.

He thought of Murray.

She bounced over to face him, her body tense. 'People like you who know where you come from, you think what's she on about? It's now that matters, people like you say. But you don't know how bizarre it is. Who was this Vermont lawyer? What if Aunt was lying and I wasn't her sister's child and I wasn't hers? Why the hell didn't she tell me and whose am I?' She was now on another tack, fingers waving in front of clavicles. 'It's like Aunt used to say about health. If you've got it you never think about it. Not until bits start dropping off; then you think shit, I've lost it. Or never had it, or whatever. People say, who needs red tape? Well I can tell you—I do. OK I'm not stateless, I'm not half-starved in some hell camp. I'm here and I'm lucky but . . .'

He stifled another yawn. 'Emmie, Miss Bowman was the most honest woman who ever lived. And you can find out. I'll help you.'

'Sure. Sure. But . . .' She paused, stared straight ahead at the misty head of Christ. 'There's a guy at rehearsals who's in recovery. I wonder if that might help. What d'you reckon?' She was now burrowing beside the bed. There was a dimple above each buttock. He put out his hand. Too late. She came up with her arms full of papers, brochures, books, and dumped them on him. 'Here.'

'Not now.'

'Oh all right.'

She rolled away. 'Her name was Candida,' she said over her shoulder. 'Aunt's. How about that?'

There were two or three surfers creaming in on the slow winter rollers. Another ambled down to join them, his wetsuit hanging from his waist in welts of rubber, his face blue. He dragged on the rest of his suit and paddled his board out to lie flat-bellied beside the rest. Patient as predators they waited for the big one then vaulted upright to sail in or crash from sight.

A bundled child in pink gumboots was helping Dad. It raced the ribbons of sand blowing along the beach, picked up driftwood, fell over, tried again, resolute in its conviction that life goes not backwards nor tarries with yesterday. It was right. The gut-slicing despair of grief had begun to fade, would continue perhaps to fade. Otherwise, he thought, rifling through the pile of guff Emmie had insisted he take home as well as Alice O'Leary's books, he would become dependent on grief and would not be able to save the world until he had saved himself from this addiction. The books said so. Neat eh.

There was information about access to co-dependency workshops to find the cause of the canker, the Inner Child trapped within, represented often by hand-held soft toys clutched by participants. The frog was particularly popular. Followed by bears.

Robin read on with increasing interest. Parents did not do well. They had a bad press. He was astonished to learn that some recovery experts believed most people in the United States have been the victim of child abuse until he discovered how widely the term was applied.

Very widely indeed. Parents abused their children by invalidating their creativity and their experiences. They belittled, they thwarted the spiritual growth of their children who could be marred both by parents who worked too hard to make money and thus did not give their children sufficient attention and by those who did not make enough money and thus failed their offspring in other ways. Solo mothers with seven or eight dependent children had frequently provided insufficient time for bonding and inadequate resource material within the home.

Nazism, he read, was the direct result of Hitler having been abused as a child.

It was all very informative, this pile of papers. Sitting around clutching cuddly toys and overcoming your dysfunctions by releasing the Inner Child was not, he read, a privilege granted only to the affluent and the safe and the fed and the housed. It was essential for the future of humankind. The Inner Child wished to fly first class in its mission to heal the world. Like Saint Thomas Aquinas it was aware that man naturally desires happiness.

As who does not? Robin sat white-knuckled in the cold car, his eyes on the oyster-coloured horizon beyond the passing ferry, his head spinning with gurus who blamed parents, politicians who blamed the poor, experts who blamed other experts and change agents with the quick fix. He wanted to shout at the watchful flattened surfers—'There is no quick fix. You can't love everyone. Just feed them.'

And where was he in all this? Ah, there you go man, there you go. What about the boy wonder for disinterested generosity, for solving the problems of the world, for getting things weighed off, for understanding that we are all different and some are more different than others and the trick is to know that we don't know.

And what about Emmie? 'OK,' he promised a group of marauding dogs cruising the pavement. Marauding. On the maraud *à la plage*. His eyes itched. He made an odd sound, something between a snort and a sob. 'OK,' he said again.

The dogs came at a fast clip, tails up, paws pacing, eyes and ears sharp for action. A bitser, a collie, a corgi with a plumed tail and another more genetically sound one, a bassett hound, its bandy legs motoring in an effort to keep up with the boys as they searched this way, that way, come on gang, she must be somewhere.

It puzzled him that Emmie had not only given this stuff house room but had wanted him to read it. Emmeline O'Malley who had been born in the state which glories in the fall then sheds the lot to regroup for next year. A state which is various and stoic as is Emmeline.

He piled the brochures, pamphlets and books back into her kete. A phrase caught his eye. There was one condition which was more resistant to therapy than all the rest. Addiction to God, he read, is more insidious than alcohol, drugs, sex, food, gambling or bad relationships. He should tell Eileen, but would not. He felt a sudden stab of affection for his mother, for the thin purple thread of vein on the tip of her nose, for her tongue which flicked, her pale hands still offering him the comfort and salvation of her fix. He must help her more; mend her fence, her shower curtain as well as his own, must shoulder her problems with promptness. Look after her better. Of course it was easier to like Maureen. She was not his and she had not drifted away, disappeared somewhere else a long time ago.

The car was tossing in the wind. The dogs were still circling. The bitser squatted briefly then bounded after the rest as they disappeared. The pink-booted infant and the trailer of driftwood had vanished. He must go and see Eileen. Now.

He inspected Alice's books. Emmeline had blown dust from them, run a finger along the top before piling them into the kete. 'I haven't read them for years.'

'Did Miss Bowman?'

Emmie was still huffing. 'Doesn't look like it.'

She handed the bag. 'I've put in a few photographs. Some of her first husband. Can't think where they came from.'

The photograph of Edwin Calder reminded Robin of a naive portrait by some itinerant Early American painter. The tight lips, the small wary eyes; the loving attention to background did not display the quill pens of old-time lawyers or the pumped-up livestock of prosperous farmers, but Edwin also had been portrayed at his workplace. He sat in charge of a flat-topped desk supported by a telephone, blotters both rocking and flat, a brass inkwell and an ornate pen-holder. His large hands clasped wooden chair ends, his boots gleamed, his pleats were knife edge and his moustache large. One or two other photographs featured Alice; standing beside the solid figure, her eyes, like his, fixed beyond the viewer. Edwin looked tough, Alice merely distracted. There was none of the serenity evident in Miss Bowman's photograph in these ones. Robin had not seen it for years but Emmeline remembered it. 'The cloak one? Yeah, that was her when she was young. I'll try and find it.'

Robin opened Alice's *Poems '47* and propped it on the steering wheel. He should go back to the flat, flake out onto the Indian bedspread (they would get a duvet later; Lisa would pop out at lunchtime) instead of bumping about in the cold car. He had finished with recovery.

The poems were not good; they were trite, bad and of little

interest except for occasional unexpectedness of subject matter among the paeans to nature.

> *I know little of Mexico, well, not much.*
> *Hearts plucked for chucking. Aztecs.*
> *There was no wheel.*
> *Montezuma declining heaven*
> *Then Frieda, and Lawrence in the new one.*

The handwriting on the inscription was small and neat, grade-school neatness with careful loops and crossed Ts. One in *Poems '47* read,

> *My darling Candida,*
> *As always.*
>   *Alice.*

Yes, well. Interesting. He looked at the other books, flicked through each title page searching like Cara for latent lights.

The Mystic Scroll (1957) was inscribed *For you.*

The Hand of Time (1959) *For you again.*

All Fall Down (1960) *No words.*

The Load (1962), thought by some critics to be her best work and by some her worst, was inscribed simply *Later.* None of them except the early poems was signed with her name. Robin had known *The Load* was her best ever since he discovered her in American Lit where she had featured briefly, very briefly, as an enigmatic fringe figure with no obvious antecedents who specialised in despair; who occasionally overwrote but usually sliced to the bone. The last book was a 'simple tale of a dysfunctional family'. A family who should have loved each other and didn't, who hated each other with self-destructive loathing, though not at the beginning, no, not at the beginning at all. The beginning was an idyll. If there was a false note in the book it was the excessive lyricism of the first few chapters, the overwhelming sense of a cornucopia bursting at the seams with tumbling children, russet apples, wide red barns and plenty. An Eden waiting to be lost as lost it was. Betrayal, violence and bitter grief took over as the writing tightened to laconic understatement. A child hanged itself. Not in the barn, that had been done before. From a tree by the river, feet touching.

Robin read on. A slip of airmail paper lay face down on page one hundred and forty nine. There was no heading and no date.

He is dead. I am coming immediately. I'll cable. Hurray.
Alice.

Robin swallowed, picked the transparent slip from the page and held it in his hand. He glanced over his shoulder in a quick idiotic gesture and laid the letter flat on the passenger's seat. Astonished, unnerved by the bonus of the Great Find, he shifted his buttocks and discovered something else. His bladder was bursting. He glanced at his watch. No wonder. He turned the car to head for the nearest Gents. Where? Kilbirnie's he knew, an ornate little edifice of a bog on a corner but could he make it. He was not going to. Impossible. Not impossible, not impossible at all. He swung the car into the Sunday calm of a supermarket car park, fell out of the car and walked stiff-legged behind a pile of battens, unzipped and pissed against the wall. There is no relief but relief. The strong head of steam, the splatter of the cascade was satisfying. He rezipped and sauntered back across the asphalt then remembered and broke into a bounding headlong dash for the car. He had not locked the door.

No one had glanced, no one had cared, or if they had had walked past his hoard with the dead eyes of the unknowing. Not surprising really.

He was still reading when the telephone rang. He had always avoided telephones, had been glad that Lisa had leaped to answer at all times. 'Sandy. How did it go? No! Tell me. Seventeen? Wow! On a Sunday.'

'Hullo,' he said.

'Hullo, dear.'

'Oh hi Mum.' He had not got there; his mother had remained unvisited. 'Hi,' he said again.

'Robin?'

He turned on the news, left the sound off. 'Yeah?'

Eileen sounded slightly breathless. 'I wondered if you'd like to come over tonight for a drink . . .'

The newsreader dipped her chin slightly, swapped her competent calm face for her competent sad face. The news from Rwanda was worse.

'A drink? Now?'

'Yes. Now.'

'What for?'

'I just thought it would be nice. There's something . . .'

He overreacted in compensation. 'Yeah, that'd be great. I'll come straight over. Great.' Wow. Gee. Hang. 'I'll bring a bottle,' he said.

'Oh, you don't need a bottle,' said Eileen.

He pulled up at her gate, aligned the wheel, got it right, did not abandon the thing yards from the kerb like some. He was tired though you don't say that and was bored by people who did. He sat at the wheel with slouched shoulders, smiling at Emmie's house. 'You're overstimulated,' had been Eileen's comment on the rare occasions when he had 'played up' as a child. It had not happened often and there had been little stimulation. He grinned again. Good kind generous Emmie would forgive him, had already done so. He must see her, tell her. Emmie, I found a scrap of paper I'd like to keep for a while. No, a letter. He would not diminish the find, nor resort to his mother's diminutives—women to girls, girls to lasses and finally littlies who were the best of all. Emmie, I found a letter in *The Load* and I'd like to keep it for a while if that's OK.

Her casual reply. Sure, sure.

He walked past the rockery which Eileen had given up on and how could you weed around those Crown of Thorns' spikes anyway. The concrete birdbath now veered slightly to the south. His feet scuffed the whiskery grass which he should mow and would. The globe above the front door was lit, its tideline of dead insects obvious. Access to Eileen's house was usually from the back, not past the dingdong of the front door.

It opened immediately. Eileen was wearing a garden print whose history he remembered. It had been created from a short sale length eked out by Maureen with a wide insert of black at the waist and black collar and cuffs. The flowers were pink and white; their stalks had been picked out for contrast. The star-spangled brooch gleamed red and gold on her left breast. 'Hello dear,' said Eileen.

He kissed her soft powdered pinkness. 'Hi.'

'Well.' She almost clapped her hands. 'Come in,' she said and darted sideways into the front room. Robin, who had not been watching, headed automatically towards the dining-room and the telly and my little papers and the crocheted afghan and the iridescent birdman on the wall.

'No, no, no, Robin,' laughed his mother, her voice high. 'We're in the front room.'

'Oh.'

'There's someone I'd like you to meet.'

'Meet,' he said.

He backtracked to the floral carpet, the unlit fireplace, the stamp album on the mantelpiece and Nana Dromgoole's books between the wild-eyed heads of the brass horses. There were one or two studio photographs but no recent ones. They cost money and snaps showed you just as much anyhow: Terence in a hat laughing, offering a black and white fish; Robin as a baby, fat-cheeked and earnest above rompers and soft white boots. Wedding groups with lasses in their slimlines and the boys in tight suits and shame-faced grins and murderous hair cuts.

All her life was here and he had seldom given it a glance but then nor had she, or not that he had noticed.

A man in a clerical collar stood smiling upon the shagpile hearth rug. Small, spry and bald as a coot, he leaped forward, extended a hand stamped with a large Band Aid and laid it, inert and flaccid as strips of playdough, in Robin's.

'Clayton,' said Eileen, her curls bobbing, 'I would like you to meet my son, Robin.'

Robin yanked his mouth back into position and shook the hand again. 'Robin,' said his mother, 'I would like you to meet the Reverend Clayton Nolan.'

'Oh,' said Robin. 'Well, ah, nice to meet you.' His eyes flicked to the Band Aid. Flesh wound? Wart? Stigmata? The other hand was naked. Nothing. Not a sign. What the hell was going on?

The Reverend Nolan fingered his collar and confided how happy he was, while Eileen bustled in and out from the kitchen to remove Gladwrap and return with Snax and paté and peanuts and nibbles which reminded her, she said, nodding her head shyly at the joke, of roofing iron. Not the taste or the texture, goodness me no. They were delicious but it was just the shape, just like roofing iron for pixies didn't they think. It was clever of them to get them wavy like that wasn't it, she would never have thought of it even. She paused for breath. 'Clayton?' she murmured.

'Oops, sorry.' The Reverend Nolan sprang forward. 'Eileen would like me to offer you a drink,' he said.

'Beer thanks. Beer.'

This was very odd indeed. No one had said so, but presumably his mother and the Reverend Nolan were good friends, possibly they planned to marry, to live together according to God's will till death did them part and good luck to them. There was a plumb bob at the bottom of his throat. Good luck to them, good on them. Good. Good. He must say something. He looked at his mother, pink-cheeked above her thundering great brooch with the rays and the sunburst of goodwill.

'Beer it is!' Clayton turned to the table with its white crocheted cloth and poured a can into a diamond-cut glass which Robin had never seen in his life before. It must have been stowed away. Stowed deep in a dark cupboard waiting for the light.

The Reverend Nolan checked his fiancée's sherry glass, clutched his whisky, and was back on track. He was very pleased indeed to meet Robin about whom he had heard so much. A tutor he understood, a tutor at the university, so he had heard. He was sure Robin would understand. Yes. He was very grateful. God moved in

mysterious . . . Yes. After his wife had left him he was for a time
. . . Yes, well. In a Christian context of course but . . . He was sure
Robin would understand.

He was now skipping about on small slim feet, touching Eileen's
arm or shoulder for a moment and then bounding away from the
strength of the charge. He was unable to keep still, there was so
much to tell, so much good news to impart. He had known Robin's
dear mother for yonks. Literally yonks. Such a worker. Dedicated
in her efforts with the shut-ins and the olds. And my ex-wife and
Eileen had once been friends, which was strange was it not. At
school, he understood. But that was before, yes well, mysterious
ways. Eileen had been a tower, a positive tower at the end. Clayton
blew his nose. His spectacles were round and gold and sparkling
with joy. 'And afterwards,' he added.

All this joy was unexpected and confusing. Obviously they did
plan to marry. A good thing. A very good thing.

More congratulatory handshakes with Clayton concluded, Robin
turned to his mother and took her in his arms. I am so happy for
you. You deserve happiness. You are a good woman.

'Mum,' he said. He kissed her cheek, misjudged it slightly and
banged his nose on something hard.

Gold had been dredged or mined, men had sweated, slogged,
half-killed themselves to produce this small round ball in his mother's
earlobe. Why bother. What did it all mean. Forget it smart-arse.

'I hope you'll both be very happy,' he said. 'And I'm sure you
will.'

Twinned at the same height, hand in hand like wedding-cake
toys, Eileen and Clayton beamed back at him.

Robin lifted his glass of beer and smiled again. His mother
blinked at the beautiful back of his head, the generous smile of her
son.

'Thank you, my boy,' said the vicar. 'Thank you.'

'Sundays are Clayton's busy day,' said Eileen suddenly. 'Aren't
they dear?'

'Yes dear.'

'You live locally, I suppose?'

'No. No. This is not my parish. Never has been.' Clayton's hand touched Eileen's sleeve. 'We met at Synod. I am here to rejoice, to meet with folk. I return to work next week.'

'To the coast,' murmured his future wife.

Clayton's hands rubbed. 'The Gold Coast,' he cried. Fingers touched again, burst apart. 'Eighteen feet of topsoil,' he crowed.

'You must come and have a meal at the flat,' said Robin. 'Next week, why not?' They leaned towards each other, murmured together and came up smiling. They could fit him in on Thursday if that would suit. Yes. Yes.

'Would you believe,' whispered Eileen beneath the global mausoleum, 'she left him for another woman?'

'Oh.'

'Wasn't it awful? And her parents were quite normal. They used to live in Miramar.'

He did not attempt to see Emmeline. So much pinkness, so much euphoric gentle joy sent him home depleted and early.

He wolfed down the steaming omelette, tore hunks of bread apart, slapped them with cheese and chewed on, his mindless and unseeing eyes fixed on the coffee-maker on the far bench which had developed some messy and expensive blockage. The silence spread in circles, flowed over the dove-grey three-piece in the lounge, beyond to the standard lamp with the coral shade because Robbie needed it for close work with all that awful marking. Lisa on the padded sofa swinging her ankle at the Renoir above the heater, which had both children and dogs and was a focal point.

He leaped to the telephone at the first ring. 'Hi,' he yelled.

'It is I,' said Spiro. 'I wish to talk to you.'

'Sure. What is it?'

'I do not wish to mention over this thing.'

He could see the hand rejecting the telephone, damning its black unreliable soul, its army of eavesdroppers. Spiro distrusted telephones. He liked New Zealand and its people but their delight in technology did not please him. Their faxes meant nothing to him, their computers, their e-mails drove him insane. You could not fight them. Computer error they say. They have lost my papers. The computer has eaten them, they say. I know them. It is they who have lost. Computers are the patsy.

'I've got a tutorial at five. After that.'

'OK.' Bang.

Robin tidied up as usual, rubbed the formica with a soft cloth for the purpose then turned to *The Load* beneath the lamp and kept reading.

Emmeline had had a calligraphy phase at one time, and the green ink was distinctive. He grabbed her letter from his pigeon-hole, his fingers tearing. It contained a single sheet of lined paper. The message was brief, the writing difficult to read.

Emmie's message was even briefer. Her 'Any use?' filled the yellow stick-on label.

> Long Creek,
> Patearoa,
> Otago.
> May 17th,

Miss Bowman,
> My wife died yesterday. She asked me to let you know.
> Wilfred Q. Hughes

No year. But why should there be and he knew when she died. Fifteen years ago, and Wilfred Q. Hughes had been much older than Alice. What the hell was he doing. The essential was to get down there, to interview the old man before he died on him as Miss Bowman had done. He read the note again, searched the page. How soon could he get there. He would need time. Days and days of time, calm serene hours with the tape recorder and the old man telling him why his wife had stopped writing the moment she married him and how he had been entirely responsible as seemed likely. He must get down immediately, get down south for a weekend, get the feel, the taste, make sure W.Q. Hughes was in good health and likely to remain so until the August holidays when the interrogation could continue in depth.

His heart was beating with the panic of the hunter who realises he may lose his quarry through his own carelessness, who sees the antlered head lift to scent the breeze and scarper.

Wilfred Q. could be a hundred. He could be dead.

Robin dreamed that night that Cara had a D-minus for Shelley. It didn't seem to add up. They didn't do Shelley in Stage One.

'Anne,' he said next morning to the secretary of the English department whose screen saver had whorls of light instead of toasters with wings or cruising fish, 'Anne, do we have telephone directories for the whole of New Zealand?'

He was rather proud of the pronoun. It indicated an intimacy, a pulling together for the good of the cause rather than an irritating interruption to a busy person from the most junior tutor of all.

She turned her head with polite interest. 'No. Should we?'

'I just wanted to look something up.'

But Anne was helpful to all. 'I'm popping down town at lunchtime . . . ?'

'No, no thanks a lot, but . . .' He drifted down the herringgutted corridor to his consoling graphics and his unfinished letter which was taking time to write. He wanted detachment with polite interest, courtesy without obsequiousness, results without guile. There were several corrections to be made.

> *Dear Mr Hughes,*
>
> *My name is Robin Dromgoole and I am a tutor in English Literature at Victoria University, Wellington. I have chosen the work of your late wife Alice O'Leary as the subject for my thesis for a postgraduate degree.*
>
> *I would be extremely grateful if it would be possible for me to come and talk to you soon about the life and work of your late wife.*

I would be free any weekend in the near future which would be suitable to you.

I enclose my home telephone number in case you prefer to ring me collect.

I very much hope you will be able to see me.

    Yours sincerely,

    Robin Dromgoole

He searched the Dunedin directory in Lambton Quay, his fingers riffling through the south for Hughes. There was a W.Q. in Patearoa. Wilfred was extant.

He sent the letter Fastpost.

Spiro opened the door with a dead fish in one hand. The Angel Fish lay limp, the billowing transparent driftings of its fins clotted, its eye clouded.

'Dead,' he said.

'I'm sorry.'

'It happens, Robin. It happens.'

They stood staring at the fish lying inert in the large palm. 'Just this moment I found him.' Spiro's other hand turned, flicked, went belly up. 'Come,' he said. 'Come in.'

He placed the fish on the slab bench, gave it a final pat and rinsed his hands.

'Coffee or ouzo?'

Ouzo, like dope, had been a disappointment in the past. 'Ouzo.'

'Good man.' Spiro poured a slug of oily liquid into a glass and watched as the water swirled to smoky opaqueness. Small marvels pleased him.

He lifted his glass to the small convex shape on the bench and drank. 'Ahh! good. Very good.' He dragged the back of his hand over the grey exuberance of his moustache, sat opposite Robin at the narrow formica table and lifted his glass again. '*Yámass*,' he said and drank.

'*Yámass*,' said Robin. The remaining fish drifted in their glass world, turned and returned to turn again. Shreds of green broke loose from an undulating aquatic plant and floated upwards. There were two ornaments on the gravel bottom, a Buddhist temple and a drowned castle where timid fish could hide. A weighted plastic frog burped bubbles.

Robin gave a quick chuck of his head towards the corpse. 'I wonder if they know it's dead.'

Spiro shrugged an acknowledgement of defeat. 'We cannot ask. They cannot tell,' he sighed. 'He was a purposeful fish, my Angel.' He leaned forward to make his point. 'That is why I like the tropical freshwaters the best. The tropical marines have such beauty, ah, such beauty. They float, they drift. What need have I to hurry, to work, to be quick. I am beautiful.' He gave a quick explosive puff of displeasure. 'They are Betty Boops those Marines.'

Betty Boops?

Spiro was still shaking his head. 'They are not working men's fish. Fifty dollars or more for each. Each! No. For me the freshwaters every time.' His tongue was busy, his face contorted, winking and pumping with the effort involved. 'I have a tooth,' he said. 'I must see the man before it is lost.'

He drank again, cradled the glass between both hands, guarded it on the table. His moustache was moving, working itself up to something. 'I have something to say, Robin.'

'Yes?'

'To you.'

'Yes?'

It was taking him a long time. Spiro hummed, hawed, chewed his moustache and started again.

A fish trailing silver streams surfaced sudden as a cork to gape, its eyes beseeching the ceiling. Robin could watch the fish for hours and might have to at this rate. He turned back, tried to help. 'Go on.'

'You are my friend, Robin, as well as my offsider. Yes?'

'Yes.'

'A friend to be trusted. A friend I could entrust.'

'I hope so.'

'What do you mean hope? Is it or isn't it?'

Would I say No I am not to be trusted? Think man, think. People don't say that. You were the one who told me. You and the fish and their agendas. But you are safe, Spiro, safe as houses. 'Robin is so responsible,' Miss Newman had told his mother in Form One. 'I would trust him with anything.' He saw the tufted mole, the sweetness of the smile. '*Anything*,' she repeated.

Rob lifted his glass again. 'You can trust me, Spiro,' he said pompously. But something was required. This was manly handshake country; covenants sealed by the clasping of hands whose weapons have been left beyond the ramparts. 'What is it?' he asked.

Spiro was now looking shy, or as shy as a face as ingenuous as his could look. He stood up, eased his crotch and sat down again.

In love as well? Getting married also?

'I wish to go home to Crete,' he said.

Robin glanced up in surprise. 'For ever?'

'No no no no, boy. For a month, three weeks is all. And I am making you an offer because I trust you.' Spiro's hands widened, arms embraced the air above the table. 'Because I hold you in my heart.'

'Offer?'

'I am inviting you to take charge, sole charge of Dionysus Caterers Ltd while I am away.'

'But I can't. My job. Everything. No.'

The beauty of the secret, the glee of Spiro's hands, the excitement of his arms reminded Robin of the bridegroom-to-be. 'That is the wonder of it,' he explained. 'I am not wishing to go until November for my niece Amalia's wedding. And by November,' one finger stabbed Robin's guernsey, 'by November the university is shut and Robin will take charge of Dionysus Caterers and grow fat with profit and I will dance.' Spiro's arms lifted, turned and dipped to plangent chords. He was home, fêted by loved ones, glad to sniff the wild thyme and to dance, to leave his trusted offsider in charge. Spiro leaned over the table and embraced him. 'Good,' he said.

Not good. Not good at all. 'But . . .'

'Is no problems.'

Yes there bloody is. Sure the lectures will be over, the place empty, but that's when you do the work, that's when you get on with it, day after seamless day of searching and unfolding and thinking. Of clearing his mind of Cara and Helen and Rebekkah and Wes and getting on with his own work. Getting something down.

I don't want to. I refuse.

Robin sat silent. One who was considering all aspects of the proposal before coming to a wise decision. 'Three weeks,' he said hopelessly.

Spiro gave him a quick elbow jolt across the table. 'Not long enough? You wish to get fat for months? No, three weeks is enough. Any more the fat arse.'

'Spiro, I can't.'

'Of course you can! Would I have let you if I did not know you could and I could trust you? You are too modest. Here you are, the best, the most reliable of men in Wellington and telling me you can't. You are strange some of you Kiwis, you say can't, can't, even when you can and know you can. For modesty you say no. No Cretan does this. No Greek. It is mad, mad. You need wings Robin, wings to lift you to the sky like my Oscar. My Icarus.'

Not a good role model.

He was eight years old, barefoot on the haircord, chewing his pyjama cord, turning up the radio for the beat and swoop of the weepie.

> 'Put silver wings on my son's *chest*
> Make him one of America's *best*
> One hundred men we'll *test* today
> But only *three* win the green be*ret*.'

He tried again. 'November's a very busy month,' he said.

Spiro was now pouring more ouzo. He turned with the glass in his hand.

'More fat on the arse. And the Wine Festival also which is the big one.'

Dionysus Caterers was Spiro's life work. He and his bride Kostoula had arrived years ago, had sailed into the unknown without words or money. Robin had heard it all. The sponsor uncle that Spiro had fought with the first day, how they ran away down the hill and past the tram terminus to sleep on the beach. Next day a job washing up, jobs washing up. Oh it was easy then. Jobs they fell from the sky in those days. How they had cooked day and night on their rented Baby Belling supplying other caterers for a pittance, for two pittances, and finally enough to 'take off on our own'. Each detail, each triumph and the one or two failures (the baklavas too messy for the mayoral function; the overseasoned stiphado) had been recounted. How Kostoula had asked a bride's mother how much her pink satin with black revers had cost and been told off by the groom. How she had asked a councillor's wife if her diamonds were real. It is different in Wellington. The wind blows and oregano must be cultivated and no pride in the price paid for anything. But despite Kostoula's despair at no babies they had been as happy as most. Sometimes Spiro wondered whether if he had stayed in Kalives he would have been happier, would have had more slabs of pleasure remembered from tavernas and scented hills and the sea. But he was an honest man. They had been happy enough and made money and he still had Dionysus. It was his life and his reason for life and he was entrusting it to his best friend Robin who he loved.

I do not wish to do this. Now come on Spiro, let's get this straight. Sure I could but I won't. You won't mind, Spiro, will you? Fat chance. Not only mind—you'd be insulted, hurt and bloody well crushed. And I could. And who else is there. Oh bloody hell. 'All right,' said Robin.

The glass was lifted, the arms outstretched. 'Good man. Good boy.'

Robin grabbed the letter from his pigeon-hole, took it to his room where nobody could see if the old man had died last week or merely refused to see him.

Like Wilfred's previous letter this one was brief but the writing was in a different hand; large, blue and on the slant. Wilfred had died. He had died and Robin was too late. Died because he should have been contacted before you dumb prick.

> Dear Robin Dromgoole,
>   The boss says any weekend is OK by him and me too.
>   Let us know when and I'll meet you with the dog truck. The airport is OK as I have to come down anyhow.
>   Best,
>   Shara Bow
>   PS. I live here.

'Emmie, hey Em, I've had a letter from Wilfred Hughes.'

'Who?' She was unimpressed. He could see the hand fiddling with the hair, the bare foot on the lino. She was probably standing on one leg. He felt she had yawned in his face.

'You know, Alice O'Leary's husband. I've found him!'

'Why can't you leave the poor old guy in peace?' said Emmie and replaced the receiver. He stared at the perfect patterning of the bee's-eye mouthpiece, the neat curve of the earpiece, the ergonomic simplicity of the thing. Stared so hard he could draw it.

The ultimate put-down.

And Emmie had done this. He sat at his desk staring at a jellyfish chugging its way across the screen saver. Why had she done that? She should not have done that. She could not have meant it. She had been so friendly, so understanding, so . . . She must be unhappy, missing Aunt. He would go and see her. Take her some flowers if the shop on the corner had anything interesting.

They had lotuses, crisp blue-petalled things drooping from vivid stalks. Perfect for Emmie: funky flowers for lotus-eaters, sharp flowers for redheads.

'For a lady, Robin?' asked Mrs Vella holding them away from the counter to drip.

'Yeah.'

'Ladies get two sheets.' Mrs Vella laid the flowers on one blue and one pink square and handed them over with a wink of her gold tooth. She was glad to see Robin was getting over it.

The rain was heavier in Seatoun. He drove up the drive past the dead harebells and narrowly missed the snail trike abandoned at the front step.

Emmie looked at the flowers thoughtfully, lifted her eyes to his. 'That's very kind,' she said. 'Why did you bring them?'

Because I did. That's all.

'I thought you might like them.'

She stared at them, touched a carved petal. 'I do. A lot. The combo of that purple with that green. Thanks.'

He realised with a flick of self-disgust that he had been expecting more. Emmie usually went overboard about any gift, however small, however ridiculous.

'Blue,' he said. 'They're blue.'

She looked at him, her face serious. 'Purple. Why have you come?'

'To thank you for sending Wilfred's letter.' She shook her head, a red toss of dismissal, of no problem, of any time. 'And why did you slam the receiver down?'

Her shoulders lifted, dropped again, encompassed all the boredom of the whole world. Emmeline was not herself. 'Come into the kitchen.'

She trailed down the hall, one exhausted hand beneath the floating stripes of her sleeve brushing the wall at intervals. The carpet runner was on its last legs.

The kitchen table was covered with papers, notebooks, ledgers, a small calculator, five biros, two empty mugs and a tin of cat meat. She picked up the tin of cat meat, smiled at it with more affection than she had shown anything else so far. 'Calvin bought it. Saved every cent, nagged a few. Now Mum buys the cat.'

She put the flowers in a straight-sided vase with an aspirin for luck.

'I'm trying to work out the money. It's odd. One of the things about not having any is it takes so much time. All that hunting for cheap stuff and checking op shops and skipping the large economy sizes because you can't afford them so you have to go back next week. But I can see now.'

She propped her rump on the corner of the table and sat massaging a shoulder she'd graunched last week. 'I can see now why rich people get mean. How you could get funny about it. Money takes time too.'

'You could get an accountant. A chartered accountant.'

She looked at him as though he had been advocating the services of a gutless green gecko. 'Oh, I don't need one of *those*. I'm just working it out. City Mission, Women's Refuge, Red Cross.'

He held on to the chair back, spoke slowly. 'Emmie, Miss Bowman begged you to be careful with her money.'

Her voice was gentle. 'It's my money now, and there's more than Calvin and I need.' She lifted her face to his once more, stared into his eyes and smiled.

'And Murray'll need quite a lot,' she said.

Eight

'Murray!'

'Yes Murray. The guy who mows my lawns. The guy with the La-Z-Boy who's doing medicine. The guy who hogs the peanuts. Murray, Murray, Murray.' Her face was inches from his, her nostrils wide. 'And Maureen, what about Maureen your mother-in-law and her red-hot Bernina. Why don't you do something to help Maureen?'

'I don't trust Murray, that's why.'

'You don't have to trust him. Just do it. And anyway,' she said, calming suddenly, 'it's a loan.'

'You won't get it back.'

They stood glaring at each other for a moment before she shook her head and turned to the stove and the coffee and the popping gas. 'Sit down.'

He sat watching her shoulderblades move beneath the thin stuff, the percolator hissing as she turned to put the still fussing thing in front of him. 'There are some things I want to say, so listen.' The shadows beneath her eyes were dark, her mouth had gone wrong but her voice stayed gentle.

'You think I'm flaky right?'

He examined the bear riding the sickle moon on his mug, noted how the water lilies on the table had darkened to purple. 'In the sense that you're erratic, yes, but I know you're . . .'

'We have two things here.' She held up two fingers in an ambivalent gesture and moved one. 'One. Who are you to judge me . . .'

'You asked.'

She scarcely paused. 'And two. Let's examine our track records. Look at you.' She lifted her hand. 'I haven't finished. In fact I've hardly started. You'll get your turn so shut up. You wanted to study zoology, you gave that up. You were going to be an ornithologist. Up to your knees in spoonbills. When did you last even see a spoonbill?'

'They've gone.'

She flung an exasperated palm at him. 'Any bird!'

'A pigeon. Last week. It had a feather on its claw.'

She was not interested in pigeons. 'Then you gave all that up. English, English literature was the thing. Books. Wisdom of the ages. Then you were going to do Henry James and ditched him for poor dopey old Alice O'Leary. Any moment soon you'll ditch her I bet. And cooking. When did you last cook anything decent? And what about the bush, tramping? The great outdoors, the call of the wild, man, the call of the wild. Where's that gone?'

He looked at her. 'Lisa.'

'And you blame the bush?'

He hoped his voice sounded as dispassionate as hers. 'You were the one who said to ditch guilt.'

'I said to face it. There's a difference. I know. No, not Aunt. There was a guy years ago when I was a kid.' She propped her face in the heel of her palm.

'Is this some bloody grief fest?'

'She's dead, Lisa! She's dead.'

There was a book called *Elephants* among the pile on the table. Its cover showed a small eye surrounded by a square map of wrinkles. 'Yes,' he said. 'I realise that.'

She closed in. 'Then grow up! It's you who are damaged. Erratic. Changeable. Not me. Not me at all.' She paused, squeezed her eyes tight. 'And leave that poor old guy alone. Leave him alone for God's sake.' She ran to the door and dropped suddenly onto her heels. 'Calvin,' she cooed. 'How'd it go, hon? How'd it go?'

If members of a family become separated they appear anxious and try to keep in touch with long distant calls called 'contact rumbles'. When they come together again they go through a special greeting ceremony which involves rumbling, trumpeting, urinating and defecating in a tight ring with heads and tails held high.

Christ in concrete, what a fool. He replaced the book and headed for the back door.

Calvin dived across the floor, wrapped himself around one leg and damn near felled him. 'Look!' he yelled. 'Look Rob. Choice eh!'

Calvin had been transformed. Ruby's birthday party had been held at McDonald's and there had been face painting. Calvin had chosen Batman's mask with extra spikes above which his recently cut crewcut bristled like lit stubble. He looked very odd indeed.

'Hi Calvin. Have fun?'

Calvin disappeared beneath the table. His voice was muffled. 'Yeah, neat.'

'Sorry,' said Emmie.

One of the water lilies wasn't going to make it. Its droop was obviously terminal. Rob nodded, headed again for the door.

'Forget it.'

Calvin was now on all fours, his arms straight, his drooping head weaving slowly from side to side. He gave a long anguished moan and lifted his painted face to explain that he was an elephant crying.

*

Robin sat in the bucket seats at the airport dredging up instances of unreliability and memories of flake. He wriggled into blue plastic, saw the skinny bunched figure pedalling behind Aunt on her upright bike, red hair dragged back, plaited too tight, the nose dripping in the wind beneath a crocheted woolly hat with bobbles. 'Emmie O'Malley with the cast-iron belly,' chanted the kids when Miss Bowman was not present. The Ramsay boys up the street (triple sons of widowed mother) waited for a clear run; chanting and pointing when Emmeline entered the dairy, springing from bare feet for a squizz through Bernie's window, mobbing their prey like starlings when she came out.

'Don't be daft,' she said kicking whichever one was nearest. 'If I had any chutty I'd give you some.' She stepped over the writhing body on the pavement. 'So lay off.' They did, and soon laid off the chant as well. There didn't seem much point when Emmeline sailed past them with her head in the air and her feet in the wide springing prance of a dancer. Who did she think she was anyhow?

She told them. Emmeline Frances O'Malley.

Why did she go to Strathmore Park?

'Because it's better,' said the skite. She stood arms akimbo, legs braced for action as she socked it to them.

They attacked with the rat-pack drive of primary and she went home bloody. She let it run, turned at the gate. 'Stare, stare, like a bear,' she chanted. 'Go jump in the lake, dumb-bums.'

Robin hopped the fence to help. 'And you, small change,' snapped Emmeline striding up the path with head high.

Yes, well. He tried again. Saw her draped over the fence in her wild period, the period which had excited Bernie but not Miss Bowman.

'What I'd really like to do,' she had confided at the fence one day, rolling a lemon verbena leaf between two fingers for the smell, 'is get a job organising orgies. There are people who do. Guy knows a woman in the States.'

He kept his face blank. Which one was Guy. The greatcoat. The pea jacket. The berk with the pony tail.

'I'd be good at that.' Her eyes, he remembered, were far away, misted with visions. 'I'd have pools, you'd need a pool don't you reckon? And rich guys. That could be a problem. Nubile slaves I could handle. And we'd have half-naked guys holding poles with feathers like *Aida*. I saw a book in a New Age shop the other day. Anything goes. There wouldn't be much point in hiring a co-ordinator otherwise, would there. It wouldn't be down-home stuff. You'd have to cater for all tastes. I've got no background in SM but the research'd be interesting. And the logistics. I suppose you'd have sort of set menus on hand and you could offer them like caterers and the clients could take it from there with their own alternatives or additions or whatever, and you'd liaise later. What d'you reckon?'

Robin stirred in his form-fitting eggcup seat.

'You got one of those sheepskin things on your bed?' said the man beside him.

This happened too often nowadays. Total strangers questioned, confided, bent his ear. Last week a man had bailed him up in a bus and told him his firewood problem. He had the pine, had got it into the shed the year before, it was the only way, but now she was too dry, see. It burned too quick and he'd have to get something more dense to calm her down. Macrocarpa was useless. Good heat but sparked like buggery. Should he go for gum or manuka? Otherwise you're just heating Wellington. All that money going straight up the chimney. What did Robin reckon?

He forced himself to turn to the sheepskin man who was small and sharp in a brown suit, brown hat and shiny shoes. An old guy.

'No,' he said.

'I had one but I flagged it away. Electric blanket now. Got an electric blanket?'

'No.'

The man puffed out his weathered cheeks, gave his considered opinion. 'Good news electric blankets. I turn mine on full bore half an hour before I retire.'

Retire. Robin nodded. It was definitely happening too often.

He took a quick glance at himself in the mirrored wall. Just the same: jeans, parka, glasses, hair. The answer came. You're on your own, Robbo, you're alone. People talk to people on their own. You haven't gone nice. Relax.

The boarding signal was a relief nevertheless.

Shara Bow met him at the airport with the dog truck. Or at least he assumed it was her; a small wiry woman stood by a pick-up with a wire cage on the back, ripping into a startled-looking policeman. She had spiky blonde hair, bright eyes and a neat little beak of a nose. She looked like a chicken in boots. Or a roadrunner belting across a desert highway to avoid extinction. Robin stopped, put his pack down to watch. This one looked unlikely to be squashed by anything. She stood, arms bare in the morning frost, her boots unlaced below khaki shorts stained with oil, her breath hanging in the air.

The cop rallied. 'Now look, lady . . .'

'Look lady is not where we're at. I've gotta meet this guy, this guy's waiting on me. OK, OK.' She glanced at a vast digital watch with knobs. 'Three minutes! Three lousy minutes is all. How's he gonna find me way over there, me and the dog truck? I told him the dog truck. How's he gonna find an unknown dog truck way over?' She gestured to the car park alongside. 'How's he gonna see it? So I stay here, right.'

The cop mumbled something.

Robin moved forward as she turned away happy. 'Are you Shara?'

She glanced up from the boot-faced cop, smiling in victory. 'Pardon *me*, officer. Hi. You must be Robin,' she said, glad to share her triumph. 'This officer was so kind, he let me park right here. First he says no way, over there, but I say maybe the guy don't know dog trucks?' She nodded. 'I thought maybe not. Get in, get in. Bye officer, bye.'

She slammed the truck into gear. The cop lifted a hand through billows of blue smoke.

'You're American,' said Robin.

'Right on the button.' She was driving fast. He sneaked a glance at her profile as she passed a bus, noted the lines at the eyes, the downward tug of her cheek. Her behind was propped on several old cushions for height. She drove with attack; weaving and diving, the custom-made dog pens rattling on the tray, they belted along the road to Dunedin.

It was a beautiful morning, a clear midwinter dazzler, a good day. The hills were rounded, the sky stone-washed. The plumes of breath expended during Shara's disposal of the cop would have disappeared long before he and his chicken-headed chauffeur headed for the hills and the air like bloody wine. People talk about their surroundings as though awareness of them happens every day when it is as rare as a roadrunner's tooth. Yeah, we enjoyed Otago. The terse directive—Enjoy. The last time he had felt as though every bone, cell, hair in his body was alive and well and present had been with Emmie at Chainsaw. After Chainsaw. Yes. He splayed his fingers, looked; still ten. He turned to the hills, the sweeps of blue.

'It's so clean here,' he muttered.

'Gets washed enough, doesn't it?'

Well, yes. 'Whereabouts in the States do you come from?'

'Oklahoma.'

'Ah.' Oklahoma. Okies, dust bowl. Depression, *Grapes of Wrath*. Oklahoma, where the wind comes right behind the *rain*. He had taken Lisa to a revival of the film. The farmer and the cowman, he remembered, should be friends. But Shara would have known even less before she came here. Anti-nuclear policy. Scenic wonders. Racial tension. Unlikely. The world whittled to a green fruit and a purblind bird on a tin of polish.

'Ah,' he said. 'Whereabouts?'

She was concentrating. 'Sulphur.'

'Sulphur. Oh. Do you like it here?'

'Sure.'

Probably she didn't like to talk while driving at this speed. She navigated Dunedin in minutes.

'Small, isn't it?' he said as they shot out the other side.

'I like it.'

'Yeah, me too. Beautiful. Stone. Trees. Grass.' He felt tempted to open the window, to explain to a father and his padded infant transfixed by heavy machinery tearing up a tree-lined square just how beautiful it was.

'I came here as a child,' he said. 'With my mother.' Silence. 'We stayed with an aunt in St Kilda.' He told her how cold the sea was and how a man had been attacked by a shark before they got there, not that that would have made any difference to the victim. He saw his aunt's moist lips, heard her voice tolling. '*Eat-en. Eat-en.* Torn apart at the waist.' 'The guy wasn't out deep,' he said.

A quick glance. 'That's nice.'

He rubbed his hands together. 'It was a long time ago.'

'Is that right?'

He sank back wondering how on earth he had got into this conversation, cast another look at her and was silent. From this angle, beneath a squash of black fake-fur hat grabbed from the dashboard as they set off, she looked more like some small sharp-nosed marsupial which can survive extremes. A rat-tailed dunnart perhaps, an endangered bilby. The spiked hair had confused him.

They drove past shining mudflats. He leaned out to peer.

'A friend of mine did a thesis on *Amphibola* there,' he said. 'A mollusc.'

'Mollusc, huh?'

'Yeah, she wanted to find out whether its nerve loop was primitive or specialised.' He was staring out the back window into the past as though Pam might still be seen upended in her search for truth.

'Which was it?'

'I don't know. I left.'

'You could've found out. You could've given her a buzz.'

'Yeah but . . .'

Yeah but what? Yeah but I lost touch. Yeah but what's it to you, chicko. That's not where I'm at. Not where I'm coming from. I don't give people buzzes. I don't do keep-in-touch.

'Tell me about your boss,' he said.

She expanded before his eyes. 'He's a great old guy. Sure, he's got his weirdo bits but we get along. We get along good, me and him and the dogs. He's the best dog man in Central. Over eighty and he can eat the rest. Eat them and spit out the pips.'

'He's a dog trialler then?'

'Is he ever.'

'How'd you get the job?'

'He advertised.' She paused. 'I don't know about that Alice lady.' She gave the wheel a sudden tug with small brown hands then corrected. 'I gather the locals thought she was a bit of a kook but I don't know. But we get along, Wil and me.'

They shot through Palmerston and headed up the Pigroot. The hills widened, stretched to the far white line of the horizon. The sky was infinite. He had never seen so much sky in his life but decided not to mention the fact.

'It's a long way. I should've caught a bus.'

'Wil said no. He said go and meet the bugger and we'll get shot of him sooner.'

Robin flung back his head. He laughed with release, with delight in gallant old pots who survive and the pleasure of being up Central where the air is.

For the first time Shara grinned back at him, the cheerful matey grin of a tough nut. Her arms were leather, she appeared to have no breasts at all, the crowsfeet at the corners of her eyes were deep cracks.

'We needed some bulk stores, but yeah, we could've got that locally. But he's the boss.'

He glanced at her again. Legs above socks, arms below sleeves tanned to dark brown; the rest would be pearly white. Behinds, he remembered from long ago, are particularly improved by contrast.

A lark lifted, a winged insect splattered tangerine against the windscreen. The wipers squirted in the silence. There was not another car in sight nor had been for miles. The old swingers from

Chainsaw should be here, grey pony tails streaming beneath helmets, their Harley Davidson burning along the open road where the wind comes right behind the rain.

Wil came to meet them at the shed with the quick swinging limp of an energetic old man in want of a hip replacement. Tall and thin, he was dressed in rough woollen trousers and faded workshirt, his arms ropes of sinew beneath rolled sleeves. His hair was a thatch of white hacked at the edges, its cut-off points blunt and sudden as a badly made wig. His nostrils and ears were also tufted, his eyes blue beneath individual stacks of eyebrow. Framed by the woolshed-red of the barn doors, hands waving to direct Shara to put the truck away now, why not, he was a powerful figure. This man did not look like some snivelling no-hoper who had destroyed the artistic creativity of his passionate wife. This was a forceful man, a man of presence. A man who belonged to the land and pitied those who didn't. Perhaps he was a bully. A hectoring humourless sod in gumboots.

He wrenched open the door to clench Robin's hand as he climbed stiffly from the truck.

'Hughes,' he said. 'Wil Hughes. Pleased to meet you. Bum gone on you, has it? Suspension's shot. Stamp your feet. Harder. Like this.' Stamping and snorting at each other they jigged on the concrete. An old black labrador lying alongside lifted a grizzled muzzle for a moment, waved a languid tail and replaced its head to yawn.

'Right now?' said Wil.

'Yes thanks. And thanks to Shara. I should've caught a bus.'

'No no. Gawd no. No. Come away in.'

The implement barn, garage and toolshed were large and well maintained, much larger in total area than the house which was a small cottage surrounded on three sides by pines. A wire fence enclosed an ex-garden in the front. Two goats on long leads were munching, their white coats haloed by late-afternoon sun. The wide expanse of the Maniatoto plain was broken by occasional clumps of dark plantation and lines of skeleton poplars. Houses were few and far between.

'Dogs,' said Shara and disappeared. Wil and Robin set off across a wide stretch of concrete to the house.

'Mind the crap,' grunted Wil. It was much in evidence as were its originators. Another surprise. Why would a man as seemingly pragmatic—as, if you could stand it, earthy—as Wil, keep such birds? These were not market-oriented hens, deep-bottomed hybrids with plenty of egg room, prolific layers with asset potential. These birds were rare domestic fowl; pure-breds of striking design and little commercial return. Birds of detail and delight, these singular creatures looked like prints from an eighteenth-century library complete with spiral mahogany ladder, not something to be found crapping on concrete in Central.

It would be Alice. Alice pining for the baroque, the extravagant. For something that wasn't entirely for goddamn use.

Robin admired, was introduced with Spiro-like courtesy to gold-lacing and spangling, to good comb and expressive eye, to silver hackles and well-barred wings. The man was an expert and a yarner as well.

'There's a bloke down south breeds them,' he said, 'but some breeds are choosy. Not for roughing it on farms. Nothing wrong with these girls though is there? A flock of well-laced Silver Laced Wynandottes in a paddock when it's green is a sight for sore eyes, I can tell you.'

'How long've you had them?'

'Two years,' said Wil lifting a blotched hand to his nose. 'The crap's a bind. I hose it down, the yard, but it's sitting there looking at you again by morning. Still . . .' His eyes searched the upper reaches of the pines. 'Alice would've loved them,' he said, 'but Geoff hadn't started then. She'd have gone for the names alone. White Silkies and Black Hamburgs, Plymouth Rocks and Silver Campines. I can hear her laugh. But you've got to keep your feet on the ground.'

They walked through the back door into a narrow porch which acted as a buffer between the backyard and the kitchen. Gumboots of varying sizes littered the floor and sat upended on sills; a stray red one lay on a kauri chest beside two old kerosene lamps with mantels intact. Individual work boots lay jumbled together except for two sets placed neatly side by side at the door. There was much wet-weather gear. Oilskins lined one wall, old cracked ones alongside two more operational ones and three checked Swanndries. Hats were in abundance; the usual sou'westers and woolly ones, three towelling, two straw and an army beret alongside khaki cottons and a dusty brown pork pie.

Assorted seed packets brown with age, garden tools petrified with caked mud and an old chainsaw leaned against a bag of pine cones and a pile of kindling. A cardboard box full of unstained wooden eggcups sat beside a washing board below a window opaque with cobwebs and dead flies. There was a pleasant smell; a dry crispness of usage and old wood, of dried mud and lavender; the latter presumably from a cocooned-looking bunch swaying above them. The range of exhibits was wide. So wide it looked like a display in some one-roomed colonial museum, some neglected pit-stop on a heritage trail for tourists. But this lot must have deepened like the Maniatoto itself, have been formed from gradual accumulation of deposits through the ages.

The kitchen was a large room with a table in the middle. Again negative space was at a premium. Horizontal surfaces were piled high with old newspapers, bills and letters had been opened and restowed in piles, used Lotto tickets were half hidden by an advertisement for sheep drench labelled Action in black felt-tip. The other side of the bench had been taken over by foodstuffs and painted tins. The Queen in majesty and Milford Sound sat cheek by jowl with tins labelled Weetbix, Cereal, Rice, Odds and Ends and God Knows. The refrigerator was an old rumbler with a rounded top. Wil opened the door for milk and the stench of uncooked overripe mutton hit the air. He closed the door without comment and sat down to pour tea from a brown earthenware pot. His voice was quiet, almost shy. 'I clean it up you know, wash the floor and that. But . . .' He lifted his arms in defeat. 'I can't keep up with it. Like the hens.' He ladled spoons of sugar, stirred for some time. 'And I can't expect Shara . . . She's an outdoor girl.'

Robin coughed into his tea. The dated phrase conjured up bosomy bikini pin-ups bronzed and anointed and laid in the sun.

There are no outdoor or indoor girls now. There are no girls. And they don't get laid. They agree, or they decline, or they are raped and/or killed. Occasionally they welcome as Emmeline Frances O'Malley had done, stepping out of silk and kicking it aside with a pink and white foot.

Robin blinked, shook his head. 'When can we start talking?' he said.

Wil paused for a moment. 'Tomorrow morning. In the front room. After I show you the frocks.'

Robin sat bolt upright at the weight on his legs. He sniffed the fusty air, tried to move his feet and couldn't as he fumbled for the switch on the rickety bedside light.

Shara was dressed in the same clothes as yesterday; only her boots were missing and her fun-fur hat. The blast of air from the door was icy on his bare chest but there was no retreat. He was naked, freezing and not in charge.

'What's going on?' he snapped.

Shara looked at him with faint surprise which irritated him further. Her hair was wet and spikier than ever. A drop of water slid down her face and ran between the small mounds beneath her shirt which were separated by a leather thong and its pendant dog whistle.

'And would you mind getting off my legs?'

Shara put up one finger to wipe another drop of water and moved slightly.

'Thanks.'

'Yeah, well,' she said, 'I should've told you yesterday but I forgot so I thought I'd get in early. I'm off soon. Wil's memory's on the blink.'

'Whaat!'

She pulled her feet up onto the bed, took her time, gazed thoughtfully at his panic.

'He seemed OK last night,' he said. 'On the ball. Won the dominoes,' he said punting up evidence.

She looked at him with the contempt he was beginning to recognise. 'You don't need memory for dominoes. You count spots.'

'But this is terrible . . .'

'Yeah, it's tough on the old guy. He knows too. That's the saddest.'

'I mean . . .'

'Yeah, I know what you mean. You're just thinking of your research about that Alice.' She was angry now. Her perky alertness was ruffled, her cheeks flushed. 'But don't you worry. He remembers every moment of every minute he ever spent with that . . . I won't badmouth her. I didn't know her anyhow, but from what I hear . . . But the old guy, now don't you get him agitated. If you get him excited his memory goes right through the roof. I talked to the doctor and he said, Shara, now don't you fret. It's just age and it's only short-term memory, names and that, and you're there for his heart pills and there's nothing to be done. It happens or it doesn't happen and it happens to everyone to some extent and don't you worry about it. That's what he said. His very words. Don't you worry, he said. So I don't. It's only names. He doesn't like names. Names bother him.' One hand flipped upwards. 'He couldn't remember Humphrey Bogart the other day. That shook him.'

'Why?'

'Yeah, yeah, but that's what gets him, see. He says he doesn't mind forgetting names of people he's known for ever like relatives. But Bogart worried him, the name was, like, all he had. No one would know who he meant otherwise. Or Gerald Ford. Sure, he's easy to forget, that's what I said. I said Wil forget it, nobody remembers that guy, and he said that wasn't the point, but I said sure it was.

'And he's such a battler, the old guy. Know what he does? I find scraps of paper all over with "Shara" on them. There'll be "Rob" too now, I bet.'

'To remind him?'

Again that look. 'What do you reckon?'

She was silent, her chin in her hand as she stared moodily at the pink ruffled lampshade on the light beside his bed. The whole room was pink. The bedspreads of the twin beds were pink on pink flowers, the eiderdowns covered in the same fabric. A mistake. Eiderdowns, Maureen had told him, must be down-proof. These ones leaked scraps of feathers, small white chopped bits drifted to the floor. The walls also were pink as was the large wardrobe. Another mistake surely; its loops and swirls and the brass teardrop handles looked like defaced Art Nouveau. Shara seemed to have settled in for a long haul. Rob sneezed and dragged on his guernsey.

'The thing is,' she said thoughtfully rubbing her nose. 'I've only got a visitor's visa.'

He sneezed again. 'Oh,' he said.

Her nose was still requiring attention.

'Do you know if Alice O'Leary did the, er, decor?' he said hurriedly. 'All this pink?'

'Naa. Most of this is Depression stuff, Wil said.' She lifted the pink frill on the bedside table with one foot to reveal a naked apple box empty except for a large chamber pot ringed with roses. 'This'll be Doris. She was his first.'

'How many's he had?'

'Three. Doris, Ivy, then Alice.' Shara picked a feather off her shorts and dropped it on the ground. 'And I just might be number four.'

'What?'

'Yeah yeah. He's over eighty.' She turned to him, pink and angry again. 'Well I'm over forty and I'll tell you something, I like it here, OK?' She stood quickly. 'Hens,' she said and left.

He stared at the white-painted door behind her. Three. Three's quite a lot.

The shower space was long and narrow and well-used; two or three discarded plastic bottles of shampoo lay on the flaking yellow concrete base beside a scrubbing brush. The walls were interesting; there were several varieties of mould present: ordinary greys, a finer black-speck one and an interesting streak of pink which he had not seen before. He dropped on his heels to touch it. More a slime than a mould. Karen would know but Karen was now preparing for the NZ Antarctic Summer Programme research into the genetic variability of Dry Valley mosses. Rob jumped up, skidded on the slippery paint and landed flat on his back on an empty discard, icy water pelting at his crotch. A Herbal Mild burped beneath him.

'Hot water go on you?' said Wil.

'Well, yeah . . .'

'Should've warned you. The hot goes dog on you if I turn her on in here.'

The old man nodded, rubbed his hands together. 'Great day for the race,' he said.

There will always be riddles, jokes, kids on tiptoe. Of course there will. Get real Raab. Lisa is dead and all grief is self-pity and self-pity is crud.

'I know that one,' he said.

But Wil, like all riddlers, was ruthless. 'The human race!' he cried, turning to the porridge heaving and thudding away to itself on the stove. Robin could feel the stretch of his smile.

'Where's Shara?' he asked after the porridge and the eggs and the bacon and the tea and the toast.

'Long gone.' Wil waved a chapped hand. 'Way out the back to fix the pump on the water race.'

'Maybe we'd better tidy up then.'

'No, no Bob, stack them up, just stack them. I want to show you the frocks.'

There was no point in asking what frocks. Wil obviously thought he had explained and Robin must keep things easy. Nice and slow and easy. For you I do special job.

The outside air hit them like a blast from a deep-freeze. Hoar frost framed trees in inch-high tinsel, furred upended buckets, transformed droppings to delicate filigreed maquettes. Wil glanced at his guest's Reeboks.

'Those things got a decent grip? This is arse-over-tip country mind.' The old man's face changed, the furrows from nose to mouth deepened, his eyes were troubled. 'What's your name again?'

Robin stared across the plain. 'Robin.'

'Wait here a sec,' said Wil and re-entered the cottage. He came back patting his pocket. 'Got the runbacks,' he said. 'She's just over here.' He headed towards a corrugated iron shed beyond the dog kennels, his feet crunching frozen puddles to slivers of ice.

The sheepdogs went mad, leaping and twisting from long chains beneath frilled macrocarpas. The noise was deafening, the yelping frenzy of hysterical finger-snapping young thrusters filmed at the stock exchange. Me. Here. Mine. Me!

Wil paused in his swinging lope. 'Get inside,' he growled. The words came from deep within. It was not a roar. It was the voice of all authority Robin had ever known or seen or read, the voice of drill sergeants and crushers, of jackboots and power.

The dogs turned, their tails curled deep between their legs as they slid back to their mini-Nissens to turn and lie with grounded paws, their eyes on the boss.

'How do you do it? No, no,' Rob said quickly at the surprise on Wil's face. 'I don't mean just shutting them up. Shara tells me you're the best dog man in the district. How do you do it? Dog trials. All that. How do you train them? Why are you better than anyone else?'

Wil gave the question some thought as he stood scratching his buttock through rough tweed. 'How does a man do anything? If I knew how I did it I would let you know.' He grinned. 'Send a postcard to the uni.'

Rob grinned back. He must watch it. This was not the moment to start liking the man who presumably had crushed his wife, killed her spirit and made her silent.

Wil turned the key. 'I keep her locked,' he said. 'I don't know why.'

The tin shed was icy cold. Robin's brain was numb and not only with frost; numb with not understanding a damn thing about dog trials or Wilfred or frocks. What frocks? And why? And why were they mucking around in sub-zero temperatures when they should be tucked up in the front room with the tape recorder and preferably six heaters going full bore and he didn't even feel the cold. He peered into the shed and sniffed. Hellish dark and smells of mothballs.

Wil pulled a hanging cord. Pale light fell from the naked bulb onto emptiness and women's dresses suspended from hangers on an iron pipe around three walls.

'Ah,' said Robin. 'Frocks.'

'And a few coats.' Wil was demonstrating the display, lurching about the shed, his arms waving in explanation as he measured each wife's remembrance.

'From here to here is Doris,' he said at the south side. 'We were married before the war. She died while I was away. Sudden. Very sudden. I got a letter in the desert. I didn't know till then. Her sister wrote.' Wil paused, his mind with the heat and the flies and the blowing sand and the two pages of thin blue paper on his knees. 'The next day I watched a Brit scrape some poor sod off a tank. Copped a mortar burst all to himself. Then the tank rolled on.

'Yes,' he said. 'The letter'd been held up. Held up in Cairo.'

He swung over to the opposite wall. 'And here to here is Ivy. Her line is longer because it was twenty years with her so naturally she had more. When I was demobbed and got the Rehab we married and came up Central. We were lucky mind.' He fingered a grey cotton with lilac spots. 'Sun dress.' He paused, his hand still on the frock, his face concerned. 'Hang on. It had a bolero as well.' He scrabbled among the wire hangers and came up with a snatch of similar material and draped it over the hanger. 'She wouldn't go into town sleeveless. "Ivy," I said, but no.' He chuckled, the indulgent half-laugh of a man who understands modesty and the fact that some women have it. 'Bolero,' he said again. He patted the ensemble, dragged hangers back and forth to show woolblends and brushed cottons, viscose and garden prints. His knowledge seemed encyclopaedic. What the hell was rayon acetate.

'She died. Sixties it was. Yes, sixties,' he said moving to the shorter wall of the rectangle.

'I don't like having Alice back here,' he said fingering a checked skirt. 'It's not chronological. She was the last and by rights Ivy should be here and Alice along that side, but then again Ivy sewed like Doris, she used to run up her tub frocks and that, so naturally she had more than Alice so it seemed sense to have,' his arm demonstrated, 'Doris this side, Ivy opposite and Alice back here.' He stopped, anxious for understanding. 'See what I mean?'

Robin nodded. 'Yes. Yes. I agree.' The knobbled fingers, the swollen joints were still stroking in remembrance. 'And I know she wouldn't have minded. Wouldn't have given it a thought. Oh, she was different, Alice. Different in every way.' His eyes were moist but old eyes often are. 'I've been a lucky man three times . . . But Alice . . .' He grabbed the fabric of the skirt. 'Seersucker,' he muttered and buried his face in its folds. 'Alice was different,' he said and lurched away.

Robin stood rooted to the floor. He had returned to the flat the day they found Lisa, had rushed straight to the laundry basket, snatched her unwashed clothes and hidden his face in them. Had roamed through the flat howling like a dog. Had refused to wash them ever again till Maureen crept in one day and took them to wash for the Sallies. 'It has to be, Robin,' she said. 'It has to be.' So why was he startled by the extravagance, the unlicensed abandon of the gesture.

It was not only the memory, he thought staring at his trainers. Wil was old, too old for such pain. Olds are meant to be past it.

Prompted by some obscure sense of loyalty he moved to Alice's wall, shoved the cramped hangers about, fingered material he did know. 'Velvet,' he said.

'Take it out. Have a good look.'

'Yes. Yes.' Robin pulled the thing out, stroked the pile the wrong way. He changed direction as Lisa had shown him, guiding his hand over the curve of her hip to her thigh. He turned the frock round. On the back of the skirt the smooth matt of the pile had been disturbed by seating. Robin shoved the hanger back quickly, gave a small dry cough. 'Well,' he said.

Wil was looking at him, his eyes bright. 'Nothing missing. Not of the ones in good condition that is. All three of them.'

'Yes.'

There were too many impossible unaskable questions. Too many things he longed to know and never would. How had it all begun, let alone continued? When had it started? When had the prefab been installed? How had Wil explained it to the successive wives? *That's my last Duchess, painted on the wall looking as though she were alive.*

Wil also had found a thing to do in remembrance. Rob gave an involuntary shiver. Someone was walking on his grave, and not only his. He moved from one foot to the other, took out another frock (Doris's side this time, to be fair): a navy blue ecru lace which scratched.

'After five,' said Wil. 'She didn't get much wear out of it.' Well, she wouldn't, would she. If they had been things of beauty in their own right, designer garments from a former age, garments made from fine fabrics with exquisite workmanship and preserved with care and space for later generations to wonder and admire, yes. Good thinking. But these—these relics from the backs of two hardworking farmer's wives who ran up their tub frocks and one who did not. No.

Wilfred was waiting.

'You don't think they might get a bit damp?' tried Rob.

'No. No. She's lined, the shed.'

'Ah.' Robin tried again, knowing he should not, knowing that the old man's pride in this hall of remembrance was genuine, that his collection of dead wives' garments was treasured, that it was not macabre, that we all have to find our own way. That it was a shrine, that one man's shrine is another man's horror story. These limp hanging deceased-estate relics appalled him, reeked of vaults and charnel houses, neither of which he had ever seen let alone smelled. And surely it was wrong to enshrine these tired garments, these empty hanging sleeves, these ephemeral *used* things.

'You could offer them to a museum,' he pleaded.

Wil's jaw thrust out, a muscle twitched his cheek. 'They're mine,' he said.

Robin walked to the open door, sniffed the air, gazed across the plain once more. 'Great country,' he said. 'Great.'

The old man glanced at a scrap of paper from his top pocket and restowed it.

'Quite something, eh Rob?' he said.

The front room was a coolstore for apples. There were no heaters; watery sun filtered through windows again masked by outdoor cobwebs onto a sofa and two chairs with wooden arms and movable backs. Large ill-packed squabs covered with something like hessian lay on bases and backs. There were smaller cushions, one for each chair, three for the sofa. The only gesture towards frivolity or the non-essential was a Smoker's Companion in the form of a painted plank-thin Egyptian slave: bare feet treading, snake band in position, endlessly proffering nonexistent cigarettes, matches and ashtray from a small tray.

There was an aerial photograph of the farm above the fireplace and nothing else. Not a book in sight. One of the biggest, most scratched poufs Robin had ever seen sat before the right-hand chair. Wil touched it with his foot. 'Suez on the way home,' he said.

Robin smiled, fiddled with his tape recorder. The long-term memory must be all right.

'Right then,' he said. 'Off we go?'

'OK.'

Robin paused. Pressed the Off button. 'There's something I'd like to ask before we begin. Will I be able to interview you again? In August say. The long vacation?'

A previously unseen cat strolled into the room, the largest angriest-looking bunch of electrified fur Robin had ever seen, a malevolent grey and black feathered boa of a cat with strong topaz eyes. A cat of character.

Wil leaned forward. 'Putz, Putz, Putz. Here Bugle, come on Bugle boy. Where you been, boy?'

Bugle sneered briefly, tore savagely at the leather pouf and leaped vertically onto the proffered knee. He gave a few desultory kneads of the coarse wool trouser-legs and curled up. Wil stroked him, murmured endearments, tickled beneath an ear which twitched with rage.

Eventually Wilfred lifted his eyes to Robin. 'Why?' he asked.

Robin explained, his eyes on the old man's. He was frank, open, he had nothing to hide. He was a trustworthy man. 'I'd like more time. I mean I wouldn't expect to stay here.' Robin laughed, a light honest sound forced from his throat by a plumed puff of air. 'I'd find a bed and breakfast or whatever.'

There was silence. A long silence during which Bugle and Wil, their expressions similar, stared back at him. 'Staying's nothing,' said Wil. 'It's why. You tell me what you're going to say and I'll tell you if you can come.'

'But I don't know. I won't know until we've talked. I can't tell you yet.'

Wil was stroking Bugle's ruff. 'Boogie woogie bugle boy,' he murmured.

He raised his eyes again and stared through cobweb. 'All right. I'll say OK for now.' He leaned back in the uncomfortable chair and stretched, his hand still stroking. 'This is my fifth Bugle,' he said still stroking. 'And this afternoon I'll show you her grave.'

Nine

Ready?

Yes yes. Get on with it.

So when did you first meet Alice O'Leary?

After Ivy died I bached for a while but I got sick of it so I advertised. *The New Zealand Farmer? The Listener?* Can't remember. *Wanted. Housekeeper. Single man. Small southern holding.* Usual sort of thing. I wasn't too struck on Alice being American at first. Or that when I rang back and asked for a photo she said she couldn't see why anyone would need a photo of a housekeeper and it was no go, so that was that. And then a day or so later she rang again and said was the position still available and she sounded so keen, well more desperate, if you know what I mean. And I liked her voice too; I'd never met an American, not even in the war, and there was a kind of swing you know, a sort of snap to it. Not ratty. I don't mean that, but . . . You know pipe bands? Lots of them round here. You know the way the kilts sort of snap from side to side with the beat? Plaits do too when the girl runs or even walks fast. Ever noticed that?

(PAUSE)

Yes. Yes, I have.

Well, her voice had that. It wasn't just the accent. Even though she was halfway bawling down the phone I could still hear the lilt and I thought that's nice. I like that. So I said, Come on down and we'll see and I'll pay, and she did straight away and I met her in Dunedin with the dog truck same as you, though a different one of course. We're talking sixty-nine now. Anyhow I took one look at her and I thought you'll do me, and that was that.

She loved Central Otago. Right from the start she loved Central. Loved the bright air she called it. It was winter then same as now. Everything about it she loved except the wind, and who does? She said our wind is lazy. Can't be bothered going round, goes straight through. She was a poet see.

Yes.

You know the first thing I noticed, well I suppose you usually do notice faces but this time it was the look, the lack of expression. Blank. Completely blank. Not prim or prissy or whatever. Just *there*; eyes, nose, mouth, nothing else. Like some sort of, I don't know, zombie. Or traveller maybe. Not an ordinary traveller waiting for a train or just padding along, I don't mean that, but I'd never seen a face, well more of an expression, like that. You know Mecca?

Yeah, I mean . . .

Suppose you got it all wrong? Suppose you were one of them and you'd got all the way to Mecca and it had taken you forever and every bean you had but that didn't matter because it was worth it. But when you got there Mohammed wasn't there. His tomb even. Well, not for you, that's my point. Everyone else, all the other pilgrims, of course they'd found it, they had it forever but you'd lost it and now you knew you'd never get it. I'd say she was one of the most lost-looking ladies I've ever seen in my life. There was a hole punched in her when she arrived here, know what I mean?

Yes. Yes, I do.

What's your name again?

Rob.

What was I saying?

Alice being lost.

Before that.

Mecca. Her arriving.

Yes. Her face told me right off. She was different.

Her loving the place was a help though. I taught her to ride and she caught on quick for someone her age and we'd head off up the back and all over. Day after day we'd be up and off. Anything, she said, anything to get outside. She wasn't much of a housekeeper I'd have to say, but she could cook a roast. Chops was the other thing but no puddings. I missed them but there you are. She liked the dog work too. She had her own dog in the end. Tip. She trained him from scratch. I showed her of course but she caught on. She was over forty mind. That's late for starting.

Forty-one.

Forty-one. How do you know?

I've looked it up.

Looked it up in what?

I've researched it.

Why?

Because I had to. I'm writing about your wife's work. I'm trying to find out everything about her and her life to help me understand her work. There are so many . . . well, things don't add up.

Such as?

Why did she stop writing?

She didn't want to.

Why?

She didn't say. Except it was gone. I remember that. I remember that because it was such an odd thing to say. She was always desperate to get outside like I said. When we were snowed in once she nearly went mad. When she was dying, well she wrote a bit then.

Where is it!

I burned them like she said.

(SILENCE)

Do you remember nothing about them? What they were. Poems? Prose?

Didn't look. Burned them.

(PAUSE)

You've no idea at all?

I said. She told me to burn them.

Nnnnh. That's very . . .

As long as she could get outside she was all right.

(LONG PAUSE)

Tell me about your marriage.

We never married. We had marital relations mind, after the first year, moved in together as man and wife. I was quite willing to marry her, wanted to in fact. I like to have things straight and I'd like to have had a child. Doris and Ivy never had any luck. I said you're not too old and I'm certainly not, but she'd had an operation so that was that. Bad luck wasn't it, but there you are.

An old *Landfall* article says she married in 1970.

Oh we told people that. But no, she wouldn't have it.

Did she say why?

She said she'd been married once and it had been a living hell. Seen a picture of him?

Yes.

Right bastard wouldn't you say. Eyes too close together. Pursed-up little duck's arse of a mouth. Never have trusted those mouths.

I'll tell you something. Once she said she had misbehaved, that was the word she used, misbehaved, and the next day when he went to the office he locked her inside and he did that for a week. And another time she ran away to her cousin and he sent the police for her and they delivered her back and he thanked them politely and took her inside and locked the door and thrashed her right there in the hall till she fell over, and then he stepped over her and went upstairs to bed.

Christ.

Yes. She described the pattern on the carpet. One of those old red and blue ones with squirls. She remembered the smell, she said. Hot dust. I believe her. I believe every word she said. She was completely straight. She hated the lie about being married, she didn't want that either, but I drew the line at letting on about that. It's a small place round here and things were different then.

She did get away from him once more, she told me. He went to England for some business trip and he took ill. Yes. I can't remember what it was, I'd tell you if I did, but he was quite ill seemingly. But he was too mean to send for her and the last thing she wanted anyhow was to go over and sit by his bedside and be growled at day after day, and in the end he was away for months and it was wonderful, she said. (PAUSE) That's what she said. Yes. Wonderful.

You remember every word.

Nothing wrong with my memory.

And you talked a lot, I gather. You must have.

Talk! You know she was the only one that talked, both of us talking sense and not just banging on. Doris and Ivy were two good women and I've never had dinner like it since, some of those blowouts, my word. But Alice, well Alice *confided* in me. Know what I mean?

Yes.

She trusted me see.

Yes.

And I trusted her.

Yes.

A lot of women just talk to women, but not Alice. We'd talk for hours, yarning away.

Did you read her books, Wil?

I have to say in all honesty, the first time round I flagged the last two away. I've never read a poem except *Drake's Drum* and stuff at school, so that didn't worry me, not liking hers, I mean. And I slogged on with her short stories but I've never seen much point in them where nothing much happens. And something did happen in

194

her first two novels. In the *Scroll* one the girl gets away at the end, and *The Hand of Time*, well sure it's sad them having to leave, but at least they're doing something. You know how I'd describe them those first two? Sad. Very sad. But yes, I read them. I can't say I enjoyed them but the people stayed in the mind.

But the last two I found tough. All those people and each one weirder than the last. A miserable pack of layabouts knocking their kids around and hating each other and whingeing and not *doing* anything. But I kept reading. I had to make myself, mind, especially *All Fall Down*. I read them. It took me a while, I don't mind saying. Lying with Alice beside me telling me to stop because if I read them I'd find out about her and I'd hate her and she didn't want that. Well, that made me keener if you really want to know, and I slogged on. Now I suppose I read them about twice a year, those last two. Not because of her being dead or anything but those people now, that pack of oddballs and nutcases, I know them better than most round here. If Nettie Rainer came in this room this moment I'd know her. Not from her daft clothes and her scraggle teeth, I don't mean that. I'd know her because I know her in my head, the poor stupid cow. Not like her, maybe, but sort of give her the benefit of the doubt if you follow me.

Yes.

It's easier to do that with books mind. Did I tell you about Alice's voice?

Tell me.

She had the prettiest voice I've ever heard. I can hear it to this day. Mind you part of it was being American and the funny words but it had a sort of lilt, a snap to it.

How did she react to the frocks? I mean as a . . .

She didn't go near them. I have to say that was a disappointment. I thought she'd take an interest somehow, but no.

Did she realise um . . . Well she must have got rid of some dresses in ten years. Had you sort of started, as it were? On hers?

She was a hoarder and I never kept things that weren't in good shape. And in the natural course of events I would've passed away first being twenty years her senior, but no. Cancer. She was only in her fifties.

Yes. I'm sorry.

(PAUSE)

When she died I had her at home. I didn't want her lying down there in Bob Gravely's fridge. I had her home, in here as it happens. She was the only one I had home. And you know what, that very night I had to go and see the vicar. He'd been tied up all day and she didn't want a religious service so there was a bit of sorting out to do, but he's a decent cove . . . name's gone . . . doesn't matter. Anyhow he's OK like I said and he'd promised to see me, but that meant I had to leave her almost as soon as she'd arrived home. You can imagine. But there was nothing else I could do. The vicar was going to fit me in after vestry as it was and I knew I had to get everything tied up that night and I couldn't think what to do. About leaving her I mean. (PAUSE) Know what I did?

Tell me.

I found a couple of old white candles we'd had by us for power cuts and I put one in each of those enamel candle-holders with handles like the old days and I lit them and put one each end. Do you think that was OK?

I think that was inspired.

Good. I've never told anyone that. You don't think it was daft?

No. (PAUSE) There's something . . .

Yes?

You described her as lost, when she arrived in 1969. Did she tell you why she was so . . . ?

(SILENCE)

No.

Didn't you ask her?

No.

Not even later when you were . . . ?

If she'd wanted me to know she would've told me, wouldn't she?

But you mean you never had even the slightest idea? Didn't you have a suspicion, a clue, the slightest glimpse of what had left her so shattered?

No.

Why not?

Because she didn't tell me.

Oh, fuck.

Alice used to say that meant the truck won't start.

Nothing wrong with your hearing.

Never has been.

Another thing.

Yes.

When did you take . . . ? Oh forget it.

When did I take her frocks over?

Yes.

A few weeks after. Why'd you ask?

I don't know.

You married?

I was.

What happened?

She died.

But you're just a kid.

She was twenty.

Christ. What happened?

I . . .

Want to tell me about it?

(END OF TAPE)

They explored the diggings first. There was little wind and the frost had gone. Wil explained the machinery in some detail: the broken-down crushers, the remains of a sluice, an old race. The function of each half-buried, rusted hunk of metal was described in full. Robin, who was usually interested in industrial archeology but not today, did his best. He listened, he nodded, he bided his time. The grass was long and dry about their feet; elderberry trees and a few collapsed heaps of leafless climbing roses fell about nonexistent houses marked by an occasional slab of stone or the remains of a fireplace. Two tall brick chimneys weathered to pink stood some distance away beside a straggle of broken fence. It was difficult to avoid Ozy-mandias, easy to sentimentalise the lives of the men, women and children who had lived here. An existence which at best must have been rugged and at worst heartbreaking had become as picturesque as a churchyard with old-fashioned roses. Reality had gone for a burton.

'Wil?' said Rob as the truck slammed into action.

'Yeah?'

'Did your wife . . . ?'

'Alice, man, Alice.'

'Alice. Did she bring any books with her when she came?'

'One or two.'

'I would've thought . . .'

'She sent for the rest. She sent to America and they came later. Months it took. Months. You wouldn't believe.'

'And where are they?'

Wil looked at him. 'I gave them to the bring-and-buy.'

A hare zigzagged across the road and dived for safety. Rob forced his voice down. 'When was that?'

'When she died. The vicar said the ladies couldn't shift many of them but he was grateful for the thought.'

'Do you know what happened to them?'

'No idea.'

'Weren't there any work notebooks—any manuscripts, *anything*?' He was begging again, whining for scraps. 'Things connected with her writing, anything, any piece of paper? I'd be grateful for any-thing.'

Wil stopped the truck. 'Here we are. She's a bit stiff this one, from memory. Might have to heave her up a bit.'

Rob lifted the gate into the paddock in front of the cemetery. There were two more larks, more sky than ever and peace for miles. He tried to remember later, struggled to visualise what it was that had stunned him about the place. He could think only of silence and a light breeze on his face and the plain below. There had been a church somewhere: a small church nearby as they walked across the paddock of dry grass.

The burial ground was square and empty of visitors; there were headstones, white pebbles, overgrown mounds, the occasional crooked or broken memorial and dead or live flowers in jam jars. All the usual appurtenances of death and remembrance were present. None of which had anything to do with his reaction to the place, his sense of liberation, of soaring release. Nothing to do either with the conviction that this was the only place in the whole world where any man or woman in his or her right mind would care to dump their carcase. He had never thought of burial until Lisa died. Maureen had begged for cremation as Lisa had hated being shut in her room worse than anything in the world when she was tiny, and please oh please Rob, and what did it matter anyway.

It was not that he wished to lie here. Quite the reverse. It was just the conviction that this was a good place. He walked to the fence beyond a couple of macrocarpas. The cliffs of the escarpment fell away sharply to the dissolving plain below; the faint lift of air moved his hair, his hands lifted.

'We've been climbing see,' said Wil. 'You probably didn't notice but we've been climbing since we left home.'

'No, no, I hadn't.'

'This is the foothills of the Rock and Pillar.'

'Oh.'

Wil was swinging away to the right. 'Alice's over here. This way.'

'Good place, Wil,' he said.

'Why?'

Robin shook his head in defeat, his eyes on the headstone above the mottled gravel centred by three crimson china roses below glass.

Alice Amy Hughes
1928–1979
Beloved Third Wife of Wilfred Quentin Hughes
Not lost but gone before

Rob felt his mouth opening and closing. Third wife of widowed husband. Second runner-up to Ivy.

This was the final resting place, this the epitaph of a woman who could freeze your gut and make you see. A woman whose characters knew that the trick is to survive, to expect nothing, to endure. To shut up and get on with it. Sometimes even to laugh because the world loveth a cheerful sufferer wouldn't you say.

Rob's rage was dry in his mouth. He concentrated on the gravel on the grave below him. Fish, he remembered, don't like their gravel too light. It dazzles them.

'Why didn't you say she was a writer? A wonderful writer. A writer that . . . It hasn't even got her own name!'

'She didn't want it,' said Wil.

And that I will not believe either.

He would like to talk to Emmeline. He would like to talk to her now.

Rob climbed back into the truck. Judgement was required, dispassionate critical analysis of the evidence available. Prejudging was out. It was no use leaping onto the wrong horse and cantering off into some subjective sociological liberated bloody sunset. Think man, think—'. . . in the bowels of Christ, think it possible you may be mistaken.' Alice might have asked for nothing else. Cancer gives you time to decide. It was conceivable. But why?

They drove in silence for a few minutes, but time was short.

'There's something else I'd like to ask you, Wil.'

A quick hooded glance.

'Did Alice ever tell you why she was so unhappy when she rang the first time? When she first arrived?'

'You asked me that before.'

So you were lying. Oh shit.

'When she wanted to get outside all the time?'

'She always wanted to get outside. She was an outside girl like . . . like what's her name?'

The worry on the face beside him, the searching hands.

'Shara.'

'Shara, like I said. Shara's an outdoor girl. Likes to be outside.'

His anger for Alice was now combined with numbness. He stretched his legs, lifted his behind, thought of the grass stirring at the edge of the cliff. In the summer there would be butterflies—small New Zealand Blues teasing wildflowers of the same colour, dipping above clovers and vetch. Possibly a Small Black Mountain. A Tussock.

He tried again.

'You never asked her?'

This glance was hostile, the voice from dog control. 'What d'you think I am?'

'I just wondered.'

It would be a flowering field in the summer. He would tell Emmie. Show her. Show her as he had meant to show Lisa. Yes.

'Going to be a corker of a frost again tonight,' said Wil. 'A black one I shouldn't wonder.'

He was right. They stood at the farm gate next morning waiting for Rob's teed-up lift to arrive. The ground was iron beneath a black frost, the plain stamped flatter than ever below the weight of the sky, the freezing air. Their breath was solid, came in chunks. Word bites.

'You'll say Hi to Shara for me. And thanks.'

'Yes. Yes.' Wil fished in his pocket. 'You can have this if you like. I made a copy at the time.' The message was brief.

> Long Creek,
> Patearoa,
> Otago.
> May 17th

Miss Bowman,
    My wife died yesterday. She asked me to let you know.
        Wilfred Q. Hughes

'I've seen this before,' said Rob.

The eyes snapped back. 'How?'

'My research. I've seen the original. But I'd like this. I'd like this very much if that's OK.'

'Keep the bloody thing.'

'Would you mind telling me . . . ?'

'I don't know do I? Not till you've asked.'

Doug would be here in a moment, burning down the road in a Holden with roo bars. 'Why did you write to Miss Bowman?'

'Alice said to.'

'Did Miss Bowman answer?'

Carved from ice the word huffed back. 'No.'

At the sight of the car Rob lifted his bag, his voice gentle. Very gentle indeed. There was plenty of time. 'Why did you keep a copy, Wil?'

The blue eyes glared. 'I'll tell you why. I kept a copy because I wanted a record. A record of every word, every single last word I'd ever said to the bitch. Got that?' He was waving, stamping about as the Holden slowed. 'Come on. Here he is. G'day, Doug. Get in man, get in.'

The handshake was a quick clench; the bugger was on his way. One hand slapped the side of the car. The face above was stern, the arm raised from the elbow in wooden dismissal. 'Late already. Late. Off you go.'

Doug was not a talker and disliked the Pigroot. They went the other way.

'We passed that Mazda at Middlemarch,' he said and little more. He drove fast and well and the power lines looped and slid beside them and the rain started and changed from sleet to drizzle to great splattering drops as they approached the route to the airport which was signposted with small painted aircraft for extra clarity of information, or perhaps for the benefit of non-English speakers, for those dependent on visual images such as the stylised signs depicting gravid female figures with suitcases which now lined the route to the maternity wing in Capital Health, Wellington. They had been installed since Calvin's birth after the regrettable incident of a *prima gravida* in a confused Laser.

The signs looked to him like pick-up points for bulbous women awaiting holiday transportation but you always see what you're looking for.

Doug was going to pick up his wife who was due home on the two-fifteen flight from Christchurch after seeing the twins, so it had all worked out quite well and Rob needn't give it a thought. Any time.

Rob sat at the airport with a pad on his briefcase making notes. Rough What-the-hell's-going-on notes. Let's-clear-the-head notes. Lists of questions asked, lists of discrepancies, lists labelled Do. Thoughts on Where-we-are-at which seemed pretty much nowhere. He liked lists, they comforted him. Emmeline had told him once that if she had achieved something which had not been on her list she had been known to put it on so she could cross it off. He had laughed loudly.

So what had he learned. Bugger all. Wilfred Q. Hughes had loved Alice O'Leary. Or had he. Wilfred Hughes was an honest man. Or was he. Alice O'Leary had not wanted any mention of her work, not even her birth name to be recorded. Or had she. Yet what would be the point of Wilfred mentioning her former life when she had been happy to flag it away while she lived with him for ten years and loved the place and the dogs, and, from the sound of it, the man himself and his bed to boot.

And Wil seemed interested enough in her work, he thought, busy with his fine point and his paper and his confusing evidence. Proud even. Alice, it appeared, had not given a damn about posterity. Not, presumably, from a Christian death-of-the-temporal-and-spirit-to-the-Lord 'perspective', but merely because it didn't matter. She knew she could do it. Or perhaps she had not given a damn, period. An interesting woman. He had always thought so.

His visit to Central had made the waters even muddier. Not a word written while Alice had lived in Central and not a glimmer of explanation as to why not. And Wilfred's sudden unexpected last-moment outburst against the good, the forthright, the gallant Miss Candida Bowman.

Rob leaned back, closed his eyes. He had been aware of the alternative explanation from the start, of course, conscious of the kneejerk answer. It all added up did it not, the wretched marriage, the cryptic inscriptions in the books, the 'He is dead' letter, followed by the lilac and the weeping woman and the bird hide and the desolation.

OK—so Alice was a lesbian given the push by Candida Bowman. A feasible explanation perhaps, but his heart sank at the analysis involved. The thought of R. Dromgoole searching for clues in such a minefield was disheartening. The baying of those entitled filled him with gloom.

And anyway he did not believe it. Alice's usual imagery was of grief, loss, despair; her sexual metaphors were often clumsy if not faintly embarrassing in so sharp a writer; locked doors, wrong keys, impaled specimens were bathetic images for sexual passion. It did not add up.

He disliked the other quick-fix answer even more. The 'buried in the Antipodes ergo death of the spirit' myth had always infuriated him, but then it would, wouldn't it. Damn and blast and bloody hell. Alice O'Leary continued to fan dance before him, teasing his mind with alternatives. The seven veils he thought, sourly turning a page of his workbook, would have been more illuminating.

She was also shaky on affirmative feminist rhetoric.

> *No woman has yet wet her pillow for her sister's grief.*
> *She was a mean woman. Even the passings of her wind were*
> *counted.*

No. Not a good choice for Suffrage Year by and large in this day and age. Not one to be dialogued with at the cusp of sisterhood. He piled his notes together and headed for the plane.

*

The man in the window-seat wore a fringed silver-studded jacket and came from Balclutha. The tip of his tongue protruded slightly as he copied recipes from his friend's *Quick Cuisine*. He had only got it for two days and the photocopier at work was on the blink so he had to snatch any chance he could get. Did Robin cook?

Yes, he had been very interested in food, still was as a matter of fact, but not as much. He found that nowadays . . .

'Any qualifications?'

'No.'

'Never get anywhere without qualifications. Got your own knives?'

'Yes.'

'Not an amateur then?'

'No but I . . .'

'Got to be one or the other,' said the man licking his finger and turning to Sauces.

The old man on the aisle side was having problems with his slab of cheese. Muttering and snarling to himself he attacked the plastic-entrapped treat from various angles. Periodically he put it back on his tray and glanced casually out the window for a few moments before pouncing again with shaking hands.

'Can I help?'

'Thank you. Thank you very much.' The tweed leaned close, stunned by expertise as Robin ripped. 'Never get into the damn things. Never. My wife used to do them for me but she passed away last year. Thank you. Thank you.'

The landing was smooth. The old was met by the not-so-young. Explanations were made. Hands shaken. Mussolini had banished handshakes in Italy but Italian men can hug. My boy Harold dropped Robin off at the theatre which was kind, and there were seats available for *Hedda Gabler*.

He sat there waiting for his love. Emmeline ran on, her frock skin-tight to the waist then puffed and gathered and full to the ankles. He sat smiling, smiling fatuously as she demonstrated speed and languor, insolence and energy, frustration, boredom and delight in malignity with the assistance of one or two others. The shot at the end did not surprise him. He had been expecting it and could now go and see her. He rose to his feet still smiling and groped for his parka.

'Honestly,' said the voice behind him. 'Why'd they set it *then*? Did you know any girl in our day who knew how to even *shoot* a gun? Let alone have them in the house.'

'Hi, Cara,' he said.

'Robin! Didn't you think that was awful? What'd you think?' Cara's mouth was working; pink lips glistened beneath a flicking tongue. She had to know.

'I liked it. I liked it very much.'

She was blocking his way, attempting marital support from a tall man beside her as people streamed around them. 'Alistair went to sleep, didn't you, Al?'

'No,' said the man, 'I didn't.'

'This is Alistair. This is Robin Dromgoole, yes, Dromgoole. He was my very first tutor. In '92.'

Hi. Hullo. Accompanied by handshakes and Robin's impatience. Emmeline didn't know he was here. She might have to rush off. Where was Calvin? He hadn't asked, he should have asked, he could have minded Calvin, would have liked to have minded Calvin except he would not have been here to do so and Emmie had been hacked off with him and his whole body was aching with longing to see her, to be there, to focus his attention on Emmeline and go home with her and Shut up, shut up for God's sake you mindless mouthing *face*.

'Excuse me,' he said edging towards the stage.

'There's something. Just a tiny thing if you've got a moment,' begged Cara. She must have been good-looking once. Still was in an anxious sort of way. He laid a hand on her arm.

'What about tomorrow? I'm just on my way to . . .'

'Such a tiny thing. Yes, yes, Al, you get the car. It's American literature. It won't take a moment but I need your advice. I really want to do American lit next year if I pass this year of course, but

I'm worried about *Moby Dick*.'

'I don't think you'll find *Moby Dick* too much of a problem, Cara.' He put a hand beneath each arm and lifted her bodily out of the way like a milk crate. 'Tomorrow,' he said.

'It's the *whales*,' she cried, her waves of concern chasing him as he ran.

He knew where to go. He had picked up Calvin once or twice in the past when the backup system had failed. He ran round backstage calling her name, shouldered his way past half-dressed men and women and nicotine and heat and the scent of flowers none of which he had sent. People were sweating, kissing, mopping, removing greasepaint and unwinding all over the place. An older woman in towelling and furry slippers sat in a corner reading *Death Comes to the Archbishop*. He seized a man with flashing glasses and a beard. 'Emmie,' he said. 'Where's Emmeline?'

'Around, darl. Mind my glass. Around.'

'Emmie!' he yelled.

She was beside him, both hands tugging at a blonde wig. 'I can't think why he wanted her blonde,' she muttered.

'Nor can I and you were marvellous. Amazing, wonderful.'

She bent over, her hair falling as she scratched. 'They itch like stink,' she said slowly righting herself to grab a brush. She paused in mid-sweep, her head on one side.

'You've seen it? Just now? What'd you think of the production?'

She was wearing a different kimono from her one at home. Not a kimono at all, a black silk thing with dragons hung loose from her shoulders. He recognised her knickers, dismissed the production. 'It was you, Emmie.' He was offering her treats with open hands. 'You've got to come down south with me next time. Promise.'

'I can't. Of course I can't.' She turned to the mirror above the spilt powder and the tubes and the sticks and the mess and the flowers and the cards from others. There was an artificial sunflower, orchids, a Gary Larson good luck moose joke from Murray. Murray. Mrs Elvsted was cleaning off make-up alongside, hands slapping and wiping and slapping again. She was smoking at the same time, removing the smouldering cigarette periodically with quick spiv fingers for ash removal, slipping it back into the grease-laden mouth, squinting through smoke and slapping some more. It all looked quite difficult. 'Shit,' she murmured gently as ash met cold cream. There was no air. Emmeline's brush strokes were angry tugs, not a sweep in sight. 'How could I?' she snapped.

'I've found the most marvellous place for us to be buried.'

She put down the pink cushioned brush and looked at him.

'We'll take Calvin. That goes without saying. In August, right?'

'Nutter,' said Emmie and slipped out of dragons.

Cara was waiting for him after his Sylvia Plath tutorial. She had laid aside her memsahib neutrals for the day. She stood four square in front of him in a scarlet tracksuit demanding advice on a good book about the Sumerians as she couldn't work out where they came in, nothing too complicated, one of those charts would do even, and also which did Robin think was the best Maori dictionary? She had an old one but there seemed to be better ones about now and she hoped Robin had given some thought to her enquiry about *Moby Dick*. It was the attitude of the book. She fingered the Save the Whales badge on her chest in explanation. What should she do? She was keen to do American lit, she liked the look of all the rest of it, but he must see her point. Could she perhaps leave that one out? Well, she'd have to wouldn't she, but would this mean she'd be seriously disadvantaged and she was sorry if she had been a nuisance last night but she had had no idea he was in such a rush and Alistair had left the parking lights on again and frankly the whole evening had been a disaster; and as for those guns, the very thought of them made her cross all over again. Not the guns obviously, but setting it *then*. She knew she'd scarcely seen him since Stage One but her course adviser was so, well, you know, and Robin had always been so kind.

Robin's mind was elsewhere. It was still humming along last night's lines of communication, sweeping across open country, lingering and swooping and backtracking for miles.

He dragged it back. Had Cara considered New Zealand literature as an alternative?

Oh yes, of course she would do that later, but the thing was she'd read most of the ones on the list already and what she wanted was to extend her horizons. To have to study things she might otherwise never have met up with, if he saw what she meant.

Yes.

Buck-passing was in order. The best thing would be for Cara to consult the Professor in charge of the American literature course.

Fingers touched her mouth. 'Oooh.'

Rob heaved on his pack, attempted to conceal smugness. 'It is the only solution in the circumstances,' he smiled. 'Good luck.'

'Robin,' called Anne laden with replacement telephones. 'There's a phone message. Your mother-in-law wants you to go round some time.'

And when did you last see your mother-in-law. 'Oh. Oh thanks.'

Maureen answered the back door, her face crumpled. She had lost her piping foot.

He took her in his arms, pressed her soft warm bulk against his, kissed her hair which was all that was available. Her face was tucked deep between his chest and arm for comfort. 'Don't worry. I'll find it.'

She lifted her face. 'And that's not all.' One hand was moving, massaging invisible oils into the back of the other one, her eyes were wet. 'It's all such a worry.'

'Let's find the piping foot first.'

The piping foot often disappeared. He knew it well, had retrieved it from beneath the sofa, from under the scraps, from deep in the wastepaper basket and, one triumphant day, from inside the refrigerator.

'I've looked everywhere,' she moaned. 'Everywhere.'

He followed her into the lounge. He had noticed before how stooped she had become but today was worse; her back was bent in despair. He had thought, had hoped, had been almost sure that she was 'getting better'. She was back in her old routine she had told him recently, and yes please, she'd love to see the Van Gogh film. She had loved the book with his pictures in the library. As long as Robin didn't think it would be too sad. And she was having people in occasionally again, though not often of course because of the time.

When she woke up in the morning was still the worst but now what she did was get straight up and get out the bike and go for a ride along the foreshore which helped, and it gave her a good early start as well. Yes. Did Robin find getting out early helped?

He agreed. He went for a run he said. He was about to say every morning but remembered this was not so.

The Bernina was pulsing once more, lengths were being transformed. She was out checking back views once more which she hadn't had the heart for till recently. And covering a bridal coathanger in the same fabric for her favourites, though not many. 'Some of them,' she said darkly, 'wouldn't have a clue.'

So what had happened to cause this relapse, this sodden imploding.

He found the piping foot beneath a tangle of bobbins in one of the chocolate boxes. She couldn't understand it; she had looked there just a minute ago. Thank you. Thank you. She reached out a frantic hand for Betty and held her tight.

'She's got a new frock,' he said hopelessly.

It didn't help. He sat beside her and hugged her, hugged both of them. 'It's all such a worry,' she said again.

'Tell me.'

'Oh Rob, oh Rob.'

'Would you like a cup of tea?'

She shook her head. 'It's Murray,' she said.

Oh God. 'Murray?'

'The thing is, the thing is.' Her head was swinging from side to side. 'Emmie's lent him all this money see.'

'But why are you worried? That's her business. Emmie told me about the money. She wants to lend some to him. It's her money.

No problem.'

The head stopped swinging. She was crying now, silently and tidily. No mess, no fuss.

'You don't understand. It's not that.'

'Then tell me.'

'I can't.'

They sat in silence for a minute, Betty's rigid toes boring into his groin.

Maureen was now mopping up. She straightened, bonged her face with tissues, blew her nose hard and turned to him. 'Yes,' she said slowly. 'Yes, I think I can tell you. I couldn't tell anyone else. Not to another living soul I couldn't. Not even to Lisa. Especially Lisa. No.'

Her arms tightened around Betty at the enormity of her confession. 'I'm scared he won't give it back,' she whispered. 'Oh Rob, oh Robbie, I'm that terrified.'

Tears flowed again. 'And it's that awful, it's that awful of me. How could I *think* such a thing, let alone say it? His own mother who loves him. Who'd die for him though I know people just say that. But you know, Rob. You know it's true, same as Lisa.'

'Yes.'

'So how can I? How can I think such an awful thing? I try and try. All night I try. But . . . He wouldn't mean to. I don't mean that, not for a minute but he might forget or . . .' The damp despairing pain above the rictus of Betty's smile was too much. Rob sat holding her in silence while she begged him for an answer.

'Oh Rob, he will, won't he? I can't say anything to him, how can I? What could I say? He's that happy down there in Dunedin, well of course he is and if I said . . . Oh Rob, *promise* me he'll pay it back later. He will, won't he?'

My friend. My gallant old boot.

'Of course he will,' he cried flinging back his head to laugh. 'Hell's fangs, matey, if that's all that's worrying you.' He clapped his hands together for the fun of it. 'Time we went to see your Van Gogh. What about next week? We'll go early, have tea afterwards.

There's a Satay Something next door. What d'you say?'

'That'd be nice. But if he doesn't, what will I *do*.'

'But only if you promise to forget such a daft idea.'

Her smile was watery. Damp but present. 'Oh Rob,' she said.

Van Gogh was an unfortunate choice. Maureen sat bundled beside him in stoic silence as the bleak images flowed before them. There were no sunflowers. The rain poured down on dark huddled figures and sad streets. The camera work was excellent.

She leaned towards him, touched his arm. 'Terrible weather,' she whispered.

He nodded, blinking, and took her hand.

They walked up the concrete beside the fence which was still holding its own, still hanging on by a thread though it had seen better days and was on its last legs and he still hadn't fixed it.

'I'll have a look at it in the weekend. We'll have a look, I promise.' She looked at him, her face a paler smudge of grey beneath her woolly hat.

'That'd be nice, dear.'

He kissed her goodbye at the back door. Held her at arms' length to tell her. 'There's something . . .' he said.

'Yes dear?'

'I've been seeing a bit of Emmie lately,' he blurted. 'I mean . . .'

She stood silent for a moment, her eyes on her hands, her fingers twisting her ring.

'Emmie's a nice girl,' she said. 'I've always liked Emmie.'

He hugged her, held her tight.

'There's just one thing,' she said. 'Later if . . . you know, if you don't . . .' She paused. 'No, not now. I'll say it later. It's too soon.'

'Tell me now.'

She touched his hand. 'No. No. Later.'

Ten

He recognised the voice immediately.

'Shara. What's up?'

'Wil's been kicked by a horse and he wants to see you.'

'Christ.'

'Yeah. He's in hospital with internal bruising. Something about the liver capsule or God knows.' She gave a long sniff. 'He's a mess, Rob, a real mess.' He could see her, a small bedraggled creature, all toughness gone. 'When can you get down?'

'This weekend,' he said hoping he could and how much was the fare and what did the old man want and God, let me get there.

'I'll meet you.'

'Thanks.'

*

The local hospital was threatened with closure. The words were seen and heard often in the media, discussed and repeated throughout the country; small hospitals, freezing works which had ceased to be viable, sheltered workshops, psychiatric units and small country schools were all at risk and some were threatened with closure. The phrase was loaded. It had a ring, a plangent echo like 'shallow grave', or 'ageing Skyhawks', or 'God's Own Country'.

There had been a stay of execution on this one. Locals had marched, politicians had arrived, drunk tea on television and departed. Wilfred greeted him with news from the front. The head doctor, the man he was under, a man who had his letters from Bombay, had told him. The proposed closures were mad. Stark staring raving mad. 'He says at the end of the day we'll all be on the road with our gall-bladders or hips or whatever looking for a bed. Ranfurly to Balclutha, Balclutha to God knows where.' Wilfred paused briefly. 'God, it's hot in here. And how are you, Tom? How are you?' The old man lay alone in a four-bed ward, his legs moving irritably beneath a cotton blanket. 'Take it off man, take it off. The heat's killing me. And sit down. I've something to tell you.' He stretched, blew out slowly. 'Now don't you worry about what Shara says. I'm OK. Just give me a week or two. Bloody sore at the time, I don't mind telling you. Got me right in the slats but I'm better now.

'Lucky Shara was there though. We were up the back cleaning out the race again. Needn't have taken the horses, just as easy have gone in the truck. Easier. Flat as a pancake out there but they get too frisky if they're not ridden. Frisky's right. I didn't know old Bess had it in her. Thought I was a goner at first.'

He puffed again, a long careful release of air. He was very pale, the skin round the mouth yellow and waxy. Even his eyes seemed paler.

What did the doctors say? Was he in pain?

An impatient movement of the legs. 'Yeah, yeah. Now shut up eh. I've got something to tell you.' The head turned. 'Where you staying?'

'Round the corner.'

'I'll get Shara to bring it down tonight then.' An ambulance wailed, was silent, then sped away ululating. If Emmie had been here he would have said it. She liked the weird ones. Wil looked at him, a quick nervous slide of his eyes.

'Haven't got that tape thing have you, Tom?'

'Rob.'

'Doesn't matter. Doesn't matter a fish's tit. Now listen. And no bloody tape recorder.'

Two nurses chattered past the window, their hair snarling and tugging in the wind. One carried a sharp-edged guitar, white and gold and spiky. She stopped suddenly, roared 'Eeelaine' into the wind and hurried on.

'I'm not going to cark or anything,' snapped Wil as though it had been Rob's idea and a useless one at that. 'It's not that. Funny you know. I never felt, all that time we were charging backwards and forwards across the desert, after Minguar Qaim, at Alamein even. Mates, good cobbers, men I'd known all my life being scuppered all round me and the Brits as well, fried alive in their tanks often enough. And never, not once, not at any moment of any day or night did I think I'd cop it. It just didn't occur to me.' His brow was furrowed. He didn't want his listener to get the wrong impression. 'Not courage. It wasn't that. I just knew I'd come home and I did, and Dorrie'd gone like I said.' He paused. Wil's surprised acknowledgement of the prospect of his own mortality filled the room.

Rob watched the pale blue curtains stirring above the old-fashioned radiator as the old man hunted up the words. He had time to note similar ones tracking between the beds for privacy, and a cardboard urinal to hand.

'That's why,' said Wil finally, 'that's why it knocked the stuffing out of me. I don't mean Bess kicking me in the gut or wherever, that goes without saying. Ever been kicked by a horse? Don't bother. A bugger like I said but it was later, when they'd had a look and said I'd probably be OK, that I thought about things. It wasn't till then that I thought Jeeze I could've gone, and I'm not getting any younger either. I don't mind telling you, it made me think. So I told young Shara to get on to you and tell you to come.' He reached for a glass of water. Rob, like all sickbed visitors, leaped to help and was dismissed. Wil leaned back. 'Where was I?'

'Telling me to come.'

'And you came.'

They grinned at each other, the slow accepting grin of men with time to talk. Presumably it might all make sense eventually. All Robin could do was wait. The tea-wagon, manned by a diminutive tea-person in a pink gauze headdress and sheepskin boots, rumbled to a halt at the end of the bed. 'Tea dear? Milk and sugar was it? All on our owny-oh today are we? Never mind, you've got a visitor, that's something. Good as gold then.' She retreated, backing and filling the clumsy wooden crate out the door with the precision of a truckie in a tight alley, then waved through glass.

Wil nodded. 'That's Betty, got a daughter married next week. They're all nice here. Two men even. But someone's always popping at you to do this, do that, get on a pan or wash or eat or whatever. Well, they have to, it's their job. But more than that. If you're not watching the bloody telly or listening to the radio or talking your head off they think Christ the poor old geezer's all on his own, better pop in. Why do they do that?'

'They think you're lonely.'

'On your own's not lonely.'

'Not if you mean to be.'

'That's right. You've got it, you've got it in one.' Wil, overcome with excitement at anyone understanding what he was on about, moved too quickly and winced with pain. 'Can't move. Hard to remember that.'

Rob stowed the empty cup on the locker behind the urinal. 'What did you want to see me about, Wil?'

'I told you, this cock-up's got me thinking. All those years ago when Alice asked me and I promised her I would—and I meant it. Of course I meant it. But I hated that bitch so much I thought I'll

216

leave it hoping she'd die and then I wouldn't have to deal with her. And now she has and I still haven't done anything.' Wil turned his head, his face puzzled. 'You ever hated anyone? Personally I mean.'

There is always this compulsion towards truth. Not virtue, there is no virtue in fussing about shades of meaning; nevertheless he did not hate Murray, he merely despised the man. He preferred to be where Murray was not. Murray brought him out in a rash. 'No,' he said.

'No. Me neither till her. Not even the Jerries. Not like that I mean. You have to when you're killing them of course. But personally. And I've never even seen the woman.' Wil rubbed a button on his striped pyjamas, examined it thoughtfully. 'You know curses?' he said suddenly.

'Curses?'

'Real curses. Damn your eyes. Rot in hell. What if there was one and they did? Think about it.' Wil was silent; the skin stretched tight across the beak of his nose gleamed yellow and waxy. The eyes were far away, the hands clenched. 'I hope there is. I hope there is for that one.' His voice was fierce and strong. 'Rot in hell,' he said.

God in heaven. Candida *Bowman*?

Wil leaned his head back on pillows, his eyes now on the peg-board acoustic tiles of the ceiling. 'I want you to contact Alice's girl for me,' he said. 'I can't leave it any longer.'

The skin on the back of his neck was crawling, his heart still. 'Alice's girl?'

'Yes.'

How in the world, the whole flaming world, had he not guessed?

'What's her name?'

The head did not move. 'Emmeline. Emmeline O'Malley she called her. The bitch wouldn't even let the child keep Alice's name. What's the difference between O'Leary and O'Malley? Six of one and half a dozen of the other but that was the point, to my mind. It was nothing but spite. That's the difference. Sinful, vicious spite, another way to break Alice, and by Christ it damn near did when she found out. Not at first, I don't mean, when Candida said she'd mind the child. Alice was grateful then. Grateful beyond words. She said so. Told me night after night as we lay together. What else could she have done at the time except kill herself and Micks were funny about that then. And besides there was the child.'

It was a long story. It went on for a long time with diversions and rethinks and thoughts of no relevance at all. The Western Desert reappeared, a ferry trip when he was a boy, the celebration in the back of the local butcher's shop the night he and Ivy heard about the Rehab farm ballot and how the hams had dripped fat when things hotted up. Both Ivy and Doris, Rob learned, were buried in the Ranfurly cemetery but fortunately there was no plot reserved for him and what did it matter anyhow.

The meal trolley was clanking down the corridor smelling of fish pie and hot metal when Rob walked out to the empty car park and the cold blaze of the stars.

He refused to go back that night. 'There's all day tomorrow,' he said, avoiding any mention of possible exhaustion.

The story rolled on next day, shunting into byways or steaming ahead until darkness. There were few names to remember and Robin did not miss the tape recorder.

Alice Amy O'Leary was born near Woodstock in Vermont in one of those villages you see pictures of in the autumn with sugar maples and clapboard houses and that and bloody cold in the winter with barns built for snow to fall off. Houses are built right in the woods with no fences seemingly, but then the trees are deciduous over there and it's blazing hot in the summer.

She was an only child, Alice, only child of—names've gone, doesn't matter. Her father ran a general store, one of those country stores with everything, you see pictures of them now as if it was history, but I can remember the same round here. Wood floors, all wood, clothes, longjohns, boots, dry goods, drench, stuff for miles. Lots in bulk then, all weighing and wrapping and tying up. People took a pride in it. Huge roll of brown paper, string, knots; quick-fingered you had to be then.

He died young, her father. I don't know when, but Alice and her Mum carried on running the store. Alice'd be good at it too. She was quick with sums, checked her change quick as a flash. Well you have to if you've any sense, but lots don't, they haven't the head for it. But she did and ran the farm books for me later and what a joy that was. I'll show you a photo of her then when I get home. All in white with her hair tied back. Long hair. That'd be the forties. Her mother was widowed by then. And the men were away, lots of them at the end, and soon after this Edwin Calder came home again. He was some sort of war hero from the Normandy landings and he was well-heeled as well. That made it harder for her later. There was this feeling about that she'd done pretty well for herself. She was twenty-five by then and a quiet girl and a country store didn't add up the same as Calder and Calder who'd been attorneys since the *Mayflower*, to hear them talk.

His mother wasn't keen, Alice said, but again that wasn't all. There was another reason why Alice felt it was her fault. She felt she hadn't loved him enough. Not the old gut-slammer, the ball-squeezer, know what I mean? But it was a long time ago. In those days if you didn't get married in Vermont by the time you were thirty you had to go and hide under the bed for the rest of your life she said. She was funny too about cheerleaders. She said she could kick high enough and her face was OK but her fanny lacked oomph. She told me see, she told me everything. Everything about her I wanted to know, and the same with her and me.

So she married Edwin Calder when he qualified and joined his father and his dead grandfather and Calder and Calder was motoring again. Seen a photo of him? Yes, well you see what I mean, and it was worse when he started drinking. One of the few things about the man was his war record. I've seen that round here. Everywhere. It's understandable mind, some returned man takes to booze and the wife feels that she wasn't there and how would she know and the poor devil's having nightmares and trying to bayonet the enemy in bed night after night. All that and not loving him enough. If she had she could have helped him, that's what she felt anyway. Don't ask me why.

And it got worse. We all know boozers, seen the poor buggers at it, who hasn't. And it got worse, of course it got worse. They had some grand wedding presents, glass bowls and crystal and that, and one night he came back blind and biffed the lot at a wall and asked her next morning what she'd done to them.

And then there was the business of no children and him roaring and screaming about the bloody House of Calder or whatever and her having every test under the sun. And finally the doctor said he couldn't do any more until Edwin was tested and that went down like a lead balloon as you can imagine, but he was and it was his fault all right and that finished him she said. Mind you he wouldn't admit it, and he'd be buggered if he was going to stand with his balls in cold water like the quack suggested, and he certainly wouldn't take on another man's bastard by adopting and by this time Alice could see that it was no place for a child anyhow.

Why did she stay? Yes well. Why do they? It was being sorry for him almost if you like, grieving for the man. For his nerve which had gone and his dry balls and his rage which had stayed. But I agree. Why? Why the bloody hell do they? Pride as well of course. The only person she told was that woman, her best friend—kicked the bottom of each other's cots out they had, that sort of friendship which had gone on for ever. So she told Candida Bowman who said leave him immediately, and so she should have. I'll give the bitch that. Alice never told her mother. She couldn't tell the poor old lady who was a real mess by now, what with arthritis and heart. Why worry her? What could she do? No one could do anything but Alice herself and she knew it.

Before that, well before that, long before she was married, she'd published those poems and he'd never once mentioned them so she knew he wasn't exactly interested. So she kept it secret when she started up with the stories. She sat beside him night after night with him coming back more and more glassy-eyed every time he pretended to go to the toilet which was often, until finally he fell asleep with his mouth open, drunk as a skunk and she could creep off to bed praying he wouldn't follow her. She told me; the watching and waiting, how it destroys you. Not the body, the mind. Fear is like ants, she said. Carting your will away grain by grain like ants with a dead moth. So what she did, or what she tried to do rather, was to sign off and write things in her head. Poetry was too hard she said. But she could think about her people, get them moving in her head. She'd sit there quiet as a brown mouse waiting for him to flake out, and in the morning when he'd gone she'd get them down on paper, or try to.

Her stories would never have been published mind, if it hadn't been for Emmeline's father—though he wasn't that then, of course. This'd be more like the mid-fifties and Emmeline wasn't born till sixty. Stephen Gilchrist was his name. He's dead now, long gone, but he was a decent enough man she said, though Christ, I think that's pushing it. Younger than Alice, just a kid, but married already; one of those rush jobs and two kids already and a pathetic little bunch of a wife. He was a law clerk in Calder and bloody Calder and wrote poetry in his spare time. Though what spare time he'd had in that set-up God knows, let alone at home. But they used to talk together at office dos about poetry and stuff, not that they had the chance often in that outfit, which was mean as cat shit. Alice said it was just loneliness at first, and probably would have stayed that way, them both being so trapped and so sort of defeated. But then Edwin went to New York for some law deal and Alice and Stephen became lovers and Stephen sent the stories off and they were accepted.

And then she found she was pregnant. Ask yourself. At first she didn't tell Stephen. Well you can guess why, and yes you're right. Because she knew what he'd do. She knew he would panic and by God he did, though mind you he was in a mess, I'll say that, two kids and a third on the way and the junior partner's wife in trouble in a firm like that in the fifties. They'd have eaten him raw so he scarpered. Took to his heels and ran and sent for his wife and kids later. And all this time Alice went on writing. Bitter stuff, as you can see, and why not? How she did it at all God knows, but then again we're all different and she said otherwise she would have gone completely flyblown. She got that one from me. I'm not proud of it mind, especially when you've seen the real thing. The Maoris have a better word for mental illness—porangi—in the dark. Benighted. But she liked it. The tougher, the more basic the word was, the more she seemed to like it for herself, know what I mean?

'Yes.'

It was different when she knew she was pregnant. Then she said it was survival. Survival for her child and herself and she turned to Candida Bowman.

Of course she would never have got away with it if Edwin hadn't packed up in London that time like I told you, and been away for so long. I think maybe she'd got sort of punch drunk by then. One foot in front of the other waiting for whatever was going to happen. And one thing was certain and that soon. She'd got past panicking. She moved in with the Bowman woman and lived in a sort of dream and walking for miles. All this she told me. Ever read the second one? That tells you something. *The Hand of Time*. Yes. It's grim but you can see that one's more . . . well hopeful. It's the only one to my mind that gets better towards the end. Ends better. She said Candida minded her, cared for her, couldn't have been kinder, she said. And then one day she handed Alice a piece of paper all typed out neat as a pin, and left for work. She ran a specialist plant nursery. Carnations, I think it was. Here, this is what I told you about yesterday. Shara brought it in last night. You can see how old it is.

THINK ABOUT IT.
1. The baby is due next month.
2. Either Edwin will be
    a) Home
    b) Coming soon
    c) Dead
There are no other alternatives.

3. In a), b) you cannot keep this child, and you can't bank on c).
THINK ABOUT IT.

SO   *4. Possible alternatives after the birth:*
        a) The child is put up for adoption.
        b) The child goes into a state home.
        c) You run away with your illegitimate child.
   5.   *a) and b) are self-explanatory.*
        c) requires clarification.
        How can you support a child? You have No money, No
        qualifications and No home.
   6. What other alternatives are there?
THINK ABOUT IT.
Someone has to.

Alice told me she sat reading and rereading the piece of paper till the words blurred. She could remember the pattern the words made, the gaps between the lines. She was in shock or something. All this, all this she told me, and more.

So Bowman came back from work happy as a clam, all smiles and pink about the edges and asked Alice what she had thought of the document. And Alice said she had found it interesting and had Candida any suggestions to make herself, because if not she thought it was one of the most vicious things she had ever seen, and the fact that every word was true did not alter that in any way whatsoever.

So Bowman takes off her boots and curls up and tells Alice that 4a was the only possible option and she has given the matter a lot of thought and it was no use Alice sitting around like a stranded whale with its eyes shut. She, Candida, would take the child after it was born and bring it up and when Edwin died, as he must soon by all accounts, Alice could move in and they would all live together.

Alice said No. She said No for a month. She went on and on and on saying no till the bitch wore her down. She had the power see. There's always one that's got the power, say what you like, and this time it was Bowman. She made promises. She wouldn't bring the child up as her own. She promised that. She would never pretend it was hers. She would be a foster parent, a foster aunt. What sort of life would the child have otherwise, she said, an illegitimate, a byblow trailing around after a New England vagrant? Who would mind it while Alice worked? What would she work at? What was she qualified for? All that. You can imagine and still Alice said No. And then she gave in. Quite suddenly, and later even when she lay with the child in her arms she still knew she had to. They didn't know then, all this stuff they go on about now how even a half-dead mess of a mother is better for the child than anyone else, and if you ask me there's a lot of muddled thinking going on there too, but how would I know? So Alice gave in. Candida had a bit of money coming from her grandmother, her garden business was doing OK and she would put in a manager for a while. Alice could see the child, though not too much as it would be unsettling and when Edwin died they would all live together, and that couldn't be long the way he was killing himself, like I said.

So Alice signed. She signed the adoption papers and collapsed next day. She was mad she said, completely deranged. Cold and shivering and out of her mind. Things you couldn't imagine giving a thought to tore her apart. A packet of peppercorns she'd taken by mistake from a store counter years ago and what could she do? She'd taken them back at once but the person who had paid for them had left the store and would be missing them and Alice didn't know her name even, or where she lived, and what could she do. She could still remember years later, when we were tucked up in bed together she could remember every minute of it all. How she couldn't sleep, she wouldn't eat, she tried to cut her wrists and made a mess of it.

And in some weird way that saved her. Well, obviously it did, she felt if she was so useless she couldn't even kill herself then she bloody well deserved to have to live. And you can see that in her books can't you? Certainly the last two, *All Fall Down* and *The Load.*

But always she knew she would have her daughter with her eventually, and that's the bit that doesn't show up in the books to my mind. You get the loss all right, I reckon, but no hope except in *The Hand of Time*. I read them and read them but I don't get that feeling in the last two, not the hope. Survival. Acceptance even. Stoicism? Yeah, that's there too, sure, I agree. You've put your finger on it. But it doesn't add up though. Not to my mind, because why doesn't the hope show up in them? It was what kept her going she said, the hope of being with her child. That and her writing. It makes you think, doesn't it? Gawd, I wouldn't know the sub-conscious if I met it in the street, but it makes you think. Did she have some sort of premonition or what?

The first shock, and even then she didn't see through the bitch, was when Candida said she and Emmeline were going to New Zealand. The climate was good the woman said, and the soil, and her grandmother's money had come through and she was going to New Zealand to start her own plant nursery, which she never did nor intended to if you ask me. She told Alice she had always wanted to leave New England, and land was cheap here, and with the climate, well, why not now she had the chance.

By this time Edwin was back home and completely dependent on Alice. She shut off, she said, detached herself, went through the motions, put him back in bed when he fell out, cleaned up after him and you can imagine that too. He was pathetic she said, though I'm damned if I'd have seen it. He wasn't violent now, just a complete wreck, a wreck of what had once been some sort of man. He scarcely knew her half the time, stared through her like glass, she said.

Sure, sure, why didn't she leave the man when her child was here and waiting? You tell me. You're the smart one. You tell me. Pity? Yeah, plus guilt I reckon. Even though she thought, even though she tried to convince herself, *knew* she had done the right thing, millions of women have half starved themselves to support their kids and done so. Maybe that was it. Maybe she thought she hadn't had the guts, had given in because she was feeble, had taken the easy way out. Hadn't had the courage. That was one bit we didn't talk about. Perhaps because she knew I'd have loved a child, but that's easy for me to say. Perhaps that was it. I don't know, I just don't know. It was part of the pact with Bowman too, though that wouldn't have kept me back for a second. I'd have been up there like a robber's dog. I don't know.

She was told, allowed, mind, to write to Emmeline no more than once a week. Any more, the woman said, and it would be unsettling. When the child could write there'd be two or three letters a year. Little formal things. Thank you for my birthday present. It has been raining here. Photos? What photos? She didn't say. There weren't any with the letters. I told you about the letters. I told you just now. The unopened ones. I did. I said. All right, all right, I'll tell you again.

When Edwin died she sent off a letter that very day to say she was coming. She told me. 'He is dead. I'm coming.' That's Alice. She never messed about. Straight as a die. Make you laugh, wouldn't it, if it didn't make you bucket. I can see her writing it. He is dead. I am coming. Wacko! So she came straight out. And when she left Seatoun, when she was thrown out on the street with no child and dead as mutton because nothing could touch her or matter ever again, you know what that bitch did? She gave Alice a cardboard box and said you might as well have these and the taxi drove off to the airport and Bowman walked back up her drive.

Alice didn't open the box till they were well up—over the Kaikouras, she said it was, all that snow. And inside the box was every letter or card she'd ever sent Emmeline since she was a little tot and every one unopened. All those years and the kid had never had a glimpse of one except for presents. Think about it. Kids love things with their names on, love them long before they can read. I've seen it. Bowman must've been pretty quick off the mark, pretty cunning to beat a kid to the mail year after year. That's what gets me. Not only what she did, but the viciousness, the spite. Never a thought to tell Alice before. I know why she did it, she did it because she was the victor and she'd won and she wanted every twist of the bayonet. I've done it and I know. The twist is part of it. She wanted death, not walking wounded.

It was Central that saved Alice. And me she said, but I don't know. And the dogs. She had her own dog you know. Yes. Real little goer he was too. A huntaway, couldn't see him for smoke.

Why didn't she go to court? Work it out man. Use your loaf. What chance did she have? This was sixty-nine remember. She had signed the papers, Emmeline was adopted. It was all legal. Oh, she begged, of course she begged, she damn near destroyed herself. Saw a Wellington lawyer who wasn't hopeful, and begged Bowman some more. Just to be able to *stay*. That was the arrangement. And there was another thing. A thing she didn't tell me till much later. A thing she told me only to stop me storming up and clobbering the bitch and bringing the kid back to her mother, legal or not legal.

Christ, it's hot in here.

She said the kid didn't like her. That was what finished it. If there had been any spark, anything other than obvious dislike . . . It wasn't only that Emmeline wasn't interested, why should she be? What's an unknown woman to an eight-year-old. And she was unknown. There was no photo of her in the house that Alice could see. Obviously no one had talked about nice Alice in Vermont and how Emmeline would like her and what fun she was. And here was another card for her, look, with her own name on it—love from Alice. And that's another thing doesn't add up. Alice *was* fun. Not at first my word, not at all, but even then she had a quickness. She noticed. Later we'd roll about. It must've been there. It's in the letters. You see it a bit in the poems but the laughs got knocked out of her and the breakdown didn't help. That's no fun believe me. I've seen it in the desert. Men half out of their minds and not a scratch on them. You're lucky if you can sign off, and that's what Alice did when she saw the unopened letters.

And Emmeline was happy in Seatoun, Alice could see that. It's a nice place she said, beach and that, and the woman, whenever she did write which wasn't often, told Alice about the good school and how Emmeline had lots of friends and was happy as a Cape Cod clam. And she certainly seemed happy according to Alice, one of those skinny kids always jumping about the place and her father's red hair. Quick on her feet, you know the sort, and by this time there was ballet as well, though what the hell that had to do with the price of fish is beyond me. But all this, all this added up, and what with the kid not liking her as well . . .

No, I don't know why the kid took against her, not really. But then again maybe I do. Alice had no fear, not physical fear. I've seen her eyeball a bull, a great thundering Hereford, and get herself back to the fence cool as you please. It wasn't that. But when she got nervous she tried too hard, know what I mean? She sort of pushed things. She talked too much and her hands were all over the place and she went on and on. Well, a lot of people won't shut up, I could show you a couple of real snorters round here, but it was different to that. She only did it when she was nervous, not like old Don down the road who can't even pour a drink when he's talking. Stand there with the bottle in his hand and your tongue hanging out and on and on till you could throttle the man.

No. Hers was different. It was nerves, it only happened when she wasn't easy. At ease. At the races say, or Dalgety's tent at the Show—somewhere else where she didn't feel at home, didn't feel easy in herself. And I can see her, that's the tragedy. I can see her putting the kid off and longing to be liked and trying harder and harder, and laughing too much maybe, or not enough, and making it worse. There was too much at stake. And she couldn't take her eyes off Emmeline she told me, the way the child moved, and everything got worse and worse and things got tougher with the bitch saying she'd fight every inch of the way and that Alice hadn't an iceball's chance in Hades, and what did she want to do to the child? Did she want to destroy her own child? Take her away from her security and happiness? And there was Alice getting more desperate every day and more shy until she would've put anyone off, let alone a bright sparky kid like Emmeline. What could Alice do? Cut her in half like Solomon? I always thought that was one of the dumbest stories I've ever read, even for the Bible. What would anyone want with half a child, mother or no mother.

I told you she'd changed Emmeline's surname to O'Malley. Yes.

By deed poll. Alice didn't even know that till she arrived in New Zealand. She went butcher's. Well, wouldn't you? Gave the woman both barrels, told her what she thought of her and how she couldn't believe it, let alone understand it. And you know what the woman said. She just smiled and said she didn't have to understand it. It was done and that was that. O'Leary to O'Malley. So near. Why not O'Connell or O'Riley or any damn thing, not Irish at all? I'll tell you why. The nearer it was the worse, don't you reckon? More rub-your-nose-in-it if you see what I mean. And my God Alice saw pretty damn quick.

Suspicions before she came out? Well there you go. Did she? If it'd been me I damn well would've. As I said I'd have been here in a flash years before, but I think there were two things. I think that she just went on day after day cleaning up after Edwin and knowing that her child was happy and she would be with her one day. And the other thing was that she trusted Candida bloody Bowman. She had ever since they were kids, she said. She was straight like Alice, and you know what some kids are like, especially girls, well they were in my day. Sneaky often. But Candida never was. One day somebody wrote Fuck on the blackboard and the whole class was kept in and finally Candida got sick of it and said she'd done it when she hadn't. She'd just got sick of it, know what I mean? Kids don't usually do that. Not when it's the strap, or not in my day.

Maybe she'd made up her mind, made up her mind even as a kid that she didn't give a stuff what anyone thought of her, that she'd play it her way. Maybe it was that and good luck to her, except for what she did to Alice. But surely Alice should have realised? That's what gets me. But then again if you trust you trust, if you don't you don't, and I'll tell you something else. You don't have to like people to trust them, and the other way round as well. And Alice admired her; not giving a damn about what she looked like, not giving a damn what anyone thought, being so independent, making her own life. Alice fluffing about with poetry and books and Candida getting on with what she wanted to do, which was grow things and to hell with the rest. She knew the woman was honest. Except you know something? Probably you haven't noticed but I've read them so often now, thought about them for years, especially the last two. Why does she go on about betrayal? Sure you can say it was Stephen, but you know what I think? I think she was preparing herself—no not that—more stiffening herself in case. Does that make sense? Well, I'm glad you think so.

And added to that there were the other things. So few letters came back to Alice and what there were from Candida so wooden, and the same from the kid. That would have been Candida, see. No little kid's going to love someone they never see unless someone tells them about that person are they? Let alone her hiding the letters. Someone who shows photos, talks. This is Nana, this is Pop, this is Alice who loves you. It's a two-way plug to my mind. I see that with nieces and nephews.

Yeah, I agree. You wouldn't think that after all she'd been through she'd have left it like that again but I saw her, and yes I can imagine, and it'd break your bloody heart. She thought it was best for her child.

It all came to a head when Emmeline had gone on to ballet from school one afternoon and the two of them were at it hammer and tongs all day and finally Alice dashed out the door and that was it. The bitch had won and Alice came south the next day.

'I saw her.'

'How d'you mean?'

'I saw her that day. I was about six but I've never forgotten. I lived next door to Emmie and Miss Bowman.'

'You never did.'

'I still do. Well, my mother does.'

Wil's grin was wide and slow.

'Then you know Emmeline! What's she like?'

Rob's head moved. 'Fantastic.'

Wil was moving too quickly, grimacing with pain and excitement. 'Bring her down man. Bring her down soon.'

'I'd like to a lot but . . .'

'But what?'

Use your head man, rub a few memories together. Here is a woman who longs to know who her mother was, who disliked her the only time she saw her as much as Alice thought she did if not more, and who loved and admired Miss Bowman. The woman who had devoted her life to her, had brought her up, encouraged her, given her freedom. He saw the bundled figures biking towards the Seatoun tunnel through the years, the corn popping, the food, Emmie's grin. This is the woman you're going to rip apart in front of her. Turn her into a monster.

No. And Emmie won't believe you or me.

'Emmeline loved Miss Bowman very much,' he said.

'That's because she doesn't know what she was like.'

'She would never believe you. Never in a million years.'

And God knows what I believe. Things had become chaotic. His mind was spinning, heading for white water on a leaking raft. The session, the revelations, the call for attendance at the sick bed had all promised good things. Things of meaty goodness on which to chew. Things which had in fact been provided and had turned into red toadstools with spots.

'She had wanted to come in August,' he said. 'Very much.'

'Well, then?'

He looked the patient straight in the eye. 'She loved Miss Bowman and you're right, her mother worried her. OK Alice was wonderful. OK she could write. OK you loved her. That doesn't alter Emmie's reaction and why should it?'

'I'm going to tell her.'

'You won't. I'll break it to her. I'll tell her about . . .'

'What the hell's it got to do with you?'

'She's my . . .' His tongue was wide; there was too much of it, thick as a cow's. 'I love her,' he said.

'Ah, so that's it then. You love her so that's all hunky dory and the truth can go out the window. The big straw boss can shield his girl. What about my girl! What about Alice? She's dead. She doesn't matter! Well, she matters to me, get it. You're happy to flag away the rest. Happy to have her daughter think she didn't care, didn't give a stuff and dumped her?'

Rob was overheated, stupid, infuriated by sense. 'She did,' he muttered.

Wilfred ignored the pain. 'Get out.' He grabbed the grey cardboard urinal and threatened barrel first. 'Get out.'

Robin stood, took the thing from the shaking hand and put it on the floor. 'Sorry, that was stupid.'

'Just bugger off will you.'

You could have killed him. You realise that. You realise he's right. You realise Emmie will have to know everything and Emmie will hate you and Emmie will never believe you because Emmie is steel from Toledo or wherever the fuck it comes from.

The old man was chewing, gnashing, glaring into his face. 'Oh, sit down you stupid bastard,' he said.

'Why didn't you tell me all this the first time I came down?'

'I told you. I kept hoping the bitch would die and I wouldn't have to deal with her.'

'You knew she was dead.'

The eyebrows wouldn't have it. 'No.'

This is where it gets tricky. His mind goes sailing along, rational, convincing, authoritative, then slips a memory cog, a cog which was operational five minutes ago and leaves you floundering. Rob/Tom, that's nothing, but the occasional unpredictable lapse . . .

'I know you did,' he said.

Wilfred switched tracks.

'Well, OK, OK. Maybe I didn't trust you then and I'm not as honest as Alice was. The odd lies never worried me. And how did I know I could trust you coming out of nowhere like that? There've been others sniffing about. Weird-looking types, all jeans and dirty hair.'

Rob grinned. 'When did the light dawn?'

Wil chewed on it for a minute and let it pass. 'It was more Bess and the kick. Ever been kicked by a horse?'

He shook his head.

'Nasty. Very nasty. It'd never happened to me before. Can kill a man any day. I was lucky, but like I said it shook me rigid and I thought Christ I'd better get on and find Emmeline before I snuff it.' The voice became petulant. 'I told you all that.'

'Tell me again about why Alice stopped writing,' said Robin, his voice gentle to disguise cunning.

'I told you all that. God, don't you remember anything? She didn't need it. She said.'

Researchers can be honest too. 'I can't believe that.'

'Nor can I sometimes, now I read them all the time but I didn't read them much before. It's only in the last ten years . . .' Wil stretched his legs gingerly to the end of the bed. 'Nearer fifteen since she died.'

'So it wasn't being stuck in the ooloo with Wilfred Q. Hughes?'

There was a gleam in the eyes, a recognition. 'What do you reckon?'

Rob shook his head. 'I don't know. I just don't know.'

'There's a hell of a lot you don't know if you ask me.'

The prescribed pills were being handed out in minuscule white origami containers; the blinds were drawn as they shook hands.

'Bring her down, boy. Bring her down and I'll give her the letters.'

It would be so easy to say yes. So easy to flannel and much kinder. 'I'll try. I'll work it out. I can't promise.'

'Promise nothing. Just do it, you drongo. Or I'll come up.'

Rob lay tossing on his hired bed, aware that he was being ridiculous, that he was behaving like some goddamned insomniac in a TV ad before his partner tiptoes smiling through the night to his side with the product and the glass of water and they flash their love across the covers and don't have to say a thing. They have the cure. Unlike him. He was a fully paid-up participant in a moral dilemma and unable to sleep. He flung himself on his back and went through it again.

There was no dilemma for Wilfred, who had loved his wife. He was an honourable man who had lied to him and why not. He had never clapped eyes on Robin before, didn't know him and disliked both smart-arses and sniffers. They were town men for starters.

No problem either for Emmeline. She knew right from wrong and was amoral which was an oxymoron. No, no, a paradox, get it right you fool, and that isn't right either because you can sleep around, not that she does now, and still be good as gold and moral means virtuous in general conduct, as she is, as well as concerned with the rules of conventional morality which she is not. She has moral courage and it is a moral certainty that she will hate me for ever if/when . . .

She will undoubtedly shoot the messenger.

He turned on the light, turned it off. Life had not prepared him for this but then what could have. Only sons of widowed mothers are not trained for this sort of thing. He could blame his mother. Release the Inner Child. Oh fuck.

Any decision, he had read recently in some corporate management magazine, was better than none. This statement, slipped among comments on front-end evaluation and income projections and an advertisement for a new voice-mail recruitment service, had surprised him. Wasn't the decision to make no decision at that point in time a decision within the meaning of the act? A decision per se to defer the big one, the hot potato, the bottom-liner to another point in time at the end of the day. And if not why not? Perhaps if he could write it down. Tabulate. He put out a leg, pulled it back.

Go to sleep you drongo. A good word, drongo. I am indebted to Mr Wilfred Q. Hughes for his permission to use the word drongo. I am indebted to Ms Emmeline O'Malley, O'Leary, for her interest in the word ululate. Would Emmie come creeping to him, smiling through the night with soporifics? Probably not, thank God. The sky was lightening beyond the thin curtains. He could get up.

The airport was not busy. A ring of men and women stood staring at a cardboard container in the foyer, their faces thoughtful as cows ringed around a still-smoking meteorite. The box had contained cheese and said so.

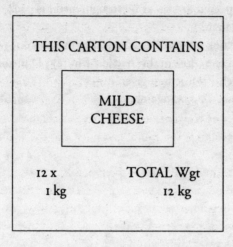

THIS CARTON CONTAINS

MILD
CHEESE

12 x   TOTAL Wgt
1 kg   12 kg

A man cradling a bike helmet gave a yap of laughter. 'Perhaps it's a bomb,' he said.

'Reuben, come here at once,' yelled a woman in a pink tracksuit. A teenager in a T-shirt labelled CREW lifted a downy upper lip and stayed. 'Rube!' she yelled again. 'You want to get blown up or something?' Rube shrugged and sauntered away, his muscular buttocks rolling with contempt.

'Can't be a bomb,' said Robin. 'It's open.'

He looked again at the label. Twelve times one kilo equals total weight twelve kilos. That made sense. Perhaps he could use the format for finding the solution. Robin shook his head. It was not funny and it never had been and there was something wrong with his gut too. Maybe he had picked up a little bug as Eileen would say.

He swung his leg and kicked the empty carton high in the air as the herd scattered.

A young Maori standing beside him dropped an eyelid. 'Easy to shift, eh. Must be a little Pakeha bugger.' He dropped his pack and took a leisurely drop-kick at the box which sailed towards the automatic doors. They opened obediently and sighed to a close behind it.

The guy peered at him as he straightened his pack.

'You OK man?'

He must look a mess. 'Me? Yeah, I'm fine thanks, yeah.'

There was one comfort. He had lost Murray's Dunedin telephone number which Emmie had given him.

'Yeah. Fine,' he said again.

Eleven

Emmeline was gathering momentum, spiralling into storm. 'I told you not to go. I said. I said leave the poor old guy alone. You go there and dig up all this mess and expect me . . .' She was tense with rage, flinging her disbelief in his teeth and his little bug and hating him.

As he had known she would.

'No!' she said.

He had prepared his case with care, had sat for hours in front of the computer getting the chronology right, sorting and dividing the evidence, correlating the events of Alice's life with the echoes from her books and his memories of Miss Bowman and the woman with the coiled hair weeping. He was going to be calm. Tactful. On Emmeline's side as always.

He resorted to cheese-carton graphics, fiddled about with arrows in an attempt to induce thought.

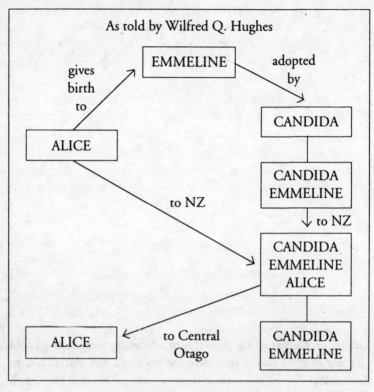

As told by Wilfred Q. Hughes

EMMELINE

gives birth to

adopted by

ALICE

CANDIDA

to NZ

CANDIDA EMMELINE

to NZ

CANDIDA EMMELINE ALICE

ALICE

to Central Otago

CANDIDA EMMELINE

Which they did and were no help. The final version would demonstrate one thing and one thing only to Emmeline. Alice had abandoned her twice. He could hear the rage—the flashing eyes, the floating hair. Betrayed! Who says she was betrayed? Even if it's true, all your dinky little diagram shows is my so-called mother loved me so much she dumped me a second time. No! I'll take Aunt.

And what other words were there? Abandoned. Left. Ditched. Went south up Central. You say she loved me. So why did she go?

Because she loved you.

He decided against the diagram.

The time charts were easier.

1947, 1948   Poems.
1953   Alice marries Edwin.
   Meets Stephen.
1956   *The White Mountain and Other Stories.*
   Inscribed: *For Candida.*
   Images of locks, wrong keys etc. Misfits. Minor disasters.
   Ellen Maybury's inflatable bra let her down. It burst on the Philadelphia flight. It was the pressure, the flight hostess explained. They should tell people.
1957   *The Mystic Scroll.*
   Inscribed: *For you.*
   Love is precious because it is rare and ephemeral and dies in the hand.
1957–59   Love affair with Stephen.
1959   *The Hand of Time.*
   Inscribed: *And again.*
   Finished while she was pregnant.
   It is best to face despair at an early age. It strengthens the heart muscles and the sky does not fall.
1960   Emmeline born.
   Adopted immediately by Miss Bowman. Emmeline's name changed to O'Malley after she and Miss Bowman reach New Zealand.
1962   *All Fall Down.*
   Inscribed: *No Words.*
   When babies open their mouths their gums are new and their teeth, they tell me, are pearls. They have not been here long.
1966   *The Load.*
   Inscribed: *Soon.*
   The bleakest of all.
   The Peaceable Kingdom is not to be found in family life.
   All grief is self-pity.

239

The book is the man, they said, the writer the work. How could they have been so simplistic, those erudite old guys, those pontificating dons, those precious belles-lettristes. So dismissive of imagination, of the creation of brave new worlds and splintered old ones.

And how do you go on T.S. Eliot then. What are your views, man, on the theory of impersonality. Let's hear it starting now for the Words on the Page Alone School of Modern Dance soon to be sashayed into the wings by the high-steppers of *nouvelle critique* and the rock 'em sock 'em finale, Death of the Author centre-stage.

Yet here he was like Cara before him, searching for babies overleaf, lovers between the lines and clues in everything.

But you have to believe in something do you not. Join some sort of dance, make some sort of decision or the bugaboo of consensus will get us all.

Alice had seen life clearly. She had looked into the goddamn pit and disliked what she saw and laughed the wrong laugh and her words stayed in the mind as did her characters. Aunt Eunice who had bought a new coat 'because she had several funerals coming up'. Her neighbour Darlene who fed her piranha fish spaghetti dipped in menstrual blood to cheer them up. The ratcatcher's astonishment when his wife left. *She didn't make the bed even, nor leave me no dinner neither.* Rats come in families so extermination takes seven days or more. *You just have to keep laying it down, ma'am, just keep laying it down. You'll get them in the end.*

The baby that had climbed up. Climbed way up the ladder and fallen on her poor baby head.

The old cop sighed. 'So how come the fingertip bruises on the backs of her poor baby knees?'

Both from her own words and from Wilfred's Robin knew Alice to be of equal fighting weight to her opponent, yet he had seen her despair; had witnessed the collapsed and broken house guest yet to receive Miss Bowman's *coup de grace* of the letters.

He tried this tack with Emmie, begged her to read the books again to find the woman. She refused. It was the last thing in the world she would do. 'But they are true, gutsy.' He held her arm, insisted. 'How can you not like them? They're you.'

She pulled away, rubbed the arm.

'I mean it,' he insisted. 'I promise.'

'Promise what?'

'You won't be happy till we sort this thing out and . . .'

'Oh, do belt up. I know you mean well but . . .'

'God in heaven, *mean* well.'

She grinned and held out her arms. Thin women's bodies are more interesting, he had always known it.

Their mouths were brushing, moving gentle as fish breathing water as Calvin appeared. He was not happy. His pants itched and Haden had got a hand gun.

Robin, overcome with love for all skinny redheads in the world, swung the child in the air.

She was reaching for her son with maternal advice. 'Hand guns are for thugs.'

Robin heaved the wriggling child higher. 'By the way I lost Murray's number, thank God. What's he doing down there anyhow?'

Her face did not change. 'Looking for a flat for next year.'

The flying feet were too near his glasses. 'Who's this Haden?' he asked quickly.

'Just Haden.'

'Has he a sister called Shelley?'

'Yeah, but she's a girl.'

They talked for hours that night. Robin encouraged her, guided her along the path he wished her to follow. He wanted her to take off on her own, to convince herself, to find the truth in his truth as his father had hoped with his mother and stamps and he with Lisa and the bush.

He had no illusions that Lisa would bless his union from beyond the grave. Stuff that John Middleton Murry crap and rightly so. He had loved Lisa, remembered her daily. She was a memory from another country where he had once loved and been happy and was grateful.

His thumb and finger tightened around his wedding ring. It was not as shiny now, a bit rubbed but still golden, still 'making a statement'. He saw Maureen fussing with her back-door key after Van Gogh. 'Not now. It's too soon. Later.' That was what she had been on about. Give me the wedding ring my daughter gave you any time you want to get shot of it, Robin. I would like to keep it now that it is no longer of any relevance to you.

Miss Bowman had undoubtedly been poured from steel.

Emmeline made it clear that she had no intention of changing the habits of a lifetime because Robin had a thing about clutter and horizontal surfaces. The front room was an exception largely because they seldom entered it. Smoke belched occasionally from the basket grate Miss Bowman had declined to use, billowed inwards like a lick of sea mist shrouding rocks. Everything else was the same; the lumpy curved reef of sofa and chairs, the rug, *The Old Shepherd's Chief Mourner, Napoleon*.

Rob nodded at the lowering face. 'Did you know he had a new chamois pocket sewn into his jacket each day so he could take snuff on horseback?'

She was drying her hair, her face hidden as she knelt, her voice muffled. 'Why is it everything you tell me is either mildly nuts or totally nuts or really interesting?'

He touched her hair. 'Don't ever get it cut.'

'OK.'

The fire was dying, the carton of red wine alongside approaching mulled wine before he risked it.

'Tell me what Miss Bowman told you about your mother.'

She was now cross-legged, tucking a foot in.

She gave a sigh, the pained sigh of the receptionist who has already explained that the consultant has no appointment free for four months and why pick on her. 'She said my mother Marie died when I was born and she adopted me.'

'Any mention of your father?'

'Oh yes. A ne'er-do-well attorney, she actually said that. I imagined him charging around New England getting the hell out of it in a ne'er-do-well sort of way. But that was when I was a child. I started getting suspicious when the other kids did. It kind of rubs off on you, like nits. You get the feeling second-hand. "Your Dad up Mount Crawford clink then?" "No, he died in Vermont." "Vermont, where's Vermont?" "Emmie O'Malley's got no daddy." You know what little snuggle-bunnies girls are. Can't think why I didn't switch to boys sooner.

'So I had my suspicions OK. And Aunt's letter confirmed them. The one I showed you.' She leaped up taking warmth with her to search in the drawer beneath the yellow-toothed ermine and the scrimshaw and the photograph.

'You've put Alice back,' he said.

'Yeah.'

'Why?'

'It's a good photograph.'

He had not seen it for years but was not disappointed; the folds of the cloak, the hood around the still face, even the hand on the staff were familiar. Wil was right. It was a pilgrim's face; it was not just the cloak. 'Wil would love that,' he muttered.

'Give it to him.'

He glanced at her stern face. 'No, I will not.'

She handed him the letter, shrugged. 'Read it,' she snapped.

Your father was a lawyer. He is dead now. My family were in timber. My grandmother stood by me and the bits and pieces we have were hers . . .

His eyes flicked over it again.

You have been my joy, and Calvin also . . .

'Emmie, it does not say that Miss Bowman was your mother.'

'It doesn't say she wasn't.'

'She doesn't mention her sister Marie, the one she said was, she doesn't give you any evidence, she doesn't . . .'

'So?'

So quite a lot. So the shrewd old bat I admired more than somewhat and who was decent to me, except at the end and I can now see why, never lost her cunning. She might as well have put Emmeline's origins through a scandal-defeating shredder as leave a letter as ambiguous as this. What had she hoped to achieve? Birth records could be traced despite Emmie's having travelled on Miss Bowman's passport. Miss Bowman had opted for delaying tactics. They had seen her out and that was the essential, though she must have hoped for a continuing effect. And would have succeeded if he had not come stumbling along like a clown on a spavined horse to rescue a maiden who preferred the dragon. Take me, take a dragon and to hell with the truth.

The letter was more skilful than he had first thought. If it had said, 'You are my child, I wished to spare you pain,' and Emmeline had checked and found this to be false the armour of her love for Miss Bowman would have been dented if not pierced. Pierced at the linchpin if armour had such things.

And if he felt depleted at the thought what would Emmeline? Feet of clay are one thing—hell, who hasn't. But feet of clay on a figure renowned for upright stance could be lethal. He leaned forward to touch the hollow at the base of the neck beside him. It was surprisingly deep.

'Do you want me to help find documentation?' he asked casually to show how inessential it was.

'No.'

His eyes were scratchy. I tried Wil, I tried. I did try. And bang goes my thesis but let's get our priorities right wouldn't you say, Wil, wouldn't you say.

Except, Robin realised as he watched the changes of colour, the sudden snaps, crumbles, puffs of gas among the flames, he would not give up. Like the yes man who finally stood firm against corruption, like the coward turned unlikely hero, he would tell the truth. The truth about Alice O'Leary which would involve telling the truth about Candida Bowman.

Calvin, he remembered, had called it Rob's thethith. It had seemed rather cute at the time.

Emmie stirred beside him.

'You'll come down in August?'

Small flecks of light glinted on her pupils. 'It would be great for Calvin. But no, how can I?'

He poked the embers, wriggled the poker. Soot fell. 'I'll ring the chimney sweep tomorrow.'

'Do that.'

They sat still, the silence sparking around the room, the smoke belching. 'Come to bed,' he said.

'No.' Her nose was scarlet from the fire, the rest of her face white. As with her feet, pink and white were localised. He put out his hand as she drew back. 'I think we should sort things out right now,' she said.

He paused, a reflective thinking-man's pause. 'Why now?'

'Because you believe something I refuse to believe and if we stay together, very gently you will muddle me into beginning to doubt, into believing something I don't believe and will not believe and why the hell should I?' She lifted her hand. 'Stop. Let me finish. It's too soon. It might always be too soon. If you take Aunt and give me some dumb-bum who shot through twice, what help is that?' She was sitting very straight, her red nose gleaming. 'I don't want to know,' she said.

'You said you did!'

'When?'

'You said people need to know their origins. When Calvin was born. You said.'

'Calvin's nearly five,' she tugged her hair back with both hands. 'You expect me to be consistent all of a sudden?' She leaned forward and socked it to him; all the frustration, the rage behind the funny-girl mask was in her eyes. 'You know me, Emmie. Flaky, disorganised nutty Emmie O'Malley is perfectly happy and so is her Inner Child so shut *up*. It doesn't want out.'

Nothing cosy here. No hearth and home stuff. He grabbed the shovel, banged about in the embers, swept up ash from the hearth with quick fussing anger. 'You don't believe that crap.'

'No, but I thought it was interesting. I like the idea of everything that's wrong with you being someone else's fault. I see the attraction, but I don't see where it gets you on account of life not going backwards but that's not what we're talking about.'

Her mouth moved with the sly glint of send-up. 'And which mother would I pick on to blame? Double whammy eh?' Her voice lifted, changed key. 'And you might at least let Aunt rot first. Stuff the truth and leave Aunt!' She leaped to her feet. 'I'm going to bed. And stop looking like that.'

He was blocking the door with wide B-movie arms. 'Let me explain.'

She scratched her lemon-scented head. 'I'll tell you what I really think,' she said finally, 'but only if you don't interrupt.'

They sat facing each other, her bare toes kneading the trotting horse beneath them. 'I think,' said Emmie, 'that one of the reasons I refuse to believe your story is that it has not missed one cliché in the book.' She raised a traffic-cop hand. 'Are you going to listen to me or not? As I was saying. Think about it, think of everything you've told me about Alice, think about those silly charts even. There is not one cliché omitted,' said Emmeline ticking off points.

'*One*. Plucky widow plus spirited daughter run country store after Daddy succumbs. Why a country store, for Chrissake? Because it's back-woodsy, gingham, wooden pegs, butter pats, forty-gallon drums of maple syrup I shouldn't wonder. Why couldn't she have pumped gas? I reckon the woman invented herself the same as she invented those cute-as-a-newt nutters in her books.

'*Two*. Plucky semi-orphan marries above herself. Wow. Gee. Shucks. Mama-in-law not pleased, she wanted the high-toned lady from Boston. *Above* herself, we're talking downmarket Henry James here.

'*Three*. Broken gallant GI hero takes to booze on account of horrors experienced defending Uncle Sam.'

'She doesn't say that.'

'I warned you. *Four*. Marriage turns out a bit of a disappointment. Gallant wife feels guilty. Why the hell should *she* feel guilty? Inner Child gone walkabout? Sense gone out the window?

'*Five*. No babies. Sorrow. Grief. But irony compounded. It's Daddy's problem, but will he accept this? No. He's a man see, and men don't mess about when it comes to virility even when they haven't got it. No other people's bastards for Daddy-o either. So no babies. Oh, it makes me toss. The whole goddamn saga makes me toss. Give me Aunt! Give me honest in-your-face and up-yours Aunt. I cannot stand *phonies*. Sentimental self-deprecating hysterical *phonies.*'

'She wasn't,' he said. 'And for God's sake stop talking. You're wrong.'

He had never seen her cry except when Aunt died.

'Emmie.'

She brushed him away. 'I haven't finished. I've hardly started. I have scarcely *commenced*.' She gave a shuddering heave for air. 'Why should I care what you say or do? I don't, I don't and you're the most uptight shit around and the sooner you shove off the better . . .' She flung away from him, cracked her head against the table, tried to stand, cracked it again and bawled against his chest. A lump of soot splattered on the hearth behind them.

She sat up later to rub her hipbone. 'Why didn't we go to bed?'

'We can now.'

Three hours. Four hours' sleep. It must have been longer but not much. 'I haven't finished, you know,' she said watching him tug on his jeans next morning with the proprietorial interest lovers take in each other's bodies.

'I've got more to say. Where was I up to?'

'Five,' he said groping for a sock.

She patted his rump, a friendly familial gesture. 'What was it?'

'I can't remember.'

'Oh yes. We've had game fatherless child, King Cophetua and the beggar maid New-England style, drunken wifebasher she cannot leave. Just tell me again why she can't leave?'

'You're being anachronistic and hopelessly subjective. "I would leave therefore why didn't she?" Think of the time. And the place.

A student of mine,' he said tugging on the sock, 'won't read *The Taming of the Shrew* because of Shakespeare's anti-feminist perspective. Another thinks *Moby Dick* has a bad attitude to whales and she's so right. They do it all the time. *Merchant of Venice. Romeo and Juliet*.' He was flat on the floor in search of the other sock. 'It's bizarre.'

'How did we get on to Shakespeare?' she said mildly.

Lisa, the Swiss and the mountains, the Maori and the bush. Robin stood silent, the sock hanging from his hand.

'What is it?'

'Nothing.'

She was still watching him. 'Why did she let me go?' she nagged him again. 'Twice.'

His mother's wedding would be small and held at Clayton's own church which would be nice wouldn't it, and would Robin please get onto Spiro and organise the catering. Nothing too grand, just something simple but nice for afterwards, just family and a few close friends.

'Yeah, sure. Can I ask Emmie?'

'Emmie?'

'That's right,' he smiled into her pink blankness. 'Emmie.'

'Well, I'll have to ask Clayton,' she demurred. That is what she was doing. Demurring. My demurring mother. My mother who has been known to demur. She would interest him till the day she died and he would never fathom her. He had waited for outward and visible signs of continued happiness on her face, but after the first glow of the announcement all had proceeded as before. Eileen's smile remained slow, tentative and rare. She bought a two-piece for the ceremony and a pair of courts to have by her for later and that was it. She made arrangements to rent her house and packed her knick-knacks only as Clayton's home was fully furnished. She made Clayton welcome and touched him occasionally.

Clayton, on the other hand, became more and more excited. He tiptoed and pranced and opened doors and helped with seatbelts while Eileen sat quietly. She often sat quietly. Once, she had told Robin long ago, she and Terence had come upon a nasty car accident around the Bays and Terence had gone to help and she had sat quietly till he returned. It was terrible he said. Terrible.

Robin wondered whether sorrow had seeped into her, filled her like a well and left no room for change. He must make allowances and did so, but wondered secretly and with shame what Clayton saw in her, which attribute it was that induced such gaiety and was glad there was one.

Clayton was growing on him as his mother had promised. 'He may seem a little, well, joky to you at first, Robin, but Clayton is a deeply spiritual man and I am sure he will grow on you in time.'

'I like him now.'

'Do you dear?' she said, her forehead slightly creased. 'That's nice.'

'I know it's late notice, Spiro, but they've just decided,' he said at the kitchen table. They discussed dates. The fact that it was mid-week was a help, and thirty people was all. No problem, no problem, and for you and your mother Robin, the mate's rates.

'Thanks a lot.'

The hands parted. No problem.

Rob's eyes, as always, followed the hypnotic driftings and dartings of the fish. A Black Neon was still hiding in his drowned castle, the green toy frog still burping bubbles on time.

Calvin would love them. The local library's vertical tank and stately Fantails were inspected frequently. Christmas; he would give Calvin some freshwater tropicals for Christmas.

He would not get them yet. Tact was required until things settled. And what do you mean by settled? Settled is that sure and certain time when all will be well, that good time coming. That time when Emmie welcomes the truth and begs him to write it. Yes. He shifted his legs and stared harder. A pink fish snapped at the frog. The inevitability of its burps must drive them insane but we mustn't be anthropomorphic least of all about fish which are cold-blooded and lacking in human emotion.

'What's happening to the fish while you're away, Spiro?'

'My cousin from Tawa sleeps in my house for the massage and feeds them while I am gone. His wife does his fish.'

They discussed the menu—simple but nice. 'Everyone in Wellington wants simple but nice. They mean rare like peacock tongues and cheap like dirt and easy on the Greek stuff, Spiro. And I will need to see the venue. Always see the venue if you can, in houses. Halls, places for hire we know: big ovens, benches, the flow. In houses it is more difficult. I arrive to take over and the kitchen is a nest for birds and an oven. No room, no room at all. The menu must match the venue. Always. Otherwise!' The hands poured the party down the drain.

'I'll have a look and let you know.'

Spiro stifled a yawn. 'OK. Sit down or finger?'

'Fork.'

'Fork. Fork is nowhere, it is between, it is a nonsense; clamp and pull and only those with strong teeth are happy. Those with bite.' He shot his bottom plate forward. 'There will be dentures. At second weddings there is always dentures. What are they to do these dentures? Ham. How do you bite ham with a fork? Clamp and pull, clamp and pull is all.' He was staring, making eye contact, begging from professional knees. 'Robin, I mean it. Ask for finger food or sit down.'

'Mum wants fork.'

Spiro leaned back in his chair, his lower lip petulant as an orchid's. 'Then fork she gets. But no ham.'

'She wants ham.'

The hands lifted from the elbows in resignation, the palms flattened in gloomy acceptance of arcane rituals.

They worked on the menu.

'The finger food for meeting and greeting and popping of corks. Asparagus rolls and club sandwiches and filo pastries for exploding. Is that simple? Is that nice?'

'Very nice,' said Robin miserably.

'And the *vol au vent* encasing the dead oyster? Very nice, very tasty—death in hot flaky.'

Oh bugger this.

'You needn't do it if you don't want to.'

'I have said I will. It is just sometimes, just occasionally, the simple and nice gives me the pricker. And for the lunch. Well now?' He gave an infuriating imitation of enthusiasm, rubbed his hands and held them still. 'Coronation chicken, why not? Ham, new potatoes, salad?' The merriment did not last. Spiro, half a lifetime of mundane food trailing behind him, sat silent.

'And then the wedding cake,' he sighed.

It was a long session. The coffee changed to ouzo, the ouzo to more ouzo as the evening turned into a training session in the intricacies of Dionysus Caterers; the books were opened, the accounting system described in detail, work plans produced, recipe and staff files, insurance, profits and problems. Spiro was not happy with Wanda. If Wanda became a problem Robin was to feel free to sack her.

'Thanks,' said Robin who liked Wanda. She was a member of some exclusive sect which made Saturdays difficult and Sundays impossible but she was a good worker.

And none of this hassle was his wish. Not one ounce of all this did he want, would have paid money to avoid. He had no wish for the distraction, the work, the sheer bind of what Spiro obviously thought was the most exciting thing that had ever happened to him, the most stimulating challenge of his life.

'Scott. Scott also may have to be watched. He does not care enough, not enough fire in the gut. Keep him on sandwiches.'

Robin dragged his mind back. 'OK.'

There's something I'd like to talk to you about, Spiro. No. Not catering. Forget catering. That's a drag but I'll do it. It's not that Spiro, but I have a problem. Calvin had had a problem last week. He missed a fight in the Wendy house. We all have our problems Spiro, and mine is a moral one. How about that Spiro? How do you go on a moral dilemma? How about intellectual honesty? On duty versus the woman I love. *Cf* Windsor. Wales. Mark Antony.

'Spiro?' he said.

Spiro rose, bent to the fish tank in benediction. 'It is late,' he said. 'Go home now, Robin.'

He turned, one hand idly scratching his groin. 'She insists on ham?'

'Yes.'

It was a warm day on the Gold Coast with a hint of spring in the air. Groups of friends and strangers gathered outside the small wooden church, told each other so. Had the visitors noticed the early prunus blossoms on the Beach Road? And the first daffodils? The daffodils were late this year which was a worry for the Cancer Society ladies, the sidesman with the eyebrows told them as Robin and his mother waited for the moment when he would escort her up the aisle and give her away.

He smiled at her, admired her jersey knit, her ruffled pink blouse, her serenity. 'Happy?' he asked.

Her smile was vague beneath grey curls and a pink meringue hat. 'Of course, dear,' she touched his arm shyly. 'It's lovely of you to fix the fence. I'm sure it was a help with letting the house.'

'And Calvin. He helped.'

She nodded, more wistful than ever. 'And Calvin,' she said. She touched her talisman star brooch. 'Who's minding him today?'

He stared at her. 'But he's here with Emmie. I told you—asked, I mean.'

Her mouth moved, rearranged itself, moved again in odd involuntary twitches.

'Not the boy, you didn't. He's so . . . You should've said, dear.'

The still house and the birdless concrete birdbath and the Crown of Thorns and his mother's sad-eyed face at his bedside after cleaning up a wee nocturnal accident, the damp sheets held well away from her winceyette nightie, her heavy-duty hairnet blue.

'You haven't said you're sorry, dear.'

'I'm sorry.'

The brush of lips, the soft cheek. 'Big boys don't wet beds, do they?'

'No.'

And they hadn't. Not ever again.

'Mum, Emmeline is my friend. Of course Calvin must come.'

She lifted a hand in quick protest.

'Well he has, hasn't he?' she said. 'It's too late now.'

The sidesman touched her arm and the organist burst into the Wedding March and the friends turned smiling in their pews to welcome them.

In fact it was not too late. Eileen could have barred the door, put up a road block. Emmie and Calvin were late. They were not inside the church. They were not coming. Emmie had sensed the bride's lack of enthusiasm, had thought better of it—to hell with them, their lack of generosity of mind and spirit, their orderly lists and diagrams and time charts and small meannesses. Their restraint.

He stood beside his mother aching with desire and rage. Emmeline would come. She had said she would. They could fornicate somewhere. Immediately. At once. Now. He turned as the door crashed open and Emmie and Calvin scrambled in. He had a glimpse of day-glo green and scarlet and turned back smiling to his mother and Clayton on his toes beside her.

The officiating vicar was one step up from the bridal party. 'Dearly beloved, we are gathered together . . .' He was an old man with a long thin face and fingers designed to bless. He was pleased for Clayton and his lady seemed a good woman. His smile creaked and flowed across his face in welcome. The congregation stirred, smiled back, were filled with goodwill and glad to have been asked. Everyone loved Clayton and he had had a rough time and the church looked lovely didn't it though it was a pity one of the altar camellias had dropped. '*Brian* does,' murmured a woman with two sticks. '*Donation*'s a much better bet but she's later.'

The vicar lifted his praying hands.

*

253

There were photographs, taut smiles, laughter and snapping cameras. Robin smiled and smiled, his eyes following Emmie as women fussed over Calvin who was looking bored and Emmie who was radiant. She looked different from the last wedding he had seen her at which was his. She was more relaxed, no, that was not the word. He watched her virtually standing on her head to enchant an old man who had seen her on TV in *Shark in the Park* and when was she going to do another one? But she was undoubtedly calmer about Aunt's death and would become more so, as long as he didn't bully her with an unwanted mother who had dumped her twice.

'You came,' he said fatuously. The lime-green clung tight, made from something which looked like rubberised silk. He had never seen her in high heels before except on stage. They were an exact colour match and so high her eyes topped his. A scarlet plate hat was clamped over one ear, her fingernails were emerald. She was distinctive, a day-glo stick insect angling its way across a field of pastels. Calvin's gear was more casual, his T-shirt Bart Simpson, his pants grey. She grinned at Rob and continued her chat with the bridegroom's sister who was over from Reefton and weren't the camellias lovely and how old was Calvin. Again the world of women tilted away from him, slid sideways to births and nuptials and small talk and survival.

Old Blue, the last breeding female Chatham Island robin, had saved her race from extinction. They are tough, females. They know more and are sillier. Can talk about anything and are scared of silence.

Spiro had done well and there were unexpected extras. The guests forked their way through whitebait provided by a devoted member of the parish and cooked by Robin at the last moment because Spiro refused. He refused loudly, vociferously and at some length. He had prepared a menu to balance, he would not fuck it up. He lost his temper which happened seldom and was alarming when it did. He slammed about shouting; his pans, his elements, all were busy. Where, where was it left he should fritter this fish?

'She caught them herself this morning,' said Robin. 'I'll cook them. It's a treat.'

'Bring her to me.'

'No. No.'

Spiro stormed into the lounge, a mad chef from stock grabbing the bridegroom. 'Where is the whitebait lady?'

'Here,' said the whitebait lady proudly, her lipstick damp with anticipation.

Robin dragged him back to the kitchen, past the still-expectant whitebaiter, past Emmie's delight and Calvin's double-handed eating habits and closed the door. Spiro came right but it took time. The perfection of the bite-size fritters mollified him until the bridegroom's sister popped in for a dish for the chocolate truffle nibbles she had brought with her all the way from Reefton.

'Why! Why? Is my food not enough? Not nice? Not tasty crap?'

The man was becoming incoherent. Robin handed a startled plate and shut the door. The thing was getting ridiculous.

'For God's sake Spiro, they're women.'

'Now you tell me.'

'They want to help, they don't mean to louse things up.'

Spiro's eyebrows were locked. 'So they help by screwing up my menu? They love by how sweet they are, how kind, how clever with the nibbles. Nibbles! By bringing food not needed they show they are nice? Balls! It is their ego massage.'

And what's yours Chuckie, what's yours? A girl's got to do what a girl's got to do. Shut-ins and olds will welcome poppers-in with food even if Miss Bowman did not, and if the girls don't pop who the hell will in this day and age and the cuts getting worse and the rich still richer. Get real man, and let the rest of us storm off shouting and the devil take the hindmost which will undoubtedly include the has-beens and the never-weres and the no-hopers and those who stink and those who drink and those who disappear without trace to a sleep and a forgetting, amen.

Never come to a wedding again unless stoned.

He glanced around, looking for sanity and repose in the form of Emmeline. She had disappeared as had Calvin. His stepfather was talking to the Reverend John who had taken the service. Eileen was surrounded by parishioners in hats and florals. Everyone was smiling except the two clerics. Robin moved over with relief.

'Yes, I agree,' said Clayton his face stern as he stared up at his friend. 'I agree with the man as to meaning, and his scholarship is convincing, especially of course to people looking for a way in . . . or out. Useful undoubtedly, but . . .'

'Exactly,' said the Reverend John. In appearance they could have been an ecclesiastical double act. Hi, High. Lo, Low. But these were serious men.

'Faith is so much more than facts,' continued the Reverend John. 'He seems, do you agree, almost to forget that. Is meaning the only point of religious consciousness? What about wonder, mystery, numinous awe? Myth even. Truth, of course there must be truth, but what are you destroying, what do you risk destroying for those who cannot and will not accept what the man says. And I don't mean only fundamentalists either.'

> '*In simple trust*, murmured Clayton, *like theirs who heard*
> *Beside the Syrian Sea*
> *The gracious calling of the Lord*
> *Let us, like them, without a word*
> *Rise up and follow Thee.*'

People alongside smiled, nodded. They knew that one.

'Quite!' said the Reverend John. 'Quite.'

Robin nodded, attempted retreat around a nest of occasional tables.

Clayton touched his arm. 'Excuse us,' he said.

'No, please go on, I'm interested.'

But like anyone talking shop, like experts in any field, Clayton and his friend preferred their audience to be informed. This was not the moment, they felt, for a quick burst on modern theological thinking with one under-read in the subject. They stood silent.

'Do you think anything will come of Church leaders taking a stance on state housing?' tried Robin.

The Reverend John looked thoughtful. Perhaps he had less faith, or fire, or was too tired. But Clayton was excited. 'Of course! Of course it will. Leadership from the top. The Prime Minister has already said he'll look into it. This is just the beginning, Robin. Just the beginning, mark my words.' He paused, glanced around smiling. 'Where's my wife? The secret of a happy marriage. Always check on your lady wife frequently.' A muscle winced at the side of his mouth. 'Yes,' said Clayton and moved away.

Robin wandered off down the passage and was confronted at the end by a pottery plaque depicting a toilet-paper roll, one ceramic end billowing, floating free as an unfurled scroll.

Calvin was in action behind the open door. He stood at some distance and sprayed. 'Hey,' said Rob. 'Stand nearer. In it, not at it. Like this.' He unzipped. 'Right up, see. Legs apart. That's it. Much better. Spot on.'

Emmeline leaned against the door frame. 'Having a demo?' she said and closed the door.

An orderly queue was forming beyond the door. After you. No no, I'm all right, after you. The bridesmaid, sister-in-law, bride and friend stopped in mid-courtesy as the three of them filed out. Eileen's fingers brushed her lips in a gesture remembered from childhood.

'Hi,' said Emmeline.

'Robin,' said Maureen tugging his coat. 'Spiro's throwing a wobbly and the vicar's fainted.'

'Which vicar?' gasped Eileen her mouth wide.

Maureen put out an arm. 'Not yours, dear. The old gentleman. We've put him in the sunporch.'

Murray had been unable to spare the time to help with the fence but Calvin had offered his assistance. He was a busy child, an inquisitive string-bean activist who liked making things go and things which did go. He liked vacuum cleaners. He poked and took apart. He reassembled. He was fearless and unpredictable and loved to help, but only with manly tasks. He hammered, he sawed, he had to be watched. The prospect of the hired concrete mixer delighted him. The noise, the thump, the revolving turnip yellowness of the thing, all these were good and were to be present for two whole days. Calvin marshalled the local kids who came to stare and was ruthless with any would-be infringements. No one could help but him and they had to stay on the footpath.

He dug useless holes with a large yellow plastic shovel which was an unexpected freebie from the local gas company. He was too short to shovel builder's mix unaided, insisted on doing so and yelled for help. He watched the rolling surge of the bowl with awe and drove Robin mad.

He was underfoot like a starving cat or a half-blind dog. He turned on the hose and could not turn it off, he poked his finger in the cement and lost a jandal, he insisted on heaving a post and dropped it on Robin's foot. The smooth cement surface of the post hole pleased him, as did his hand print.

And then he got sick of it.

The local kids had left long ago, wearied, like Lady Lucas, of delights in which they saw no likelihood of sharing. Emmie was at a costume rehearsal all day and there was still no sign of her. The wind which had been blowing sand about all day had dropped to a gentle breeze by the time Murray drifted out to watch progress. He had been working hard.

Robin, sweating and silent, his back bent, his head down, continued easing the last post into its concrete puddle.

'Like a hand?' said Murray.

Robin centred the post with care, picked up his shovel and turned to his neighbour. His eyes were stinging with grit, his glasses steamed, his back broken. 'No,' he said.

Murray yawned, scratched an armpit and yawned again. 'Only trying to help. Couldn't afford two lost days. Not at this stage of the year. I told you. If you'd made it May it might've been different. You arty bastards've got no idea of the pressure on med students at this time of year.'

The post was straight and true and the last one, striding down the drive like telephone poles across Central Otago. Now only the timber remained, the actual making of the fence plus staining and staining again. Rob laid his forehead against his last post for a moment to remind himself that the guy was Lisa's brother. It did not work. 'How much interest are you paying Emmie on your loan?' he said.

Murray searched for the answer inside his mouth. His tongue moved wide and deep as he explored his palate, moved to the right, bulged to the left and found it.

'None.'

'Why the hell not?'

'She didn't ask for any.'

'Didn't you insist?'

The tongue was thoughtful. 'No,' said Murray, 'why should I?'

Rob, his hands still gripping the post, moved his head from one side to the other and stared down the road to the unseen sea. Son of a bitch would not be accurate. 'God, you're a shit,' he said finally.

Murray was unconcerned. Insults, even as a child, had never penetrated. He was impervious, above and beyond censure. He knew where he was going and where he was coming from and had always done so. The hand, large and clean and spatulate, was scratching again. Scratching quite strongly. Robin kept his eyes on it; it was safer than the face and he had to look somewhere. He lifted his head sharply at the tone of voice as Murray asked his question.

'Have you told Emmie about the letter from that Alice woman to old Bowman in *The Load*?'

He had forgotten. It had slipped his mind. He would do so but it would not be as easy now. Not easy at all. Not at the moment. 'How do you know about it?'

'I borrowed the book the week before you did.'

'Why?' said Robin wondering if the man was lying but why should he be.

Murray shrugged, a large flop of beef and elbows. 'Just a theory of mine,' he said.

Robin, still staring as the hand moved downwards, wondered once more why he disliked the man so much. OK he was smug, imperturbable and up himself. But lots of guys are up themselves. Some of my best friends are up themselves. This one is different.

This one doesn't even know he is up himself. He is just *there*, larded, unctuous, and close at hand, checking out my resource material. 'What theory?' he snarled.

'Old Bowman was a lesbian.'

'*Wow.*'

Murray was not deflected. 'I never liked the woman and that letter proves it, to my mind.'

'Why on earth?'

'"He is dead. I am coming. Hurray." Pretty obvious, wouldn't you say?'

'No. I wouldn't.'

'There wouldn't have been many lesbian mothers around then, not single ones. That's why she came out, I reckon. Both of them. Alice and Candida.' He paused, looked thoughtful, considered. 'What a crew.'

The prognathous chin, the short upper lip, the solid thighs; all had got it wrong but that was not the point. Robin was sweating more than ever, rage was trickling down his legs, adrenalin was pumping the sweet bliss of hatred through every hollow vessel. 'So why did Alice marry Wilfred Q. Hughes?'

'Wanted the farm, wouldn't you say?' Murray turned to go. 'You'll have to tell Emmie. Morally bound to, I'd say.' He strolled to the pavement and glanced around. 'Where's Calvin?'

Christ! Rob dropped the shovel and ran. 'Calvin, Calvin, Cal–vin!'

Murray removed the paper from the letterbox and checked the front page. *Sewerage decision imminent.* He strolled up the path.

Calvin was asleep on the wide verandah with his kitten in his arms. Robin, panting with fright, just stopped himself from shaking the child awake, from roaring and demanding explanations. Apologies even. People should not disappear. Not ever, not for one second should people disappear without previous advice having been given and received.

He lay down beside the child and closed his eyes. The light behind his eyelids was blood red with black spots. He would clean up later.

He explained his concern to Calvin when they woke. He explained that when people love other people they want them to be safe and people have to tell other people where they're going otherwise people . . . He got bogged down and sat silent, his slack hands hanging. Calvin hugged the apricot kitten and looked at him for some time without expression. He took his mother by the hand when she returned and told her that Robin had growled at him and to come and look at his concrete. The kitten put one paw in the last post-hole which was still wet and howled a thin high threnody. It took some time to clean her up as well.

Twelve

The northerly was flinging white petals and mangled buds across the yard to the porch. The clothesline whirled, laden with ballooning towels, hammock sheets and shirts gross with air. Unmatched socks and a pair of underpants lay beached on concrete.

Emmie extracted a petal from Misha's half-empty saucer. 'Why does the wind always wait till the cherry's out?'

'Equinoctial gales. Look at the catkins thrashing pollen about. Rebekkah'd be beside herself.'

'Rebekkah?'

'My first tutorial.' He blew out, a long exhalation of relief. 'I'll never forget that lot.'

Emmie knew his tutorials' names and some of their problems and all of their essay topics. She might do English some time when she was old—but what about the fees.

Get the money back from Murray for starters. He did not say it. Murray was a mine shaft, a gap they circled but did not explore.

As was Alice.

He was working steadily on the novels. Emmeline continued to be amiable but uncompromising. He could work on the oeuvre, she said, till he was blue in the face with narrative structure and nit-picking symbolism—but leave Aunt out OK. And me.

Which meant he would have to leave out the life entirely. He had worked it out though. Hell yes, Rob had worked it out. He would complete his literary analysis first. Then when Emmie read the letters, changed her mind and embraced the truth he would sort out the rest and rewrite in depth which is what you write in. In the moments of sanity which sometimes sneaked up on him at dawn he realised how difficult this method would be, if not impossible. And there were other worries. Would the letters convince? Would she read them? But these were night thoughts. During the day he saw that there was a great deal to do on the works themselves; focus, analysis, concentration, all were required. Enough in all conscience as Maureen would say. More than enough. Yes.

'I must go and see Maureen,' he said.

Emmeline laid another damp petal alongside the saucer of milk. 'When are you going to give up your flat?'

He grinned at her. 'Next week.' There were better subjects for concentration: shared abandon, the squelching wonder of it all, geography of body and mind. He was happier than he had ever been in his life.

They drove across Kilbirnie to take Spiro to the airport, Calvin on the lookout for Cs and Robin cursing himself. His own stupidity had landed him in this and now the man was about to go, to swan off to his own remembered hills leaving his offsider to carry the can and dree his own dim little weird at Dionysus as promised. Emmie patted his knee. 'Cheer up.'

'C! There!' screamed Calvin from the comfort of his booster seat.

Robin swung the wheel, overcorrected, nearly hit a dog.

'For God's sake don't *do* that.'

A glint of steel to the left. 'Do what?'

'Shriek behind me. I know he's not used to cars but . . .'

'Maybe you're not used to kids.'

'A car is a lethal weapon.'

'Anyway I yelled too.'

'I'm used to you.'

'Hhh.'

They drove on, their faces blank with assumed calm. 'It was one, wasn't it, Mum?'

'Sure it was,' she said. 'C for Calvin and Casey Total Exhaust. Good one. Look! C for Chain Nail Truss. What's a Chain Nail Truss?'

'I'll tell you some time,' he muttered.

She gave him a sharp glance, waved with enthusiasm at the two figures waiting on the distant kerb. '*There* they are, hon.'

Calvin was fighting with his safety belt. 'Now we'll see the fishes eh.'

'Not today, Cal,' said Rob.

'But I told him we could.'

'You didn't tell me.' He switched off the ignition. The small finality of the click filled the car followed by Calvin's wail. 'But Muum . . .'

Her safety belt hissed back. 'We've *plenty* of time, plenty.'

'We have not. If I'd known, if you'd said, I'd have started hours ago.'

Robin had met Andoni before. He was large and bald like Spiro but his moustache lacked the exuberance of his cousin's; a thin organic strip clung to his upper lip, formal and groomed as a black bow-tie. Spiro stood looking expectant beside a suitcase and a small grip. Why were those in the front seat silent and Calvin roaring in his throne behind and when were they going to get out? He opened Emmeline's door in encouragement. She hopped out, kissed him and turned to Andoni. 'How *very* nice to meet you,' she said, glad to know there were two decent men left in the world.

'Why is your son weeping?' asked Spiro nervously. Children were beyond him. They were inexplicable and too sudden and he had an aircraft to catch which doubtless even now was sitting on the tarmac at Rongotai with its nose in the air waiting for him. He had never travelled without his wife before and the arrangements, the packing, the remembering and doing of it all had been much more confusing than he remembered. Also he had slept badly and his eyes were sore and worst of all he was not sure whether the whole thing was not an act of madness, a dreadful mistake out of which he could no longer extract himself with honour. He moved from one foot to the other. His voice was agitated. 'Does Calvin also come?'

The problem was explained amidst Calvin's bawls and Emmie's over-reactive smiles. Robin said nothing. He tried to right Calvin, who was now performing (another of Eileen's remembered pejoratives) flat on his back on the footpath, and was greeted by flying feet. Spiro stood looking at his watch, his mouth busy.

'Why,' said Andoni dragging his eyes from Emmeline's legs, 'do not the boy and the mother come up to see the fish and drink coffee and you two go to the airport and Robin comes back?'

The relief. So simple, so tidy, so wise. Spiro embraced his cousin and kissed Emmeline on both cheeks. She had helped out occasionally at Dionysus when he was short-staffed and he liked her; her cheerful speed pleased him. He shook her hand in final farewell, embraced Andoni once more and waved at Calvin's back now disappearing safely up the steps.

Robin watched her face. She seemed cheerful but then she also liked the fish, was happy for her son and had gone off her lover. He swung Spiro's suitcase into the boot and slammed hard.

She waved as they left but he was not reassured.

They could walk around holes, avoid the ruined mine shafts of too much Alice and too little Candida, fuck themselves silly and count the world well lost for love, but nature, he remembered from primary, abhors a vacuum. Things grow over holes and disguise them, branches are laid above sharpened spears. Things change.

Emmie seemed more ready to leap to her son's defence than formerly as though to demonstrate something. That Robin must learn the ropes. That there are different forms of passion.

Spiro was not going to waste a moment of the journey. He dragged a new recipe for sun-dried tomato pesto out of his pocket. He had found it beneath power bills when he was tidying his desk in case the aircraft fell from the sky. It would be very useful indeed for Robin. He was to keep it with care and feel free to use it while he was away. Feel free, said Spiro again.

'I've got a good one, Spiro.'

'This is better.'

'Shove it in the glove box.'

'But will you remember it?'

Probably not, but I don't need it and won't use it and when you ask for it on your return as you undoubtedly will, all will flood back and I can get shot of the thing. It occurred to him, not for the first time, that discussions about even the simplest arrangements with Spiro were invariably lengthy. Spiro liked to explore alternatives—to pontificate, to unbutton and have his talk out like Dr Johnson.

'Yeah, sure.'

Spiro looked at the glove box and pressed the button. It opened with a slow yawn to reveal a half-eaten piece of cake, a video of a Russian *Lear* where the treatment of the Fool was particularly interesting, a plastic bottle, a dead banana and a sun hat.

'I can't put it there!'

'Try the dashboard.'

More doubt, more anxious hesitancy as to safety, procedure, access. And this was the man who, on his own ground and untormented by helpers other than his own team could feed five hundred with a flick of his wrist and time to spare.

He was now on to the catering for the Wine Festival. Rob did realise the size of the operation, the meticulous planning required, the work? Days, days they would be working, the whole team. Rob had been there last year, he reminded him. He remembered, did he not, the size of the task, the enormity?

Yes, he did.

Not only the food, food they knew, food came last, on the day itself, five thousand individual pieces and all had gone last time. Robin must remember that people eat all day. They graze, the public, graze like cattle from morning till night. And it was not only the food. Its preparation they knew. But the planning, the transport. Robin had considered had he not, the equipment? Now was not too early, not too early at all, to plan the transport, to arrange the details for the erection of the marquee. All, all must be in its place for the arrival of the five thousand pieces which was just the start.

'And of course the problem of not knowing. Never to know how many. Thousands there maybe. Fourteen, fifteen vineyards, maybe more this year, who knows how many will come to Dionysus? It is not only for us, for the food. It is the wine they are coming for, and for some the screaming music which luckily I don't hear and nor will you this time because of being flat out and the Boss also.' Spiro gave him a comradely thump on the shoulder. 'Boss,' he said again and leaned back to chew his moustache. 'Simple but nice. Now is the time when they are right. But simple to eat on plastic plates does not mean simple to make ahead and simple to keep coming and coming all day while the wine flows and the crowd gets happy and the noise more.' He paused. 'You have the menu from last year safe?'

'Yes, but I'm going to alter it a bit.'

Disbelief flooded Spiro's eyes, dropped his mouth. Disbelief and anger ticking. 'It is not to be altered. I spend days, weeks, with the balance, the subtle, the goodness. For days I was working to bring it all together and easy to eat as well.'

'We can't do exactly the same again every year, Spiro.'

'We haven't. Second time only is this one.'

Robin waited at the roundabout and explained carefully. 'Spiro, if you give me the responsibility of Dionysus you have to give me some freedom with the menus.'

'Why?'

'Because I'm in charge. I don't mean I'll change anything unnecessarily, hell no, it's the last thing any sane man would do. Your menus work. We all know that. But I must be free to make minor alterations if I want to.'

More chewing, an angry huff. 'Why?'

Because responsibility is power? Bugger that. Because I get bored making crostine for thousands. Because Emmie makes the best blini in the world and she's said she'll help.

He tried another line often mentioned by Spiro. 'Because cooking is a creative art.'

'Which is it you change?'

'Blini instead of crostine.'

'Your Emmeline's speciality. She is helping then, she and her blini. Now you are talking. No more the agenda fish hide.'

They stopped at the airport, Spiro's shoulders still heaving at his wit. He embraced him, dropped one eyelid.

'The blini for this time,' he said. 'Go with God, you and your angel fish.'

'Sure,' said Emmeline flaked out in a bikini trying for a mini-tan. 'I said I would if we can find a sitter. But what I'd really like of course is to take him too.'

She sat up to anoint herself with the Cancer Society large economy-size sunscreen. It was, she explained, the only one where you could combine protection with donation to a good cause and wasn't it a clever shape. You could get drunk with power pumping the stuff, like striped toothpaste when it started and every kid in town was squeezing.

'Although of course,' she said lying down again beside Misha's semi-clotted milk saucer, 'nothing really works with redheads. Don't worry,' she yawned, covering her face with Aunt's old straw hat which was etched at the rim with something black and suspect that looked like ergot but presumably was not. 'I said I would and I will.' She lifted the hat slightly to glance through chequered sunlight at his face. 'But he would so enjoy it.'

She could not mean it. He loved the thug too but this was ridiculous. 'No,' he said. 'No.'

The hat was back in place. 'Oh, we'd have to find someone to mind him all day. I realise that, but someone'd jump at the day out. I'll ask Thea.'

But Thea and Ruby were going to Eketahuna that weekend to see Gran who had been a bit off for some time and didn't seem to be picking up as quick as Mum and the rest of them had hoped. Thea was sorry but there it was.

Other sitters also declined. Maybe if it'd been next year. But no. They were tied up this time.

Calvin was into finger food and Emmeline gave up fighting about vegetables in the weekend. She slapped the meat in the sesame bun, neat as a pin and ready to go. 'It would have to be someone he knows well, of course. Murray, for instance,' she said licking her thumb.

Robin gave a short squirt of the Cancer Society can. It was a good shape, a miniature white plastic petrol container destined to save the day. He rubbed the stuff into his palms, sniffed. Lisa had had aloe-scented hand lotion. He had never smelled an aloe but then who had in Seatoun and you have to believe something. 'Calvin,' he said, 'doesn't like Murray.'

She was watching him. 'How do you know?'

He was silent. He didn't even know whether Calvin liked him, though he had hopes.

At home, sir, he is all my exercise, my mirth, my matter.

Now my sworn friend, and then mine enemy, my parasite, my soldier, statesman, all.

And Hamnet had died and here he was still hunting for clues in the text and Emmeline waiting hamburger in hand.

'I don't.'

'You'd think they'd work out some way to make the sesame seeds stick on,' she said licking again. 'And who else is there?'

269

He could see Calvin having fun, belting around the beaten grass with his water bottle, his pumpkin smile wide beneath his dumb French Foreign Legion sun hat, his arms covered with Total Block. He would certainly enjoy it. Kids should enjoy things, they should learn to enjoy things early as Calvin had done. Robin's Inner Child kicked. His mother had not taught him early enough, possibly because she had not had much to enjoy herself at the time, but what excuse was that.

'I could ask Maureen,' he said to Emmie's shoulder.

'Isn't she a bit old?'

'I'll ask.'

The house needed painting, the downpipe on the south side was green with mould. Perhaps he could steamblast it some time but that would remove more paint and he was damned if he was going to paint it while Murray lay around like a Palatine, a word he had been meaning to check for some time to see if it meant what he thought.

He turned his attention to the fence which was more satisfying; a good fence, a strong fence, a fence of class. He laid his palm against it as you might on the neck of a promising colt from the home farm.

'Hello Robbie!' called Maureen, shoving the casement window open beside him with a small explosive puff. 'It sticks,' she explained.

Nobody else called him Robbie now. He had never liked the Bobbie/Robbie stuff. But the connotations, ah, the connotations. Those he had loved and still did. Charles Lamb had been sorry when there was no one left to call him Charlie. 'Hi,' he called loudly.

'Come in dear, come in.'

Murray, fortunately, was not at home. His exams were over and, as he told them, he was quietly confident, though of course you can never trust the sods. As usual he had taken a week off study immediately prior to the first paper. He found it invaluable.

Rob looked at Maureen's smiling face. How could he have been so idiotic as to have thought for one possible moment he could have asked her. Excuse me Maureen. Could you see your way to minding the child of my de facto, my lover, the light of my life, while she and I work side by side as we were destined to do from earliest childhood but unfortunately I did not have the wit to notice at the time. Though you do realise Maureen, even though it doesn't look like it, that I loved your daughter dearly.

Maureen tugged open the back door which also had a tendency to stick and waded towards him.

He took her arm, held her firm. 'What on earth's happened?'

'Oh, it's my silly knees. Come and I'll tell you. No no no. I don't want an *arm*.'

They progressed slowly into the ziggurat room. Maureen crashed straight legged onto the sofa; the over-stuffed cushion on which Betty sat bounced slightly, upending her into Maureen's lap. She took the battered doll and kissed her, her hands busy fluffing out the few inches of skirt with practised hands. 'Silly old me,' she murmured.

Why do they do it? he wondered. Old men never do. They have more sense. Their ailments or accidents—self-inflicted or otherwise, are never silly. Their backs, if and when they go on them, may be cursed but never belittled. No one tells an old man that he must be furious with himself for having hit a head, twisted an arm or thrown his back out yet again. Such trials descend on old men, are inflicted from on high and must be born with courage.

'It's my own silly fault,' said Maureen yet again. 'I told you I'd been biking again. Well, I overdid it. You see these things you know. In the hairshop. When I go for a cut I see them, those little papers Eileen used to hand over the fence and I miss them my word, but it was a lovely wedding wasn't it. Every time you pick up a paper now they're at it, old as you like, all busting themselves getting fit. Men and women. There was a man last week, eighty-seven, he said, and fitter than he'd ever been in his life. Works out three times a week, runs all over and his wife as well, though she's only seventy-nine but trim as you like. They all say it makes them happy, gives them a 'positive attitude to life through exercise,' they say, and I thought that's you my girl, that's what you need. Mind you I couldn't afford the gym and that, but I doubled up on the biking and then trebled and pretty soon I was going for miles and I did feel better, that's the sad thing. And then blow me down I woke up one morning and there's my knees up like balloons and painful as all get out. It doesn't seem fair somehow.' Maureen stretched out her legs and tucked back her skirt in demonstration of her stupidity.

Her knees were certainly enormous. Swollen and shiny, the fat jowls and bulging foreheads of truculent politicians and bald babies stared back at him. 'I've always been wide behind the caps,' she said, 'but look at the *fronts*.'

Yes, she did have pills. The doctor said they would go down in time and to keep them up. Frankly Maureen couldn't wait to get shot of the silly things.

They sat contemplating the affected areas for a few moments while he murmured his sympathy. He could not ask if Murray had taken over the cooking. He could only hope.

She bounced Betty on her thigh a couple of times. 'Robin?'

'Yes.'

'You and Emmie.'

'Yes?'

'If you would like me to have it . . .' She brushed his wedding ring, her fingers snatching away as though singed. '. . . Any time. Not now, I don't mean. But if you would like me to later I would be very happy. Rather than just, well, put away somewhere, you know what I mean?'

She was smiling at him, smiling widely at the one she loved. 'And it looks as though it's all going to turn out all right with Murray and the loan and that, doesn't it?'

'Yes.' He couldn't look at her. It was impossible and his eyes were wet. 'Maureen,' he mumbled. 'I . . .'

'I'm glad I mentioned it, then,' she said quickly, bouncing Betty with renewed vigour. 'And would you check the letterbox on your way out, dear. It's never anything but long envelopes with bills but I'd like the *Contact* if it's there.'

*

He had rung Wilfred and Shara several times. At first when Shara answered she was cautious, speaking in the guarded tones of doctors talking over their patients' heads as they lie listening with polite interest trying to memorise phrases such as 'unacceptable angulation' and 'external fixation' so they can ask nurse after.

'He's fiiine,' she said, drawing the word out so that Robin would get the picture. He was OK. Like fine-*ish*. He was getting there. 'Sure,' she said. 'It's just like, you know, he's got a way to go yet. Yeah. Yeah, OK. You hear that? That's Wil, he says he's *fiiine*.'

But latterly her tone had changed. She was cheerful. Everything was good, good, great, yeah. When was he coming down? Tons of room. Yeah.

Wil rang. 'So when are you coming down? When're you bringing Emmeline and the boy?'

'Wil, I . . .'

Emmeline paused beside him, the tissue half-way to Calvin's leaking nose.

'I'm a box of birds now. When are you coming?'

'Wil, I told you. I said. I said I didn't know how Emmie . . .'

Emmeline took the receiver from his hand. She did not snatch or grab as he did in attempted retrieval. 'Leave me alone,' she hissed. Calvin, his nose still leaking, looked up, clung to her leg.

'Mr Hughes?' She was polite and crisp and devastating. She explained that she was sure that Mr Hughes had loved Alice O'Leary very much and she believed most sincerely that for some reason Alice had told him this odd story about herself and Miss Bowman. She continued calmly through the muffled contradicting exhortations from Central. She had never heard a word about Alice O'Leary being her mother, she did not believe it for a moment and as far as she was concerned the matter was at an end. She had been loved by Miss Bowman and had loved her back, a woman who had devoted her life to her and although she hated to disappoint Mr Hughes, let alone hurt him in any way, she could not do it. Come and stay, she meant. No, she couldn't.

Calvin was clinging tighter. 'Mum?'

Robin tried to seize the telephone as she dropped her left hand on the burrowing head. Her voice was no longer calm. Yes, she had hoped they might have been able to come and see him but now, in the circumstances . . . Her voice caught, got stuck in her throat. 'I, sorry, I . . .' She handed the receiver to Rob and hid her head in her hands.

So this was where it had got them, all the pussyfooting around mine shafts. They should have explored them, all of them, got to the bottom of the things, roared and screamed and let the echoes rage. What had they been afraid of? Why had they been so shy when every mound and crevice was known? And poor old Wil still clinging in silence to the other end of the line from Central.

Calvin was now crying, his nose unchecked and streaming.

'Wil,' said Robin. 'I'll write. Yes. Yes. Bye then. Yeah. I'll write. Bye.'

He replaced the receiver, listened to the small sound. It's the small sounds. Clicks, snapped twigs, boots on stone. 'Why the hell did you do that?' he said to the eyes above the hands.

Calvin was now howling at the unknown, burrowing like a liane between them.

'It's all right,' he said finally. 'It's all right. Forget it. It's all right.'

He dropped on his knees to Calvin. 'What's up, matey?'

Murray would be happy to come and mind Calvin for the day if it would be any help. He realised it would be a full-time job but if it would be any help at all he would be happy to. And he was not that struck on the wine aspect. Wine had never been one of his things. Nobody enjoyed a good Müller Thurgau more than he did, but in his opinion there was a lot of bull talked and written about the stuff, and he could take it or leave it. Besides he had always been very fond of Calvin, he said, bending to wipe the upturned nose with a decisive jerk.

'So that's all right,' Emmie told Rob beneath the duvet which was getting too hot now it was summer. He moved his legs slightly. They still had not discussed things properly. Had not had the flamer to clear the air. He had not even discovered why she had bounced at Wil, except for vague mutterings about exhaustion, and she was never exhausted. She did not know how to be exhausted, but certainly things had caught up with them. Emmeline had a part in a children's play called *Manu and the Kelpie* and his own life had gone mad with food and faces in endless combinations. People pecking at food, stuffing themselves with food, swigging and eating, eating, eating. Eating on the move like ruminants or squeezed onto narrow chairs or queuing at the buffet with already laden plates for just a touch more. A sliver of torte perhaps. A smidgen of pastrami. A bean.

They set off at daybreak in the Dionysus van to pick up the team, Emmie and Calvin in the front because of the hills. Murray sat in the back among the spare seats and the five thousand pieces. The marquee was upright, the power on, utensils at the ready, all the gear and tackle and trim of their trade was waiting in the Wairarapa.

Murray, having chosen the best seat before the other clowns arrived, had time to tell them that he'd never seen much point in all this fussing about food. Give him a good steak any day. He patted Calvin on the head. 'Comfy, son?' Calvin did not reply.

Wanda, as usual on Sundays, was unavailable. Her place had been taken by an unknown quantity called Serena, a tall rangy blonde who looked anything but. She laughed a lot as she told them in a high thready voice about some of the more gracious functions she had helped out at—the Yacht Club stayed in her mind, as did Government House. The kitchens, she told them, were out of sight. Scott, who Robin had moved from sandwiches of necessity, stared at her in silence. The rest, both regulars and casuals, nodded politely. The regulars had been forged in the heat; Merle who could do anything, Ron who was a tower of strength and Jayne who was quick off the mark.

Robin drove slowly over the long curving bends of the Rimutaka Hill. He had travelled in the back of the van many times and knew its reluctant sway, the sickening lurch of its rear end towards the edge and the cliffs of scrub and ragged bush below. No one must be sick, especially Calvin.

Serena became silent as climb and bend followed descent and sweep and the van churned upwards once again. Hadn't Dionysus got a minibus, she asked faintly.

'No,' said Scott.

They made it all in one piece.

The Wine Festival was in full swing and Dionysus was on top of things but only just.

As usual at this stage a routine had not been completely established. Things were both fluid and disorganised and would soon become hectic. People were shouting, falling over each other's feet; the vineyard owner's dog had discovered the rabbit fricassees waiting for more secure storage. They had been saved from destruction by a quick kick in the haunch from Scott who was immediately abused by Serena, Merle and an apoplectic passer-by who asked Scott what he thought we were *here* for if not to love those weaker than ourselves and she was going to report him to the SPCA immediately. Robin, who shared her sympathies but was glad the rabbit fricassees were safe, tried to keep out of it but failed. A full-scale row developed; the team were at each other's throats.

Robin exercised crowd control, his palms raised to restrain the mob. Scott, his face expressionless, dropped a carton. Black plastic plates skidded across the trestle table onto beaten grass to lie in shuddering piles around the ankles of his detractors.

'Wash them,' said Robin. 'And that's it. All of you. Now get on with it.'

Murray departed hand-in-hand with Calvin in his Foreign Legion hat, his mini-Total Block in his pocket. They would take the courtesy bus, explained Murray, just get on and off where they liked, case the joint, go where the spirit moved them, wouldn't they, Cal?

'Yeah,' said Calvin inspecting a thread of grated raw carrot left over from Emmie's farewelling hands.

Serena took over front of house. Out of the corner of his eye as he assembled for presentation, which is all, he watched her transforming the trestle tables behind which the hordes would jostle as they ordered rabbit fricassee or lamb fillet with polenta or maybe just a simple but nice blini or two with spinach and walnut salad. Serena seemed efficient as she anchored the cloths with clips, rerolled some of the hundreds of knife/fork/napkins-to-go which had slipped a bit, dealt with plates and studied the flow. 'Hey, Rob, this OK?'

They worked it out together. If they come this way?—yeah but what if they . . . ? He had done it dozens of times, worked it out as Spiro had taught him. 'A caterer is only as good as his flow.' No jams. The effort is no use if they can't get at it.

And paying on the spot would take time even with token money. 'And what about the posies?' said Serena. 'Where's the posies?' 'Oh Emmie's done pumpkins and stuff. Look.'

The first of the bell peppers, the last of the pumpkins gleamed together on straw platters. Pink potatoes shone beside ruby tamarillos and crisp apples from the cool store. Emmie's mounds of polished fruit and vegetables were cornucopias in the round; symbols, if you could stand it, of glowing abundance and plenty. A harvest festival in spring when every leaf was sharp and green and still unfurling.

The music was blaring and thumping alongside. A band he didn't know—Sinking Lid. Rock and roll meets country. Not bad. He would have a look later. The wine buffs and bibbers were already in action in the marquee alongside. The experts sampled, tasted with discern-ment. The more enthusiastic bibbers did not bother. They were into it.

The tents, the noise, the streaming crowds trekking across flattened paddocks and dusty paths reminded him. Miss Bowman had once taken Emmie and him to an A and P Show in the Wairarapa; a long haul by train and bus to every wonder in the world and a Mermaid in a Bottle. There had been no vineyards then, no heady decisions required as to nose or body or aftertaste. There had been meat pies and candyfloss and picnics and hot water from the stand behind the *Women's Rest* and a beer cavern beneath the Grandstand labelled *Gentlemen Only* where, Miss Bowman told him, he would be fortunate enough to be admitted in due course providing he behaved always in a gentlemanly and chivalrous manner.

Emmie was polishing her final pumpkin; she could make even a Green Triumble shine.

'Not the asparagus,' he yelled. 'Rebekkah's bringing the kids.' She turned to laugh, waved a hand. 'Love yah,' she yelled back.

'Hi, Rob!'

He glanced up. Rebekkah was followed by a man with a child clamped to each hand—a man so neat, so struc-tured as to appear slightly surreal. Threads of hair were plastered across his scalp, the middle button of his blazer was buttoned. Even his blond beard was a production; bits had been left out, shaved where beards normally are not. A man, it was clear, who spent time on his image.

'And this is Wes,' said Rebekkah fondly. 'We finally got it all together, didn't we, love?'

Wes agreed. It had been and still was part of an ongoing process but he and Bekk were finally learning to communicate. They had both taken counselling for dialogue skills and empathic listening between partners. The thing was to be pro-active.

'Great,' said Rob. 'Great.'

'Hey,' roared Wes grabbing Haden and Shelley whose out-stretched hands were about to deconstruct Emmeline's pumpkins. 'Watch it, you lot.'

'I bet his other dame shot through,' muttered Emmie above swirling cream and the roar of the hand beater. 'Why'd she take the creep back? Kids, I suppose. I dunno . . .' The rest was drowned as she switched to High.

Queues were forming; there was no time for words. There was heat, sun, grass, dust and action. They were, as Spiro would have told them, flat out like a lizard drinking. Chaos was contained, panic averted, the five thousand pieces were diminishing by the minute.

'We're out of tapenade!'

'Here.'

'Profiteroles!'

'Here, dummy.'

Merle and Rob were now side by side at the table. Emmie was in charge behind the chest-high structure dividing the cooking area. He glanced at her occasionally; was greeted by a grin, a wink, a snarl. He was ready to understand, even to accept her rejection of poor old Wil. He would accept anything. His heart melted through the soles of his Reeboks as his hands and the rest of his mind ticked steadily and he nodded, smiled, took tokens and nodded again at the orderly crowd which was becoming less so. Undoubtedly there would be some fat on the arse for Robin and he would give them all a bonus and have a party. He paused, his splayed fingers momentarily steady on token money. He and Emmie would have a party. A minor orgy. Jesus.

Someone was shoving, yelling, elbowing his way to the front through mutters and stirs of dissent. 'Piss off,' said a blonde in a floral hat guarding her polenta.

Nothing stopped Murray. He stood before them, his face grey and oiled with sweat. 'I've lost him,' he said.

He should have fought her. Insisted. Not that shit. Don't come. Stay home.

'Merle. Get Ron to help you till we get back, OK?'

'Sure,' said the startled face.

He would find him. Find him first, bring him back and tell her then. No. He grabbed the keys of the van. '*Emmie*,' he yelled.

The three of them squeezed in the front and shot off down the road.

'Someone'll have seen him,' he said. 'Those announcements at shows. Kids get separated all the time, remember?'

'Yes,' she said.

'I just turned round,' said Murray, 'and he'd gone.'

'Yes. He is quick.'

He couldn't even drive fast. Calvin could be anywhere; alone on the tracks beaten on the verges, outside paddocks, lost in the dust of the vineyards. Found. Found by someone decent. Someone responsible. Or otherwise. The etched image of a child walking away hand in hand.

She clutched his arm as they swung a corner.

'Christ!' yelled Murray two vineyards later. 'Look.'

Robin pulled onto the verge.

She was scrabbling over Murray's knees, her hands on the door handle.

'No!' yelled Robin.

He grabbed her back, slammed her against the seat.

She was fighting, clawing, teeth bared. She was getting out. Going to join the child and the man walking beside him.

Her nails were biting his arm.

'Listen. I'll park the van behind that shed. You stroll back. Casual. Easy. "Hi." Murray and I'll come back otherwise we'll lose him. Get it?'

'What if the guy's, you know, helping?' said Murray.

'Then we won't thump him, fuckwit.'

'And don't look as we pass,' he told her.

She clenched her eyes.

Robin signalled, turned slowly in behind the shed. It was bigger than a garage, a large barn backed by hawthorn.

She was out running before he seized her arm. '*Walk*. Just walk. And go round the other side of the shed.'

She was distracted, whimpering. He held her arms tight. 'Calm down.'

'Hh.'

'Calm down. Now!'

'Yes.' She strolled away.

'We'll give her a minute or two,' said Rob.

Murray, his mouth hanging, was silent. 'And you drive,' said Rob.

'Why?'

'Just *do* it for Chrissake. Pull over beside them. Calm, slow, we're looking at the view.'

Murray swung the van onto the road by the laughing crowd waiting for the courtesy bus at the gates of the vineyard and the group of three further along the verge. Emmie was on her knees, her face hidden.

'Now!' he said and jumped from the van as the guy took off. Robin had one glimpse of tight-faced terror and the man was away, wide shorts flapping as he sprinted down the road.

He was going to lose him. Pop music was belting above Calvin's wails, his glasses were fogged, his breath rasping as he threw himself at the slight figure and flattened him. He had hold of one foot only, its trainer slipping from his grasp, when Murray arrived, climbed into the shallow ditch and sat on the guy.

'Take him away,' he hissed over his shoulder.

'Come on, Cal,' said Emmie, tugging her reluctant child.

Robin climbed up from the spreadeagled figure, moved to the head and began thumping it on the ground. Thumping from rage, from despair, from loss of innocence.

'For Christ's sake,' said Murray, 'you'll kill the poor sod.'

A guy in a passing truck went for the cops. They handed the captive over, stared at the stained face, the T-shirt labelled *Instant Arsehole*, the tick of fear beneath the eye, the ordinariness. The dreadful pitiful ordinariness. For the first time in his life Robin was glad of Murray's presence. He might indeed have killed the guy. Left him to die face down in docks and plantain and crushed grass.

Emmeline and Calvin appeared. She was talking talking talking, explaining that when people love people they have to know where people are and people must stay with the people who are minding them and ask them for an icecream if they want one, not just go off with someone else without telling.

They climbed into the van, Murray in the back.

'Let's get one now then,' said Calvin.

*

Rob drove with one hand, hers clamped by his side, Calvin on her knee.

'Did you see his T-shirt?' she muttered behind Calvin's back.

'Yeah.'

'He shouldn't have had that T-shirt.'

'Forget it. It's just words. Letters.' He thought quickly. 'Like the ones Japanese wear. *Boogie ladder. Hopper girl,*' he said making shut-up faces above Calvin's head.

'He wasn't Japanese,' she said bleakly.

Murray sat silent, his smirk unseen as Calvin handed his mother the raspberry ripple. 'Want a bite?'

'Thanks hon. Thanks a lot.'

They parked the van on the road and walked past milling crowds and safely grazing sheep to the vineyard and the Dionysus tent beyond.

The vines were in new leaf; pin-sized green grapes stood upright on stalks, like spores on the fruiting body of some particularly unattractive fungus. Straw surrounded the roots; they were cherished these vines, cherished and precious and time consuming for their owners.

Rob was looking for distraction, finding things to show her. Men in wide-brimmed Man from Snowy River hats new since last year; men in baseball caps, designer straws, panamas. Where were the hats of yesteryear—the towelling, the canvas, the floppies? Rob caught sight of a yellow towelling in the distance and was reassured.

The shimmering silver of the bands' tent roof was glinting like a sunlit glacier above a middle-aged woman who swayed alone, arms high to snap the rhythm. Soon she must dance, join the kids, but not yet. The band had changed. A torch singer was belting out her somebody-done-somebody-wrong song, her hair grey beneath her black garden-party hat, her elegant twenties gown swinging, her voice deep and true. 'Look at the bow on her behind, Em. Just on the curve. Any good?'

'Yes.'

He got marks for trying. 'Yes,' she said again.

'*You're so rich / that's the answer,*' yelled the trouper. The applause was long and loud. The singer acknowledged it, bowed graciously beneath her feathered hat, swept her long skirt from side to side in recognition of their good taste and discernment.

'I'll go on,' said Rob.

'Just one more.'

The next song was unexpected. The husky contralto was deeper than ever, pregnant with warning above the tooty beat of the electric organ. The words were advice from a soul who had been there, had been down to the woods today and received a big surprise. It would have been safer, she confided, to have stayed at home.

Emmeline's face was motionless, deadpan as a woman in a blue movie. 'I should have killed that man,' she said. 'Why didn't I kill him?'

The food had disappeared but the packing, the sorting, the cleaning up took time. Serena was declared a good find by Merle, Ron had taken a slice out of a finger but no worries. Murray and an unchastened Calvin jigged by the dying embers of the band. Murray, as he told them, felt it was the least he could do.

It was late when they set off and there was little sound in the van as they crawled over the Rimutakas. The hills were dark, the scrub deepening to black in the steep valleys below.

Calvin fell asleep as the van left Featherston and was not alone. As Serena explained, they were all pooped.

'Rob,' said Emmie.

He changed down, hugged the curve. 'Nnn?'

'The old man, Wil.'

He was concentrating, didn't take it in. 'Yeah?'

'I'll ring him shall I? When we get home?'

He was grinning his head off. He heard his voice still grinning at the tight bends, the sharp-angled curves of the road downhill.

'It'll be too late for him tonight. Tomorrow'll do, hon.'

Thirteen

She explained her reasoning when they were in bed, made the
situation clear. He lay prostrate beside her, his eyes staring through
blurred gradations of light to the dark untidy corners of the room.
He knew the tone in her voice, put a hand to the floor for his
glasses. All senses were required. Concentration.

'It's not that I've changed my mind about her or anything.'

He would not have thought his body could have sagged further.
Not in bed. 'No,' he said.

'I just think I was a bit tough on the old guy.'

'You do, huh.'

Her face was anxious. 'You too?'

What the hell did she expect. 'Yeah.'

She gave the duvet a quick tug. 'After today I feel I ought to give
them a chance. Hear the evidence or whatever. Find out. Does that

make sense?'

He anchored his half. 'Yes.'

'It's nothing to do with you being so ace or anything. But after today . . .' She moved beside him.

'It's over, gone. I promise.'

'It wasn't Murray's fault,' she said as cramp seized his thigh.

He shot out of bed, his face manic as he pumped up down, up down till the pain faded. 'Then whose was it?' he gasped, watching her face as he crawled back beside her. 'Miss Bowman'll haunt you if you start that crap. We're not going to take on that boyo's guilt. It doesn't exist for starters.'

She ran a finger down his nose. 'You tell me things I need to know.'

'Balls.'

'Well, something.'

'OK. Something.'

His eyes were closed when she spoke again.

'There's no safe place now, is there?'

'There never was.'

'But you tend to think, when you were a kid . . .'

She lay on her back beside him, her eyes open, her arms stiff, obviously, rigidly un-asleep.

'Are you awake?'

'Nh.'

'Me too.' The pause was long. 'Tell me the history of the world.'

He dredged himself upwards, did what he could. 'First there was the Big Bang or God or both.'

'Then.'

He could hardly get the words around the yawn. 'Science or people?'

'People.'

It is a truth universally acknowledged that the history of homo sapiens as we know it . . . The consensus of opinion on the origins of man holds that . . . He was drowning in sleep, sinking, groping for lifelines. 'Africa,' he murmured.

'Lucy?'

'Yeah, Lucy, others. Lots . . . others.'

Wilfred was blown out of his mind. Like Spiro he collected idiomatic gleanings from other lands. It must be universal. At Rongotai an exchange student from Germany had come smiling to his friend Robin to tell him that he was so far up himself that Helmut was unable to call him cowboy any more.

Wilfred was still shouting down the line. 'But why *not* till after Christmas? Why not now?'

'I can't leave Dionysus and Emmie's in a kids' play.'

'A pantomime,' roared the voice. 'I saw one once. Couldn't make head nor tail of it. Weird Brit thing. Put her on the line boy. Put her on.'

Emmie took the receiver warily, held it at some distance. 'Hello, Wilfred.'

'I've worked it out,' she said later. 'We'll be flat out till after Christmas. I'll just forget the whole thing. Let it sneak up on me like summer.' He knew what she meant. The warmth which now seemed constant had been skulking and reappearing for weeks.

The refrigerator art had brightened. Images of sun and sand and matchstick heads in pink seas covered the door. The black smudges, Calvin told them, were sharks.

Postbank staff were busy, their faces glum beneath red festive nightcaps trimmed with white. They had not been consulted. Nor did they think nightcaps were the answer. Carol singers busked in green cassocks and work boots before a window decked with artificial snow and angels and Donald Duck seesawing in endless metronomic union with Mickey Mouse. The lights were up in Oriental Bay.

There were other signs of summer. Young women in filmy grey or black habits slashed to the thigh strode down Lambton Quay in boots or sat laughing with lunch and lovers at Oriental Bay as joggers rolled by beneath the Norfolk pines. Thin strappy frocks above T-shirts were long and postulant-like, but according to Emmie things would get better in high summer when the shirts were abandoned whereupon their wearers would be virtually naked above and shrouded below which would be interesting wouldn't it, and would Rob take Calvin to see Santa and for God's sake watch him. Haden, she said, had already been.

'Hold my hand,' he said giving a quick sideways skip to avoid a skateboard on the crossing.

'Naa.'

'No cool yule then.'

Small, boneless and hot, the hand appeared in his. Calvin's mind followed no obvious thought patterns; he was interesting, a one-off job like his mother but less predictable. Rob grinned at the thought, glanced down at the orange bristle beside him and met the cool gaze beneath.

Emmeline was undoubtedly busy. She scrambled from rehearsals for *Manu and the Kelpie* to radio plays, from voiceovers to TV commercials for cheese and one next week for toilet cleaner but what the hell, they paid well and anything would be better than those green things dangling from the rim waiting for extinction from one squirt of whatever it was. Any moment soon she hoped to graduate to drench. Drench and dip are prime time—when the farmers are having their tea.

The university was empty, Robin's marking finished.

The essential quality of poetry is that it makes a new effort of retention and 'discovers' a new world within the known world. Discuss this statement of D.H. Lawrence in relation to his own poetry.

As always he had been depressed by the depths and heartened by the peaks and pleased by the dark horses, the late starters, the also-rans who had pulled through against form.

As always he had fought for the deserving in post-examination grading sessions. They had done much better during the year in assignments, look at their records again. He insisted, would not be dissuaded and they passed. One of them who reminded him of Cara, generous in her triumph and unaware of its cause, sent him a card of the kotuku nesting in splendour at Okarito. She was going to have a go at American lit next year. *Moby Dick* was not mentioned.

His thesis languished as he had known it would. Dionysus Catering had taken over and November had been as busy as Spiro had predicted. 'Every year they start earlier for Christmas. Soon it will be October we are sweating, then December dead as mutton.'

So his thesis was on hold, on the back burner and possibly down the tubes. It all depended on what happened down south. Emmie was right, he thought, watching Calvin perched on a wide red satin knee in Santa's Cave between Toys and Children's Wear. There were too many variables. No point in thinking about it. Not at this stage.

Santa's boots were impressive, wide Cretan broad-nosed ones inadequately trimmed with cotton wool. The red pyjama suit was slippery, not a good choice, for knee work. Presumably the poor guy would have expired in wool. The beard was more con-vincing, false but not ridiculous, the hat a sumptuous squash of red with a cockade. The face was doing its best, nodding with encourage-ment, smiling incessantly between steel-rimmed specs and silver curls. Calvin, was it? That was an unusual name. Calvin. We don't get many Calvins do we, he asked a passing elf. And what did Calvin want for Christmas?

Calvin told him in some detail. The list was long and compre-hensive and did not include freshwater tropicals. Father Christmas winked at Robin above Calvin's head. He should not have done that. He should take more pride in his work. If F. Christmas, sweating among tinsel streamers, silver bells, edible Christmas trees and smiling elves, could not sustain a willing suspension of disbelief who the hell could.

Calvin did not like his gift. He already had a ball at home he explained, and attempted an exchange, but Santa had disappeared. He had gone, said the elf, to feed the reindeer. Calvin's gaze was more cool than ever, his disbelief total.

Robin took Ruby and Calvin to see *Manu and the Kelpie*. They liked monsters and impersonated them frequently, roaring and shaking and munching air at each other with stiffened fingers. This one, however, was a noble mythical water spirit. An object of awe and reverence not given to drowning travellers, at least not in this play. Nor did it appear in the form of a horse. This kelpie was a long-tailed creature, all shimmering greens and brackish weeds as it writhed and undulated its saving destiny across the stage. There were no shudders of fear or dread from the audience, no frissons of pity or terror. This was an amiable monster, glad to be befriended in its struggle against the evil forces of open-cast mining by a Maori boy called Manu and his friend Rosie played by Emmeline in brief shorts and a cap full of hair.

Like some other morality plays *Manu and the Kelpie* had its jokes, most of which fell flat with good reason. Calvin and Ruby preferred the slam bang of slapstick, the cut and thrust of action drama.

The best bit was the fight at the end when the kids won eh.

Spiro had had an excellent time in Kalives and was glad to be home. The best of all; good to go, good to come back. To be once more with the work and the fish. He had danced, drunk, kissed and fought. A ball he had had, and would have another one quite soon, now he knew Robin would turn up trumps. He had always known Robin could do it. Spiro had extracted this competence, on which Robin could look back in his darker moments which we all have even when we think they will never come again. 'And I have decided to buy a cellphone,' he said.

'But you hate phones.'

'For talk, I hate them, not for work. The bridegroom is a mechanic in Chania and has a share in a drycleaning business. Two jobs he can run.'

He presented Robin with a reproduction Attic vase depicting a priapic satyr in full cry after his fellows. Emmeline would be interested. Also Calvin. A gift for the whole family.

The Dionysus books were examined with care, menus inspected, new ones discussed. Robin's heart expanded. It was over—and now for Central Otago. He dragged Calvin from the hypnotic fish, from the driftings and dreamings and sudden decisive dartings, embraced

Spiro and headed down the hill.

Andoni had left a note on departure. He had enjoyed his time in Wellington and felt much better for the change. The fish had been fed that morning in case the aircraft crashed. He wished to know all and would ring.

What Emmie was going to do was simply to enjoy the holiday. She couldn't think when she had last had a holiday—I mean *gone* on one you know? Packed a bag and shoved off somewhere. And Rob deserved one, not only Dionysus but look how much he'd done during *Manu and the Kelpie*, and boy, a hand in need is a hand indeed and not only a hand and why didn't he come over here right this minute.

And one thing she would promise. She would give Wilfred a chance, a fair crack of the whip. She would just sit still and listen, hear the old guy out and then she would make up her mind about the whole thing. Quietly, soberly and in the fear of God Emmeline would consider the evidence, she would not become emotional. Robin need not worry.

The holiday did not begin well. Robin, alarmed at the thought of Calvin in the back seat for two whole days, had insisted they fly and hire a car in Dunedin. Also he had scruples about Emmeline paying her share with Aunt's money. Truth was one thing—knives in the back of the deceased, as Eileen might have said, were a different thing again.

Emmie went disorganised on him at the last minute; she was still flinging things into the suitcase as the taxi arrived, still grinning maniacally at Calvin as she explained why his new trike couldn't come but it didn't matter as they were going to have *fun* and had anybody cancelled the mail? No—well maybe she better, oh, he *had*. Great.

'The cab,' said Robin, 'is waiting.'

She was not much better at the airport, skidding around hunting for Wet Ones in case You Know Who is s–i–c–k, not that he will be of course, and great, she hadn't seen a *Metro* for months.

'They have them,' said Robin, 'on the plane.'

'Yeah, but . . .'

'We are boarding *now*.'

He sank into his seat. Emmie was staring at her boarding pass, her face puzzled. 'Why am I Bombgardner all of a sudden?'

'Because you've got the wrong boarding pass.'

'How in the world did I do that?'

'I have no idea.'

Mrs Bombgardner, large, blonde and draped in palm trees and bananas, surfaced from the seat in front. 'Now how in the world, Elsa Bombgardner, did you turn into O'Malley at your age?' They laughed, they were happy, they agreed it was the oddest thing but they guessed they were on board now and that was the main thing.

Calvin loved airports; aircraft, balloons, heavier-than-air machines delighted him. He sat wide eyed and beaming as the plane took off, liked the wrinkled sea below but took against the mountains the moment they appeared. Those hills were horrible. He did not like those hills. He began to bawl. He wanted to get out. Now. Right now. Immediately.

Alice had opened the box of her unread letters above these mountains where her grandson was now 'creating'. Robin, as Emmeline told him, had an overdeveloped imagination but was pragmatic as a boot. With which he agreed, prided himself. No fey Celtic stuff about Dromgoole he remembered as the hairs on the back of his neck crawled. No ghosts here.

The man in the seat opposite Rob moved to the back. Emmie attempted comfort, the flight attendant sweets. Calvin clutched them in one fist and kept bawling. Tears shot from his eyes, splashed and fell again. But what is it, hon? What *is* it? I want to get out. I want to go away. Now.

'You don't think he's going to turn into a little shit, do you?' muttered Emmeline.

'Not a chance. Here Calvin.'

Calvin did not pause.

'Throw the little bugger over here,' said a voice behind them. Robin turned in fury.

'Hi,' said Clyde.

'What the hell are you doing?'

'Wishing I'd brought my Walkman.'

'OK. You come and shut him up and I'll do the smart stuff.'

'Right. Move over.' Clyde ambled into the aisle, tugged his track-suit pants, sat beside Emmie and took the momentarily silenced child on his lap.

'Hi,' he said. He told him his name was Clyde and did Calvin know about hydroelectric power stations and dams because he worked on one called the Clyde, named after him, because it was his and Calvin, was that right, Calvin, should come and see it some time. Clyde could show him the control room and the generators and the turbines and did Calvin know about penstocks? Had Emmie got a piece of paper? He drew diagrams with a felt pen. There was nothing in the world like dams and water under pressure. Wait till Calvin came one day and they opened the tailrace. Did Calvin know about tailraces? People talk about them as though they're normal. They are much more than that, they're super-normal. Did Calvin know about Superman? Yeah. Well, tailraces are Superwater. Water like all the water in the world, more water faster than anyone could believe, that was what happened with tailraces and dams.

Calvin, calmed by technologies beyond his dreams, lay still.

'Best day's work you ever did, chucking me out,' said Clyde.

'I didn't.'

'Well me, then. We'd just discovered Diane was pregnant. I couldn't handle it. I had to have my dinky little degree, my As and Bs and all that shit like I told you. Not kids. There was a heavy scene. A real slammer and Diane threw me out. I couldn't handle that either. I got blind, can't even remember where I got the knife.' Clyde shook his beautiful shaggy blond head in disbelief. 'God, what a clown. It was the shirt that saved you. Still got that shirt?'

'Yeah,' grinned Robin.

'Nice shirt. Like I was saying, I chucked it and we came south. Best thing we've ever done. Buster had a stinker of a cold so Diane didn't make it up to Auntie's funeral which was sad. She was a feisty old girl but glad to go. She told Mum. "I'm ready to go Edie," she said.' Clyde was talking, relaxed, in charge, he would yarn for ever. 'They change every day little kids, y'know that? Ever been to Cromwell? Pity about the drowned bit but it's a nice little town. Orchards and stuff and the pay's good.'

'Plenty of apricots?' asked Rob.

'Yeah, sure. Tons. D'y'want some?'

Wil came swinging across the concrete to greet them, one hand out to grasp, his khaki hat crumpled in the other. He was not smiling. He looked older, bleached and spare as a dried river bed.

He shook Emmeline's hand. 'Pleased to meet you,' he said and looked down at the grin beside her. 'And what's your name?'

'Calvin.'

'Calvin. If I don't remember you tell me.'

'OK.'

'Come away in.'

They progressed in silence across the yard, Calvin detouring to embrace the labrador. The old dog clambered to its feet, licked the face and collapsed once more.

The air was warm around them, the dogs quiet, the breeze drifting across dry paddocks to the pine trees. There was not a rare fowl in sight. 'Mind the crap,' said Wil and was silent once more. Unease stirred around them. This was not what Rob had expected. He had told Emmie how delighted Wil would be to see them. How he loved kids, how excited he would be, how he was a great old guy.

Emmie strode beside him in silence, her head high. Half-way across the yard she started babbling in praise. In praise of everything. How much she admired the cottage, how cute it was and look at the view and they certainly were happy to be in Central, weren't they Rob? She had never even been to the South Island before could

Wilfred believe. She could see just from Dunedin and the Pigroot that scenic-wise it left the north for dead just like everyone said, and they were so right.

She couldn't imagine how anyone would want to live anywhere else. Rob had told her it was freezing in winter but she wouldn't mind that either. She liked a summer life, sure, but being a redhead summer was a bit of a drag even with Total Block, and Calvin was the same, poor little sausage, and anyway she liked the cosiness of winter. Close the door, light the lights, all that. She could see it was different for farmers, they couldn't do that, could they? Out in all weathers, weren't they?

'Yes,' said Wilfred.

Every sort. Yeah. She realised that. Those shots on TV of un-seasonal snow storms. Dead lambs, starving cattle, the lot. But didn't Wilfred agree? Didn't he agree there was something about winter?

'No.'

Nothing put her off. She was frenetic, could not, apparently, keep either still or quiet. Sidestepping, gushing at labradors, prat-tling. Nothing would stop her. 'Don't worry Cal,' she said lifting the child from mess underfoot and restarting him on a cleaner route. 'It's ornamental fowl. A higher class of crud altogether. Not many people have ornamental fowl.'

She flashed Rob a rictus grin, included him in her embarrassing attempts at goodwill and social concourse. 'Do they, Rob?'

He couldn't believe it. Her. Wilfred. Any of it. 'No,' he said.

Wilfred was moving stiffly, his left leg swinging wider than ever. He stopped suddenly without explanation. Emmie, taken by sur-prise, ploughed into him, apologised endlessly and made it worse.

He stood silent, not looking at her, his mouth clamped tight as he gazed over the plain and waited for her to shut up. Rob stopped beside him, the suitcases held well above the ground.

Calvin was now playing a form of free-range hopscotch among the droppings. Eventually, without explanation or comment, Wilfred moved on through the airlock porch to the kitchen.

'Make the tea will you?' he said crashing onto a chair. Bess's kick had certainly aged him.

Emmie was now banging on about the mess and muddle of the kitchen. It was wonderful, a real *farm* kitchen. Did Wilfred know she'd done a TV ad for drench? No she couldn't remember which one. Not just at the moment, which was mad, but she would. Probably about three in the morning ha ha.

Robin began to hope for Shara's return; a counter-irritant of any sort would be welcome. He could not join the conversation, ask after Shara, about Doug who had given him the lift to Dunedin, about anything or anybody. Once or twice he opened his mouth and shut it again as she continued to behave like some sort of Mad Hatter hostess entertaining the old man in his own kitchen, making him welcome in his own home with hysterical overreach.

She was on to horses, the shock of being kicked by and how awful. That was one thing she could bet on. One thing which would never happen to her, no way. Not in a bull's roar. She had never ridden, never even sat on one, could he believe. Boy, she could see why the Brit cops use them for crowd control. Give Emmeline long batons any day.

Rob could feel his teeth, his locked jaw. 'Emmie,' he hissed.

She turned to him, her eyes bright, blinking, her mouth all over the place. 'Yes?'

Wilfred was laughing. Or something like it. The process was drawn out and appeared painful. It began slowly, forced its way into wheezing guffaws which turned to gut-wrenching explosions of mirth or grief.

Calvin, who knew about jokes, grabbed another chocolate biscuit and joined in, yelping with excitement and spraying crumbs.

Wilfred's head was shaking, his eyes streaming, his hands clutching his sides like F. Christmas on a Ho-ho-ho jag. Calvin's finger followed the old man's pointing one. 'Mum!' he yelled.

'And you say,' gasped Wil, 'you say you're not her daughter.'

*

There were explanations of course. Explanations called for and given. Emmeline was not pleased. She sat stiff-backed and demanded them. She had not come all this way to be made a fool of, not that she minded that, never had, but she hadn't wanted to come in the first place—or ever. And what Wilfred thought he was doing behaving as though she was some long lost Anastasia figure she couldn't imagine. And as for Rob sitting around like a spare lemon and Calvin—Calvin could be quiet this *instant*, like now.

Wilfred apologised. He should not have done that. He hadn't meant to upset Emmeline, not for a minute. It was just the whole thing was a bit of a shock if you like. He'd never even seen a photo of Emmeline and then to see her climbing out of the car a dead ringer for Alice though the hair was wrong . . . It had knocked him for six. Had caught him between wind and water, left him speechless, and then, and then, and then . . .

The old man was mopping his eyes again, leaving wet patches on a large checked handkerchief.

And then to see her, to see her behaving exactly like Alice (hang on lass, hang on), like Alice in Dalgety's tent or at a wedding or wherever, when she was nervous. No, it was too much.

He shook his head, picked up Emmie's hand and held it. 'Too much,' he said. 'Forget it, lass. Won't happen again. Just have a holiday. No sweat. Just relax.'

'I am relaxed,' snarled Emmie.

Shara was at the doorway in stockinged feet, her arms cradling a large half-dead lamb. 'Shoot, that water race,' she said. 'I still say we need a fence.' She glanced around counting heads. 'Come and help, boy.' The lamb was installed in a carton beside the hot-water cylinder. Shara explained about bottle feeding and frequency of same. Calvin's grin was constant. A lamb of his own, a lamb none of the other kids had, a lamb called Spud whose tail jiggled when Calvin fed him. Misha had never let on whether she liked him or not.

The time he could spare from Spud he devoted to Shara. They disappeared for the day (You've got to let him, Em. Yeah, I know. I know), Calvin crowing like a sun-screened rooster from the pommel end of the saddle, Shara behind. They saw a dead sheep with a lamb's feet sticking out its bottom and a hawk eating a lamb. Shara said she didn't know whether the hawk had killed it or not but Calvin reckoned it had, his hand demonstrating the killer dive.

Is that a soldier hat, Wil? Yes. Can I have it? For now you can but only inside. Why not for always? No. Did you have a gun in the war? Yes. Did you kill people? Yes. Where is it? Handed back. Haven't you got a gun at all then? Yes. Where? The cupboard was unlocked, the empty twenty-two and three-nought-three inspected, the differences explained, the mechanisms demonstrated. Can I have them? No. Do you use them? Not often. Calvin nodded at the face peering down the empty barrel. 'Getting a bit old, I suppose.'

Emmie and Rob took over the food to Shara's delight. It was the one thing, the only thing, that got up her nose about Central. Not being able to call up a Thai, a Mexican, even a goddamn pizza. Not even a deli-to-go. She had never been into food, let alone fixing the stuff. It was like, you know, the worst thing, the pits, knowing that every day after you've kicked off your boots you have to cook something dead and what was worse you have to think about it. Sure there was never anything but mutton, but would you broil, or baste, or fling bits around in a skillet? She couldn't face it, except she had to, it was part of the deal. In fact when she'd first arrived it was the deal, and she had to say Wil was the unfussiest guy in the world. He'd eat anything and sometimes had to. So sure Em, sure, she's all yours and Rob could come and help clean up after she killed.

'How do you think he is?' asked Rob hosing the sweet stench of blood from beneath the dripping carcase.

The fluorescent light turned Shara blue, her nose purple.

'I think he's more frail, like he has little naps. I go in an hour later and he's still out for the count with his mouth open. That kick didn't do him any good.'

There wouldn't be many women you could ask. 'How are the

matrimony stakes?'

'Naa. He's too old. Before Bess maybe, and all this razzmatazz about Emmeline. He's gotten to the stage of one thing at a time, emotion-wise as well. I'll stay, mind. I like him. I'll look after him, but then it's good-night nurse.' Robin, now busy with the straw broom, glanced at her. She was compact, sinewy, androgynous and straight as a die, a 'lovely little outdoor worker'. 'I'll miss him though. I like the old guy.'

Wil had rescued their arrival from near disaster and Emmie tried to do the same. There was the obligatory visit to the frocks. The shed was now stuffy, the smell of moth balls and unaired frocks more obvious in the heat. Emmie, finally speechless, stood in the middle, her hands twisting with misery or something like it, while Wil, oblivious and proud as ever, conducted his guided tour, explained the relative positions allocated to his ex-wives' garments—the reason why Alice had fewer than Doris or Ivy being that, unlike them, she was not a home dressmaker. He invited Emmeline to feel, to handle, to admire and praise.

Robin stood close to her.

Wil had never again alluded to Alice as her mother, had never forgotten Emmeline's name, nor indeed Calvin's. He seemed, for all his frailty, to be in a state approaching euphoria. Controlled euphoria. He was not going to muck things up again. He tried to keep his eyes off Emmeline and often achieved it. She was his guest, she was here on holiday.

They were being made happy, welcomed up Central for the farm holiday of a lifetime, but Robin was conscious of the tension at the end of the line. Something was ticking like the reel of an old western clicking from sprocket to sprocket as the charge snaked along the fuse to the keg at the head of the canyon and the camera flicked back and forth from the tense faces of the bad to the unknowing innocent good as they rode onwards. In *High Noon* it had been the clock at the railway station. Wittgenstein, like Emmeline, had loved westerns. He had read it somewhere.

They swam in the creek, picnicked on boiled mutton sandwiches and discussed next day's plan beside the Smoker's Companion. Their only failure was the Gold Trail.

Calvin, having expressed mild interest in panning for the stuff, lost interest and demanded to get back to Spud. And there was a gate up the back needed fixing and he and Shara had to check out the race again and why couldn't they go home to the farm and stay there?

'This is heaven,' she said scrambling up from the creek. 'But it's false pretences.'

He was on his back watching the sharp leaves cut the sunlight to pieces. 'Yes.'

'Why do you always agree? Why can't you tell me I'm wrong? And now he wants me to look at letters or something.'

'I know.'

'So why didn't you tell me?'

'Because he wanted to. Hey—I've got a note of Alice's I should've given back to you. From Miss Bowman's copy of *The Load*.' A Freudian flicker. He had not wanted, still did not want her to do a Murray. To get it all wrong. So he had forgotten. Forgotten temporarily, for six months.

She was standing now, drying herself with her knickers. The patterns of light and shade were interesting, her trunk dappled as a plane tree's.

'What's it say?'

'"He is dead. I am coming. Hurray."'

She paused, one hand across her breasts like a pared-down version of an Edwardian postcard labelled *Summer Days*.

'Lovers?'

'No.'

'It's a thought though.' She stood silent, dredging up memories. 'Naa. I was only nine but . . . No. There was no affection, no tenderness or loving welcome. Anything but, from memory. Nothing in their mien,' she said sending up the word. 'Nothing at all. Just

299

Aunt being tougher than ever and Alice moping about like a wet hen.'

'There was nothing in their *mien*,' he said removing a thread of green river slime from his foot, 'because they were not lovers and never had been. By the time you saw them they were not even friends.'

'You know he wants to leave Emmie the farm,' said Shara as she flung the shovels into the tray of the truck. She was dressed as usual— boots, shorts, bleached shirt. Her arms and legs were tanned leather, the mahogany V of her neck edged with white.

Not that. 'No,' he muttered.

'Yeah.' She swung the truck out the gate and headed straight into the sun, her eyes squinting up the track as she changed the subject. 'The race needs a new ram. It's junked out completely this time.' She was giving him an out, a chance to leave it there. It was not his problem. She just thought she would mention farm legacies in passing.

He looked at her sharp little face, her kid's hands clamping the wheel, wondering why he found her so attractive, liked her so much, why she had become one of the few people of whom—when he walked into a room and she was there, drinking her beer, checking her Lotto ticket, standing on her head eating lettuce because Calvin wanted to see—he would think, 'Good. There's Shara. Good.'

She was, you could say, centred. She had got it all together. Slice her where you like; longitudinal, sagittal or transverse, Shara would stain true throughout. He could not ignore her confidence.

'How do you know?'

Not a glance. Eyes still peering ahead. 'How d'you reckon? The guy told me.'

'Emmie wouldn't accept it.'

Now she did look at him. The pitying glance, the half-sneer of one confronted by the unfathomable ignorance of someone who does not understand about land.

'I know,' he insisted.

'And what about Calvin?'

He jumped out to open a gate. Had time to think before he slammed the door shut. 'All kids love farms, that's nothing.' He put a hand on her knee, removed it immediately. It had turned into something unattractive, unwanted as a dead toad, a sloughed-off skin. 'Don't worry,' he said.

'Me? Why should I worry?'

He told Emmeline in the shed later. They had reached the stage where everything was discussed automatically. It saved having to charge out shouting to reverberate hills and the answers were more interesting and conceivably there might be understanding, discourse, the exchange of thought.

'Who said?'

He was head down cleaning a shovel. 'Wil, according to Shara.'

Emmeline heaved herself onto the work bench, ran a hand along the vice. 'You could crack macadamias in this,' she said.

'They'd be squashed.'

She wiped the back of her hand in a slow outward curve beneath her nose, inspected threads of hair. 'We'll have to go home. It's bad enough being here under false pretences without this courtiers-hissing-in-the-wings stuff.'

'"I thought the King had more affected the Duke of Albany than Cornwall?"'

She looked at him with something like despair. 'Well, you'd know.'

Central Otago was on slow bake; heat shimmered above the plain, the creeks were low, even his hayfever had dried out. Calvin's sunscreen had to be renewed hourly. He was a pinker shade of pale, Emmie a proud ecru, Robin tanned to a crisp. They looked as healthy as Aucklanders or Australians or other outdoor persons at risk.

Wilfred and Calvin appeared to enjoy each other's company. They devised games, walked together each morning to collect the paper from the gate so Wilfred would have all day to fulminate about its contents. The first time Rob saw their back views disappearing hand in hand down the paddock he pulled the pink-rose curtains shut quickly. She saw his face, sat up. 'What is it?'

'Nothing.'

She was out of bed beside him, tugging at roses. She hid her head on the back of his neck for a second.

'We still don't know the date of the hearing.'

'It takes time.'

'Yes,' she said. 'Yes, it does.'

The ground rules of the minefield game were simple. Fowl droppings were mines, the explosion of which was euphemised by Wilfred to the pop of a deflated balloon. They laid the path together, Wilfred wielding scissors, Calvin laying masking tape to indicate safe passage. Inspection was made each morning for enemy action and adjustments made as required.

Wil straightened to greet them. 'Minefields,' he said, 'are messy.' His eyes were very blue. He had been there and he knew and he had nothing to hide. They stared at masking tape and bird shit.

'Calvin and I are going to his Gran's grave this afternoon. Anyone coming?'

'No,' said Emmie.

She would not. She had said right at the beginning that she would not. OK, OK, she was prepared to accept the fact that Wil hadn't meant it, that Gran had just slipped out, whatever that meant, and how anything could slip out if it hadn't been there in the first place was beyond her. Wil had promised he would play it cool. Gran wasn't cool. Gran was hot as hell. The whole thing was too much. She had had enough, she didn't mean to be ungrateful but he kept changing the rules like that shitty game. They'd had a wonderful time and he was a nice old guy, she meant it, but oh Rob, let's go home now. And she was going anyhow.

The skin beneath her eyes was damp, her hands moving. Emmeline, like Shara or Aunt, was tough, but when she was nervous, bewildered, when life was beginning to fray at the edges, it showed.

'Don't worry,' he said. 'It'll be all right.'

So that's another thing solved wouldn't you say, man, wouldn't you say.

They told Wilfred they would be going home on Friday. They stood shoulder to shoulder carrying the banner of solidarity between them and thanked him profusely, Emmie smiling, Robin not. He was disgusted with himself. And God. Eileen's God, Miss Cranborne at Sunday School's God, the God who died for us and gives us the peace that passeth all understanding when we forget self for the good of others, right.

He had given away the guts of his thesis for Emmeline and was happy to do so. Hell, yes, more than happy. So why did he feel like a plucked capon, something emasculated and by no means at peace? Because his work, his work which was not done, was important. Not important in the overall scheme of things whatever that was, but important to him. His. And not only his. That was one of the main reasons for his frustration. He had discovered something of interest which would illuminate the work of Alice O'Leary who was a good writer and undervalued. Something which should be said. And here he was giving that away and he should feel better, not worse. Infinitely worse. An ineffectual angel banging and bleating away up Central. His anger started with himself and moved on. Not for the first time he wondered how anybody who did not believe in God could be infuriated by Him.

The old man had watched them in silence, eyes hooded, mouth turtle-clamped. He was detached, dry as a sunbaked stone.

'You haven't read your mother's letters.'

'Don't call her my mother.'

Wilfred stood there, stood there hatless in the sun stroking his axe handle, the blade glinting as he changed hands. 'My wife then, and she wasn't that either. I want you to read Alice O'Leary's letters.'

'Sure,' said Emmeline. 'Sure.'

*

'Mum,' said Calvin licking tomato sauce off a slab of luncheon sausage. 'There's butterflies, Wil says. Blue butterflies. C'mon Mum, come on.'

They set off in the truck. Shara had disappeared as she often did at weekends, leaving no message or evidence of her existence except small work boots side by side in the porch. If asked on her return of her whereabouts she said she had been mucking about and the race was OK again now but it wouldn't last, no way. So why leave her working boots behind. Nobody asked.

'What's the matter?' whispered Emmie in his ear.

'Nothing,' he said staring out the window. How could she be so obtuse as to be unaware that his great find, the heart of his original research, was being forfeited? Or perhaps she had noticed and had chosen to ignore it which would be worse. No, she would not do that.

And what did he want her to do? Gush? Fall about with thanks? It was his decision. He was behaving like one of those bozos at Spiro-catered pre-Christmas functions. (*Have you booked yours yet?*) Guys winking man to man across tables as they overdosed on illicit cream and pork chops and advised each other not to let the wife see. Whose coronary is it anyway?

But she might bloody well notice.

'I will read the letters,' she told him as they climbed out at the cemetery. 'I said I would.'

It was not enough. 'Great,' he said.

Wilfred was right about the butterflies. Clouds of small blue ones rose round their ankles as they walked through grass dried to straw. They were an exact match with the pale blue wahlenbergias as he knew they would be. A redheaded kid chasing blue butterflies in a silver paddock, he thought sourly, is a pretty sight.

Emmie had given him up and was walking beside Wilfred. They moved towards Alice's grave while Calvin crashed about searching gravestones for Cs and Rs for Ruby and Hs for Haden.

'Why are some of them crooked?' said Calvin, his hand tilting.

'Subsidence,' snapped Robin and strode to the cliff edge. He

304

now had bloodymindedness to add to stupidity, the stupidity of those who seethe in silence and expect others to determine the cause, to glance inside the head of the wounded and understand.

Spiro's fish were wrong. Words could help, it was just a matter of finding them and the time and the place. Nothing more. Easy. Robin stood staring across the plain to North Rough Ridge and Raggedy Range beyond, his chest tight with self-hatred. He stood there for ten minutes or more watching the heat haze, the dark shelter belts, the river. His breathing slowed, became regular, unnoticed as a sleeping child's. He had a momentary glimpse of how life should be, could be. Anything seemed possible, levitation became an option as his arms moved and he felt again that extraordinary weightlessness as though wings could sprout and human beings could change and everything would be all right and he must find Emmie immediately to tell her, because she might not have noticed that this was a good place. That there are good places. He ran to join them, dodging graves and tussock, bounding around fallen headstones surrounded by warmth and sky and the bleached-hay smell of summer. It was important that he bring the news as soon as possible.

They scarcely glanced at him. They were busy talking.

'You said you weren't married,' said Emmie.

'We weren't.'

'But it says wife. Third wife.'

'I lied.'

She took that one on board in silence. 'And why didn't you mention her books?'

'Rob said that too, didn't you?'

'Yes.'

She was very still. 'Let's go back and read the letters,' she said.

Wilfred made formal, almost ceremonial, arrangements. He escorted Emmie to the front room, handed over the cardboard box in silence, moved the Smoker's Companion to one side, plumped the hessian cushion on the sofa where he thought she would be most comfortable because she would have more room and did not explain for what. He promised her she would not be disturbed, that he would look after Calvin. It was time the hens were fed anyhow and she was not to worry on that score and heaven knows where Shara'd got to. Come on, Rob.

Rob glanced at her. She nodded. She would examine the evidence in private.

He headed up the track to the low curve of hills behind the house. Emotional trauma, landslides, would be taking place in that musty hessian-coloured room; the only friendly charge, if any, from a plywood Ancient Egyptian with his hands out. Rob wanted to rush back, to burn his goddamn notes. To help her.

He tried to work things out but failed. Thought happened inside, grim hacking stuff undistracted by spur-winged plovers and sprouting cowpats and an unknown fungus on a fallen pine.

Shara was striding towards him in mud-stained Nikes. It was early evening, the air soft above burnt paddocks, space infinite, time running out.

The sheep tracks were empty, the animals silent beneath the last of the sunset. It had not blazed; a trace of pink cloud, a few streaks of grey, a flattened sun balanced for a few moments on the edge of the world before sinking. Nothing spectacular.

For once Shara wasn't squinting against the sun. Her crowsfeet were milky white, her eyes brown. 'Where do you go to on Sundays?' he asked.

'I walk round the farm.'

'Why not wear boots?'

'Because if I wore them I'd work. There's always something. This way I just look.'

She gave a large sniff, a long drawn inhalation, a short puff out. 'Emmie's reading the letters, isn't she?'

'Yes. How'd you guess?'

'I figured she would after seeing Mom's grave.'

Her head was at shoulder height beside him, a crisp loner with insight.

'The letters prove it,' she said.

'I haven't read them.'

'Wait till you do.' She kicked over a nodding thistle, attacked the root with muddy shoes. 'I read the lot when Wil was in hospital.'

You did, huh.

'Emmie wouldn't accept the farm. I've told you that,' he said.

'Get real,' said Shara and strode on.

Emmie was waiting with the box in her hands. 'Hi, Shara.'

Shara lifted a hand and marched into the implement shed. They could hear her slamming about inside.

'Come round the front,' said Emmeline. Geraniums and a few sun-scorched daisies crackled against them as they passed. For the first time in memory the front door was open. Drifts of cobwebs brushed their hair as they walked through to the stuffy room.

Her face was stained and damp, her nose pink, her voice sharp with effort. 'You're right,' she said.

She shoved the box into his hands as though she hated him, them, the battered cardboard. 'Here. Read them. I'm going to howl my head off.'

'Emmeline.'

'Read them.'

The writing was bold; black, spiky attenuated shapes lay diagonally across the page in the latter ones. The early ones were printed in lower case in the daft way adults do in letters for little kids too young to read them.

The letters were short, lively and of no literary merit. No mute inglorious Edward Lear awaited resurrection here. There were sketches to illustrate: a tortoise, a barn, a hysterical stick Alice jumping over a crescent moon at a letter from her daughter.

Each letter began *My darling child.* There were early two-liners in cat/mat rhyme. Mock rhymes appeared later when Emmie could get the joke.

My tortoise
Is full of porpoise.
He doesn't mess about
When the lettuce comes out.
He heads across the grass with action
For lettuce is a star attraction
For all Hard Tops who love the good things,
For all small girls that extra luck brings.

And yes, there was the text, the goddamn subtext, even in the worst ones.

Even a hen
Can say When,
Even a stoat
Can say Won't.
Whereas a Paradise Bird on appointment
Can turn out a grave disappointment
There's no telling. That's
fine, yes. But quelling.
It's better when animals soar
And not nearly as much of a bore.

The last letter was written just before Alice left for New Zealand.

My darling child,
I can't write sense. I am about to explode with happiness.
You and Candida will have to stick the pieces together when I see
you in Wellington. I hope you'll do a better job than poor Humpty
Dumpty's medics!

It was signed as always *Your loving friend, Alice*. Nothing heavy.

Robin sat holding the empty box for some time before restowing the letters and heading for the pink bedroom.

She was asleep. Well, that was good. That's the best thing, isn't it, when you are emotionally drained. My partner is emotionally drained. Sweet Christ, my sweet partner. She sat up. Letters skidded from the unbalanced box, cascading to the floor like plastic plates.

'You all right?'

That cockeyed half-smile. 'Well, it's a bit of a shock.'

'Of course, yes.'

She stroked pink floral cretonne, gave it her full attention. 'It's *how* she wrote. All that fun stuff, all longing hidden. So happy. That's what gets me. Not even signing herself *Mother* or *Mom* or whatever. Alice didn't know Aunt had ditched her. And it's not only that. Think of the effort she must have made not to muddle me, to write cheerful letters without hooks, no "love me because I'm your mother and I am miserable" tags.'

Her face was whiter than ever against the rioting pinks of the pillow roses. 'I couldn't do that. Not for eight years. Not for eight weeks. And not one of them *read*. Think about it.'

She jumped up from the bed, grabbed a towel. 'I'm going to have a shower.' She turned at the door. 'And where does it leave Aunt?'

She said the same thing in the kitchen after Calvin had gone to bed and they sat around the kitchen table. Moths banged against the lighted window, a morepork called, Blake the labrador and Bugle lay sleeping muzzle to muzzle.

Shara stood up. 'Night,' she said.

'No, no, Shara, don't go,' said Emmeline.

No fuss. I go or I don't go. I do it or I don't do it. Shara sat.

Emmeline explained, her face lit by the fluorescent light blinking above the sink and the hundred watt overhead. Wil had to realise, she said, speaking slowly and carefully, that although she believed Wil, and Rob, and most of all the letters (how could she not), Wil still had to realise the whole thing was a shock and when she had finished the letters she couldn't move, had sat poleaxed for half an hour but still he must realise . . .

The old man's face was shadowed. The violet opalescence of the light above the sink did not affect him, he had his back to it. That was all very fine and large, he said. He had realised it would be a shock. He had made allowances for that, but when was Emmie going to come off her high horse?

High horse?

High horse. What about Alice? What about her loss, her misery, her torture at the hands of that woman? What about that then? 'What about my girl!' said Wilfred, his fist clenching, a spoon jumping. 'What about Alice!'

'Yes,' said Robin.

Shara looked at him thoughtfully. Emmeline lifted her chin.

Her head was high, her hair catching every glint. 'I agree she was my mother. No one could read those letters and not agree. They're . . .' She was gulping now, swallowing, 'they're the best thing I've ever had and the whole thing is heartbreaking, but can't you see? It was *Aunt* who brought me up, fed me, biked for miles, loved me silly. I will not,' said Emmeline, 'hate Aunt.'

'You don't have to,' said Rob.

They stared at him, Emmie blankly, Wilfred enraged, his face still halved by shadow.

Shara was sitting beside Rob. She was so small that much of her was beneath the table, her whole head was flooded with light: a sharp-nosed nocturnal animal blinking in the glare of revelation. She lifted one hand, swept her open palm against Robin's in a misdirected high-five. 'All *right*!' she said.

'We're all nuts,' begged Rob his hands wide. 'All slogging on. Crashing about. Getting it wrong. They both got it wrong. Weak? Vicious? Saint? Bitch? How do we know?'

'We know what she did,' said Wilfred.

'I'm talking to Emmie. Take both.' He was insisting now, hammering it past her staring eyes into her head. 'Why can't you love both for Chrissake?'

'No,' said Wilfred. 'I'll never accept that.'

'Then don't. I'm talking to Emmie.'

They went on for hours. They wouldn't stop. Shara went to bed and Robin missed her; her steel, her sense, her lack of imagination and her calm.

How would you feel if some false friend had stolen Calvin?

She didn't steal. She offered. And how many would?

Many women, hundreds. She wanted a child.

You think, you think . . . *Try* bringing up a child on your own.

I wish I'd had the chance. But I wouldn't steal one.

Aunt did not steal. Did she Rob?

She probably didn't mean to originally. But yes, she did.

You say that? You say that to *me*?

The letters, he said. The unopened letters.

They reached a compromise eventually, from exhaustion—from sense—from whatever it is that occasionally, just occasionally, enables antagonists to agree to differ. From affection despite all.

Wilfred produced a bottle of Glenfiddich he had been hoarding and they lifted a glass.

Emmeline would accept the evidence, she would find out all about Alice and love her as she deserved to be loved, would tell Calvin about her later as long as she did not hear one word, and she meant one word, against Aunt.

'Your hair's wrong,' said Wilfred, 'but otherwise . . .' He turned and passed the bottle. 'There's a toast,' he said. 'More of a ladies' toast, if you like. I taught it to her and she loved it. When we had a drink and it was just the two of us she'd say it, say it to me. Only when it was just us, mind.' The old man lifted his pale amber glass to Emmeline.

> *Here's to you, and to you, and to you again.*
> *If I hadn't of met you*
> *I couldn't of let you,*
> *But I met you*
> *And I let you*
> *And if I met you again*

I'd let you again.
So here's to you.

They left the following week with Calvin bawling his head off. They would come the same time next year. Earlier, if there was a chance, but definitely next summer. They would come every summer.

They didn't, of course. Not every year. But they meant to.

Barbara Anderson

ALL THE NICE GIRLS

Devonport Naval Base, 1962. Her husband away at sea, Sophie Flynn's life is becoming rather complicated. She has two children to nurture, the captain's wife to minister to, her wayward sister to keep an eye on, and an elderly neighbour to nurse. A perfect naval wife, she does all this and more. And then she falls in love with the commodore...

'Sharp and clear, Anderson's writing is marked by a vibrancy that has brought the critics out in superlatives'
Marianne Brace, *Independent*

'A romance with a dash of feminism, a depiction of rocky marriages and a comedy of manners...Anderson is a delightfully acute observer of human beings'
Kate Bassett, *The Times*

'The setting and style are highly individual. Light but not trivial, serious but not pretentious, this is a very enjoyable novel'
Jessica Mann, *Sunday Telegraph*

'A highly gifted novelist...Sharply intelligent, direct, poignant, she freeze-frames human emotion and guides her plots with a serene disregard for pretensions. Above all, her writing is alive, real'
Sophie Kershaw, *Time Out*

VINTAGE

Anne Tyler

LADDER OF YEARS

On a beach holiday, forty-year old Cordelia Grinstead, dressed only in swimsuit and beachrobe, walks away from her family and just keeps on walking...

'Her best book yet'
Roddy Doyle

'Every scene breathes with intimacy. Lifelikeness almost lifts the characters off the page. *Ladder of Years* ruefully contemplates the unhaltable passage of time. But, scintillating with *joie de vivre*, it also offers an intensely appealing way of passing it'
Peter Kemp, *Sunday Times*

'Anne Tyler's novels have three qualities that make them special: they are funny, they are sad, they are intelligent'
Nick Hornby

'Dialogue top-rate, people alive to the fingertips, places as real as next door – you don't get a finer comedy of manners than this'
David Hughes, *Mail on Sunday*

VINTAGE

Also available in Vintage

Margaret Atwood

THE HANDMAID'S TALE

The Republic of Gilead allows Offred only one function: to breed. If she deviates, she will, like all dissenters, be hanged at the wall or sent out to die slowly of radiation sickness. But even a repressive state cannot obliterate desire – neither Offred's nor that of the two men on which her future hangs...

Brilliantly conceived and executed, this powerful evocation of 21st-century America gives full reign to Margaret Atwood's devastating irony, wit and astute perception.

'*The Handmaid's Tale* is both a superlative exercise in science fiction and a profoundly felt moral story'
Angela Carter

'Out of a narrative shadowed by terror, gleam sharp perceptions, brilliant intense images and sardonic wit'
Peter Kemp, *Independent*

'The images of brilliant emptiness are one of the most striking aspects of this novel about totalitarian blindness... the effect is chilling'
Linda Taylor, *Sunday Times*

VINTAGE

A. S. Byatt

POSSESSION

A ROMANCE

Winner of the 1990 Booker Prize

'A massive, complex story about a literary mystery which turns into an emotional voyage of discovery...the novel is a triumphant success on every level – as a critique of Victorian poetry, an unbearably moving love story and a satire on the modern 'Biography Industry'...*Possession* will be the sensation of the year'
Cosmopolitan

'*Possession* is eloquent about the intense pleasures of reading. And, with sumptuous artistry, it provides a feast of them'
Sunday Times

'On academic rivalry and obsession, Byatt is delicious. On the nature of possession – the lover by the beloved, the biographer by his subject – she is profound...She is ripening into our best novelist'
Evening Standard

VINTAGE

Georgina Hammick

PEOPLE FOR LUNCH
AND
SPOILT

'Remarkably fine short stories...Old favourites (class, pre-
mature widowhood, schoolgirl crushes, the Generation
Gap) acquire fresh life in her skilful and original tales'
The Times

'Gaps – emotional, cultural, social – are what Hammick's
characters usually stare at each other across. Comedies of
misapprehension modulate into little tragedies of alien-
ation...Hammick has a sharp mimic's ear for the tell-tale
turn of phrase and a narrow eye for the give-away detail'
Sunday Times

'She has commonplace themes, and big ones; humiliation,
guilt, dishonesty, stagnancy...Hammick's cameos of social
cruelty are acutely funny and enjoyable'
Observer

'Sly observation, robust compression and a nice range of
chaos and panic on the domestic front'
Guardian

VINTAGE

Also available in Vintage

Mary Morrissy

MOTHER OF PEARL

'At once heartbreaking and invigorating...One of the best of the latest generation of Irish fiction writers'
John Banville

'A dazzling display...A formidable first novel'
Clare Boylan, *Irish Times*

'The story of a stolen baby and two mothers who have between them created her, Morrissy's book is as dark as a hope chest and as carefully worked as a christening shawl...you read agog, to the very last word. Quite a book'
Lisa Mullen, *Time Out*

'A slap-bang terrific new novel...With great lyricism, skill and insight, Morrissy explores the darker sides of the maternal instinct. She paints an indelible picture of one tragic woman's desperate search for home and family'
Val Hennessy, *Daily Mail*

'Unsentimental, powerfully emotional, even-handed and generous, the novel has a rare compulsive quality. It's extremely unusual for a book to bring tears to my eyes these days, but *Mother of Pearl* managed it...It is a very fine novel indeed and deserves wide recognition'
Carol Birch, *New Statesman & Society*

VINTAGE

A SELECTED LIST OF CONTEMPORARY FICTION
AVAILABLE IN VINTAGE

☐ ALL THE NICE GIRLS	Barbara Anderson	£5.99
☐ THE HANDMAID'S TALE	Margaret Atwood	£6.99
☐ POSSESSION	A.S.Byatt	£6.99
☐ THE MATISSE STORIES	A.S.Byatt	£4.99
☐ NIGHTS AT THE CIRCUS	Angela Carter	£5.99
☐ WISE CHILDREN	Angela Carter	£5.99
☐ PEOPLE FOR LUNCH/SPOILT	Georgina Hammick	£6.99
☐ NOW THAT YOU'RE BACK	A L Kennedy	£5.99
☐ MOTHER OF PEARL	Mary Morrissy	£5.99
☐ A LAZY EYE	Mary Morrissy	£5.99
☐ OPEN SECRETS	Alice Munro	£5.99
☐ LADDER OF YEARS	Anne Tyler	£5.99
☐ THE ACCIDENTAL TOURIST	Anne Tyler	£5.99
☐ ORANGES ARE NOT THE ONLY FRUIT	Jeanette Winterson	£5.99
☐ THE PASSION	Jeanette Winterson	£5.99

- All Vintage books are available through mail order or from your local bookshop.

- Please send cheque/eurocheque/postal order (sterling only), Access, Visa or Mastercard:

☐☐☐☐☐☐☐☐☐☐☐☐☐☐

Expiry Date:_____Signature:_____

Please allow 75 pence per book for post and packing U.K.
Overseas customers please allow £1.00 per copy for post and packing.

ALL ORDERS TO:
Vintage Books, Book Service by Post, P.O.Box 29, Douglas, Isle of Man, IM99 1BQ.
Tel: 01624 675137   •   Fax: 01624 670923

NAME:_____

ADDRESS:_____

_____

_____

Please allow 28 days for delivery. Please tick box if you do not   ☐
wish to receive any additional information
Prices and availability subject to change without notice.